Preserve
Emma Ellis

Preserve is a dark novel. Readers should be aware it contains references to sexual assault, self harm and suicide.

This novel is written in British English

Cover by GetCovers

Chapter 1

10 years after the Great Unrest

Your life length is in our hands.
One of the core values of XL Medico

***

At first glance, the body looks quite serene. His face relaxed, unsmiling, eyes closed, black hair curling round his ear, some colour in his cheeks. The Preserved always keep their colour, like the skin is still alive even after their souls have departed. It's as if they're made of plastic. As inert as a mannequin.

When Ava walks round the other side, she sees what killed him. The bus hit him square on the left side. No amount of preservation drug will save you from your brains spilling out.

Pres-X restores youth; it doesn't make its takers bullet-proof. She hopes they don't want an open casket.

'How many years since he took Pres-X?' Ava asks Max as he loads up the files, the computer taking its time as always.

'Ten years. Literally just finished regressing.'

'Shame.' She peers closely at the body. It'll never stop being weird. Ninety years old, and he looks like he's in his twenties. Well, half of him does.

'The wife will be in later,' Max says. 'Maybe put her off viewing immediately. Unless she wants to mix her vomit with his brains.' Ava smiles at his poor-taste comment. He smiles wider. 'Oh, and the flower delivery is due shortly.'

Max gets to work. The corpses of the Preserved rarely need much attention, though this one will take a little longer. Push what's left of his brains back in and sew it up. A short infusion with top quality embalming fluid to stave off the ashen complexion of death even longer, and keep the cheeks rounded and plump. Ava leaves Max to it. Despite a lifetime working in a funeral home, she's never developed a stomach for that bit. Client facing, that's her domain.

She walks through the reception area, past the display caskets that smell of oiled wood instead of the formaldehyde stench of the cold room. Wilting lilies droop in their vases. The expense to replace them seems pointless when business is so quiet, but how bleak would a funeral home be without flowers? Not enough clients to justify the expense, Max reminds her every time the delivery comes. Not enough people dying these days.

Not enough with a high Life Score, anyway. The algorithm that assigns every citizen a wealth number at the age of twenty-eight dictates everything from where you can get your coffee to where you can live. Where you can have your funeral is no exception.

In the window, Ava checks her reflection. She prefers to concern herself with the effects of ageing that she can detect without the need of a mirror. That is, until she has a Preserved coming into her work. She pinches her cheeks and smooths her hands over her less than smooth forehead, trying her best not to look twice the age of the ninety-year-old widow due in soon. The transience of youth long behind her, a distant memory of a time when her knees didn't creak, her hair was absent of its spindly silver streaks, and her eyes functioned efficiently. Not that Ava cares. Smooth skin would only serve to please onlookers. Or perhaps make them pity her less.

The wife comes in sooner than expected. Her regression clearly completed also, the bright pinkness of newly Preserved skin no longer showing. Even in grief, she appears well-rested and radiant. Her sadness makes her glow instead of grey. The silk handkerchief she holds to her nose is embossed with the XL Medico logo, as is her handbag. With that and her youthful skin and thick glossy hair, she's a walking advert for the drug Pres-X.

Ava puts on her most solemn face, unnecessary as her face is naturally so, and greets the widow.

'Mrs Constance. Please, take a seat.'

The furniture is heavy and padded enough to rival any 800 plus domestic home. Ava's father made it all out of refurbished bits and bobs but chose good quality materials, and laboured day and night to make the finish perfect with ornate engraving and real silk upholstery. The funeral home looks exactly like it should cater for the Society's wealthiest, even if the staff are all far below their clients' Life Scores.

'Fifty years we've been together,' Mrs Constance says through sniffs. 'We were just starting anew.'

Ava doesn't speak but nods her practised nod. There is something familiar about Mrs Constance, her face one Ava recognises from years ago that she can't put a name to. Often the way with the Preserved. They look like every wellness poster and beauty commercial going.

'Pres-X was supposed to give us decades more. I mean, look at me! I look like I'm fresh out of college. But he's gone. All those decades we should be having, gone.'

'I am so sorry. It's such a tragedy.'

'It's not fair. Just not fair. He was only ninety years old. Too young.'

When her sobs are subdued, Ava hands her the catalogue, watches her browse floral arrangements, shows her around the caskets. She says her usual explanations, and when the timing seems like she might as well get it over with, she hands her the quote.

'Thirty thousand pounds for a funeral!' Mrs Constance says and drops her handkerchief.

'I am afraid the costs are substantially higher for Preserved.'

'Why? Just because of our Life Scores, we should pay more?'

'No. Not at all.' Ava sits back, her posture more defensive than she intends. 'I'm afraid the cremation process is more. The furnace needs to burn a few hundred degrees Celsius hotter and for twice as long as a non-Preserved. The energy costs are very high.'

'They never told us this when we had our treatment. It was probably in the paperwork, but I was old then. I didn't retain information so well. Ted dealt with all those particulars, you know?'

Ava knits her eyebrows together and upturns her mouth, making her most pained expression. She's not without sympathy. She's swallowed back enough tears from her own grief over the years. But her sympathy comes with a pang of envy. Mrs Constance has enjoyed so many years with a companion. To have had someone to care about still at such a great age seems unimaginable. Unfair.

'Our crematorium and service rooms are all on site, so it's completely hassle-free for you. I can give you a tour if you like. I am sure you have heard about the premier embalming we do here. Mr Constance will be beautifully rested. It sounds like he was a wonderful husband.'

'He really was.'

Mrs Constance's pain is like ripping the plaster off Ava's own. She's in the wrong job, she thinks for the millionth time. Her father's business was never meant for her. Not yet anyway. She should work somewhere cheerful or around less people. But so few companies offer work to women of her age. She's still fertile, just. Still too dangerous to be around.

'Well, let's bury him,' Mrs Constance says. 'He'd like that.'

Ava's shoulders slump. Explaining this never gets easier. 'I'm afraid that's not an option for the Preserved. The Pres-X drug gets into the soil and its effects there are unknown. The other option is to not have a solo burn. Some people opt to pair up or more.'

Mrs Constance's eyes widen, and her plump skin tightens around her jaw. 'Mix my Ted's ashes with those of strangers? No. No, I couldn't bear it.' She grips the arm of the chair, bleaching knuckles, toned forearms tensing.

'I assume you have no prepayment plan in place?' Ava asks, knowing the answer already.

'He wasn't meant to die now. He was meant to have another sixty years at least.' She picks up her handkerchief and sobs again.

'Such a tragedy.'

'We have never been wealthy,' Mrs Constance says when her tears have calmed for a moment. 'Not excessively, anyway. Our Score only scraped the treatment level. I worked at XL Medico. We got an employee discount for Pres-X. I'm only a 700, as you can see on my file. I expect even you have a higher Life Score than that.'

Even you. Ava bites back her wince and decides not to divulge her mediocre 520 Score. Still, her empathy is genuine, and her naturally solemn face drops to appear even more so. 'Mr Constance is welcome to rest here for a week while you have a think. There's no need to decide immediately.'

'I can't have him cremated in some mass grave. I simply can't. Who would the others even be? Would they even be all from this funeral home? Yours is the only in the county that is exclusive to 700 pluses.'

'I can't guarantee. We don't divulge such information out of confidentiality. But since so few 700 pluses pass away, I must warn you it's most likely it would be mixed.'

'My Ted, cremated with paupers? No, I can't. I simply can't. There must be some payment plan. Some discount for senior citizens?'

Mrs Constance wipes her nose with the XL Medico handkerchief again, her makeup smearing against the cream silk. The last part of their conversation replays in Ava's mind. Did she say employee discount for Pres-X?

'I am afraid no senior citizen discount is possible,' Ava says. 'The details of the payment plan are on the quote. Why don't you take a few days to think about it? You can come and visit Mr Constance tomorrow.'

Mrs Constance nods and stands. If she is dissatisfied with the customer service, she doesn't show it. Her preserved skin continues to glow, her expression set to neutral. She takes an elegant hand and tucks her sleek hair behind her ear, smiles to reveal her pristine white teeth and healthy gums. 'Thank you. You've been very kind. I will see what I can do and be in touch.'

Ava walks her to the door. Her back stiffens, and she struggles to stand while Mrs Constance, almost half a century older, springs up with ease. Ava opens the door for her, the hum of the busy pedestrian traffic and buses filling the room instantly, and Mrs Constance makes her way out onto the street. In her cream heels, she walks as quickly as all the other young people in the pedestrian fast lane.

Ava doesn't even close the door before the sirens make her jump, blaring down the street, beeping all others out of the way. The shiny black cars, the symbol of the government—the Eyes Forward logo—emblazoned on the doors, park right outside L.M. Funerals.

The men exit the cars, two from each, their blazers embossed with the same logo as the cars and walk right through the door Ava is holding open.

'Can I help you, gentlemen?'

One of the men steps forward, his suit so sharp it looks like it would cut skin. Perhaps that's what caused the scar down his chin. The others linger, herded behind like sheep. 'Who is in charge here?'

'Me,' says Ava. 'I own this funeral home.'

He doesn't introduce himself. The Eyes Forward staff never do. It's like they're one being. All stiff suits and grim faces.

'It should be Luigi Maricelli,' he says, no intonation or emotion in his voice. Might as well be a robot.

'That was my father. He passed some years ago.'

The man looks at Ava's hand, her implant glowing orange, revealing her fertile status. He makes no attempt to disguise his glare, nor his disapproval. 'There is no man we can speak with, or a woman of safe age?'

Ava shakes her head. No need to mention Max down the hall. His front of house skills are limited to cleaning and signing for deliveries. 'No. This is my business. There's just me.'

'But you are not of safe age to be conversing with men.'

'I'm not far off.'

'Well, that explains the aircon in here. Or do you keep this area cold for the bodies?' He and the other men all chuckle as Ava grits her teeth.

'I prefer it cool,' she says, without a hint of annoyance.

'Very well. We shall talk. You must sit and face the wall as we do so. I'll not have my men tempted.'

She does just that. Obedient, as always. It's not the first nor likely the last that such a request shall be made. As if one look at her forty-nine-year-old face would make men jump on her. Perhaps pinching her cheeks is more effective than she thinks. She smiles to herself as she ponders this and wipes her eye as the sting from their aftershave subsides and her eyes finish watering. She hears them pull the chairs away from the table, the groan of the wood as they sit.

'This is strictly confidential. The Eyes Forward requires your service. Your Society requires your service. Your government has called upon you. You will sign an NDA and you will obey it. Is that understood?'

ment. If I can assist the wonderful Eyes Forward, I'd like to help.' She sweetens her tone for that last bit. A little flattery goes a long way.

The suit rustling is louder. *Good,* she thinks, feeling a little more powerful. *Let them squirm.*

'You are not of safe age,' the man says. 'Your implant shows you are still fertile. The labs have men on their staff. We can't risk you creating another burden on the Society.'

'I can do night work—to fit around my duties here. I will work alone, at whatever time suits your other staff.' She waits for them to answer, but there is only silence. She imagines what their facial expressions are: contemplative, disgust, impatience, approving? She wonders if they can decipher her own anxiousness from the back of her head. *Sod it.* She's been a good Society citizen forever. Opportunities like this are rare, and so, without a moment more thought, she decides on her stance, Mrs Constance's words sounding over and over in her head: *employee discount.* 'Or else you can just confiscate my formaldehyde-rose as I assume you will do anyway. But you will not be able to make more without me. It's my recipe. I will not hand it over, and your labs will waste a lot of time and resources trying to figure out how to make it.'

Huffs of breaths and more crisply pressed suits crackle from behind. Ava resists fidgeting in her seat, tensing through her restlessness, body buzzing from her boldness. To make Eyes Forward representatives squirm is the sort of thing many would sacrifice half their Life Score for.

'Very well, Ms Maricelli,' he says. 'We have ourselves a deal.'

Chapter 2

Ava's home is nicer than most people expect, in a better neighbourhood than they assume she lives in when they see her surname and—when her father was alive—heard his accent. Immigrants don't do so well in the Society. In a neighbourhood surrounded by families whose lineages date back to before Britain was rebranded as the Society, she has never fitted in. She cycles home past the houses where the other first- and second-generation immigrants are more common, cardboard in the windows to make up for crappy insulation, bikes locked up outside, stripped of any part that can be taken. The Eyes Forward logo adorns every street corner and bus stop there, *All Eyes Are Our Eyes* written underneath. To tell people that the Society Police operate everywhere, as if people need reminding. The Eyes Forward have been in power for about fifteen years. The centre ground, a worthwhile compromise, everyone seems to think. Including Ava, mostly. The days of left and right politics ripped the country in half, the Eyes Forward were the glue to bring it back together.

She continues to cycle up the hill where the cafés get higher and higher in their Life Score clientele, where the litter is old wrappers of branded products rather than government-issue ration packets, where the looming Eyes Forward symbol becomes sparser. Fewer criminals around here to remind, no shady alleyways to conceal the crooks, until she arrives at her own street. Trees are still abundant, sighing under the weight of leaves yet to drop. Some real grass remains in front gardens, interspersed among the gravel and plastic foliage. The pedestrian traffic thins, and buses are more frequent. Still, what use is a nicer neighbourhood when she is still below the 750 Score required to fund Pres-X treatment?

Suzanna is at her front door as Ava walks past. In the six or so years they've been neighbours, Ava has never seen her without a face mask and rollers in her hair, always preparing for some night out that never seems to happen.

'Ava, dear. You look tired.'

'Hi, Suzanna, nice to see you.'

'You can get aloe vera creams on credit if you buy in bulk. Help your skin and your Score.'

'Thanks, Suzanna. I'll bear that in mind.'

'Have you thought about a kombucha cleanse? I can leave you some if you like. I have too many anyway. Morning, noon, and evening sachets that you mix with a hundred millilitres of water and sip over an hour to get the best effect. Shall I write that down for you?'

'It's fine, Suzanna, really.'

'I think it says the precise dosage on the packets if you forget. I bought a thousand packets on credit and upped my Score ten points.'

Every time Ava sees her, she has some beauty tip, or Life Score tip, or like today, both. A double whammy of useless nonsense that Ava nods and smiles at. Keeping credit maxed out may indeed help boost her Life Score, but she sincerely doubts some plant secretions will do anything to enhance her life.

Zia is home as she always is. Ava still calls her Zia, the Italian word for aunt, one of the few words she remembers from her father's lessons. Zia limps across the living room with the TV turned up full volume, dusting surfaces that don't need dusting, rearranging cushions that don't need rearranging, and greets Ava when she comes in.

'Dinner is in the oven. You have a good day?' Her English vocabulary is perfect, but her accent is still as strong as it was when Ava was a kid, bouncing off each syllable and rolling every R.

Ava kicks off her shoes and turns the TV down. 'Fine, thanks.' She gives Zia a peck on the cheek. Ava doesn't hug her, she never does, too scared of bruising her parchment-thin skin.

'I saw the news about that bus crash, with a 700,' Zia says, shouting, not noticing the TV has been turned down. 'The victim yours?'

'Yep. He'd had Pres-X. Just finished regressing.'

The cushions are the opposite way around now. Zia considers it a moment before putting them back to where they were.

'The cushions are fine, Zia. Really.'

'How's that lovely girl, Mandisa? I haven't seen her in a while.'

Ava clenches her jaw. She should be used to Zia bringing up Mandisa by now. But the constant reminder makes moving on a damn lot harder. Of all the things Zia remembers, why Mandisa? 'We broke up a year ago. I'm sure she's fine.'

'Oh, that's a shame.'

Ava braces herself for the next bit of conversation. She knows it's coming. It's always the same. Zia peers closer at her, puts her reading glasses on, and inspects Ava's face like she's a piece of damaged art. Not just in passing, like Suzanna. Zia inspects every inch like looking for cracks in the crockery, searching for some flaw that needs filling. Ava's never cared about looking her age or older. Every line is a badge of honour, she thinks. Surviving the Great Unrest a decade ago is something to feel proud of, not cover up with delusion and chemicals. But Zia's frequent reminders let her know she is not as desirable as she perhaps once was.

'You'll leave it too late if you don't meet someone soon. Your mother aged quickly. You're like her, take after her side. You'll get wrinkles very soon.'

'Get? Ha. I've got plenty. And I don't care. I can only see them when I put my reading glasses on and look in the mirror.'

'But other people can see them.'

'So?'

'You want to be a spinster forever?'

Ava pulls her face away and resumes staring at the telly. 'Actually yes,' she replies, too quiet for her aunt to hear. 'Happily.'

Zia walks back into the kitchen and commences rearranging the crockery. 'Dinner will be in an hour,' she calls from the kitchen. Ava only half-listens. She knows what Zia's saying already. 'It's a bean dish. I saw it on that cooking show. You know the show your dad likes? Maybe he'd like some.'

Ava doesn't have the heart to remind her, yet again, that Zia's brother died a decade ago. She gets up and walks to the kitchen doorway. 'I know. Listen, Zia—'

The crockery is all out on the side now, Zia paying little attention to Ava.

'Zia!'

'Yes, dear. Oh, I'm making that bean dish for dinner. I saw it on that cooking show. You know, the one your dad likes?'

'Great, listen. I've got an opportunity with work. You just need to keep taking your meds. Do those brain exercise things. I'm going to get you Pres-X soon, really soon. I know it.'

'That's nice, dear.' She smiles and looks at Ava, except not really at her, but through her, as if Ava is a puff of smoke. 'How was work? How's Mandisa? I've not seen her in a while. Why don't you two have a baby? That would be lovely.'

Ava mutes a sigh and returns to the sofa, reaching for the remote control. 'There are no more babies, Zia. Hardly any in ten years. The Enough movement won, remember?'

'Oh, yes, of course. I was wondering why I hadn't seen a baby in such a long time. That's a shame. Your parents always wanted grandchildren. Your Zio and I never made time to have a baby. I wish we had. You know what, I saw some bus crash on TV, a 700 plus. The victim come to you?'

Ava turns the TV back up. The high volume should keep Zia's brain engaged, or at least distracted from Ava and her personal life. The conversation repetition can go on forever otherwise.

An XL Medico advert dominates the TV, its soft piano jingle too loud in the speakers, but Ava doesn't turn it down. She stares, unblinking, and listens to the overly soft voice of the narrator. Across the screen are young-looking people, Preserved, clearly, from their attire, the usual kind of adverts associated with Pres-X. Only this advert is different from the last. The product is different.

Pres-X-2. Coming soon to the Society! No need to struggle through middle-age. Pres-X-2 can be taken from the age of 45, as soon as hormone levels allow in women, and give you back the body of a twenty-year-old.

Keep ageing at bay, the Pres-X-2 way.

(Sterilisation mandatory for all women. Exclusively for 700 pluses.)

Chapter 3

14 years before the Great Unrest

It's hard for most people to imagine a time before Pres-X, before every citizen would strive to Score 750, the milestone when Pres-X becomes possible. Like there was once a generation of people who couldn't imagine a life before cars, then smart phones. A life before antibiotics, when the smallest infection could be fatal. Modern day trivialities such as bacteria were the world's biggest killer. Now, with a high enough Score even time isn't a death sentence.

Of course, at first the sceptics outnumbered those who hailed it as the miracle innovation it turned out to be. And some of those sceptics never regained their faith. For some, their desire for a natural life wasn't just a bluff. It stayed with them to their end. Such people viewed mortality in the same way some people once viewed poor mobile phone service: a fact of life but better than the new-fangled alternative and all the supposed health threats. Like good phone reception is the devil's work. There is a subtle difference between these two groups of tech-haters. The mobile phone service haters became quiet when nobody died. The Pres-X sceptics became *angrier* when nobody died.

There is literally no winning against sceptics.

That is what Ken said to Lucia, much to her dismay, writing off her concerns as nothing more than the ramblings of a mad woman. Like God had some say in the matter, like she loved the idea of her maker so much she was impatient to meet him. Ken would rather put off that encounter. Sinful, Lucia had said to him. Not God's plan.

There was no convincing him. She wanted to call it a mid-life crisis, but he was past that. She wanted to call him a lot of other things too, but there was no sense in being impolite. It's not like he was ever going to have the treatment, she was sure of that. He was a coward, and not a rich one. This would be like his phase when he thought he could get rich as a DIY influencer or the time he thought he'd win some Society award if he complained to the council enough. Notoriety, he said he wanted. To not just be someone whose name disappears like dust.

Dust doesn't disappear, she'd reminded him. It gets cleaned away. She cleans it away.

That's not the point, he'd said.

After forty years together, the arguments get tedious.

He went to investigate the new 'wonder drug', as he'd called it. The thing set to cure all their ails, as Lucia stayed at home and read her book. Just before she was going to bed for an early night, she watched her husband from the upstairs window as he walked toward their home. Slower than he used to be, his limp was worse. No less handsome though, she thought. The moon shone full over the semi-detached on Lowfield Road. Its silver rays glinted off the head of grey hair below.

She walked down the stairs to greet him at the door. Past the photos that hung on the walls of their lifetime of holidays together, smiling faces in front of snowy mountains and cyan blue lakes, a beaten-up old camper in the background, romantic crumbling castles and plates of food that, if she closed her eyes, she could still taste. Even all these years later.

She paused to look at one. Her dewy smile, a glass of wine.

Still, that was years ago. Things had changed.

Lucia opened the door to welcome the man she used to know. His lines dug deep with grumpiness these days instead of laughter like before. He blamed his knees, usually. Or his back. Noise, or lack of it. Politics. There were many reasons.

'Dinner's on the side. Just heat it up. You want some wine?'

'No. I'll be pissing all night,' he said as he walked through the living room, still wearing his shoes, bringing gravel in across the freshly vacuumed carpet.

'You have fun?' Lucia asked, trying to not look at the carpet.

He sat in his chair, the one he always sat in now, a separate one, where he could not hold her hand.

'Yeah,' he said, a little lighter in his tone. 'You know, I did. It's true, what I'd heard. This drug. They can cure us.'

'We're not sick. My blood pressure is exceptional for my age. Even your prostate is normal.'

He winced, like her words were some malady. 'Can cure *age*, I mean. Make us young again. Turn eighty, and then like that,' he clicked his fingers, 'all those years can go back.'

She held her head a little higher, rounded her shoulders back. 'But I'm only sixty. You're thirteen years older.'

'Exactly. When I'm eighty, this drug can make me young again.'

'You're not listening to me. I don't want to be married to some twenty-year-old. You going to turn into some twenty-year-old overnight while I have another thirteen years to go.'

'It takes up to ten years to fully regress.'

His Berkshire twang made the word 'regress' sound like he'd banged his funny bone. And he'd said her accent was still hard to understand.

'So, what, in ten years you'll only be twenty-five years younger than me?' She said this with such conviction, although not entirely sure her sum was right. She watched Ken screw his face up to count the years, but didn't give him the time to check. 'Twenty years of our lives between us spent "regressing", as you call it.' She rolled the Rs as if there were several in a row. Just for emphasis. 'And it doesn't stop you getting sick or having an accident. Twenty years could all be for nothing.'

He waved his hand at her, scoffing and scowling.

She sat on her chair, too forgiving from the hours she'd spent in it. Two half-read novels tucked down the side. 'When we married, you said you wanted us to grow old together. What changed?'

'Arthritis.'

She smirked. 'The rest of you might be slower, but your tongue certainly isn't.'

'It'll be wonderful, though. Don't you think? We get to do it all again. Remember how gorgeous you were forty years ago?'

She certainly worried more about her looks forty years ago. Whether she actually looked better then was beside the point. And she thought she was doing all right for her age. The customers in the café always said so. 'We've had our time, Ken. Why can't you look to the future? The past is done.'

'We could have a kid if that's what you want. It makes everything young again, your insides too.'

'Oh, don't be so ridiculous.' She snorted a laugh. 'Have a child, us? Now? In this world? Now you're really being daft. Frankenstein science this is. It's vulgar.' Maybe years ago, she would have liked a child, but they always had other priorities. Time slipped away. She loved being an auntie though. Ken hadn't even ever helped babysit her niece when her niece was little, such was his dislike of her side of the family.

Lucia stood and put his dinner in the microwave, since he clearly wasn't going to do it, and poured herself a small glass of red, only a dribble left in the bottle. He might end up pissing all night if he had a glass, but her bladder was just fine.

'Well, I'm going to have it,' he said.

'How, exactly? It'll be for the richest. Life Score is all anyone cares about anymore. No way you'll qualify.'

'I'll get a job.'

She choked on her wine. 'A job! You were counting the days till retirement. It's only been a year. What sort of job can a decrepit old builder do?'

'I'm going to work for the government. I filled in an application form online.' He said this as if he thought that was actually possible instead of utterly ridiculous.

'The government?' At least her impression was right when he started going on about this youth drug.

He'd gone mad.

'Yes, the government. As a PR person—for the working classes. I'll be checking everyone is doing their bit for the Society.'

She'd read about that, about what they'd been asking people to do. To betray their own people. Yep. He'd definitely gone crackers. This was the new mid-life crisis. A three-quarters life crisis? End of life crisis? The press would come out with some term for it. They always did. 'You're going to be a Society Police snitch, some spy for the Eyes Forward? You hate the Eyes Forward.'

'I voted for them. Otherwise it's bigots on one side, fascists on the other.'

She took some breath in sharply, like she'd been winded. 'You said they go against everything you believe in. Remember when they first got in and said people should be demonised for travelling? You said the devolved economies was a stupid idea, that they should never have disbanded the police. Your brother lost his job over that. Where are your loyalties, Ken?'

'I'm loyal to my knees. And my future, our future.'

'You're loyal to whatever old age crisis you're having.' Old age crisis, that would be it. She'd remember that term. Perhaps she'd write to the press and suggest it. 'Just accept it, Ken. You're not a young man anymore. You have more years behind than ahead. That's nature's way. We had a good life, didn't we? Let's just enjoy what's left.' She gazed at her husband. He still looked like the man she married. They'd both changed over the years, but they were still *them*. Wasn't that enough?

'I'm not done, Lucia. I have a lot to offer the Society still. As a young man again, I can do a whole lot more.'

A beep comes from the kitchen. 'Your dinner's ready, love. Set the table, will you?'

Planting her hands firmly on the sofa to push herself up, Lucia stood and went to the kitchen, waiting for Ken to oblige and set the table. When he did not, she got on with it herself, including laying out the wine glasses, then opened a fresh bottle, filling her glass to the brim. So much for her early night. She'd drink the whole bloody bottle if he didn't want any. More wine might have made that conversation a bit easier to bear.

Chapter 4

10 years after the Great Unrest

As night draws in, Ava prepares to leave. Dressed in black, she checks her phone for battery, then loads up the Society Police app so it's ready to go. She scrolls through social media before leaving—all the places she shouldn't be looking. Dark web socials where gangs state their intentions in code and cryptic messages. Food stores, usually. The chic little vegetable boutiques down the alley off the High Street, the 700 plus deli next to the 800 plus café on Church Street. Even the budget supermarket on Honey End Lane doesn't always escape the looting. The low Score gangs know that paying off the security is cheaper than a grocery shop.

With her bike lights off, and her gears oiled so as not to squeak, Ava sets off into the night. She puts her headphones on for the journey, the radio playing more adverts than music, but it keeps her awake. She's way past going to gigs and moshing with the crowds, but when the baseline kicks in, she can zone-out and reminisce about what it was like to have loose knees and no hangovers. Her bike is black, but the gold and pink lettering on the side stands out. Where it once said AVA.M, it now only says VAM. Her dad painted them on when she was a kid, and as much as they may make her stand out against the dark night, she's never had the heart to cover them up.

She pulls her sleeve down over her hand to hide her implant's glow so as not to give her position away. It's illegal to hide it. She's supposed to declare her fertility status for the whole Society to see—part of the peace agreement after the Great Unrest a decade prior. The Enough movement insisted eggs should be frozen and girls be sterilised in childhood until the population decreases. The implant and the rules around it were deemed a more palatable compromise. The orange colour alerts any would-be attackers that she's in her most fertile time of the month. It's supposed to put them off, the ideology states. No one wants to fuck a fertile woman. No one wants to create another drain on the Society and its precious resources. A less personal crime would be more favourable to detect. Crimes she can observe and record from a safe distance, instead of under the heaving mass of some pervert.

A life spent in martial arts training means she's happy enough patrolling the darkest streets and alleyways. Shady corners with spying vantage points over the riskiest businesses. There is always some crime to detect somewhere. Crime seems like a big word when most of those she detects are low Life Scorers looking for food other than the powdered rations they are provided. The Pro Grow rallies from the time of the Great Unrest certainly went a long way in educating the Society that everyone needs to consume less, though that lesson has only been forced upon those with little other choice.

Many people wonder how the daughter of an immigrant father has a Life Score in the five-hundreds. Twenty years of nights doing her bit as Society Police is how. Though she never tells. Reporting crime may be in the hands of Society Police, but everyone hates a snitch. No wonder the streets are so unsafe.

She glides down the hill to Church Street. A hit on the deli is imminent, if her understanding on the dark web forums is to be believed. They talk in riddles and symbols, but she's sussed most of it by now. Frozen meats, nuts, vegetables pickled in fancy vinegars are what they're after. Food that lasts and tastes good. The low Scorers love such a place. The expense of food for such a population in a world where less and less can grow means most food shops are catering solely for the higher Scores, banking the profit—what little they make—rather than shut their doors or sell at a loss to the low Scorers. The rations are meant to suffice, so the Eyes Forward say. But since when was being sufficient actually sufficient?

Hiding in the shadows, she takes her headphones off and waits. In the corner of the window, the deli window's alarm light flashes. Buses roll past less frequently now the hubbub of the day is over. Her phone vibrates in her pocket. Dan is in the pub. Come join us, he says. His calendar is clearly not tuned in to her implant. She would love a drink, but such things are illegal for a woman's orange time. Can't risk women letting their guard down, the aphrodisiac effect of alcohol, less inhibitions, women saying things they normally wouldn't. A toxic mix for the Society and its procreation laws. The laws are all that stopped the Great Unrest a decade ago. The Enough movement made their demands, and creating life became more tightly controlled than Suzanna's kombucha cleanse routine. Women should be grateful, they said. This way they get to live instead of being beaten to a pulp by enraged population-fearing meatheads. This way, fertile women are still allowed to roam the streets, pre-curfew at least. They can still live normal lives.

Normal lives. They actually said that.

That was a decade ago. Ava rarely thinks of it now. The loss of her parents in the riots made her desire peace, whatever the cost. That's how she justifies her actions for the Society Police. She's doing her bit. Keeping the streets safe. It's a philanthropic thing, she tells herself. The right thing to do for most. Noble. Useful. The lower Scorers who she snitches on should know better anyway. The extra points are just a bonus.

Ava can kid herself sometimes.

She checks the time. Ten-thirty. She waits.

She's about to give up and move on to the food wholesalers when she spots some figures skulking in the shadows. Thin, of course, and small, so likely young. The stunted growth from food shortages in teenage years. She's seen this gang before, recognises one's limp and another's stutter. Ava has played a hand in getting some members prosecuted in the past. They never learn.

Lifting her phone to record, Ava zooms in, her latest model picking out their faces even in the dark. Sad faces, malnourished. She shifts a little, dislodging the pang of guilt she has for turning in the Society's poorest, and steadies herself. She waits for the breaking glass, but they're clever this time. A gadget points at the alarm system, somehow disabling it. A crowbar to the door. She catches it all, filming live, uploading in real time. Her mind's eye sees her Life Score increasing. This'll give her ten extra points minimum, maybe more. She holds her breath as she watches and films the group make off with bags of produce, enough food to feed their families for weeks. Lavishly packaged delicacies, fragrant jams, and spicy chutneys. She licks her lips. Even her Score isn't enough for her to shop in such a place. One day, though. She'll get there one day.

A scuffle of footsteps behind and she spins around, too slowly. He's on her before she's had time to think. All hundred kilos of him, forcing his girth against her. His hands pushing down on her wrists.

'Hold still and it'll be over quickly.' Drool drips on her as he speaks.

She goes limp, lets him think she'll cooperate, that she's too small and weak to resist. His saliva trickles down her cheek and she swallows a gag. It's worse than the vinegary body odour his armpit is ramming into her face. He puts both her wrists in one hand as he reaches below to unbutton himself and she takes her chance. She grits her teeth, kicks her legs, wriggles, and spits in his eyes. She jumps up, looks side to side, her phone, it's face down and out of reach. It won't be recording this. This is a fifty-point attack for sure. She shouts his description.

'Caucasian male, one hundred kilos, full beard, get off me you pig! Wearing . . . wearing. . .' His hand goes to her throat as he slams her into the wall behind, a warm dribble of blood tracing down her neck, the uneven brickwork behind digging into her spine. Her voice is reduced to a rasp. 'I'm on Church Street. . .' Her voice diminishes to almost nothing as her vision darkens. '. . .I'm orange.'

He eases off at this, his eyes go to her hand, and he yanks back her sleeve. 'Shit. You bitch! You should have said. You shouldn't cover that up.'

'Grey jacket. Black jeans. Black trainers.' Her voice returns to a throaty clarity, and she drags herself along the wall, away from his grasp, then grabs her phone as her right leg kicks him square in the bollocks. He doubles over as she holds her phone with one hand, punching him in the nose with the other. She's filming now as he takes a moment to stand. 'Bloody nose, bloodstains on his jacket, smells like alcohol.'

'You fucking bitch! You should have that implant colour on display. This is entrapment. Hanging around street corners. You're past curfew. This is your fault. You're the one trying to make a burden, not me.'

'Rip in the left pocket of his jeans, missing canine tooth on left side, full head of hair, maybe mid-thirties, tattoo on his right wrist. . .'

'I'll find you later, bitch. I'll recognise that piece of shit bike,' he shouts over his shoulder, running away now, but she keeps filming, keeps describing until he's out of sight.

When he's gone, she sits and steadies her breathing, then tries to calm her racing heart. She holds her sleeve to the cut on the back of her head. It's not so bad. She's had worse. She wipes her knuckles on the pavement. Her neck and head throb, and she coughs to clear her burning throat, reaching for the bottle of water on her bike. Each swallow stings. The night breeze chills her through the new holes in the back of her clothes, yet still she has sweat to clear from her brow.

She looks towards the deli again. The gang has gone. The shop door has been closed. No one would even notice till morning.

She sits a moment longer, composes herself. Her logical brain kicks in, and she checks herself over for more injuries. That was sloppy. She should have been on guard. That was close. Too close. She checks her app, and it confirms her video was uploaded. She writes her description of the events. Two crimes, one category five, one category three. She grins, elated. Such men are going to assault women anyway, she might as well be the victim, since she can most likely fight them off. And banking the extra points towards her Life Score by giving evidence through the Society Police app means she's done her bit for the Society. One more predator caught. One other woman likely saved. And a few more Life Score points for Ava.

The pervert was right though. She's past curfew, and that'll cost her. They'd strip her of points if they caught her, but by doing the Society Police work, they'll probably just lower her reward. A few more breaths later and she's back on her bike, lights on now, implant on display. Grazed hips crunch with every pedal stroke. Her jarred neck keeps her more upright than is efficient, yet her mind doesn't linger on the pervert. She thinks only of Zia. Fifty points, maybe. It could all be worth it for fifty points.

Chapter 5

Ava's new job at XL Medico starts Saturday, according to the curt email she receives from their HR. The demand from the Eyes Forward has portrayed her as a burden instead of an asset. When an email opens with *we regret to inform you*, it's never going to shine a positive light. She'll be working alone, mostly, as the Eyes Forward insisted. Her implant is still glowing orange, and she needs to be *out of harm's way*, the email reads. She scoffs when she reads that, imagining the harm she'd do to anyone who tries anything, workplace or anywhere. Despite her aches and bruises from the other night, her right hook and sweeping kick still functions perfectly well.

She stops by Beanies café on the way to grab her usual coffee. The staff know her order as soon as they see her face—medium cappuccino with chocolate. Probably a common order, Ava tells herself when she feels like she stands out too much. It's not good to stand out in the Society when *All Eyes Are Our Eyes* is plastered on every street corner. She lifts her shoulders, tucks her chin in, be a brick, a wall. Camouflage is armour. She bets they make that coffee for everyone. And by the looks of the place, it's hardly busy. No queue on a Saturday morning and too many staff twiddling their thumbs. It seems hers isn't the only business drying up. It's a 400 plus café. Maybe they'll start catering for the sub 400s too. She squirms at the thought. Bumping into the hooligans she tracks at night is enough to put her off coffee.

The XL Medico building is in Central Reading, having moved out of London several years prior. Slightly cheaper rents and away from the rowdier riots, they'd said. The Great Unrest from a decade ago left them, like many businesses, wounded and on alert, London's suburbs becoming more attractive.

The building cuts through the sky like a glass blade, several stories higher than anything else in the town, with better security than almost anything else in the Society. She parks her bike out front and shows her ID at the door to a security guard whose facial expression makes her feel like he is moonlighting as Society Police and trying to find her guilty. Her ID is checked and double checked before the security guard radios ahead and lets her through the turnstiles.

Being the weekend, Ava expects to find a deserted building, echoey halls, and an empty lab where she can get to work. She finds none of those things and instead has to raise her voice to be heard at the reception desk over the noisy chatter and air of excitement. Far too much commotion for a Saturday morning in a lab. After gestures and another round of ID checks, the receptionist issues her with a staff badge and directs her to where she will be working.

'There's no one from that department to show you around, for obvious reasons,' the receptionist shouts over the din, her eyes darting towards Ava's implant. 'All the management are men, and well, you know. Please be sure to keep your distance from other employees and do not converse with anyone—in case your current situation offends.'

'Sure,' Ava says through gritted teeth as she pins the badge to her front and makes her way down the hallway.

Far from being deserted, the hallways are rammed. Lines of people with the Eyes Forward logo branded on their clothes walk in both directions. One of them she recognises from the funeral home, that scar down his chin impossible to miss. He doesn't acknowledge her at all and keeps his eyes forward, literally. Some others clock her and tut, shake their heads, give her a wide berth, and recoil their noses. She picks at her cuticle on her thumb as she hears their remarks. The ridicule never seems to get old.

'What is that doing out and about? Did you see the orange?'

'They have unsafe age women working here?'

'Let's assume only on the weekends. Seems careless for such a big company.'

Ava keeps walking, head up and wearing her most polished poker face, looking overhead for signs to take her to the correct lab. She keeps her posture straight, not cowering from the comments, her fists clenched and her jaw tight.

When she finds a room with the sign *Formaldehyde* on the door, she goes in, shuts it behind her, then leans on it a while, taking some deep, calming breaths.

'Pigs. The lot of them,' she says out loud, anger calming her where tranquillity fails.

The lab is cold. Freezing, in fact. *Good,* she thinks. If she's going to get some work done, it's going to heat up a lot. She rummages around the lab, finds the burners, flasks, tubular reactors, all she needs. It's clean, more spotless than the lab area she maintains at the funeral home, each shelf meticulously labelled and orderly. She smiles at the organisation, and her tension dissipates.

On the desk at the front is a printout from the lab manager. *30 litres of formaldehyde-rose. Leave the lab as you found it.*

Very welcoming, she thinks. Underneath are the details of the concentration needed of formaldehyde-rose as an ingredient for Pres-X, but in her head, she can't get past the volume. *Thirty litres.* They took about that much from her funeral home. They said one body's worth of formaldehyde-rose is enough for several thousand doses of Pres-X. Pres-X-2, she assumes, is what they're wanting it for. That embalming fluid puts a healthy glow back into a corpse. Ava can only imagine what it'll do to a living person.

She does the maths, crudely, in her head. Even if a single adult body's worth was just one thousand doses, the thirty litres they already have would make hundreds of thousands of doses of Pres-X-2, and they want her to work three nights per week plus

Saturdays. Assuming the target will be the same, that's looking like a million doses a week. Produced by this lab alone. She pauses a moment while setting up the equipment to scratch her head and think. A million doses a week. Is that volume normal? How many 700 pluses who qualify for Pres-X-2 financing can there be?

Buried in the depths of her mind are the latest stats of the demographics of the Society. She strains her forehead to recall. Roughly one hundred and twenty million people in the Society, down several million from its peak (although still not low enough, according to many). She's sure from half-listening to news updates on the population demographics that one hundred and twenty million is the latest figure, but such stats generally drown out as background noise as she helps Zia in the kitchen and makes sure she's not about to set fire to the apartment. But one hundred and twenty million, she's definitely heard that number before.

The figure she's sure about is that ten million Preserved people already exist in the Society, certainly no less. The ten million milestone was celebrated across every 750 plus establishment in Berkshire. The 'end of death parties' with Preserved people dressing up as people from history, deceased celebrities, and politicians were meant to commemorate their own extended life expectancy. For the sub 750s, the festivities were branded as poor taste and general mockery. But the Preserved didn't care. Parading around more like students and youths than the wealthiest citizens with the most life experience.

So, ten million already Preserved. She banks that number in her mind. And another hundred and ten million left in the Society. Only about ten per cent of those have Life Scores over 700. That's just over ten million. She smiles at her mental maths, despite its crudeness. It doesn't make sense, though, maybe her maths is wrong? She'll make enough formaldehyde-rose for the entire eligible Society in just ten weeks.

The glassware is all connected. She finds the gas to connect to the burners at the back of a cupboard where she'd already checked, her brain not being as efficient as it should be with her mathematical distraction. Surely, they're not about to ship the stuff overseas? She shakes her head at the thought. No one exports anything these days. Too much paperwork, too much aggro, too much risk of annoying another country. Formaldehyde-rose will only keep at quality levels for eighteen months, two years at a push. Fifty-two million doses of formaldehyde-rose a year, and for what? Demand must be way below that level of production.

Unless. . .

She freezes, eyes widening at the thought that has just entered her head. No. It's so unlikely she can't comprehend it. She blinks away the idea, disbelief forcing some sense into her.

But maybe. . .

Just maybe they're using formaldehyde-rose for original Pres-X, and they're about to allow lower Life Scores to take it, the original formula, anyway. Maybe production is cheaper now, and so the less wealthy will be able to finance it. Maybe just over 600. Ava pauses for a moment as she thinks: maybe they're releasing it under the National Health Service. That would all be a massive boost to the finances of XL Medico. Sure, there would be outrage from the highest Scorers, but it's widely rumoured that XL Medico bankrolls the Eyes Forward.

During the Great Unrest, the Enough movement promised to buy out XL Medico and commandeer the supply of Pres-X. The takeover was blocked, but not without some compensation for the cause. Curfews on women, displaying their fertility status, all being part of the deal to prevent pregnancies. The Eyes Forward pandered to so many demands from Enough to keep the peace. The Enough were mostly comprised of the highest Scorers, mostly Preserved or aiming to be Preserved once they hit eighty years old. It doesn't seem so absurd that the rich in power want to get richer by selling more of their most valuable product.

Maybe...

Ava shakes the thought away again. The Enough movement wanted to ban babies and reduce population. Preserving more people would go against that. But still, a million doses a week is a lot for such limited demand.

She lights the burners, then raids the fridges to find the last ingredients she needs. Spurred on by a hope, the nonsensical faintest glimmer that maybe, perhaps, she can finance her aunt's treatment sooner than expected. False hope, more than likely. Zia is eighty-two years old and as her mind is ageing quicker than her body, her window for successful treatment is narrowing rapidly. Ava can get to 750, eventually, or 700 if she gets an XL Medico employee discount. With enough Society Police work, she might get lucky in just a year or more. But if Zia's mental decline happens too quickly, she might be too far gone for Pres-X to work. That's her biggest fear, that she won't make it on time.

That she'll lose the last family member she has left.

Thirty litres turn in to forty before she calls it quits for the day. The lab has the sickly-sweet chemical scent of formaldehyde-rose, living up to the name she gave it. It's the sort of smell she'll have to exfoliate off her later. She cleans up, leaving the lab as orderly as she found it, then cycles home still on a cloud of maybes and possibilities, not noticing the chilly air or the looming rain. The dark night sky serves to calm her excited mind after the glare of the fluorescent lights in the lab. After just a few pedal strokes, her phone pings, telling her that a successful ID was made of one of the gang members who looted the deli. She's been awarded five points. She tuts at the low number, less since she was breaking a rule herself. A bylaw, not a proper law or else she'd have her own points deducted. But maybe, just maybe, she doesn't need to hit 750 after all.

Zia is asleep when she gets home, curled up on top of her bed, slippers still on, dinner burned in the oven, the fire alarm seconds from going off. Ava opens the window to let the smoke out, batting at it with a tea towel, then puts a blanket over Zia and turns the TV down, its volume at head-splitting level.

In the oven, she salvages a little casserole from around the scorched bits and couples it with some bread and cheese. Both a bit past their best; she's had no time to go shopping lately. From the detritus of food packets and crumbs on the floor, it's clear Zia has found enough to eat. A partially drunk cup of tea is on the table sitting in a puddle, a half-eaten biscuit swimming in the spill.

Before cleaning up, she flicks channels, listens to the daily population stats, which confirm her guesstimates weren't far off, but nothing yet about an extended roll out of Pres-X. Ava's heart sinks.

Doesn't matter. Back to plan A.

Zia appears in the doorway, her hair sticking out on one side and trailing down her neck on the other, the other half of the biscuit collected in the ends.

'Morning, dear. Shall I sort us some breakfast?'

'It's eight-thirty in the evening, Zia.'

'Ah, all right then. I'll make a cup of tea.'

Ava wipes her eye, clears the table, then takes the used teacup to the kitchen. Her chest aches as she watches her aunt forget where the tea bags live, then get upset as she searches the wrong cupboard for mugs. For the hundredth time, Ava whispers a promise to her. *I'll get you that Pres-X. Soon. Somehow.*

Chapter 6

'Long time no see. Where you been hiding?' Dan asks as he orders some drinks. The barman serving is one Ava recognises from last time they drank in this bar. The same one Dan had his eye on, and by the awkward way the barman avoids eye contact and his cheeks flush, she knows something transpired last time he was here, when Ava's implant was orange and she couldn't make it.

The bar staff gestures to check Ava's implant and she lifts her hand, displaying the green glow for the staff to see to prove she is allowed to mingle with men and consume as much alcohol as she damn well pleases. 'Usual restrictions kept me away,' she says to Dan. 'A non-alcoholic drink didn't really appeal.'

'Still glowing green at your age?'

It surprises her too. The hormone detectors and temperature gauge are supposed to be accurate though. Any month now, surely, she'll be deemed barren enough to do away with regulations. She rolls her eyes at Dan's quip. Her oldest friend hasn't said a sensible word to her in years. That's why she still likes him so much. 'Believe me, I'm ready to be safe age. Any day now.'

'Well, at least you don't have to worry about that at work. It's not like the corpses will impregnate you.'

She pays with her card, the bar man doing a double take when he sees she's not paying on credit.

'You sure?' he asks.

Ava nods and taps her card on the machine.

'Everyone is paying with credit at the moment. Max out credit, strive to Score. Everyone wants to get their hands on the new Pres-X-2.'

'Not everyone,' says Ava, and takes her drink. She's witnessed enough people lose everything when their debt spirals. That's what the Eyes Forward don't tell you. Strive to Score, but they'll take the lot back. And with Ava's immigrant family history, she has no family name to fall back on.

They sit in a booth in the corner that opens out to a view of the entire bar. A place where Ava can hide in the shadows and Dan can people-watch, though with his back to the bar, obviously wanting to avoid eye contact with the barman. One more awkward ex-conquest they'll now have to navigate their evenings around. Ava slides her glass along the sticky surface and finds the least mucky patch of the bench to sit on.

'So, I was in the supermarket the other day and guess who I saw?' Dan says.

Ava winces, immediately aware of the answer. 'By your tone, it can only mean Mandisa.'

'Yep. All snooty, nose in the air, like hitting 600 makes her the fucking queen and she should be worshipped for being in a 400 plus supermarket. I don't know what you ever saw in her.'

Ava knows, however hard she tries to forget. It wasn't all Mandisa's bewitching smile and swishing hips. Someone with Mandisa's level of ambition excels at all they do. Her academic brilliance spilled over into being a perfect partner. She delivered affection with precision perfection, doted on Ava in a timely, efficient manner, and exhumed from Ava a helpless neediness for lust. Even her breakup was the flawless routine of 'it's not you, it's me, it's just bad timing at the moment,' spiel. A high achiever in every aspect. Ava mouths her name. Mandisa. She always loved her name—a groan of pleasure followed by a subtle hiss. It has a succulence to it.

Ava shakes her head and snaps her mind from its daydream. 'She was nice, once.'

'You wore colours, once. How times change.' He smirks and eyes her outfit. Her usual baggy black clothes are often his in-spiration for teasing. With her choice of attire and her lank, dark sheet of hair that has less life in it than the bodies in the cold room, she looks like she's in mourning and Dan, in his tailored jackets and pressed trousers, looks like he's the one running the funeral home.

Why does she always have to be reminded of Mandisa? She broke up with Ava almost a year ago when her Life Score in-creased and meant she could go places where Ava could not. That, and Mandisa arriving at safe age created a divide that

Ava's affections couldn't penetrate. The freedom that came with Mandisa's Score and menopause meant that after seven years together, when Ava was imagining a lifetime together, Mandisa was imagining her Score reaching the moon by working for companies that don't berate her fertility and socialising in places where she wasn't viewed as a hazard. Every woman dreams of such things. But most don't have another woman to drag them down and keep them in the gutter. Ava is still too poor. Too fertile.

'These bruises,' Dan says, noticing her purple neck. 'I assume that's from another pervert.'

'Nothing I couldn't handle.'

'I don't doubt that for a minute. But you're asking for trouble dressed like that. Wear something fitted, that's what the advice says. Figure-hugging clothes are harder to remove.' He lifts the edge of her jumper and holds it away, showing how a whole other human could fit inside. 'Plus, they know you're young.'

'I'm forty-nine. Not some spring chicken.'

'You know what I mean. Dress like a Preserved. All low-neck lines and short skirts. No one will touch you then. You look broke. They know they can get away with it.'

Ava doesn't respond, opting to sip her drink instead. It's not like she thinks Dan is wrong, he isn't. But she doesn't want to feel like some polished ornament on a shelf. She knows she has more to offer the world than her modest tits and hips. And she doesn't want to be mistaken for a Preserved. One look at her sagging jawline would clear that up anyway.

The bar is quiet, Sunday night being less than peak time. It's the one non-segregated bar this end of town and every time Ava comes here, it feels like a treat not to have to prove her date of birth. Premenopausal and postmenopausal women can mingle with such ease—as long as the premenopausal woman isn't in her orange time of course. If she was on the lookout for a new woman, she could find one from either end of their timeline. Not that Ava wants that. As much as it hurt when Mandisa broke up with her, she understood. Ava doesn't always want to be surrounded by women all younger than her, her own safe time seeming to take forever compared to others. She still has to prove her Life Score on entry, obviously. That goes without saying. It's an over 400 only bar, which gives it some diversity without admitting the lowest Scorers that trawl the streets looking for trouble or food. She's unlikely to need to upload her Society Police app here.

Looking at the customers, some are clearly Preserved. None with a fully pink face. They tend not to socialise for most of the first decade after treatment, until their regression has com- pleted and the pink hue of their skin disappears. Although, to a keener eye, a few patches can be seen in those who have opted to venture out earlier. Ava remembers when Pres-X first came out and the pink skin was explained. She found it intriguing that no matter what colour the skin was when they took Pres-X everyone went bright pink. And rather than socialise with racial anonymity, they all hid away. Some claimed their identity had been taken away, others were more honest and said they looked ridiculous and were looking forward to their first outing when fully regressed. Understandable, really. She'd hate to stand out so much. And ten years of being a hermit seems like a small price to pay to be young again. She looks at Dan now and tries to imagine his rich earth-toned skin turning bright pink. He'd shut himself away for sure. He'd never find clothes to match.

It's near on impossible to tell a Preserved just by looking at their faces. The clothes can be a giveaway, but that's not certain. The mannerisms though, are the easiest tell, and Ava and Dan delight in guessing who is and who isn't. The Preserved look young but always have an air of unease in such places. For most, it's been a couple of decades since they last socialised in bars. They order drinks that are almost obsolete now, lager and vodka, pink wines and weird liqueurs. Now fresh-faced and as attractive as they've ever been, they either skulk nervously in the shadows or parade around like a dog in heat. Delighting in their own aesthetics and sure that everyone else delights in it too. Polyamory among the Preserved is common, so the rumours go, their extra years giving them the desire to experiment.

'I can screw whoever I want,' one ninety-year-old whispered in Ava's ear one evening.

She corrected him. 'No. You can screw whoever wants to screw you.'

The idea of consent is outlandish to someone with such a Life Score and who checks their reflection in their pint glass with every sip. Ava's comeback resulted in an arse squeeze, which resulted in her left foot landing squarely in his crotch.

She reported him on the Society police app and was told she'd been entrapping him, and since she was in an unsegregated bar, she should expect such attention. The app sent her the auto response headlined *Educating women for the betterment of the Society* and included 'helpful tips' such as wearing tight-fitting clothes that are harder to remove and not smiling too much. She'd almost thrown her phone out the window when she'd read that.

'Him.' Dan points to a man wearing a white T-shirt too small for him, clutching a glass of something vibrant orange. 'He's definitely Preserved. And timid. Perfect.'

'What a catch.' She laughs. 'Gold-digging isn't what it used to be, you know. The rich come with a lifelong commitment now. Not just a few years of arse-wiping and dribble-mopping. You're not going to inherit the family jewels any time soon.'

'The wait for inheritance might be worth it for the added libido,' he says, bouncing his eyebrows.

'Well, that's pretty much all you'll have in common with someone fifty years older than you.'

'You are particularly grouchy today. Maybe you really are nearly at safe age.'

She punches his arm. Not too hard, he'd probably snap.

'Anyway,' he says after he has feigned a broken bone. 'If I fuck them well enough, maybe they'll gift me some points.'

'No one seriously gifts points.'

'They do sometimes. And I'm after that Pres-X-2. My complexion isn't half as bad as yours, but taking twenty years off would be great.'

'Well, I guess you were a virgin until you were twenty-five, so you have those years to make up for.'

Dan holds his heart. Always one for theatre. 'Anyway,' he says when she's stopped laughing. 'I don't see you striving to Score.'

She doesn't tell him about her Society Police work. She never tells anyone, though she's not sure how Dan would react. Understanding? Maybe. Berate her? Most likely. The good work she is sure she's doing still makes her a snitch. 'I'll have you know I maxed out a credit card just last week.'

'Ooh! Quite the big shot!'

Ava laughs and looks around the bar. The timid Preserved guy seems to be coming out of his shell a little and is talking to a woman standing next to the bar. A group of forty-somethings are sitting in another booth, clearly with the same agenda as Dan. Competition to bag a high scoring Preserved seems fierce. Ava does a double take as she spots Mrs Constance in the corner, sitting alone. Her hair, a waterfall of caramel curls, is half pinned up, the other half flowing in glossy locks over her bare shoulders. Three days a widow and she looks just like that. Red-eyed and lost. She sips her drink, nursing every drop, or else maybe trying to acquire the taste. Her quivering bottom lip tells Ava she's likely swallowing back tears along with the drink.

'Good choice,' Dan says, following her gaze. 'Also Preserved and timid.'

'I'm not eyeing her up. She's a client at work. She's not timid. She's sad.'

'Mixing work and pleasure? Go for it. She looks lonely. There are plenty of rich Preserved looking to experiment with some younger meat. I'm going to find me one.' He necks the rest of his drink and stands up.

'Have fun. I'm going to go and speak to that woman. See how she is.'

'Use some of my chat-up lines. The oldies love them.'

Ava bats him away with a laugh, then makes her way to Mrs Constance, catching a side view of herself in the window and instantly regretting it. She never peers at herself for long, only ever indulging in the briefest glimpses to update her perspective on her aesthetic changes. Though now she fights the urge to inspect and scrutinise, like slowing her pace to gawp at a car crash. Next to Mrs Constance's glamour, she feels like even more of an eyesore than she does with Dan.

Mrs Constance looks up as she approaches and smiles with recognition. Ava sits next to her.

'Mrs Constance. I just thought I'd come over and see how you're doing?'

'You're a sweet girl. I'm doing as well as can be expected. Thank you for asking. I'll be in on Monday to arrange things for Ted. Maybe visit him too.'

'I'll have the visiting room all ready for you.'

Mrs Constance's delicate floral perfume is invitingly subtle. Probably meant to be a tease on the senses, but Ava itches and fidgets to angle her nose away. She might as well be caked in mud next to Mrs Constance's chic. Not that she cares, she reminds herself. She has no time to make an effort. And no need.

'You're still not safe, I see,' Mrs Constance says as Ava lifts her drink, exposing her wrist.

'Nor are you now.'

Mrs Constance's implant glows green like Ava's. The one downside of Pres-X, the press says. Women's youth comes with fertility.

'I'd forgotten what a bore that side of womanhood is,' Mrs Constance says, wincing down some of her drink. 'When I was safe age before, there was no such thing as "safe age". We didn't have to be on show like we do now. I'm thinking of getting sterilised. Seems sensible. Since all the new Pres-X-2 takers are going to have to be anyway. I guess there's not much point now for you. You look like you're almost safe.'

Ava flinches at the words. She's beginning to regret coming to check on Mrs Constance. That's twice in one evening she's been reminded of her weathered skin and greying hair. She considers responding by telling her she's gay and why the hell should she pander to such crap, but thinks better of it and puts her hand to her chest as if grateful instead.

'You know,' Mrs Constance continues, 'I thought I'd come here and meet some old friends. Thought there might be some people I knew from years ago. We didn't really meet up with anyone the last ten years while we were regressing. We were looking forward to having a young person's social life again. But now I just feel out of place. I have so much energy, but I just want to hide away.'

'Being young comes with self-consciousness, I seem to remember.'

'You know, you're right. I remember spending hours worrying about what I looked like, if someone would like me, what people thought of me. It's all coming back. All those insecurities.'

'I'm sure it just takes a while to adapt.'

Walking into the bar is a group of young women. Obviously young, not just Preserved young. They look comfortable and are dressed modestly. Ava hadn't considered the truth in her words as she'd said them. Sympathetic nonsense rolls off her tongue easily. That side of small talk comes with her job. But as she watches them lift their chins, posturing confidence yet their eyes film over with insecurities, she feels wiser than the ninety-year-old sitting next to her.

'See that man there, in that awful jacket,' Mrs Constance says, nodding towards a Preserved man that is so un-timid, Dan would run a mile. 'I think he's my neighbour. I've not seen him since he had Pres-X. He always used to brag about what a handsome man he was in his youth. It seems he was telling the truth. Awful man though. Used to chat up the postman, the milkman, the gardener, his maid, just everyone really. Notorious. He'll be a nightmare Preserved, chucking his seed around like it's some delicacy.' She recoils her nose and lifts her drink. 'Awful man.'

Ava laughs and watches him wait in ambush for the young women to step a little closer. 'Sounds it.'

They sit silently for a moment, watching the scene fold out in front of them. The old Preserved eyes up the women with an exaggerated neck and pouts his lips. The young women turn their back, then walk away, him trailing after them like some loyal puppy. He should try some people who are after Pres-X-2, Ava thinks. But his arrogance clearly does not appreciate tactics.

Mrs Constance faces Ava and edges a little closer. 'What do you suggest, dear? To help a Preserved woman fit in again?'

Ava ponders a moment. Imagines how her aunt would adjust, what advice she would give her. The world has moved on, while Zia has been mostly stuck indoors. Ava wonders if she'd even know her way around the town these days. Keeping her aunt alive is all Ava has thought about. Childhood memories of time with Zia, holidays, cooking together, and gossiping about neighbours. Their bond has always been strong, stronger than that she shared with her parents even. Yet how Zia would cope with the change hadn't crossed her mind, her fear of losing Zia thwarting all else.

'I guess just immerse yourself,' Ava says. 'Meet people, gain confidence. Try and remember how you were years ago.'

'You know, I think that's great advice.'

Chapter 7

13 years before the Great Unrest

Ken's fascination with Pres-X didn't wane as Lucia hoped it would. It seemed more tenacious than his other phases, and there were times when Lucia thought he was going to go through with it. When he put his back out moving the sofa, when he couldn't find his reading glasses, when he had to turn the telly up louder.

'If only I was young again,' he'd say and curse, making a show of all those inconveniences being so much worse than they actually were.

Lucia ignored his rants, fetched the ibuprofen and a snack so he didn't take them on an empty stomach, lent him her reading glasses, and passed the remote control. She smiled through pursed lips as she did this, thinking how trivial these things were to fix, all the while reminding herself he was thirteen years older; he was bound to be suffering more. She justified his grumps and groans until she felt like they were ageing her ten years herself.

Then one day, when she'd had it up to here with his whining, she did what she rarely did.

She got mad.

'For God's sake, Ken.' She wasn't even sorry for using the Lord's name in vain, such was her rage. 'When are you going to stop moaning about everything?'

'You don't get it, Lu.'

'I do. I damned well do. I was speaking to my brother about all this crap—'

'Your brother's an arsehole.'

'Ken! How can you say that? You haven't even seen him in years. Him or his family.'

'Well, I can't understand a bloody word he says. His accent is worse than yours.'

Lucia held her hands to her cheeks and took a step back. One hint of anger from her and he reacted like this!

'See, this is the problem. People are against Pres-X because there are so many people already. But if there weren't so many bloody foreigners—'

'Don't you say another word! How dare you refer to me that way. Fifty years I've lived and worked in this country. Fifty years!'

'Well. . .' he said as he angled away from her. 'You're the exception. No one travels anymore. The Society put a stop to that. Devolved economies, it was a masterstroke.'

'You hated the devolved economies!'

'I've thought about it more, and actually, it was brilliant. Why spend money anywhere else? So tell me, why we have to keep all the foreigners is beyond me. Should have shipped them off home when everyone stopped travelling. They'd like that, all of them, to be with their families. I'm only thinking of them, Lu.'

She screwed her face up at this. He hadn't thought about it more, he'd been told about it more from those Eyes Forward brainwashers. Forty years together meant she definitely knew when her husband was lying. He certainly wasn't the sort to give a crap about other people's family lives.

He faced her again, his eyes sad under his bushy eyebrows. 'Come with me, Lu.'

'I don't want the bloody drug.'

'No, not that. Not yet anyway. Come with me to a meeting. Listen to what they're saying. It'll open your eyes, I'm telling you.'

'You want them to wash my brain like they washed yours?'

'Please, Lu. Just do this—for me.'

She could never resist those pleading eyes. That was why she married the old git.

'Fine,' she said, arms folded, head turned away. If she was going to go, she'd make it as much of a chore as he made turning up the TV.

***

The meeting was the next day in the local pub. The pub where Ken had never taken her before. It's more of a man's place, he'd always said, insisting he preferred the pub opposite. But as he walked in and knew the bar staff and the customers, it was clear he'd been frequenting the establishment for some time. Far from being just men, it was very mixed, though a higher Scoring establishment than what they were used to. That was the real reason he never wanted Lucia to go there, she suspected. He didn't want to pay the high Score establishment drink prices for her.

The tight git!

Eyes Forward representatives made up part of the crowd, identifiable by their pristine suits and the government logo on the front. They greeted Ken with handshakes and familiarity.

'About your job application with the Eyes Forward, Ken,' one of them said.

'Yes?' Ken's eyes were wide and eager.

'You're in.'

Lucia was sure it was only his dodgy back that stopped Ken doing a skip just then.

'Oh my, boys, you're not going to regret this. I am a man of the people. I will be your voice here among the masses.'

'Great, Ken. That's just what we want.' His voice lacked the excitement that Ken's had.

Ken took Lucia's hand then and squeezed it like he hadn't done in years. He even leaned in and kissed her cheek. It made her jump, that bit of contact so alien she'd assumed a fly had landed on her.

'This is going to mean great things for us, Lu,' he whispered in her ear. 'I'll be a shoo-in for treatment now.'

She turned her head away, not wanting his affections over something so awful. This phase will pass, the drug will never get approved. That was what she kept telling herself. God would never allow such a thing.

There was a low stage at one end of the pub, the kind that drunk people singing karaoke would usually frequent. That night, though, there was a projector screen lit up with the XL Medico logo.

'Starts in five minutes, Lu. Let's get a seat.'

That was not going to be possible, Lucia realised. The place was packed and getting even more so, and it wasn't like any of the people sitting were going to give up their seats. They all looked about their age. They waded through the crowd and propped themselves up on a wall by a speaker, so Ken didn't have to strain to listen. Lucia sipped at her wine frugally. She listened to the murmurings in the crowd and wondered if Ken could hear it. If he could, then surely he wouldn't be agreeing with all of this.

'People just need to stop having babies if they want fewer people. Sterilise the lot of them.'

'Send the foreigners back to where they came from.'

'As long as the low Scorers don't get to live longer, I don't see the problem. They don't deserve it like we do.'

If it wasn't for the precious wine in her hand, Lucia would have covered her ears. She stood there biting her lip, wishing she could shut her ears as she could her eyes.

A man appeared on the stage, sharply dressed and grinning like he wanted to show off new teeth. He probably did, since he was the youngest person in the pub. He tapped his hand on the microphone, making a horrible thud noise that was far too loud for Lucia right next to the speaker.

'Welcome, ladies and gentlemen,' he said. 'Lovely to see you all this fine evening. And so many new faces have come to listen. First of all, for the newcomers, let's go through the science.'

He clicked a button on his laptop, and on the screen was a picture of a tortoise. Not one of those normal little ones, but a giant one, standing next to a group of scientists in their white coats. The tortoise came up to their waists.

'This tortoise is called Highlander. He's nearly two hundred years old. It has long been known that tortoises don't age. They are, what we call in scientific terms, negligibly senescent.' He over enunciated the last two words, as if Lucia would remember such technical garble anyway. 'In humans, our senescent cells accumulate rapidly in later life, causing us all sorts of problems. Stiff joints, wrinkles, weakening muscles, looking at a few of you now, I need not go on.'

The crowd chuckled at this. Lucia rolled her eyes.

'These senescent cells do not accumulate in tortoises. Their DNA forbids it. Our scientists have managed to extract that DNA from tortoises, a completely natural product, and weave it with some clever chemicals to make this wonder drug, Pres-X.'

Lucia's jaw tensed. *Wonder drug? Pah! Load of nonsense.*

'People, I am here today to tell you the most exciting news. That Pres-X is going to be rolled out across the Society! We have extensively tested it on the 950 pluses for a decade and can confirm its effectiveness and safety.'

There were gasps of joy across the room. Couples and friends embracing and wiping away tears of happiness. Lucia looked around, shaking her head at the madness. It was like some cult.

The man raised his hands to shush the room. 'As anticipated as this is, the rollout will be slow. We do not have the stockpiles needed of the drug, so naturally, we will have to start with the higher Life Scores. But rest assured, in good time, everyone in the Society will be given the chance to have Pres-X.'

He went on and on, that man, so long that Lucia had to get another glass of wine. A large glass. To take the shock away. To numb her against the madness.

When it came to the end, the man asked if anyone had any questions. Lucia raised her hand.

'The world needs people to die. Where're all these extra people going to go, hey? We need to make room for the young.'

The man softened his smile. 'We are curing a terminal illness here. Time is a terminal illness. Would you say the same if we were talking about cancer?' He spoke like he was addressing a child.

Lucia squared her shoulders and narrowed her eyes. She would not be spoken to in such a way. 'You haven't answered my question.'

'There are ideas, among the Eyes Forward, to encourage limited breeding. I think we can all agree, the lives of the living come before those lives not yet created.' He gestured around the room, and some of the audience gave a cheer. An actual cheer!

'Babies?' Lucia's words caught in her throat. 'No more babies?'

'Just less. A little more control over such things is sensible, in this day and age. Any other questions?'

There were other questions, but Lucia didn't hear them. The room spun around her with all the nods of agreement. Or maybe it was the wine. She held onto the table and looked at the floor. Better than looking at that man. Better than looking at any of those awful people.

They left the meeting, or rather, Lucia rushed out as soon as it was not too impolite to do so, making the sign of the cross over and over again. Ken trailed behind her, slowly, still listening, waving at people.

'No, Ken. No,' Lucia said as soon as the fresh air hit her face and she could breathe properly again. 'You can't do that. You're going to turn yourself into a tortoise.'

'Don't be daft,' he said, as if *she* were the mad one.

'A zombie tortoise. That's what you'll be.' She did the sign of the cross several more times as she said this, then grabbed and held onto the crucifix dangling from her neck.

He swatted his hand toward her, like her words were an irritation.

'Humans live, then they die,' she said. 'That's how it has been for billions of years.'

'Humans haven't been around for billions of years.'

'You and your quick tongue!'

Chapter 8

10 years after the Great Unrest

Ava elbows her way through the crowds to get to the funeral home door on Monday morning. Not only the usual pedestrian lanes, but a gathering of twenty or more, just standing, waiting outside the home. Loitering. In the way. *Rude*, she thinks as she forces her way through with an array of excuse mes and apologies.

'Can I help you?' she asks the crowd as she stands in front of the doors, raising her voice to be heard over the buses and general chatter. No one responds. Instead, they continue standing there, obstinate, avoiding looking at Ava. 'Right, well, okay. You're blocking the entrance to my business. Maybe move on. Please.' She adds the pleasantry at the end as an afterthought, and it comes out like a squeak.

They don't move on, much to Ava's annoyance as she grasps the door handle and hoists herself through the last members of the crowd as they stand steadfast. The body heat emanating from them creates beads of sweat across her hairline as she squeezes through. There's not much she can do about it. She doesn't own the street.

'Max.' Ava calls out when she gets through the door and he appears from the cold room, dark hair slicked back. He, for once, looks almost as well-groomed as one of the finished cadavers. 'Do you have some new celebrity status you've not told me about? What's with the crowd outside?'

'It's not me. They're all Score-diggers.'

'What?'

'They're waiting for some high Scoring widow or family member. They want to befriend them, date them, get gifted points. To qualify for Pres-X-2.' He adds smoochy noises at the end, as if Ava doesn't know what dating is. To be fair, it's been a while.

Ava slaps her clammy forehead. 'No, tell me that's not really a thing. What are our clients going to think?'

'They'll like it, probably,' he says with a shrug. 'I mean, life as a Preserved widow or widower is reported to be quite lonely. Or promiscuous. Either way, they'll like the attention.'

Max has been dating a psychology student for two months now and ever since, he seems to stitch together behaviours as well as he can a corpse. Ava was happy for him when he first met her. His sinewy body has gained some bulk since they met—dinners out instead of dodging his nan's never-ending vegetable stews. His ashen complexion is not the permanent feature Ava took it to be. A bit of romance has given him some colour. Just a bit. He still looks as if he's had a lifetime of trauma that his girlfriend's studies are yet to help him recover from.

'That psychology student girlfriend of yours talks a lot, doesn't she?'

'Never shuts up.' He smiles, and is that a blush? 'Anyway, come and see what I've managed to do.'

Ava follows him to the cold room, past the vases of wilting flowers, whose sweet smell is on the turn from pleasant to having an undertone of rot, and she must remember to chase up the next delivery, sure it was due a few days ago. In the cold room laid out on the table is Mr Constance. His head is well patched up, the stitching subtle, and mostly, he looks sleeping rather than deceased. Max stands by, changing out of his apron, revealing his creased shirt underneath. Presenting himself better has only stretched as far as ironing his sleeves, it seems. Ava inspects the body and nods in approval at his handiwork. His usual slumped shoulders round back, a hint of a smile disguising his dwindling gloom.

'Took a while, since she wants an open casket,' Max says. 'I was in at seven o'clock this morning to finish it up. But he looks all right, I think. I added some fake hair, see? Makes that side of his head look less concave.'

'You've done a good job, Max. Well done.'

'Got all the brains back in too. So, he's more or less complete.'

'Again, good job.'

He hangs his apron up and stands on the spot, fidgeting, looking at the floor. 'I was thinking. . .'

'Right. . .' She narrows her eyes at him.

'Pres-X is obviously getting more and more popular with the 750 pluses, and this funeral home is a 700 plus. I'm a bit concerned about my job, to be honest. Not many 700 plus are dying, and there'll be even less with this new Pres-X-2 coming out. That's for 700 pluses.'

'It's more of a cosmetic thing.'

'But still, banking on middle-aged rich people dying is a bit of a gamble. Our client base is simply too small. When this funeral is done, we've got nothing else. It's only this old guy in here. He looks lonely, can't you tell?' Max mocks a frown, holding his face right next to Mr Constance. Ava rolls her eyes, and he continues. 'Anyway, perhaps we should lower the Life Score requirement? I reckon a new licence should be easy enough to get.'

Ava nods. 'Thanks, Max. It's being considered. Please, don't worry about your job.'

'Maybe we could do pet funerals? I reckon rich old people would pay as much for those as they do for humans. I used to groom my dog, clippers and everything. I know how.'

'That's not a bad idea, actually. Let's research that some more.'

Max's chest inflates slightly. He stands a little straighter as he starts to tidy up. Max worrying about anything is the last thing Ava wants. He's been her apprentice for two years and during that time, she's seen him blossom at work but continue to taper mentally. His new girlfriend may have lifted his moods and tidied up his presentation, but his trauma is more tenacious than that. His humour can't hide the lines up his arms. They're red-raw some days. Fresh and angry. Ava leaves pots of antiseptic cream around the funeral home where he can find them. A subtle gesture and less awkward than trying to talk to him about it. Yet her heart aches to see it. Another youth grown up an orphan after the Great Unrest. A product of the factions that formed and divided the Society. Peace may have been negotiated, but the sadness and loss remains. At least Ava was an adult when her parents were killed. At least she understood what they were fighting for.

'Can't rely on the Preserved walking out in front of traffic all too often,' he says, a poor attempt to lighten the mood. 'Although the crowd outside certainly seems to think such accidents happen more frequently than they do.'

'I wonder if we can get some council order to keep them from clogging up the front door,' Ava says. 'It just doesn't look very professional.'

'As I said, I think it'll be fine. Have a look down the High Street. It's the same at any high Score place. Our crowd is quite small in comparison.'

'Really? Well, I'll go have a gawp and get some coffee. You want one?'

Max shakes his head and wheels Mr Constance into the viewing room. The flowers in there are holding up a little better, or more likely, Max has rearranged them to put the worse-faring ones out the front. She leaves Max fiddling with the lighting settings and blankets as she leaves.

The Score-diggers are still loitering, and she pushes through with all her strength, stepping into the pedestrian slow lane, too lazy to be quick and work is quiet enough without her for the extra minutes. The stroll takes her past the deli that was broken into, its shelves restocked, and door repaired. All ready for another looting. A new Eyes Forward poster plastered up outside, the walled-in eye the main feature, the Society Police slogan *All Eyes Are Our Eyes* underneath. A little feeling of pride bubbles up, giving her more spring in her step, that she's helped halt the criminals who did the damage, the slogan inspiring her to continue her good work.

The High Street is the busiest she's ever seen. Where the pedestrian traffic eases up, it's because everyone is filing into shops, credit cards ready. Peering in the windows as she jostles past, Ava sees full baskets and empty shelves. Several times the pointy corner of a box filled with purchases jabs at her from other people in the walking lanes.

A few minutes later, the lane detours from her usual route and takes her past the monument of the Eyes Forward. It's been a while since she's been in this part of town and the change makes her freeze on the spot, much to the annoyance of the pedestrian traffic behind her. After a few shoves and tuts, she steps out of the lane into the standing area, cordoned off by white marks on the tarmac and metal bumps to prevent any spillover. It's marginally less crowded than the walking lanes, and she takes a few breaths as she stares for a moment. Old scaffolding still lays at its base, the modifications so recent that the statue shines, almost entirely free of bird shit, the pond around it containing clear water and a few discarded pennies. Rising up from the pond is a massive sculpture of the same eye, but rather than the walls on either side of it like usual, there are hands. A copy of the XL Medico logo. A mishmash of the two. Underneath a new slogan. Not one she recognises from Eyes Forward, not the usual *Strive to Score* or Society Police slogan. Instead, it says: *Your Life Length is in Our Hands.*

XL Medico's partnership with Eyes Forward isn't a rumour anymore. It's a confirmed coalition.

On the building and storefront walls behind the monument are adverts for credit cards, loans, consumables to be purchased on credit, all the things Society citizens can do to max out their funds and boost their Life Score. They're targeted to those unlucky enough not to inherit such a Score from wealthy parents. For those who, like Ava, didn't go to the right schools to guarantee her a high Score to start with. And by the looks of the crowds, it's all working. Pres-X-2 has lit a fire within the Society and people are literally burning through every penny and bit of credit they can get.

She stands on her tiptoes and peers higher over the crowd. Scuffles break out in shops, stripped bare of all their wares and people fighting over the last things they can spend their credit on. Ava takes it in, the whole scene, a mixture of inspired and appalled, and starts to think. She could do with some new clothes, some shirts for work and comfy trousers for cycling in the evenings. Perhaps she should get Zia something, some new slippers, and a cardigan before stocks run out completely. She could probably get a new credit card. She's usually so frugal with credit, but if everyone else is getting offered more credit, then she will likely qualify for more too. She needs to up her Score, but that's for Zia, which makes it fine. There's nothing wrong with that. It's for Zia, for her health, not the cosmetic treatment of Pres-X-2. She makes a mental note of the credit card company adverts across the road. She'll apply as soon as she gets back to work.

At the 500 plus café, she grabs a couple of sandwiches that expire tomorrow. The lettuce is a little past its best, the relish soaked halfway through the bread. But still, they look satisfying enough. No doubt the leftovers from two days prior at the higher scoring café. If they're not bought today, they'll get moved to the 300 plus café, then when past their sell by date, the sub 300s get a look in.

Max's nan, Erin, is at the desk when she arrives back at work. Her long grey hair is plaited in the style that everyone wore once. Max is arranging the new flowers that have just arrived, the old ones already discarded. He doesn't look like the type to take much joy in floristry, with his tenacious gloom and ridiculing about the expense, but he always jumps up to help with that task.

'Ava, dear. Lovely to see you.' Erin walks over to greet Ava, a stick steadying her. 'How's your aunt?'

'She's okay. Not really able to get out and about these days.'

'Well, tell her I said hello. I still remember that lovely after-noon tea we all had over at the Forbury. You remember, dear?'

'I do.' Zia won't, but Ava doesn't mention that.

'Have you met anyone? I know Zia is so keen for you to settle down. You're not getting any younger, dear. I met my Lance when I was almost forty. How I wish I'd met him sooner. I would have liked more years with him.'

'Do you want to sit down, Erin?' Ava says, dodging the sub-ject. Her love life is no one else's business. Ava supports Erin by the elbow, Erin's peach cotton sleeve wrinkling under her grasp, and walks her to a chair.

'Max has met someone. Have you heard?' Erin asks.

'I have. She sounds like quite the catch.'

Erin moans and pants her exhales as she sits, flapping her blouse as she gets comfortable. 'It was exhausting getting past that bunch outside, even if they were all telling me how lovely I look. I walked all the way here. Bloody buses are terrible this morning. I waited for three and I still wasn't able to get on one, so busy. But I got to see that monument, have you seen it? It's ghastly. This bloody drug is taking over the world.'

'It's saving so many people, Nan,' Max says. 'It's a good thing.'

'Utter nonsense. You heard this, Ava, dear? My grandson, it's all he goes on about. Trying to get me to take it. Carrying on like I've got some Score of 800. Nonsense. Utter nonsense. I don't trust it. Not one bit.'

'You've got a 650, Nan. You're so close.'

Ava's eyes widen. '650. My, Erin, that's an impressive Score.'

'Oh, pish posh,' she swats her hand at Ava. 'What does it matter? We all make do with our lot, don't we? Though I'd hate to be one of the really low Scorers. I see them rummaging in the bins down the street next to ours. Searching for scraps, I suppose. Doesn't seem fair to me that so many don't have enough food and get in trouble for trying to eat, while others get to live forever. It's broken. The whole Society is broken.'

Ava nods, her smile dips, and her face heats up. She doesn't feel guilty for her Society Policing, but secrets threaten to reveal themselves in reddening cheeks and averted gazes, instinctive reactions Ava's never learned to disguise.

An array of compliments erupts from the crowd outside, snapping all their attention and providing a much-needed distraction. Wolf whistles and cheers.

'You look gorgeous!'

'Let me take you for dinner. Show you a good time.'

Over the crowd, Ava can't see why the commotion has happened, but after a moment the crowd parts to allow Mrs Constance through, and she makes it to the doors and Ava leaps to greet her.

'Lovely to see you again,' Mrs Constance says as she hands Ava her coat. 'Quite the crowd out there. A bunch of darlings, really. All so polite.'

'Yes, they all seem well-mannered enough,' Ava says. Surely Mrs Constance can see the crowd for what they are? Ava opts not to tell her.

'I've thought a lot about what you said, and you were absolutely right. So wise for a woman so young.'

Too young to be accepted, too old to be desired, Ava thinks as she hangs the coat, its soft cashmere doing little to take away the prickling feeling from her skin.

'Can I get you a cup of tea?'

'No, thank you,' Mrs Constance says, a little quieter. 'Ted always loved tea. I'd hoped we'd go to that little tearoom on the boat on the Thames when the weather gets a bit nicer. Just one more thing he'll never get to do.'

They've had many Preserved widows and widowers come in over the years, talking of the years stolen, the memories they still had to make but would forever be denied. The unpreserved talk more of the times they'd shared, the happy moments they'd had, instead of yearning for what will never be. A contentment for all they had shared, like the extra years ahead leave a taste of dissatisfaction. The devastation is often tinged with a hint of excitement though, a new freedom, like the shackles have come off. Ava sees that tinge in Mrs Constance now, her eyes glinting not only with tears but with adventure. Once again, born anew.

'Oh, my. Erin, is that you?' Mrs Constance walks over to Erin, who strains to stand, scowling and backing away.

'What do you want? I don't know you,' Erin says, folding her arms across her chest. 'I don't know anyone so young, certainly don't know any Preserved.' She says *Preserved* through lips so pursed the word barely comes out.

'It's me, Erin.' Mrs Constance continues to advance until Erin has her back against the desk. 'It's Felicity. My maiden name was Merriweather. You remember me, I'm sure. We lived on the same street for a while, down Richmond Street. It was about forty years ago. Remember? I lent you some shoes for a wedding once.'

Erin looks Mrs Constance up and down, slowly, chin tucked into her neck, wide eyes turning narrow. 'Well, I don't want your shoes. Heels like that at my age, no thank you. I'll see you later, Maxy. Ava.' Erin bolts for the door quicker than Ava's ever seen her move.

Mrs Constance's back arches, her chin goes to her chest. Ava spots the signs of someone weak with grief and shock, and darts to her side and supports her by the forearm, leading her gently to the chairs.

'We were good friends once. She didn't even recognise me.'

'There, there. Have a seat. I'm sure it's just been a bit too long for her.'

Max looks over and mouths *sorry* as Ava waves away his apology. She can only imagine how Mrs Constance would look unpreserved. Even forty years ago, she would have been middle-aged, her black hair greying like Ava's with the frizz that comes with it, her even skin blotched and loose. Poor Erin must have been so confused.

'We were supposed to meet again with old friends, together, Ted and I.'

'Can I get you a cup of tea?' Ava offers again.

'You're a good friend. I'm pleased we can be friends.'

The corner of Ava's mouth upturns at this, quite unsure if she feels like Mrs Constance is a friend and not a client as Max passes a cup of tea. Mrs Constance stares at it for a while, the steam condensing across her cheeks, beading on top of her makeup, hiding any tears.

After a few sips in silence, Mrs Constance wipes her eye and says, 'I'd like to go see my Ted now.'

Ava shows her to the viewing room and leaves her to it. The room looks as lovely as it can. There's the smell of fresh flowers, relaxing music, and Max found the perfect lighting setting. Mr Constance is draped in a fine blanket, and there's a perfectly comfortable seat for Mrs Constance to sit on with a box of the finest tissues at the ready.

A couple of hours later, Mrs Constance re-appears. Even her Preserved skin can't hide the puffiness fresh crying brings. She sits at the table with Ava and takes the quote paperwork from her handbag.

'My job in XL Medico was business development,' Mrs Constance says. 'Did you know that?'

Ava shakes her head. 'I did not.'

'It was where Ted and I met. I was his boss for a while. So many years ago now. He rose above me, of course. Promotions went his way easier than mine. I never got to enjoy the benefits of being safe age in the workplace. By the time the safe age rules came in, I was almost retired. You're the boss here?'

'I am. It was my father's business. He died during the Great Unrest. It's just me and my aunt now.'

'She's an elder, I assume. Preserved?'

'Not yet. I'm working on it.'

Mrs Constance nods slowly at this. She's clearly in no hurry to leave. It's often the way. Returning to the empty house is one of the worst parts of grief.

'Business must be tricky for you,' Mrs Constance says. 'Not so many 700 pluses dying these days. I hope you have another form of income?'

'We're branching out to pets.'

'Sensible. I'll keep you in mind when my Stanley passes. He's getting on a bit.'

Mrs Constance retrieves her phone from her handbag and shows Ava some photos of a cat. A ginger boy with a weepy eye and a face more judgemental than most humans.

'Handsome boy,' Ava says.

'He is, isn't he? Quite the comfort at the moment. I'm hoping Pres-X gets licensed for pets. That would be wonderful, don't you think?'

'I'm sure.'

'Anyway. I've taken a job back at XL Medico, since my sterilisation is booked in, they were delighted to have me back. And I thought it would be good to come out of retirement. Keep me busy, you know. Although they still don't like people my age doing too much. They don't want the Preserved stealing the jobs of the young. That was part of the peace agreement with the Time's Up protestors during the Great Unrest, I believe. But I have expertise which they can utilise for part-time hours. And it's a wage as well. So, I'd like to give my Ted the send-off he deserves. I'll go for the full deluxe package, please.'

Ava smiles. 'Perfect option, Mrs Constance.'

'Oh, please, call me Flick. We're friends, after all. And I'll take out the finance, please. The extra credit should boost my Score. Even now I can strive to score and make the Society proud. Imagine, perhaps if I keep maxing credit, I could get to 800, even 900. Wouldn't that be wonderful? To achieve 900 in my Ted's memory.'

Ava loads up the paperwork. 'He'd be very proud of you, Mrs—I mean, Flick.'

Chapter 9

Another of the deli robbers have been IDd, and on her way home, Ava gets the message to say she has another five points. 530 now. Not bad going. The attacker won't be prosecuted though, the message says, since she was out after curfew for her orange time. She'd asked for it, is the gist of the message, and she should be grateful they don't deduct more points for that rule breach. Attached to the email is a document containing details of appropriate behaviours for fertile women. She shakes off the rage. There's no point being angry about what she can't fix. She can't have long left until she's safe age, surely.

It's a small boost, but she's still so far off, and with business being so quiet, she's going to need to grab every point she can. She'll have her usual time at the funeral home, three evenings and Saturday at XL Medico, which leaves three evenings for her Society Police patrols and an entire day off. Manageable. Exhausting but manageable.

By the time she gets home, another message pings her phone. Not the happy ping to tell her new points have been awarded, but the ominous, foreboding gong of a warning message. She groans, braces, then opens it.

Warning. Causing pedestrian lane obstruction by failing to keep moving. Monday 18th March 12:34. Next offence will be points deducted.

Accompanied with footage, of course, of her doing just that. Society Police patrolling the bloody pedestrian lanes at lunch time. She groans again and slams her finger into the 'accept' button. Still, at least it's only a warning, until again, the gong sounds. Surely, it's just the same message, not another warning.

Penalty notice for obstructing pedestrian traffic. Monday 18th March 12:37.

Ten points deducted.

No! Seriously? Her groan turns to a whimper. The appeals process is nonsense and won't get her anywhere. Three Society Police caught her on camera standing by that stupid statue outside the white lines for all of three seconds before she stepped within the standing zone. Ten points deducted when she is awarded nothing for catching a rapist. Erin was right. The whole Society is broken.

Ava drags herself up the stairs, too lethargic to move quickly. Suzanna is at her front door, just standing in the doorway, her face covered in some pale green goo.

'Don't mind me, dear. Just getting some fresh air.'

'No worries, Suzanna.'

'You look a bit peaky. You should try some vitamin face masks, like these.' She holds her hands up either side of her face. 'I can buy you some if you like. Trying to max out my credit.'

'No, thanks, Suzanna. You keep them for you.'

'I'll leave some in the hallway for you. Had to give Nelson across the hall some furniture earlier. Bought too much and don't want the refund to count against me, you know? Really need to up my Score.'

Ava is halfway up the next flight of stairs by now, heavy feet scuffing, landing with a thud on each step, Suzanna's voice diminishing behind her. She calls down a thank you and gives a thumbs up, not waiting to hear any more.

The flat feels hot enough to boil water and as soon as she gets in, she turns the heating off, then opens a window, sweating from that minor effort. Zia closes the windows after her and tightens her cardigan around her.

'It's boiling, Zia.'

'It's not even summer yet.'

'Feels like it.' Ava checks the smart meter, and her jaw drops when she sees their energy usage. 'You've had the heating on all day, I see.' Learning that only makes Ava hotter. She grabs a cold drink from the fridge, then holds it to her hairline, getting a little relief.

'Having a flush, dear? It's about time.'

'No. The heating is on full blast.'

'I remembered something today,' says Zia as she sets the table, knives and forks out for some dinner Ava is sure doesn't exist.

'What's that?'

'That boy. You dated a boy. What was his name?'

'Nikos,' Ava says and puts the cutlery back away.

'Yes. He was a nice boy. Had some European in him, so your dad liked him. What ever happened to him?'

'I've no idea. I was about twenty at the time.'

'You used to wear colours then.' Zia pulls at Ava's black shirt and peers at it, as if searching for hues that aren't there. 'Now you look so gloomy all the time.'

'I run a funeral home,' Ava says and pulls her shirt away.

'I think I preferred you dating boys. It would be nice if you had a baby. I'd like you to have a baby. Your parents died for your right to have children.'

Ava swallows back a sigh. 'No, they died from a stampeding riot because no Society Police were doing anything about the Enough rallies and riots during the Great Unrest. And now the ring leaders make up half of the Eyes Forward. So they walked over everyone, it seems.' Her tone is too harsh, she knows this, but her temper is too withered to hold back. The TV isn't even loud enough to justify her raised voice.

'They never supported them, though. That Enough rabble. He would have loved to have been a grandpa. But his time was up, and he accepted that.'

Ava replaces the soft drink and swaps it for a bottle of beer and her shoulders sink when she realises it's the last one. She opens it anyway, holds the cool bottle up to her face, the condensation trickling down her neck.

'It's not happening, Zia. Not a chance, like I've said a hundred times before. I'm almost at safe age. Baby licences are impossible to get, and unlicensed babies are not treated well.'

'But still—'

'Plus, I don't want a kid. Don't even like them. Now, can we please get back to the question of dinner? There is a very cold casserole sitting in a cold oven.'

'Oh.' Zia's hands go to her mouth. 'I must have forgotten to put the oven on. Are you mad?'

Ava laughs, then swigs from the bottle. 'Of course I'm not mad. You should have just left it out on the kitchen counter. It probably would have cooked then since the flat is hotter than the oven. Perhaps we should order in tonight, save this for tomorrow?'

'Whatever makes you happy. You know that.'

Ava grabs her phone, ordering from their favourite pizzeria, one still standing from years ago, when her dad was alive and used to say it's almost as good as Napoli. She's only been able to order from there recently, when her Score tipped over 500, and it's as good as she remembers from years ago.

Zia gets the cutlery out, then sets the table again, looks at the casserole in the oven, and turns the dish over wearing oven gloves. Ava doesn't tell her again that it's cold. That they don't need cutlery. No point in having the conversation again.

'You should dye your hair a bit, you know,' says Zia, not even looking Ava's way. 'You've a lot of greys showing.'

'So do you.'

'Well, I'm old. No point looking safe age when you're not actually at safe age.'

'I'm not far off.'

'I know. You haven't got long left to have a baby.'

Ava necks another gulp of her beer. Every night. The same thing. Over and over. In the mirror above the mantle, she checks her hair. Salt and pepper, heavy on the salt. Nothing wrong with looking natural, she thinks. Every woman older wants to look younger. Every woman younger wants to be older. What's wrong with just being her, here and now? Not wishing her life away, nor yearning to turn back the clock. Everyone the world over seems to be hurrying through life, then want to do it all again. Ava swigs the last of her beer slowly, savouring it. Enjoying the taste, the coolness on her tongue. Let that last a while longer.

She watches Zia rearrange the cushions for the hundredth time, rearrange the cutlery, look confused at the casserole they have just discussed, and her heart aches. Zia remembers so much and has so much more still to give. It's only the day-to-day things that confuse her. Shoes on the wrong feet, where the tea bags are, the time of day, little things that stifle her enjoyment and make her not want to go out. Physically, she's great for her age. A little slow, but she has better knees than Ava.

When Ava's finished her beer, she shifts one of the chairs to the corner of the room to make a little space, then loads up her training app, punches out some reps, and works her muscles until they pulse and cramp. She's trained in martial arts for decades and her form may not be at its peak, but it's enough for her to not fear the streets. Women have always lived in fear, like it's just expected. But not Ava. She fears no man or molester. The only thing she fears is being left alone. The only thing she fears is losing her Zia.

Chapter 10

Keep ageing at bay. The Pres-X-2 way
One of the core values of XL Medico

***

During her night shifts at the lab, Ava surpasses her targets again. She must have made enough for a million doses already by now. If they had more staff, they could make even more still. She counts the lockers. Seven staff—for the whole lab. Why would such a massive company be so frugal with its staff? Frugality is probably about right. No company this big gets rich by indulging itself with such things as adequate staffing levels.

Down the corridor, XL Medico's new product is being manufactured. The product designed to save the Society, the adverts say. A new antidepressant with the power to turn even the bluest of blues into sunshine days. Who needs therapy when you have B-Well? From the gleeful faces in the adverts, it looks like they mainline it, and from the excitable greetings Ava receives walking past their lab that evening, she assumes they've all had free samples.

The corridors are quieter this evening, the Eyes Forward not doing their inspections. Her footsteps echo down the hallway, the fluorescent lights bouncing off the white walls more dazzling without the array of black suits to dull the brightness. A staff canteen is in the centre of the building. At this time of night, it's served only by vending machines and a kettle. There are cups on the draining board left stained for the cleaners to deal with in the morning and crumbs across the tables. *Shoddy for a lab*, Ava thinks as she fills the kettle, empty but still warm to the touch from its previous user. Sitting at a table, a couple of lab staff are drinking from paper cups, hushing their voices only slightly as she makes her brew.

'It would be such a demographic shift. That's my issue with it.'

'Supposed to be survival of the fittest. If they give Pres-X to just anyone, it's survival of everyone. That's a slap in the face for evolution. Even the bloody cleaners and criminals will have access.'

'Surely, they'll draw the line at people with a record.'

'I dunno, Sanj. They're just thinking about the money, not much else.'

The kettle boils too quickly for Ava to eavesdrop anymore. She pours slowly, craning her neck to listen, but all she hears is the trickle of water. Momentarily, she eyes a seat at the table next to them. Would it be weird to sit there? Alone and in such proximity? Would they stop gossiping? She checks her watch and sees she hasn't the time to sit and idle anyway. She makes her tea, then skulks away.

Could it be... No, she can't let herself get excited. That little snippet of conversation could be about anything. As promising as it sounded, it was a rumour. A rumour of a rumour. Plan A is still all she has. Work harder, strive to Score.

After three hours sweating in the lab, making enough formaldehyde-rose to embalm the number of staff present after hours, she cycles home, slowly, exhausted. The extra work taking its toll, and the bump in her wage packet not showing for another month at least. Her Life Score is irritatingly stagnant. No chatter on the dark web that would make a stake-out worthwhile. She is in a ditch, like low-mid 500s is the best she can achieve. For every point she has to claw up a smooth concrete wall, bloodying her hands and ripping her nails. She stretches her neck out, which cracks and stiffens even more.

The bars are full to bursting, late night eateries also rammed, filling the streets with smells of fried food and sweet treats as well as the noise that comes with such commotion. Posters everywhere with lit-up advertising, encouraging the Society to max out credit. Spend, spend, spend! Strive to Score and stay young. Ava groans. She has no energy to go for a drink and pittance left in credit to max out, still having not gotten round to applying for new credit cards. She squeezes her eyes shut, shakes the negativity from her head and tells herself she'll get there. Her credit limit will increase when her wages come in. Zia is doing well, well-ish. There's a ton she should be feeling positive about.

She stops at the traffic lights, willing them to change quicker as her legs cramp. The spring evening is cool, and she's under-dressed. She puts her hands in her pockets and forces a shiver to warm up her core. Before the lights change, he's in front of her, the same pig as the other night. His nose is still swollen, and his beard clearly has not been trimmed.

'Told you I'd recognise that bike. Green now are you, bitch.'

Her heart stalls a moment. Too tired for even startled reflexes to kick in, she takes a second to realise what's happening. Before lashing out, she clicks her phone in her pocket. She's loaded up that app a million times before and doesn't have to see what she's doing. She says nothing, only holds her phone in her pocket in one hand and clenches her fist with the other.

He reaches for her breasts with one empty hand, a knife in the other. 'Now keep still this time, like a good girl.'

With her clenched fist, she punches his jaw, taking out the other to film the aftermath. He shakes it off, clearly surprised at the power in her left hook, and Ava's pursed lips smile a little. Perverts shouldn't underestimate women. He ignores the phone and lunges at her as she punches him once again, hearing her knuckles crack. She wobbles on her bike and stabilises herself with one foot, lifting her left foot to kick him once again in the bollocks and uses that as momentum to get going. Screw the red light. She cycles off, reciting her description of the man again. She's green, there's no curfew. *Fuck that pig.* She uploads the video and makes it home, her heart racing all the way.

Zia has fallen asleep on the sofa again, the 24-hour news channel still blasting on the TV. Ava puts a blanket over Zia, then sits on the arm of the sofa, turning the telly down so she can hear it without being deafened.

She slumps herself down, willing her heart to slow and her panting breaths to ease. Adrenalin takes a while to ease up, so she closes her eyes, counts to ten, then reminds herself that she made it home. She stretches out her fingers, opens her eyes, and admires the red-raw bruising across her knuckles. If her hand is that sore, his face must be throbbing. She smiles and hopes his face is mangled enough so he can never smile again. Fat chance of that, she knows. The guy was solid. He'll probably have a broken tooth at best.

Still, it's a win.

She looks up at the TV, feeling calm now and quite proud. She blinks a few times and leans forward, closer to the telly, quite unable to believe it. The rolling headline across the bottom of the screen confirms it, as does the newsreader. It's true. It's actually true. Original Pres-X is to be offered to everyone. The Eyes Forward have deemed it a right to have access to the life extending drug for all its elder citizens. It'll still have to be financed, but the finance packages are set to suit all Life Scores, but only original Pres-X for the over seventies, not the new version.

Ava feels light at the news, and her eyes well. Zia, her Zia will live. Longer, anyway. Ava won't be left alone. Her wave of relief is short-lived though, as the dates take away some of her joy. The treatment will start trickling through the Life Scores, and with Ava's Life Score, she won't be eligible for finance for six years. *Six years.* She looks at Zia sleeping. Her shoes are off, the apartment is at a normal temperature, nothing burned in the oven. Her mental decline is a rollercoaster, and it seems that today, Zia has fared pretty well. But in six years' time, who knows if she'll cope with Pres-X? Brain exercises and the pills the doctor gave her a couple of years ago can only do so much.

How long can she wait?

Chapter 11

10 years before the Great Unrest

Working in the little café Lucia should have turned into quite the gossip. But she never did. She'd make small talk and enjoy that, but getting into the nitty gritty of things, discussing all manner of whatnot was something she had actively avoided. There was always too much else to do. But with all this new Pres-X business, she had a new interest in current affairs quite unlike one she'd had before. Not since her youth, anyway. Back then she joined marches to try and help human rights, the planet, all sorts. But since nothing ever got better, she'd written off idealistic attitudes as a mindset for the young. It was their world, going forward. She'd had her time.

But now, things were different. Now, older people were being presented with choices.

The pink faces still came out in public at first. Whether they were embarrassed or not, who could tell with their fuscia complexions. She laughed. Everyone did. But now she thought it scandalous. Those people parading themselves at having done something so ghastly, against nature. Against *god*. God had been absent from her life for a long time but now, she felt his presence everywhere, shaking his head, disapproving.

□She must do better.

□She'd heard of callings. Like when people join the priesthood. She'd never imagined at nearly seventy years old, she'd find hers.

□So she started keeping her ears open, listening for the people who felt the same way. Not the jealous ones, who couldn't afford it and wished they could have it. Not the young ones who were only concerned about what this would mean for their intended families. She felt for them, of course. But they had an ulterior motive. Less pure. No, she listened for the ones who were appalled. Disgusted with the unnatural state of things. Who did not believe that living humans should be pickled like beetroot and onions. Who believed that humans were not tortoises.

□It didn't take long to find some like-minded people. There was Thomas who worked in the dentist across the road and came in to buy his coffee in the morning. Mo, the dog walker and her 6 dogs that would all sit so nicely under the table with barely a grizzle or growl between them. Therese, who was like Lucia and thought it was terrible, but secretly, as her partner Nicola was all for it when the time came. And Lucia was fairly convinced after speaking to the pair of them quite a bit— both separately and together— that Nicola was having an affair with her hairdresser Ella. But she couldn't prove anything. Both Ian and Steve worked on the housing project across the road and would come in to buy their sandwiches every day, a full English breakfast on Fridays, they both agreed with Lucia. So that was quite a few really, and Lucia only thought of the idea a week ago.

□The idea. To counter the nonsense. To create a voice for common sense.

On Thursday evenings the café was open late for book club. Lucia took part, well, she attended, though was never really sure if all the points they made were accurate. They dug deeper into the characters than she liked to delve. Often she didn't manage to finish the book club books and so she'd look up the endings on the internet. She could always start the book, but to finish it in a week was a bit of a slog, especially when she still had last week's one to finish. And the week before. Her ageing eyes couldn't scan the pages quickly enough, and her slowing brain took a while to absorb it all. She loved the characters usually, and she was quite capable of making up her own ending to the stories. When that medieval knight ran off with that slave girl, she didn't care for that at all. She much preferred her imagined events of a duel between him and the other knight and lopping each other's heads off. But she went every week as they drank tea and finished off whatever cakes from the café needed eating up. Rather they ate them for free than sell them on to the sub 300 eateries. And it was her evening out. Away from Ken and his gripes and groans. No TV. No news. And she knew she wasn't the only one who went just for the company and not the book.

Since she was still technically working in the café up until the end of book club on Thursdays, alone, no other servers ever attended, no one would notice if she let a few people in the back door just as the book club people were leaving, and they sat around in the staff room discussing their woes with regard to the new drug that was 'changing the world,' so Ken said.

At nine p.m. just as the last book club member was leaving, (Derick. It was always Derick. Lucia often thought he was sweet on her and wanted to go back to her place like they were teenagers. Either that or he had just forgotten where he was. He used to work nights and seems like his body clock was forever tuned in to staying up till the early hours. Lucia's was not.) She locked the front door with a yawn, and opened the back door. Seven people came in and sat in the staff room. No cake, unfortunately, that had all been eaten by book club, and she made a mental note to hide some for their next meeting. If they had another meeting. She hoped they do.

Mo with just her own dog in tow, a little Jack Russell called Dennis, Thomas, Therese, Ian and Steve, along with their partners Keisha and Selina, sat down or stood, there weren't enough seats in the staff room for them all, and stared at Lucia somewhat expectantly.

'Welcome,' said Lucia. And then it dawned on her that she hadn't really thought much beyond that.

They all waited silently for a few seconds, even Dennis who usually barked enough to fill any quiet moment voiced nothing of note at all.

'So,' said Thomas. 'My neighbour Maurice, I saw him yesterday. Bright pink face.'

'No!' they all gasped.

'Yep. He's such a nice old gent and he's gone and done it. His wife died last year and I think he's having a crisis. He saw me staring. I don't suspect he'll show his face again for a while until that pink has calmed down. Looked like he'd had an accident with strawberry milkshake.'

And they all laughed. Through the broken ice they shared feelings of dismay and disgust at the state of things.

Little Dennis fell asleep after a time as the humans all chatted and gossiped for well over an hour.

'It just seems to me,' said Mo, 'that when your time is up, it's up.'

That was what the group decided to call themselves after that, the Time's Up.

Chapter 12

10 years after the Great Unrest

A week later, they start offering pet funerals and business has picked up, but Max isn't doing great, Ava realises as soon as she gets to work Friday morning. She kicks herself when she sees the state of him. Tired, withdrawn, like he's shut away, behind a door somehow. She's been busy at work, distracted with her other work and hadn't even considered how the new business plan might be taking its toll on him. He lost his beloved dog last year, and it broke him. The funeral home has had three pet funerals the past week, and Ava hadn't even thought to check on him.It was his idea, she reminds herself. He wants to do it.

He has bags under his eyes, red marks blotting through his shirt from new wounds underneath, and his clothes hang off him like he's lost a couple of kilos at least. Ava sets a coffee on the table in the cold room and leans against the side.

'Feel like I haven't seen you in ages, Max. You seen the news on Pres-X? Your gran must be pleased.'

He doesn't look up but continues working on the poodle, clipping its claws, then trimming the fur. 'She's a 650. She could get another hundred points by using up some credit, or I could give her a hundred. She could get treatment right away if she wanted. She just doesn't want to.'

'I'm sorry.'

'Don't be. She doesn't want it. I can't force her. I'm destined to have no family.' He sniffs a little and takes a step back, admiring his handiwork on the dog.

'Oh, Max.'

He smiles. It looks as fake as the one he puts on for clients. 'I'll be fine. When B-Well comes out, I reckon I'll be right as rain.'

'Next dog that comes in, how about I deal with it? You do front of house.'

'No, please. I mean, it bums me out, sure, but I like doing it. I wish I could have done it for Winston.'

Winston was sixteen years old when he died. He was adorably affectionate the few times that Ava met him, but his rancid breath made it hard to pet him for long. The incontinence that came with such an age made Max's work clothes smell like pee. Max would have only been a small kid when he got Winston. Life without the dog would have been beyond his memory. The dog helped him cope when his parents died. The grief he felt when Winston passed, he said, was worse than when his parents did. He was older, all too aware of the permanence it meant, no childish notions of rainbow bridges and the dead still being present. Max saw Winston's death for everything it really meant.

'Well, okay,' Ava says. 'Maybe we need to book you an appointment with that therapist again.'

'She's not working anymore. You didn't hear? Did your therapist not tell you?'

'I don't have a therapist.'

He looks surprised at this, pulling his chin in and knitting his brows. 'Okay. . . whatever. Well, no therapist is working anymore. No point with this drug coming out. If you read what it says online, they all got payouts from XL Medico. Redundancy payments, basically, approved by the Eyes Forward. There's retraining available in other fields. Erm, teaching and care work, I think is what they're offering. Therapist is not a licensed profession anymore. Conflicting therapies, they said. Be better to use the same approach across the Society.'

'Sounds like something the Eyes Forward would say.' Eyes Forward with that damned hybrid statue with XL Medico. She thinks this but doesn't say it. No point upsetting Max.

'I think they just don't like the idea of patient confidentiality,' Max says, and Ava raises her brows though the surprise is for herself, how she hasn't considered such a thing before. 'All eyes are our eyes,' Max says, making air quotes at the Eyes Forward slogan.

'What about your girlfriend?' Ava asks.

'Frida? What about her?'

'She's doing a psychology degree.'

'Yeah. So later she can help with the studies of B-Well. That's one of the other jobs being offered. Research. I don't think she wanted to be a therapist anyway. She's more academic.'

Ava wants to smile but resists. She can imagine Max with a creative, maybe an environmentalist or maybe even a care work-er. But an academic? That seems absurd. Probably what people thought when she and Mandisa were an item. Mismatched, like a shirt she'll never grow into. Still, opposites attract. Perhaps Max's mismatch will work out for the best. She hopes so, any-way. 'So, when do you start on B-Well?'

'Dunno. Being my luck, they'll probably only offer it to the high Scorers for ages.'

'You know, I'm doing some work there. Maybe I could get you on a trial or something? No promises, but I'll ask.'

He smiles more genuinely at this, though she thinks he's probably right. The high Scorers get first dibs on everything, though with Erin's Score being so high, Max's outlook is a hell of a lot more promising. Erin can gift her points to him, but that would take her out of the running for Pres-X. There's only so much a Score can finance.

At least she and Zia don't need B-Well. They're not the most relentlessly cheery people, but they're fine. That's one less thing her Score has to finance. The stagnancy of her points grates on her, and she decides to invest in some new spyware. A phone upgrade and a long lens maybe. These aren't needless purchases. They're things she can actually use. Investments, really. Pay on credit to up her Score, then catch more crooks with her Society

Police work and up her Score even more. She sits at the front desk with a fresh cup of tea and loads up the computer. New credit card pop-ups fill her screen almost instantly and she applies, gets accepted straight away, then starts shopping.

Everything is out of stock. Beyond out of stock—even the back-orders are out of stock. She groans and holds her head in her hands. Her plan foiled, and now she has excess credit to use up. Unused credit doesn't look good. Why didn't she check first? She kicks herself. Everyone must be wanting to get on the Society Police game and up their Score. Her usual quiet job is going to have some competition. The news reports say how great it is that 'spending is trending.' Everyone is working towards the same goal, they say. A truly cohesive Society. Ava grits her teeth at this. It's just not true. Everyone wants to look a bit younger. What she wants is for the last member of her family to live.

Everyone would think Ava is nuts for giving her Score to Zia. She'd be back to square one to get her own Pres-X-2. A youthful exterior so much more important than functionality of the interior. But Ava doesn't want it. She doesn't care about middle-age, about looking like she's lived and survived and that the effort of this has withered her past her aesthetic best.

On the wall opposite the desk hangs a picture of her parents, to give the place a family business feel, her father had said to her. She wasn't working at the funeral home then. She was still doing her chemistry masters. Despite this, a young Ava is in the photo with her parents, smiling, well-dressed, ambitious. Her father was so convinced that Pres-X would get banned that there would be a shortage of funeral services for the high Scorers. 'It'll never take off,' he'd insisted when Ava tried to educate him. 'People want natural lives, not some artificial zombie-maker.' It was a little over a year later that he and her mother were trampled to death, caught in the middle of a Time's Up stampede and an Enough riot—one side trying to stop people living too long, the other trying to stop more babies being born. He never lived to see that Ava was right, that Pres-X would take over the Society, his business acumen as outdated as his views.

Ava walks over to the picture to inspect it more. He still had dark hair, not a sprout of grey. Her mother too. Ashy blonde locks looking sun-kissed rather than time-tinted. In her mind's eye, they look how they always looked. The immortality of memories has warped her perspective. She's never realised before. They must have dyed their hair. Even her parents, with their belief in a natural existence and natural lifespan, coloured the evidence of their years away.

***

At XL Medico that evening, Ava gets the chemicals going, then leaves the bubbling liquids behind to walk down the corridors. The B-Well lab is easy to find. It's the only other lab working after hours, and the only lab with multiple staff who sound loudly pleased to be working. Ava swallows back a hint of envy. Her lonely workplace may scratch her itch for science, but to work among other chemists, to indulge in the camaraderie of a truly scientific community would be a real dream come true. She shakes away that feeling, stands straight and moulds her face to appear professional instead of the ever-present congenial expression she's so used to portraying, then knocks. After no response, she lets herself in.

'Well, hello there,' one man says, a wide grin plastered across his face. The grin falters quickly as he eyes her wrist. 'I wasn't aware fertile women are allowed in here.'

'I'm green.'

'All the same. Safe age women are far more, well, agreeable.'

The woman behind him nods in her stereotypical agreement while waving her golden, glowing hand in the air.

'Anyway,' Ava says, ignoring their discontent. 'I was hoping to ask if there are any trials going for the new drug, B-Well?'

'Not now,' the man says. 'All been done. Its roll out starts next week.'

'Any chance of some samples, I've a friend, low Life Score—'

'Not to worry,' he holds up his hands, once again wearing the same grin. 'Everyone will be allowed it. All Scores. The entire Society. New statement from Eyes Forward. They're funding it all on the national health, not even having to self-finance. Isn't that wonderful?'

A little trickle of relief spreads over Ava and the muscle knots in her shoulders loosen. 'Great. Yes, it's wonderful. Thanks for the news.'

She walks back to her lab, alone but lighter. The corridors feeling slightly airier than they did before, a little less suffocating. She has one less thing to worry about. Max should be pleased.

After bottling up her thirty litres, Ava cycles the longer way to avoid the pig she reported. Her phone beeps as she arrives home. Her Society Police report is rejected. That man she reported is too important, apparently. *Upstanding member of society. This is clearly a misunderstanding,* is what it says. One bit of good news followed by a bit of bad. The universe's way of righting itself. She makes a mental note to carry a taser next time she cycles that way. If she can't have him prosecuted, she'll burn his eyeballs out instead.

Chapter 13

Mr Constance's funeral was a week ago, and they have no more in the diary. No human funerals, that is. No one is dying. No one with the required Life Score anyway. And if they're rolling out Pres-X to everyone, lowering the Life Score of the business may not even help. Ava puts her elbows on the desk and rests her chin in her hands. There's a guinea pig in the cold storage, a cat, two dogs and a hamster. Max has spruced up their fur, thickened their whiskers, and Ava has prepared the services. Hamster coffins aren't going to pay the bills. With her dwindling bank account, everything she has done to increase her Score will be whittled away.

The vases are empty, and the reception feels and smells too sterile without them. 'Guinea pigs don't need flowers,' Max had said. Rightly so, but the ambience needs them. Even when just dealing with pets, the job is depressing enough without some floral arranging to look forward to. Ava uses the company credit and orders a fresh delivery, strongly scented ones, a hit of colour. The lack of joy she presents in her clothes doesn't mean she wants to be surrounded by gloom. Some biscuits, too, for the clients—dog and human, for when the living pets attend the ceremonies. The flowers should work wonders to mask the smell of those visitors, as well as the embalming and coffin odour.

At least the calming atmosphere is maintained within the thick glass windows. The noise from the crowd outside is dim when the doors are closed, though their body heat steaming up the glass is a constant annoyance. They're still there, waiting and eager to chat up a high Scoring recently bereaved. The owner of one of the dogs actually accepted a date with one of the Score-diggers yesterday. That funeral is in four days' time. Ava wonders if the Score-digger will be in attendance, tissues at the ready, a consoling arm of support. She shivers at the seediness of her thoughts.

Ava browses the internet, maxes out the last of her personal credit on two credit cards to keep her Life Score up, spreading the repayments out over the next year should help someway in maintaining her Score. Perhaps she can get more hours at XL Medico. The demand will certainly be there. Another lucky night as Society Police would be useful too. Her day off with XL Medico is tonight, so she makes her mind up to go on patrol. Sleep is for the 700 pluses, she justifies.

'Max, you want anything from Beanies?' she calls down the corridor to where Max is still grooming cats.

He comes out of the room, brushing ginger fur from his apron. 'What'd you say?'

'Coffee from Beanies?'

'Oh, no. Thanks.'

Ava stops a moment to look at him. His usually styled hair is less so. The colour in his cheeks that his new relationship brought is fading. 'How you doing? Have you had your B-Well yet?'

He keeps his eyes on the floor. 'Got my prescription today. But you know the dose is Life Score linked, so I only get thirty milligrams. Nan keeps trying to give me her points so I can get a higher dose, but she needs that for the Pres-X she's still refusing.'□

'Shit, Max. I really am sorry. But hey, thirty milligrams is better than none. I'm sure it'll help.'

'Yeah. Maybe. We'll see. Actually, Frida is doing her dissertation on it. You might see her around XL Medico to go through data.' His chin lifts a little at the mention of her name, his mouth upturns just a little. The relationship is still blossoming then, at least.

'You'll have to bring her in to say hi,' Ava says. 'So I know who I'm looking for.'

'She'll be the one talking everyone's ears off and asking tons of questions.' His lips curl up to a full smile.

'Ha. She sounds lovely.'

Stepping out of work onto the busy pavement, Ava elbow-barges her way through crowds of Score-diggers. She makes sure she's keeping up with the lane she steps in, no dawdling, nothing that could get her more points deducted. Across the billboards, the speed minimums for each lane are displayed, flashing neon, reminding everyone. There must have been a few reports for them to go to that trouble. Ava keeps looking around, checking for Society Police cameras in her face, but sees none. Based on the lack of spyware supplies in the shops, she assumes they've all got hidden cameras.

Round the corner on to Cross Street and a man nudges her, then whispers in her ear, too close, too familiar. 'That woman over there plans to rob you, just so you know. Better give her a shove first.'

Ava doesn't lose any speed but keeps walking. The woman turns around to face Ava, keeping pace, headed in the same direction, narrowing her eyes at her.

'If she doesn't, I might give you a squeeze,' the man says, grimy breath making Ava recoil.

It's then she looks down and sees it, the glint of a not-so hidden camera lens on the man's lapel. The woman has her phone in her hand, by her side as if she's not using it, but the camera is pointing up at Ava. They're trying to rile her, to get her to stop, lash out, anything to report to the Society Police. She swallows, bites the inside of her cheek, and maintains her direction and pace.

'You should hear the things that woman says about you. Your family too. She's going to hurt them all.'

Them all? She definitely doesn't know Ava's family then. Certain of her convictions, Ava keeps walking. Ahead in her lane, a heated exchange begins. Two guys screaming, chests pressed against each other as they keep walking. Through the gaps in the people, Ava sees their red faces, fists waving in each other's faces. A heavy shove pushes her out the way as the man forces his way through, lifting his lapel to film above the crowd. The woman ahead is holding her phone high up now, catching the action ahead. Ava rummages in her bag for her phone, cursing herself for being so slow. By the time she has it in hand and the Society Police app loaded up, the exchange has cooled down and there is nothing to see.

Dammit!

She arrives at Beanies to grab a coffee. She's been going to that café for years. It's the only one that doesn't burn the coffee and serves it with the right amount of milk. Her usual coffee shop now has a new sign hanging: '600 plus café.'

What!

Ava approaches the counter, flustered from outside but broiling with rage.

'Kris, what the hell?'

'Sorry Ava,' Kris says, his usual flushed complexion now looking more guilty than endearing. 'You not a 600?'

'No, but I've been getting my coffee here for years.'

'Shh, just keep quiet. I'll do it this once.' He glances over his shoulder before retrieving a cup. The milk steamer hisses, sounding as angry as Ava feels.

'Why the change?'

'Boss is worried about the demographic shift. You know, more lower Life Scorers living longer.'

'And that means he needs to price them out?'

'It's just business, Ava, that's all. The high Scorers have had some of their perks made non-exclusive to them. Just trying to keep them happy. Give people something to aim for.'

'That's bullshit of your boss,' Ava says, avoiding looking at Kris, her gaze on the brown liquid coming out of the barista machine instead. 'I'll have to walk all the way to Cuppa-go.'

'They're over 700 now.'

'What!'

'Everywhere is the same to keep peace with the high Scorers being put out about this whole non-exclusive Pres-X thing. It's incentivised—by Eyes Forward. Without having to strive to Score for Pres-X, people have nothing to aim for. They can get Pres-X-2 or just wait it out and get the regular Pres-X. The Eyes Forward don't want them thinking like that. They want people to work hard and take Pres-X-2, to stay productive, not get old—still got to strive to Score. We have to keep ambition alive.'

'You sound like you actually agree with this nonsense,' Ava says with a groan, slumping against the bar.

He pours the foam, exactly the right amount, exactly as she likes it. 'I don't disagree. I'm hoping my Score is high enough to take Pres-X-2 by the time I'm older. You must be itching to get your treatment.'

'Not really.'

'Whatever. Here you go.'

He hands her the coffee, and she takes it with a mumbled thanks.

'Where am I going to get my gossip and current affairs info from now, Kris?'

'Watch the news like everyone else. Sorry, Ava.'

Sitting in the café, it's clear it's for over 600. Or will be. . . The furnishings are being reupholstered, pictures dusted, and woodwork painted. Her shoes feel tacky against the freshly varnished floor. The window's long serving fingerprints have been wiped away.

She leaves with her coffee rather than sit and feel like some poor eyesore and sees that Kris was right. New 700 plus signs are being hung in every eatery, some going as low as 600 but otherwise, to say the area was gentrifying would be an understatement. Through the crowds everywhere that are denser than ever, she hadn't realised. Even the 500 plus corner shop has upped to 600.

She shoulders her way through the crowds back in to work, impolitely, though apologising in case her body language gives the Society Police any cause for alarm, somehow only managing to spill a drop. The gathering outside her work thins briefly, their attention drawn elsewhere.

'There's one! Where are they going?'

'Excuse me, miss. You look lovely. Fancy grabbing some food? I'll treat you.'

'Ignore him. He's horrible. Let me show you a good time.'

Ava glances behind her and there's a Preserved woman calling in to the 600 plus deli across the road. No, 700 plus now. Her face still has a few patches of bright pink, not even attempted to be concealed. Rather than duck quickly into the deli and get out of sight of the onlookers, she pauses, smiles, then gives the crowd a wink. They all follow, leaving the space outside the funeral home the emptiest it's been in days.

Ava rolls her eyes at the madness and gets back to work. What little work she has, which is putting the order of service together for Jack the poodle and browsing pet coffins on the wholesaler's website. Erin arrives soon after Ava, looking flustered with her hair coming loose from its plait and dust from the streets coating her shoes. In her hands is a lunch box for Max.

'He left without it this morning,' she says.

Ava calls to the cold room for Max and he comes over, blushing when he sees the food.

'I am capable of sorting myself out a lunch.'

'I just don't want you to miss out. I wouldn't have bothered if that crowd was still outside, but I managed to walk straight in. They're back already though, I see. How is that not illegal, hounding people like that? They should all have points deducted.'

'I couldn't agree more,' Ava says.

Max takes his lunch and goes back to the cold room without saying another word. Erin watches after him, her face drawn and chin down. When the cold room door closes, she turns her attention to Ava.

'How are you, dear? How's business?' Erin leans on her stick.

'Ticking over. Don't worry about us. And you? You should qualify for Pres-X soon. That's great news, isn't it?'

'Yes, yes. Anyway, I really want to talk to you about Maxy. He's not right, is he?'

Ava nods. 'He does seem low, more so than usual.'

'I just don't understand it. He has this new girlfriend. Has he told you?'

'Briefly. Is it serious?'

'I don't know. But you'd think he'd be on cloud nine. She's quite pretty. Seems rather charming actually. Lovely manners. But he's just so sad all the time.'

Ava's lips twitch as she chooses her words. Does Erin not see the problem? It makes her wonder if Zia is so clueless. Actually, she doesn't need to wonder that. 'I think, Erin, if I'm being honest, he's worried about you. Worried you won't take Pres-X.'

Erin snorts a laugh. 'Why would he worry about that? Of course I'm not going to take it. My husband and my daughter, Max's mum, they're all waiting for me somewhere. When it's my time, it's my time.'

'But you're all he's got.' Ava says this with a lump in her throat. A worry she knows all too well.

Erin's face is still then, blank, expressionless. 'Ah. I see. But he's a young man. I'm just his old nan. He doesn't need me.'

'I think he needs you more than you think.'

'Nonsense. He doesn't even need me to bring him sandwiches. He has his B-Well prescription now. That'll perk him up a bit.'

'I hope so.'

Erin gives Ava a smile as she leaves, bracing herself to face the crowds outside. She grimaces as she walks, her limp mostly concealed by stubbornness and grit. Ava shakes her head. How can she not want to take Pres-X? The pains that come with her age, the tempo, the fog. . . how can she not want rid of all of that? It's not the same as the nonsense of Pres-X-2. Original Pres-X is so much more than that. It's more time with your family.

With Erin gone, Ava sets to work cleaning the place. A light dusting and vacuum are all it needs, nothing like the clearing up of glassware and benches a busy lab would require. Pat the dust out of the upholstery and she's almost done. Bored again. Working so many hours for so long in a job that interests her so little is beginning to take its toll. This was her father's vision, not hers. She wanted to study art until her father told her she'd be wasting her time, so she pursued science instead, and loved that even more. She's keeping his memory alive, that's all.

The heavy furniture, ornate picture frames, crystal light fittings, they're all the exuberance of wealth he envisioned for his career's future. Ava is living in the shadow of his memory. She knows this, but that shadow is all encasing. A memory. That's all we are ever destined to become, for the shortest time at least. Ava barely knew even her grandparents. The memory of us is as mortal as our flesh, it only lasts a little longer. The quiet hours in the funeral home give her time to ponder such dark thoughts. That of her own mortality and the lack of anyone to remember her. She can picture in decades to come, after she's long gone, the L.M. Funerals sign outside crumbling into obscurity, repainted over with a logo of some discount store, the kind everyone needs once in a while. A conversation between two people outside debating what was here before the discount store, neither certain nor being able to agree.

She puts the vacuum down and decides to buy some beers on the way home.

***

By the time Ava gets home that evening, she has a mental list of just one place where she can buy food. If that ups its Life Score, she'll be relying on powder rations. The dehydrated fluff has always been a staple for the lowest Scorers. *Sustainable for the planet and you,* the packaging says. If it was up to the Pro Grow campaigners from years ago, it's what everyone would eat. Perfectly balanced, planet-friendly dust. She swallows back bile at the thought of it. No more fresh food, no more treats, beer, Zia's questionable casseroles. Someone of her Score shouldn't be subjected to such depravities. It won't come to that, she assures herself. The Eyes Forward won't let it come to that.

'What about that nice girl, what was her name?' Zia asks when Ava moans about it at home. Zia seems more lucid today. The flat isn't baking hot, and the oven is on at the right temperature. No tea spills.

'Mandisa?'

'Yes. She had a high Score, didn't she?'

'Yes, Zia. That's why we broke up,' she says, making a cup of tea, cursing to herself as she realises she forgot to buy beer.

'She was lovely. Single, at your age. Just seems a shame, that's all.'

'I'm more likely to meet someone when I'm safe age.'

'Safe age. Pah. We never had such a thing when we were young. Getting pregnant is hardly unsafe. We protested against enforced sterilisation for girls, you know. We did that for you, so you'd have the choice.'

'I've made my choice, and that ship has almost sailed.'

Zia leans in close, peering at her in that way she does. 'You do look flushed, dear. And you are quite irritable. And your skin looks dry. And all this black. I suppose it's slimming, black clothes, but you don't need to worry about that. Are you ill, dear? In the mind I mean. Worried about your silhouette like some girls do?'

'No, Zia. I'm fine.'

'You might meet someone if you wore nicer clothes.'

'I've met too many widows to want to meet someone. No amount of happiness is worth the grief.' She bites her lip as soon as she says this, hoping Zia doesn't remember her own grief.

Zia plonks herself heavily on the sofa, a grunting exhale escaping. 'Your *Zio* wasn't the best husband in the end. We had a lovely life until then though. But he changed in the end. I grieved for the man that he used to be, not the man he became.'

Ava freezes, her breath catches in her lungs. It is the most coherent thing Zia has said in years. Ava never knew her uncle, only met him a handful of times. According to Ava's father, he hated being called 'Zio', the Italian word for uncle, and when Ava was a girl, her father insisted she use it. A culture clash, her mum would say with her usual air of apathy. Easier for them to keep their distance. There's only ever enough oxygen for one alpha-male in a room.

'Still, your parents would want you to meet someone, instead of worrying about your Score all the time. They never cared about that. Live while you can, until your time's up, they said.'

Ava nearly spits out her tea. 'Say that again. Did you say time's up?'

'Yes. At those meetings, that's all anyone said. I might make a hot chocolate, dear. Want one?'

Ava's jaw drops. She needs a moment to think, but if Zia loses her thread, who knows if she'll get her back to this conversation again. 'No. And have you got some photos of these meetings?' Ava asks. A long shot but worth a go.

'Probably some, most certainly some of the rallies. Check the hard drive. The folders on there. Might be some. How about a camomile tea?'

'Sure.'

Ava grabs the laptop and plugs in the hard drive. Album after album of family Christmases and birthdays, photos of when she was a kid, learning to ride a bike. None of Zia, well, hardly none. She was always behind the camera, the one shouting cheese and waving and smiling more than anyone else. And then, out-of-date order, at the bottom of all the lifetimes of memories, a folder titled TU.

No. It can't be.

But she loads them up and there they are. Her parents. Over ten years ago, a few years before the Great Unrest. Time's Up meetings, it must have been. When Time's Up was in its infancy, just a few members, a couple of signs protesting against the life extension. One of the factions of the Great Unrest who organised and partook in all manner of protests to try to stop the rollout of Pres-X, to try to ensure there was room for more babies instead of just long-lived elders. Were her parents really some of the founders of Time's Up?

The meetings were small at first, then, as Ava scrolls through, they became larger, bigger crowds, more attention, more . . . riotous, and alongside them, someone she recognises, sat right next to her parents. The top half of his face is concealed under the brim of his hat, but that chin, she knows. She's seen him walking the halls of XL Medico, coming into her funeral home and telling her they want her stock of formaldehyde-rose. Only he looks younger now. Seventy years younger, still with that same scar on his chin.

Chapter 14

With all score requirements increasing everywhere, the gangs must be planning more raids. Ava's certain of it as she checks for noise on the dark web. Sure enough, there's call signs she recognises, and she gets on her bike and makes her way to Beanies, of all places. Revenge raids, these are likely to be. Not for food, but to show that the low Scorers are not happy.

Her favourite dark alleyway hideout is inaccessible. A heap of bikes, no lights, no reflectors, are lined up at the entrance. And inside the alleyway, the bikes' owners all piled up on top of each other. Spy cameras point at the high street, long lenses on tripods, not a square inch left for Ava. She curses and tries the next spot and finds it much the same. With pointy elbows, she shoves herself into the middle of the group, ignoring the tuts and cursing around her.

She doesn't have to wait long. They arrive in droves, Beanies, Cuppa-Go, sandwich bars, pastry shops, and they take their baseball bats to them all, smashing windows and spray painting over the new Life Score requirement signs. They should have seen it coming, really, thinks Ava. Cutting off the lower Scorers from every outlet, incentivising it was hardly going to go down without consequence. Still, she's not one to side with thugs and with her phone in her hand, the night setting on, she strains to reach over all the other Society Police trying to catch the action, sure she's getting more footage of the backs of people's heads than the crime in front. But they're all new at this, whereas Ava is an old hat. They stay to the end, keep recording every minute, whereas Ava memorises descriptions, and after the initial on-slaught, stops filming and has the footage and her description uploaded before any of the other Society Police have even put their cameras away. She smirks. *Amateurs.*

She climbs out of the crowd, hauling herself over not-so-stealthy bodies and equipment, then cycles home before the roads are crammed with everyone making their exit, mentally counting up her points as she does so.

Outside her apartment block is a vehicle she hasn't seen in years, the yellow stripes like a wasp, its passengers just as vicious. Bailiffs. They can't be for her. She keeps up with all her repayments. She locks up her bike in the storage downstairs and steps as silently as she can up the stairs. Suzanna. Her door is open, and there's wailing from the inside.

'I'll pay it all back! I will, I promise.'

'It's too late for that now. You've missed two weeks of payments in a row.'

'I'll get more credit. I know I can get more. Please, don't take my points.'

'We have a court order to take your points and your possessions.'

'This is a death sentence. You know what that means. I'm a 640, hear me? 640!'

Ava pauses only briefly to look. The rollers in Suzanna's hair have come out, her curls hanging limp over her shoulders. Her face mask is smudged, off-white gloop collecting across her brows.

'There's a place for you in a sub 200 building south of the river,' the bailiff continues without a hint of emotion. 'You may take one bag of clothes. The rest will be sold.'

'But this is my home.'

'It's a home for the 500 pluses. I'm sorry, but you must leave.'

'Ava!' Suzanna spots her creeping past, up the stairs. 'Tell them. Tell them I'm good for it. Have you any points to spare? Please? I'm so close to getting Pres-X-2. So close. Please. I can't be a sub 200. I just can't.'

'I. . . I'm sorry. I can't do anything.'

Suzanna drops to her knees and wails so loudly, surely Zia can hear it over her telly.

'I really am sorry.'

The bailiffs lift Suzanna by her armpits, then haul her down the stairs, her feet dragging across the floor as she screams in denial the whole way down.

Chapter 15

7 years before the Great Unrest

'This book club of yours is going on later and later,' Ken said one evening as Lucia arrived home just seconds before midnight. He'd gotten even grouchier over the last couple of years, if such a development was possible. Where Ken had become grumpier, Lucia had blossomed with her new friends and social life, her interest in the world, and her renewed ability to stay up late.

'Well, if you ever read a book, you would know there's lots to discuss.' It wasn't an accurate comment. Ken had read lots of books, just not lately. As if Lucia reading meant he couldn't or didn't want to anymore, like he didn't want a common interest.

Ken shuffled up to bed now. Why he waited up for her, Lucia wasn't sure. She never bothered staying up when he was out with his Eyes Forward colleagues, spying for the government and berating new parents. The latest campaign to put people off having children was all his idea, apparently. Although Lucia suspected his stupid old brain that can't even make toast would never think of such a thing. Cutting Life Score points for every child born and upping the Score requirements for all the nurseries. It was stated on the news and on TV adverts as Ken nodded away from his seat proudly. When she'd heard it, Lucia wanted to throw the telly at him, the old bigot. Just wait until Time's Up hears about this, she'd thought. Not even the shame of it being her own husband who'd suggested such an initiative would stop her from speaking out about it. She was so mad that she met Mo and Keisha that very evening rather than wait until Tuesday.

Of course she hadn't thrown the telly at Ken. She'd ground down her molars and told him he was stupid and opened her book instead of watching any more. He didn't even notice her anger. Instead, he'd said his initiative was sure to reward him with some Pres-X soon. It was still only available for the 750 pluses and even with the boost in his Score since he'd started his spy work, he was a way off the 750 requirement.

'I'll qualify for a staff discount,' he'd claimed. Although with his eighty-first birthday approaching, Lucia wondered if he'd been hoodwinked, or if he'd changed his mind. She hoped it was the latter.

Lucia sank down into the sofa and took her shoes off. Walking all the way back so late was doing her feet in. No buses ran so late. It's good for you, she'd tell herself. A bit more exercise was a good thing. The hum of the electric toothbrush started upstairs, and Lucia reached for her book that was stuffed down the side of the sofa cushions, still half unread.

'You coming to bed or what?' Ken called down from upstairs.

'In a while. Just going to sit up and read for a bit.'

'Bloody books. Suit yourself.'

Lucia didn't want to read. The book was rubbish anyway. All clichés and too much smoochy stuff. Instead, she really wanted to digest the meeting she'd just had. It was marvellous. Over the years, the Time's Up membership had grown significantly. So much so, they pretended to be another book club on Tuesdays so that they could take up the entire café and start as soon as the café closed at seven p.m. They read classic sci-fi from the 1900s, if anyone asked. A genre so unpopular, no one else would want to join them for the purposes of book club alone. That was Thomas's idea. Quite a clever one, they all thought.

Tonight's meeting hadn't started well. Poor Mo came along carrying Donny, who was recovering from a sprained knee after chasing a squirrel. Lucia had assumed Mo's tears were about Donny, and Lucia almost cried too. She'd become quite attached to little Donny, and he often snoozed on her lap during the meetings now.

'The bastard,' Mo said. 'Three years together and he dumped me. Can you believe it?'

'Oh, darling. Come and have a seat,' Lucia said as she pulled out a chair for her. Mo's relationship had been somewhat turbulent over the last few months, but it had really seemed like they'd sorted things out.

'He said it's too risky, being in a relationship with "the likes of me". He actually said that. He said we might accidentally have a baby. He's so worried I'll get pregnant that he'd rather dump me than risk it. I've told him I don't want kids—another dog would be nice, a friend for Donny—but he doesn't believe me. Said I'm at "that age" when I'll change my mind. I said he should have a vasectomy if he's so bloody worried, and he said it's not him who's the problem. It's not men's hormones that need to be kept in check, and that if I'm not willing to be sterilised, then I obviously have another agenda. Can you believe it! Dumped for not being willing to have surgery.'

'The bastard indeed,' said Keisha, shaking her head.

Keisha and Ian actually wanted children, but with all the hormone crap they put in the water now, it hadn't been possible for them. It was everywhere, the news was saying. Hormones pumped into the water supplies, into grain, flour, oats, everything. Every time Lucia baked cakes for the café, she felt guilty that she was sterilising people with treats. But she could hardly not bake cakes.

'Better off without him, love,' Lucia had reassured her. And she really was. Mo was such a sweetheart. She didn't deserve to be taken for a fool. And she was only in her early thirties, so she had years of being attractive still ahead of her, not a single line on that lovely face of hers.

What had started as a sad meeting quickly turned into something quite exciting. There were so many new attendees now that Lucia had a hard time keeping up. She hardly remembered their names at all. She definitely should get some new glasses. Seeing a little clearer would help her remember, most likely, but she never seemed to have the time to visit the optician. One of the new members had such a sweet, singsong voice. Quite distinctive. Once conversation had moved on from Mo's love life, and they'd all said their sympathies, they'd started their usual naming and shaming of pink faces they had seen, of how the Society's demographics were more and more off-kilter, how hard it was to get an appointment anywhere, staffing issues everywhere, when that lovely little voice spoke up.

'The Eyes Forward are rolling it out to their staff soon, I've heard,' she said.

Lucia stopped passing around the cake she'd been cutting up, her bones freezing in their positions. After a moment, her jaw relaxed enough to speak, and she rasped out a single word. 'When?'

'Soon,' the nice young lady said. 'Really soon.'

Chapter 16

10 years after the Great Unrest

The confirmation emails for the vandals comes through just the next day, and Ava's score is bumped up to 570. A big jump! Even with her apparently now outdated spyware, she managed to capture seven of the perpetrator's faces and the app managed to ID them. Nothing custodial, just the usual Score deductions for the first offenders and a few more for second offenders. A link to a new Eyes Forward post details how they intend to divvy up charges to avoid custodial sentences, and the punishment is harsh. Harsher than jail time. The new line of treatment makes Ava shiver and struggle for breath. No Pres-X. Ever. A death sentence they'll wait until their old age to receive. All the vandals are so young that such a thing probably won't register. It'll be years before they'd qualify. But Ava is shocked. She feels less like Society Police and more like an executioner. She has just helped sentence the young hooligans to an early death or at least not an unnaturally long life.

The small print details how they can win back their right to Pres-X, with great difficulty: years of obedience and Striving to Score in a manner that Ava can't even contemplate. And if they commit another crime? No B-Well. Any low Score vandals who need B-Well will be left depressed to roam the streets. More likely to reoffend, thinks Ava, and take their rage out on the Society. A poorly thought-out plan. Custodial sentences are brought in after that, the new information says. No one wants prisons populated with a load of low Life Scorers living out hundred-year sentences. So keep their life expectancy sub a century, strip them of their happy pills, and lock them in a cell instead.

A chill creeps over Ava. For years she's worked as Society Police. Snitching to Score got her and Zia their apartment, their nicer-than-rations groceries, good pizza, better coffee. Now all her hard work is making her feel like the villain, and for what? Her Score is too low for many of her favourite things but still higher than the hoodlums, yet she feels like them. Still far away from Pres-X and likely to be back on rations soon.

She grits her teeth. The usual uplifting elevation she experiences with a Score bump is absent. Instead, she is hollow. She squeezes her eyes shut and replays the images of the hooligans trashing the high street, scenes she has seen so many times of the low Scorers raiding food stalls, their skinny arms reaching for delicacies. *No.* She tells herself. They deserve their punishments. They are the criminals. She can still remember the stench of the latest pervert's body odour as he slammed his hefty weight onto her. The upstanding member of the Society with no punishment. He'd get Pres-X. Maybe the B-Well will make him less of a thug, she hopes. There has to be a rationale to the system.

An XL Medico advert pings across the screen as she scrolls their 'your life length is in our hands' mantra, which is seemingly quite redundant when it's the Eyes Forward who can take your chance of getting Pres-X away. But it doesn't matter. Not a jot. Ava and Zia both have clean records. Minor offences is all Ava has ever been in trouble for—a mis-parked bike, lane dawdling, and she cycled through a red light once. Nothing that'll matter. They know better, are good citizens. No point even trying to break the law when All Eyes Are Our Eyes. She knows this too well.

Checking the Pres-X release dates again, for the fifth time at least, it shows the wait list time is the same. Six years before Zia will qualify. A plan B, but the likelihood is she'll have degraded too much to qualify by then. Stupid, she curses. Why line up people by Life Score? Why not age or need?

She makes her way to XL Medico for her weekend shift. She recognises some of the people at the front reception desk, though frustratingly none are Chin Scar. She wants to look at that scar again, confirm it really was him in the Time's Up photo. No such luck. As she scans her pass and enters through the gates, Mrs Constance is standing with them, wearing a smile, laughing in such a way it reminds Ava of playground flirting. She flicks her head back, then brushes the man's arm. Her tinny giggles hit Ava's ears like nails on glass. Despite the audible onslaught, Ava gawps like she's watching a bike crash.

The lab is disordered. Its usual pristine glassware is still unwashed and lab coats are tossed in a pile, uncollected by the technicians or cleaners. Computers not shut down properly and items tossed in the fridge all higgledy-piggledy. Ava stops just inside the door for a few minutes, taking it in, stepping in and around the chaos, shoes squeaking on spills on the floor. The note on the desk is missing. Is she to assume that her job today is to clean rather than make formaldehyde-rose? Looking at the mess, they, whoever the weekday staff are, probably just forgot she's working today.

She gets to work putting the lab back together, a task that uses up over an hour of her precious time, then gets to work setting up her equipment. Just as she has the burners on, the lab doors open and Mrs Constance comes in, radiant, her sharp skirt suit fitted to perfection, her employee lanyard hanging from her neck.

'I never had the chance to thank you for the service,' Mrs Constance says, tucking her hair behind her ear, flashing the gold of her implant. She must have been sterilised now.

'It was a beautiful service. Lots of lovely words spoken. He was obviously a popular man.'

It sounded like a pleasant service, though Ava didn't see any of it. Eyes Forward were everywhere, and so Ava faced the wall the entire time. None of them asked her to, but if such a request came up, it might detract from the ambience.

'He was. Truly. More gloaters than mourners though. Ex colleagues and current colleagues who just want to gawp at a dead Preserved. We haven't any family. Not many friends, really. Some old colleagues. Such is the way.'

Ava smiles her practised smile, replying with sympathetic words as always. 'You did him proud.'

Mrs Constance nods, looking forlorn for the briefest of moments. 'I didn't know you work here,' she says, glancing around the lab.

'Just part-time.' Ava watches Mrs Constance take a few steps around the lab, clearly not someone who knows what any of the equipment does, though rather than a look of awe, she appears vacant, lost in the space. 'How are you doing?' Ava asks.

Mrs Constance stops, then cocks her head as if searching her memories. 'When we first took Pres-X, another seventy years or so felt like it would fly by all over again. Whizz by. We talked about if we would get a second dose, one day, if that's an option. Now all those decades seem like forever.'

'It's a fresh start, maybe.'

'Perhaps. I'm getting there. Everyone seems so much nicer now than they did at first. A few weeks ago, I felt so self-conscious being Preserved. In the bars I felt like I stood out, like some unworthy old woman. Ignored. Now lots of young people come and talk to me, even walking in the street. I've been asked out more times than I can count.' Mrs Constance's tone picks up as she says this, excited, enraptured with her recollections.

'Perhaps now I've stopped crying quite so much, I look fresher. What do you think?'

I think the Score-diggers are hounding you, is what Ava wants to say. Instead, she uses her well-oiled poker face and smooth as silk voice. 'You look lovely, and it's nice people are being friendly.'

'I suppose it's because more young people are taking Pres-X-2. We are becoming more accepted. Although theirs is more cosmetic, not quite so required as for us older people, to save our joints and hearts.'

Ava just nods.

Mrs Constance looks at the floor for a moment, a little more colour seeping into her cheeks. 'I was thinking of asking you out for a drink, since we had such a fun time the other night.'

Ava swallows, finds her mouth suddenly dry. 'Oh, well—'

'Ted and I always wanted to experiment a bit. You've a nice face, mature, and your figure seems quite lovely under all those large clothes. And your advice was so right. Immerse myself.'

'Mrs Constance—'

'Flick.'

'Flick.' Ava clears her parched throat. 'I don't think that would really be appropriate, mixing work and pleasure.'

'But the funeral has happened now.'

'We both work for XL Medico.'

'Different departments though.'

'All the same.'

'Well,' Mrs Constance tosses her hair over her shoulder, raises her chin up a few degrees. 'Lots of people seem to find me attractive. Desirable. If you're not interested, you could just say so. I have plenty of Life Score points going spare. I'm up to 780 now and this job will bump me up several points as well. I was hoping to gift some to you.'

Ava's pause reveals her surprise and temptation. She looks at Mrs Constance. She is beautiful for a ninety-year-old, she thinks as she bites her lip. But no. That's all wrong. She can't sleep with her for Life Score points.

'I've been taking B-Well,' Mrs Constance says, a haughtiness in her voice now. 'You heard of it? The wonderful new drug XL Medico is making? Ground-breaking. Thought for a while that I'd just go without it, but I'm so glad I didn't. I feel like me again. Adventurous, alive. A lot of motivation. So, just think about it. We have a connection, I think. You understand me in a way so many don't. Anyway, thank you again. I'll leave you to get back to it.'

Ava watches Mrs Constance leave, sure she is swinging her hips more than she was before, and waits for the door to close behind her before she lets out a breath. No. She can't think like that. It would be wrong, too wrong. Mrs Constance is just grieving, that's all. She blinks away the thought as she gets to work, making her thirty litres, assuming that's what is required of her, and leaves the lab in a much more orderly state than she found it.

Shaking off the weirdness of the day, Ava makes for the exit as her phone pings—a happy sounding ping instead of the dread of the warning messages from the Eyes Forward. She reads, then re-reads, just to check she hasn't made a mistake, but there it is in plain font. A happy message from the Eyes Forward, actually congratulating her for her role in the Society. She's the top performing Society Police user for the month and has been awarded an extra twenty points! She air-punches when a voice calls her name. A voice she hasn't heard in quite some time.

'Ava?'

She turns, slowly, and is suddenly aware that she's wearing threadbare clothes and her hair is a mess, stuck to her sweaty scalp. 'Mandi. What a nice surprise.'

Mandisa looks perfectly flawless, as she always did. Her hair glints like moonshine on a river, and her makeup is perfectly applied, not even a crease in her clothes. It's been a year since they split up, when Mandisa's Life Score was too high to bother with Ava anymore. Ava's breath stops, but her heart races. Mandisa steps closer. She's more beautiful than Ava remembers. The hibiscus of her perfume ignites memories that Ava's tried to forget.

'I wasn't aware you're working here.' Mandisa gives the softest of smiles. 'Not doing the funeral home anymore? I guess there's no point now.'

'We're doing pets, mostly.'

'Nice.' Mandisa nods, her eye contact elsewhere for a moment.

Ava shuffles on her feet, adjusts her weight as a brief silence hangs clumsily between them. 'I'm just part-time here, in the lab. Making formaldehyde-rose. Nothing compared to the advanced stuff you're probably doing.' Mandisa always was a brilliant chemist. One more thing she could lord over Ava.

'That's great,' Mandisa says, her eye contact is back, sparkling, intense. 'You always wanted to use your chemistry degree more. How's your Score? I'm soon to take Pres-X-2. Booked in next week. I'll be one of the first Desirables.' There wasn't a hint of brag in her tone, more informative, like she is reading out a party invitation.

Ava inspects Mandisa's flawless skin some more. The minimal signs of ageing look natural on her, like she's lived a life of joy instead of struggle. The truth on show, Ava thinks as she struggles to see what the benefit of the anti-ageing drug will be.

When Ava doesn't reply, Mandisa fills the silence. 'How's your Zia?'

'Old and getting older. She won't last the six-year waiting list she's currently on.' Ava inwardly kicks herself for sounding bitter, but she can't help it. The sour taste from their split has never gone away. If Mandisa had married Ava when she'd asked, perhaps now Zia would qualify for Pres-X. Perhaps Zia wouldn't have burned herself on the oven the other day, wouldn't have flooded the bathroom when she forgot the bath was running, wouldn't have forgotten that Ava's dad is dead. She hates that most of all, having to tell Zia all over again that her family is dead.

'I'm sorry,' Mandisa says, her eyes darting to the floor.

'What do you want? Besides to show me your Head of B-Well Product Development employee badge.' Ava could hardly miss it. The gold badge adorns her lapel like a jewelled brooch, her hair over her other shoulder so as not to cover it up.

'Nothing, really. I just saw you and wanted to say hi.'

'Anyway, I best get on my way.'

'Ava?'

She turns and waits for the next line. Mandisa steps forward, closing in on Ava's retreat.

'Tell Zia I said hi, will you? She was a good friend. Tell her I remember those rock cakes she used to make.'

Ava tuts at this. Zia has never made rock cakes. She swallows her pride, and her eyes linger on Mandisa for a second more than they should before she replies. 'Sure, I'll tell her.'

'It's really nice to see you, Ava. Hopefully we can see more of each other now that you work here.'

Ava grunts, turns on her heel, then marches towards the door, a heavy feeling lodged in her chest. Mandisa. Awful Mandisa, boasting and showing off and parading herself around just because she looks so lovely. Fancy asking what her Score is anyway. How rude and nosy. Mandisa clearly still lives in a bubble up in high Score land, looking down on all the sub 700s like they're peasants. Ava kicks her bike as she unlocks it, then cycles away, knuckles bleaching from gripping the handlebars so tightly.

She stops by the supermarket on the way and buys a packet of hair dye. Black to match her original colour. She applies it as soon as she gets home, gritting her teeth as she rubs it through her ends with her clenched hands. Her back twinges as she leans over the bath to rinse, even more so when she stands straighter after. It takes ages and leaves stains on her top, but she does it. Salt and pepper hair now just black. She checks it in the mirror and nods at the result, the lack of silver streaks making her hair look like an abyss of darkness. That ought to shut people up for a while.

She runs her fingers through it, the odd patch she's missed imperceptible and the texture softer, improved. A silver necklace jingles from her neck, and she wipes some dye from it to prevent it tarnishing. It was her mother's necklace, handed down a few years before she died—a delicate chain with a floral pendant that has lost its shine but not its appeal. Funny how a colour can be so coveted in crafted metal, yet when produced by the body, it's scorned. She wipes the last of the dye from the chain, then polishes the pendant on the towel she has ruined. Still, she looks a decade younger. Paler, maybe, so she applies some makeup to balance that off. A touch of colour, highlighting her cheekbones, disguising the under-eye circles that match her hair colour too well. Not bad. Desirable? Probably not. But younger, sure. Her implant still glows green, hormones stubbornly holding out. If her hormones think she's young, maybe it won't hurt to look so.

Chapter 17

Dan's house is closer to the river than Ava's, and as she cycles there to meet him for dinner one evening, he messages, saying to meet him at a different address. It's an estate that backs onto the hillside with a view of the river but high up so there's zero flood risk. It's the sort of estate you wouldn't even know was there, the sort that caters to higher Life Scores than either of them have. New man, it must be.

She turns her bike lights on as she weaves down the lane, flanked by entrance gates to properties more grandiose than almost any other part of town, rare flowers wafting their sweet scent across the street. Real flowers, no fake ones in sight that Ava can tell. If they are fakes, they're extremely good ones—even the insects are falling for it. Towards the end of the lane, she comes to the property name Dan gave her. Hillside Cottage. Hardly a cottage. Its width spans the width of several apartments and is as high as an entire block. She counts three balconies as she enters the grounds behind huge hedges, perfectly pruned, and various fruit trees lining the path. She parks her bike outside, doesn't bother to lock it, then tucks in her T-shirt.

'Ava!' Dan calls from the doorway and greets her with open arms and air kisses. His aftershave is different. Less chemically, more musk. Pricier, probably.

'Dan. What the hell? New man I assume?'

'Yes.' He grins so widely he could be a jester. 'And he's an 890.'

'890! Blimey,' Ava says, letting out a long breath.

Ava follows him along the stone tiled floor, past framed paintings lining the walls and shelves of antiques. Her eyes are so wide as she takes it all in, they begin to sting and water. She wipes her eye on her sleeve, looking down as she does so and sees—is that real gold in the stone tiles? Wow. She's scuffing her soles on actual gold. In the lobby—there's actually a room the size of Ava's apartment that Dan calls the lobby—an elderly man limps over, supported by a stick and puffing for breath. His tailored clothes fit him in the way they always do for the wealthiest elder citizens. Made-to-measure and expertly ironed. And he looks elderly, his lined face hangs even as he smiles, red semi-circles from drooping lids under his eyes. Though he has the bright pink face of a Preserved, he's obviously in the early stages post treatment.

'Ava, this is Jeremy. Jeremy, Ava.'

Ava smiles and says hello but doesn't go in for as much as a handshake. Elders bruise too easily. Jeremy looks like he would crumple.

'I think, actually, I might have to leave you two to it,' says Jeremy, his voice trembling more than his body. 'I'm very tired. I am so sorry to be rude.' His accent reminds Ava of old black and white movies from over a century ago.

'Not at all,' Ava says.

'You rest up, my lovely,' Dan says. 'You'll feel right as rain in no time.'

Ava eyeballs Dan all the way to the dining room, which is for quite a long time given the size of the place. When they sit at the dark wood table on two of the uniquely carved chairs, so heavy and sturdy they would make Ava's funeral home chairs seem like flatpack garbage, Ava can wait no longer. 'Spill then! Who is this guy? What are you playing at?'

'He's a sweetie. And he'll be hot in a few years.'

'Yeah, but now—'

'Don't go all judgey on me,' he says, folding his arms across his designer shirt. Brand new by the looks of it. 'I applied for this job at the university. Really want to up my Score and get Pres-X-2 and this job would really help. But it's a catch twenty-two. They say Pres-X-2 is a requirement for the job. Not just for women, men as well.'

'Just for women?' Ava says, wincing. He didn't sound sarcastic.

'You know what I mean. Anyway. . .' He waves his hand, dismissing her offence. 'They've done studies. Students learn better if the professor looks younger, and with the amount they're charging for tuition fees these days, they want the best, you know? So, I had to up my game. I've been going to every bar, using every dating site, but all the ones who have finished regressing are snapped up already.'

'All the ones? They're people, Dan.'

'All right, Miss Easily Offended. All the *people* who have finished regressing. I figure Jeremy is a good investment. He had his treatment just last week. His libido isn't even too bad and that'll only improve.' He bounces his eyebrows.

Ava laughs. 'And you reckon he's going to gift you points?'

'He's already said so. Got no family, doesn't need so many points now. He wasn't even going to bother having Pres-X. Can you believe it? But when they opened it up to lower Life Scores, he thought, what the hell, why not? If the paupers are doing it, so should he!'

Ava rolls her eyes. Dan's candour is as crude as ever. 'And how does Jeremy feel about being used for his Score?'

'Look, I've been honest,' he says. 'And he's shown me pictures of what he looked like in his youth. The guy was hot! Check it.' He takes out his phone, then loads up a photo and shows Ava. He's right. Even Ava can appreciate Jeremy's once good looks. 'It's like having a flower and waiting for it to bloom.'

Ava laughs again. How poetic. 'So, when's your treatment?'

'Ha! Next week.'

'Next week! Wow! You don't waste any time.'

'Hey, life is short, so they say.'

'Oh, the irony.' She gives him a playful punch on his arm.

Dan looks up, gaze wistful, as if seeing his youthful self flying high. 'You've heard what they're saying? What they're calling the ones who have taken Pres-X-2? Young-looking people, decent Scores. That'll be me. I'm so looking forward to being a Desirable.'

That word again. Not an adjective, a noun, with a capital D. It makes Ava flinch.

'And look at you, making the effort now. Did you think I wouldn't notice?' He picks up some of her hair and twiddles it around his hand.

'I just thought, well. . .' She stumbles over her words, quite unsure how to answer. She's still not even sure why she did it.

'It looks great. When your implant goes gold, you'll almost pass as a Desirable yourself. You look like you're finally ready to move on from Mandisa and meet someone new.'

Mandisa. She definitely wasn't the reason why she dyed her hair. Nope. Definitely not. It was for Ava to look like she's not safe age, to suit her hormones. That was it.

Dan starts prodding at his cheeks, lifting his brow line, stretching his jawline. 'Get ready to see me looking even more gorgeous. Come round for dinner after?'

Ava nods. 'Sure.'

***

Desirable. All the way home, that word grates on Ava. She didn't catch it when she first heard it, when Mandisa said it, but now that she's heard it again, it's gotten to her, is stuck in her mind like some annoying song. She tries to mouth the word, but it makes her lips twitch like she wants to bare teeth. Desirable for men means looking young. For women, it means looking young and being safe. Her cycle home is slow, yet she's burning hot, gripping the handlebars tighter than needed. *Desirable.* As if the only condition to being desired is youth. Her skin itches at the thought. She wants to shed it, to grow into another, to cast off the feeling of being undesired. Not to be younger, no, but to shed her current skin and to arrive in one in which she is comfortable again. Is there ever an age where it's possible to just be, to live in a skin that fits just right, not too tight nor too loose? That's a level of comfort she can never imagine, as much as she pretends she wears it already, a level of comfort that baggy clothes can't compensate for. The discomfort of age is no worse than that of youth, only she grows more tired of it. The days dig in and snag, however many there have been.

She screeches her bike to a halt outside of her apartment building, and kicks it after dismounting before rattling it against the bike stand as she grabs the lock, slamming it into place and tutting over and over to herself. *Desirable. What crap.*

Chapter 18

With the funeral home still too quiet to make a wage, Ava makes her mind up to be proactive, and visits XL Medico during a weekday, making use of her current green time. Based on the state of the lab last time she was there, there's a good chance the lab is understaffed. Freshly washed hair with no greys, a dash of makeup to balance it off, wearing her smartest trouser suit. All to make her look presentable, employable, to give her confidence to ask for more hours.

She did not make an effort in case she bumps into Mandisa, definitely not. She didn't dye her hair for Mandisa, to look younger, to match Mandisa's youthful and soon-to-be more so appearance. Mandisa's beauty isn't even why she loves her. No! *Loved.* That ship sailed long ago. She squeezes her eyes shut to force out the thought. Past tense. Everything about her and Mandisa's relationship is past tense. She didn't love Mandisa for her looks. She loved her for. . . well. . . she can't really think of why right now. And doesn't want to.

It doesn't matter, since Mandisa is not why she's going to XL Medico today. She's going to find more hours to earn more money and strive to Score. Like a good citizen of the Society. She holds her head high as she scans her card and walks in without raising any eyebrows, then makes her way to the lab.

Feeling a touch more glamorous than usual, she walks through the corridors a little taller, tucking her hair behind her ears rather than letting it fall over her face. The perfume she applied earlier is still teasing her nose, emitting none of the old gym clothes malodour from last time she was in these corridors. And she must admit, she feels better for it. She has a spring in her step that a trickle of extra belief in oneself can bring. She's at XL Medico for work. Just for work. Mandisa and her 700 plus score aren't even on her mind. Nope. Not one bit.

The staff in the lab are frantic. The mess Ava saw when she last worked was nothing compared to this. Spillages and boiling over glassware, nothing where it should be, all combined with yelling and the smell of something burning. Ava tiptoes in, her bit of extra self-belief eroded by what a nuisance her turning up unannounced is likely to be.

She clears her throat. 'Hello?'

One man stops what he's doing, his face red with impatience as he looks her way. 'Who the hell are you?'

'Ava. Weekend staff.'

'Right. The formaldehyde-rose chemist. Well, what do you want?'

'It just seemed a bit chaotic in here last time I worked. I wondered if you needed any more help during the week.'

He looks down at her implant and his eyebrows raise with surprise. Whatever effort Ava put in to making herself look younger, her face clearly still looks like she's at safe age.

'A green implant?' he snorts. 'Don't make me laugh. The last thing we need is another unsafe woman around here. Unchecked hormones are what is leading to the mayhem. *Feelings and sensitivity,*' he says, this last bit with a fake whiny voice that makes Ava want to smack him. 'Get the hell out, will you? Before you cause more dramas than we've already had. If you know any men or safe women, send them over.'

Ava stands in the doorway, so angry she's sure steam is coming out of her ears.

'At least have the decency to face the wall.'

Instinct makes her shoot him a look with eyes like lasers before she complies. A few deep breaths, then she counts to ten, and the steam fizzles out.

'And no Preserved women either,' he says. 'The last thing we need is some disguised hag going through another few years of being fertile.'

'Disguised hag? You know you help make Pres-X, right?'

'Yeah well, doesn't mean I think it's always a good thing. Fertile and Preserved women are nutcases. It's like working with a load of bloody Joan Porters around here.'

Joan Porters? Ava folds her arms to get her clenched fists out of his sight. 'Who the hell is Joan Porter?'

He snorts a laugh. 'You seriously haven't heard of Joan Porter?'

Ava shakes her head.

'Well. The Joan Porter effect is real and happening. Watch the bloody news, why don't you. Let's just say for some people, Pres-X is a blessing, and for others. . .' He makes an exaggerated shudder noise. 'Being young again doesn't mean they have to go all predatory. I've got nail marks on my shoulders from trying to escape Preserved women. Like they think they're some fucking gift to us all. It's bad enough in the bars, but I'm not putting up with it at work too. No wonder they've altered the recipe for Pres-X-2. Wean them into youth slower, rather than the shock.'

'I think the predatory behaviour works both ways,' Ava says, remembering the attack and the arse squeeze in the bar.

'Yeah, whatever. Anyway, we're rushed off our feet here. More product would be helpful but it's not up to us. Targets are high and getting higher for everything. You make the formalde-hyde-rose, right?'

'Yes.'

'Well, that output needs to double, at least. And since your stubborn little arse won't share the recipe, I don't see what choice they have except to insist you work more. Be careful what you wish for, that's all I'm saying.'

'Double?' Ava almost shrieks and snaps back to face him.

He raises his eyebrows, her surprise mirrored in his. 'You not get the memo about output? It's all over the XL Medico info streams.'

'No. . . I'm not on the XL Medico intranet yet.'

'Lucky you. Anyway, NDA and all that. You can read all about it when you get access. Enjoy living in blissful ignorance for now. Work is about to get even harder.'

Ava leaves the lab, a mixture of anger and excitement whirring inside her. Pissed off at the awful lab guy, but his smarmy, cocky, dickhead mouth has just told her she's more than likely to get more hours if output is set to double. Double is more than she bargained for, but she could cope. She'd have to.

On her way down the corridor, she walks past a load of executives, Mrs Constance in tow. Ava skirts the edge of the corridor, looking away, her black suit not at all helping her camouflage into the white wall. Of course Mrs Constance sees her. Ava would never expect she could be lucky enough to escape, like some dirty stain on a polished surface. She says nothing, just looks at Ava, a pleasing smile as she tilts her chin up and down to take her all in, and she grins, then winks as she walks by. Under her sparse makeup, Ava can feel her cheeks reddening. Mrs Constance's approval is not what she was hoping for.

Chapter 19

6 years before the Great Unrest

Lucia laid out the rock cakes she'd made specially, along with all her other café duties. The rock cakes had gone down well at the last meeting, not too sickly sweet for that time of night and enough fruit in them to make them seem like a decent enough meal replacement. Some of the people who attended the meetings came straight from work and often hadn't had any proper dinner yet, so Lucia thought they'd need the calories to fuel their in-depth discussions. A few of the rock cakes were a bit bigger than others—she'd never developed the knack of making things look even. All the cakes in the café were a bit wonky, but that just made it clear they were homemade.

Lucia had been busy in the café all day but had made time to bake an extra batch for this meeting, since two others were coming. She couldn't believe it when they said they'd come, and she kicked herself for not inviting them earlier. She hadn't known how much they hated the way things were going, but when they opened up the new funeral home in the town centre, not just any funeral home, an exclusive funeral home for the 700 pluses, she knew they must have felt the same way as she did about Pres-X.

Keisha and Ian arrived first, Keisha sporting her bump that was really starting to show.

'Look at you!' Lucia held her hands to her face, then placed them on Keisha's tummy. 'You're getting so big!'

Before their chat had even got into full swing, Mo arrived, little Donny in her arms, propped up on her belly. 'And you too,' Lucia said and took Donny off her. 'This dog is getting as fat as you. You shouldn't be carrying him.'

Mo had accidentally fallen pregnant by her ex-boyfriend. It was quite a shock at the time. Even more of a shock that she'd decided to keep it. But now, she was radiant.

Mo laughed and sat, rotating her sore ankles. 'I'm thinking about getting Donny a pushchair, but I'm worried about the abuse I'll get in the street if people think it's a baby.'

'It's quite obvious now you're having a baby,' Lucia said.

'Yeah, but two babies. You know people have had their houses vandalised?'

'I read in the news. Terrible.'

'All to make room for the Preserved.' She clicked her teeth and took Donny back, who curled up on her lap. 'You know my dickhead of an ex actually tried to have me fired?'

They all gasped. 'No!'

'Yep. Said I was in no fit state to work. That if I wasn't willing to have an abortion, I wasn't dedicated to my job. I'm not even asking him for money. We haven't been a couple for ages, besides the one night, you know. I want nothing to do with him!'

'Bitter,' Keisha said. 'That's all he is. What did your boss say?'

'Not a lot. Yet. But you know, they're going to take away all our rights. No maternity cover, no job protection if you have time off to have a baby, no flexible working. None of that.' She listed all these terrible points off on her fingers, swiping her hand through the air as she did so. 'It's just speculation at the moment, but it'll happen, I'm sure. I'm just lucky my mum can help.'

Keisha shook her head. 'We always imagined we'd both work after having a baby, but the way things are now, we couldn't get a nursery place. Ian might have to take time off. They're saying it's more acceptable for men. They're guided by logic and not by hormones. They're less likely to lose their job and more likely to find one afterwards. You know employers can now refuse to employ mothers? It actually said that in the news.'

Lucia started handing out cakes. People needed sugar to help deal with such things. 'I came to this country over fifty years ago, and I hardly recognise it now.' She slammed the plates down a little too hard.

More people arrived, so many now, and Lucia felt pleased she'd made double the usual amount of rock cakes. All those people whose names she could never remember. Their faces in soft focus under artificial lights. She recognised Luigi and Daphne instantly though. They came, just as they had promised.

Lucia grabbed their wrists and pulled them to the front. 'Everyone, we have two new members. This is my brother Luigi and his wife Daphne. Oh, I know. Why don't we get a photo? Keisha, you're quite arty. Write Time's Up on that piece of paper, nice and big, and hold it up.'

Keisha did just that, and Lucia organised all the people, telling them where to stand to make the most of the cramped space. 'Now say Time's up!' she said with a smile and took a photo, plus another for good measure. She held her phone to her chest, a feeling of pride at what she had created.

'Now you get in,' Thomas said, and he took a photo with Lucia included, right in the middle.

'Wonderful. Thank you everyone,' said Lucia, a happy tear in her eye. 'Did you know that Luigi and Daphne have just opened that funeral home for the 700 pluses? That's how sure they are this drug won't be around for long.'

Everyone murmured approval at that.

'I don't know, Lucia,' Thomas said. 'Every person over eighty on my street has had it now, I reckon.'

'That's because you live in the poshest area there is.' Ian smirked.

Thomas rolled his eyes. 'I'm just saying. And Society snitches are everywhere. I almost didn't come today, worried there'd be a spy here. We should start vetting people.'

'Erm, we already have been.' The young lady with the sweet voice stepped forward. 'I work for XL Medico and have a lot of access to the Eyes Forward. Let's just say I've checked all of you out.'

'And who checked you out?'

'That's enough,' Lucia said, as stern as she had ever been. 'New people, I agree, should be vetted. But those of us who have been coming for so long are obviously trustworthy. And I can personally vouch for Luigi and Daphne.'

'Well done on the funeral home, mate,' Steve said to Luigi with a much lighter tone. 'When I start bumping off these Preserved scum, I hope they go to you.'

'Stop that!' Lucia said, even more stern now. So much so, she surprised herself. 'We are a peaceful group. We're not going to be killing anyone.'

'If anyone harms my wife and kid, I certainly will,' Ian said. 'I'd rid the Society of any of its elders. They're all a waste of space if you ask me. Preserved or not. And they'll all be Preserved soon, you mark my words. All of them.'

'Not a chance,' Luigi said. 'It's eugenics. They don't want the low Scorers getting their hands on Pres-X. This is the same old elitist crap we've had for generations. The rich get, the poor don't.'

'Rich or poor, no one should have Pres-X,' Mo said. 'It's just not right.'

'Exactly,' Lucia said, glad the conversation was back to where it should be. She could always count on Mo. 'That's why we're here, to stop Pres-X. Stop it for everyone.'

Chapter 20

10 years after the Great Unrest

At work on Monday, Ava had arranged funeral services for a goldfish and a hamster before midday. The 750 plus pet business is picking up so much, she considers putting prices up. If she can make enough profit on deceased pets, maybe the lack of deceased people won't matter. Not so much, anyway. Still, it's only a small amount of business, not enough to fill the hours, let alone the bank balance.

She leans back in her chair and gazes at the framed photograph on the far wall. Her father looks so serious in that photo, not that he was ever some jester, but he certainly had more wit and warmth about him than that photo portrays. She wonders what he would make of his business now, offering pet funerals. He was dumb enough to start an exclusive funeral home just as Pres-X came out. So convinced was he that Pres-X would tank, he invested in this place. She tuts to herself and shakes her head. Damned fool. So convinced was he that the Time's Up would win, Ava now realises, and kicks herself for not understanding this sooner.

She idles away a few moments, scrolling through celebrity news. There's plenty of gossip column hype about Pres-X-2, both embracing and condemning. Those denying they've had it when they clearly have, as well as those citing their excitement to take it soon. One of the latter is the popular singer, Monika Skye, a star for as long as Ava can remember. Her song *Life Without You* is one of their most requested funeral numbers. Ava checks her bio, almost fifty, and her complexion is holding up well, better than Ava's anyway. In a lot of her many, many selfies is her aged, small dog, Theodore, all grey fur and cloudy eyes. One celebrity pet funeral could be great for business. Ava clicks follow and wonders how inappropriate it would be to send her details for their services.

Just as she is debating this, the front doors open. In her celebrity stalking mindset, she hadn't even noticed the cars pull up outside, blocking the entire bus lane by the sounds of the developing commotion outside.

'Can I help you?' Ava stands.

They don't need to introduce themselves. It's the same sharp-suit wearing Eyes Forward groupies that came to ask her to make formaldehyde-rose a few weeks ago, the man with the scar down his chin still leading the way.

'We've come to congratulate you on your recent Society Policing achievements,' Chin Scar says.

Ava tries to avert her gaze from his chin, but her eyes flick to it every other second. It's definitely the same one. This man must be the one from the Time's Up photo. The scar is identical. *What a hypocrite!* She pushes that thought to the back of her mind. Now is not the time to confront him. Now is the time to be professional. 'Thanks,' she says. 'And?'

He raises an eyebrow, his eyes darting from her face to the wall, a silent instruction, so obvious it's not worth the effort of speech. Ava turns her chair around and plonks down heavily with the quietest of huffs. The chairs on the other side of the table scrape against the floor. But no knees creak like hers did.

'The Eyes Forward feel it is imperative to congratulate women on their achievements, to let them know that, even when at unsafe age, the Society appreciates their contribution. The history books may be full of many men doing great things, but we must never forget the few women that are the accessory to such accomplishments. Women may be silent in the history books, but they are not without use. With your Society Policing, and the amount of formaldehyde-rose you have been making, you are one of those women who is a true asset to the Society.'

With her back to the men, it's hard to judge his sincerity. He sounds earnest, but he could have a smirk on him to rival that late night newsreader. Ava notices a smudge on the wall, a little flaw in the paint. She must get around to cleaning it, to make it gleam, professional, perfectly presented. She squeezes her eyes shut and forces her mind back to the here and now. What did he say? An asset? 'Right. Good to know I am doing my bit.

Be awful if the Time's Up and Enough were to start the Great Unrest again. It was so terrible last time.' She waits for him to divulge a hint of discomfort. Guilt. Nothing. He's as robotic as ever when he replies.

'I understand you are doing pet funerals now. A savvy move, I must say, given the prospects of your usual business.' It would sound like a compliment if his voice wasn't as monotone as a bus engine.

'Do you have a pet you'd like a service for?'

'That's not why we're here.'

'No way.'

He doesn't acknowledge her sarcasm. 'Is anyone else here? This is confidential.'

Ava shakes her head. 'Just me.'

'Very well. Here with me is Doctor McGellen,' Chin Scar says, 'from XL Medico. He will explain the particulars.'

'The output needs to be greater. The demand for Pres-X-2 is far more than anticipated.' The doctor's voice is somewhat higher. If she didn't know he was a man, she wouldn't be sure. 'The astonishing and welcome consequence of this new wonder drug is that so many people are striving to Score, the nation's wealth has increased more than we imagined, and so more people are eligible.'

'It is a wonderful advancement for the Society,' Chin Scar says. 'Soon we will have an almost entire nation of high Scoring young people, and sterile, since women being sterilised is a condition of treatment. No more citizens battling with middle age. None of the cosmetic issues with that time of life. You must appreciate this benefit.'

'No more attitude from the Time's Up, then?' Ava says, unable to bite her tongue.

A small pause from them, and Ava wishes she could see his face. Is he blushing? She chews on her lip, itching to interrogate him further, ask about her parents, about what changed his mind.

'The factions of the Great Unrest era are long gone,' Chin Scar says. 'The Eyes Forward have united the country, and we all work towards a common goal.'

A united country? She ruminates on this a moment. He's not wrong, not entirely. The factions are not vocal anymore, but how did the Time's Up get so silenced? They were as noisy and riotous as the Enough in the Great Unrest. She shivers to think of this, of her parents being part of the anarchy. What did the Eyes Forward promise the Time's Up? From what she can see, none of their demands have come to light. She can't let the lull in their dialogue last, can't let them think she's overthinking. 'The common goal, as you put it, is to have the Society completely populated with Desirables?' Her tone is sweet, an innocent question.

'That would be a most pleasing outcome. The Society's Desirable citizens will be the envy of the world, even more so than already.'

Ava mutes any sound of her annoyance, feeling quite the envy of nobody. 'Appreciate how hard it will be for me to double the output. I'm sure Doctor McGellen can understand.'

'Indeed,' the doctor says. 'The Eyes Forward are grateful for your service.'

'So, I will require staff. It won't be possible to do this alone.'

'I will assign you a lab partner who is happy to work with an unsafe woman,' Chin Scar says, hissing on the 's' when he says unsafe. 'I think there is a homosexual man in one of the labs who may agree.'

'And I will need to work more hours, obviously. And be paid accordingly.'

'Your hourly rate will extend to the extra hours, of course.'

Ava grins widely at this, resisting the urge to air-punch. She can see her Life Score creeping up before her eyes. But the Eyes Forward are here. She has so many questions and can't fight the urge to ask one more. She knows they won't stay long, so she reaches for the question at the forefront of her mind. 'You're not worried about the Joan Porter effect?' She waits for him to answer, senses his awkward shifting behind her, the air becoming instantly stuffy.

'I'll have someone meet you tomorrow evening for your shift,' Chin Scar says.

That's all. They make for the doors before Ava even stands, leaving her elated yet frustrated. Unable to ask Chin Scar about her family or another name she's insanely curious about but with stifled knowledge. Her stomach knots with more unease than joy. That was too easy. She wanted more hours and now she has them. Life doesn't work that way usually, not for her Score, her gender. She was ready to plead her case, to fight for her hours, yet they just landed on her lap like some gift. Her moment of elation dissolves into suspicion.

She sits, facing the chairs where they had sat, pontificating ulterior motives and dastardly outcomes. She shakes the dread from her. More hours, higher Life Score, Pres-X for Zia. That's all that matters. The Eyes Forward can use her all they want if that's the pay-off.

But still. . .

She can't help it, her thirst for answers. It's what led her to study science. What would happen if she mixed together all the cleaning products she could find? Almost fainting and a day-long headache, as it turned out. But still, her desire for answers was unabated. What did her dad used to say to her when she was a kid asking a million questions? He'd do the sign of the cross and shout: *Damned Eve ate that apple! You women! Curiosity kills the cat!* Well, this cat works in a funeral home, so that's mighty convenient.

Joan Porter, who the hell are you?

Chapter 21

Down to Life Scores of 650 already for Pres-X, ahead of schedule, the news says as it hails the headline. Efficiency in the Society, another accomplishment for the Eyes Forward. Ava's eyes widen at the news, 'ahead of schedule' sounding like exactly the sort of thing she needs. Her chest deflates when she learns just how ahead of schedule they are. Weeks, mere weeks rather than the months and years that Zia needs.

Zia seems older by the day. She struggles to get out of bed, wheezes with every step while holding on to the wall for support. Twice in the last few days Ava has had to grab her to stop her falling. Guilt itches away at her every moment she's out of the apartment. A million worries torment her. What if Zia has fallen? What if she burns the place down? One option would be to find a carer for Zia, but that would eat away at Ava's Life Score and take away the chances of her funding Pres-X. The more she's away working, the more likely Zia is to have an accident, but she needs to work to up her Life Score. Whenever Ava thinks of this predicament, she either yawns from exhaustion or clenches her fist with anger.

It's not fair.

At her next shift at XL Medico, she has a lab partner, and they produce fifty litres of pure formaldehyde-rose. It should have been sixty, but her partner is not another Ava. He's a lab tech who knows where everything is stored but has little clue about how to assemble it. Having help with the cleaning and organising is still useful, but on her ride home she's beyond exhausted. She's too tired for any Society Police work. With that, and the funeral home, she's flat out. Arranging many cheap funerals for wealthy pets is proving to be more hard work than the much less frequent and more expensive 700 plus human funerals. The embalming may be easier, but the sheer volume is hard to catch up. She decides against sending details to Monika Skye for her dog. The extra business the attention could generate may prove unsustainable.

She cycles to work in the morning on tired legs, hoping to roll down the hill rather than pedal when the bus in front of her slams on its brakes. Ava screeches to a stop and curses, then shuffles forward past the tyre skid marks on the road and leans over to see around the bus.

In the road is a woman, maybe eighty years old, in her night-clothes, stepping in front of buses. She has the tell-tale pink skin of someone recently on Pres-X but hasn't started regressing yet. She's walking back and forward, obstructing both lanes of traffic, muttering to herself. Buses in both directions honk their horns, a bottleneck of cyclists congregating and shouting at her to move over. The anger in the morning rush hour is heating up about to boil over. Those that aren't in a hurry take their phones out, Society Police apps loading up. Catching someone blocking traffic is worth at least five points. Ava checks the time. She's going to be late. Society Policing will have to wait. She gets off her bike and leans it against a lamppost and runs over to the woman.

'Hey! What are you doing? Get out of the road.'

The woman doesn't answer, but walks again in front of the next lane of traffic. More honks and angry shouts and gesticulations from the jam.

'Hey!' Ava runs to her, takes her by the arm, then tries to drag her back towards the pavement. Perhaps she'll even be awarded points for her actions, she wonders.

'Leave me be!' The woman attempts to shake her arm free. 'It's my time. It's meant to be my time.'

Both Ava's hands are gripping her now. Luckily she's light, not much to fight against. 'This way. Out of the way. Come on.'

They make it to the pavement, and the woman crumples to the ground. Already Ava's fingers have left purple bruises on her arms.

'I'll see her soon,' the woman says through quiet sobs. 'I miss her.'

'Who?'

'Cheryl. She died three years ago. I'm supposed to see her at the end.'

Ava's impatience melts away, the woman's broken heart reminding Ava of her own. She sits on the ground next to her, sidling up close. 'Where do you live? I'll take you home.'

'Be quiet!' She holds her hands to her ears, her watery eyes wide. 'Stop shouting at me! It's so loud.'

Ava strokes her arm, an attempt to soothe her as her sobs become a little louder. When she removes her hands from her ears, she shields her eyes, then after a time she goes back to her ears again, all the while muttering to herself. 'Make it stop. Make it stop.'

'Why don't we go somewhere quiet,' Ava says, wracking her brain to think of such a place. The poor woman clearly needs some rest and some peace.

When she gets no response, Ava searches for a number for social services on her phone, then calls them. The phone rings off the first few times with no answer nor messaging service. She tries again and again, all the while the woman sitting next to her shivers. On the fourth attempt, she hears from an exasperated-sounding call handler.

'We'll come and collect her. Everyone is busy right now. It'll be a few hours.' Ava swears she can hear a sigh or huff between every word.

'Few hours? I can't sit with her for that long.'

'Then leave her.'

The call handler says this so matter-of-factly that Ava nearly chokes at that response and backs away from the woman, hoping she didn't just hear that. She holds her hand close to the mouthpiece, attempting to block the sound from her as she speaks. 'But she'll cause an accident.'

'So? Just tie her up or something.'

Ava's poker face is quite unaccustomed to such comments and she stifles a gasp. After a deep breath to keep her voice calm, she tells them the address of her workplace and hangs up. She's definitely not going to tie up an elder citizen in a crisis, nor can she just leave her. The bus and cycle traffic is flowing again, even the pedestrian traffic is too heavy for someone rogue walking. The orderly streets are no place for a breakdown. In the end, she opts to chain her bike up and take the woman on the bus to work. A funeral home doesn't seem like the most ideal place for her, but it's all she can do.

The woman stands without too much complaint, and after gentle coaxing from Ava, using such a soft and gentle voice, she's worried she'll attract a kitten rather than one of the Society's elders, they get on a bus. It's not a long walk from there, the bus only shaving off a minute or two at Ava's usual pace, but it seemed a hell of a lot easier than dragging and sweet-talking the woman the whole way. She sits next to Ava, hugging her body for the journey, still muttering words to herself that Ava can only just decipher.

Ava tries to make small talk, voices reassurances, asks her questions, but the woman doesn't respond. Her head jerks and shakes. Rarely are her eyes open. The acceleration of the engine makes her jump, and the laughter from other passengers causes her to retreat further into herself and slam her hands once again against her ears. Ava tries not to stare, though her concerned eyes can't help but glance over her. Unwashed nightwear, the ends in tatters. Her hair knotted and wild. Her bright pink skin dotted with perspiration. The ten-minute journey feels more like ten hours, but eventually they arrive at the funeral home and with wobbly paces, Ava encourages the woman to alight the bus and follow her.

'It'll be quiet and peaceful in here,' she says, then shouts at the crowd outside to part and make way. Even the sight of one of the Society's elders in a crisis isn't enough to make them reel in their compliments and barrage of one-liners.

'That colour looks great on you.'

'That nightgown is very flattering.'

'Looks like you need to be shown a good time.'

Ava is not gentle or polite this time. She grunts and curses and uses one fist to punch everyone out the way while the other hand grasps the woman's forearm and drags her through, all the while worrying she'll either let go of the woman and leave her behind or snap her arm off.

After more brute force than she's used to using outside of her Society Policing, she makes it through the doors. The woman squints in the dim lighting and recoils from the soft music, still muttering, both hands now gripping Ava's tightly.

Max stands from the reception desk and darts over to assist. 'Whoa! What's the plan? Coax them in alive and lure them into a coffin?'

'Funny, Max.' They sit her on a chair in the waiting area, and Ava fans herself with her shirt. 'Found her playing with traffic. Make a cup of tea, will you?'

Max nods and runs off faster than Ava has ever seen him move.

'It's so bright,' the woman says, moaning and trying to bury her head into her lap. 'Turn the lights down. I can't bear it.' Her nightie crinkles at the waist, and a slipper falls off one foot. Her bright pink skin extends to every extremity, Ava notices as the woman curls her toes underneath her foot, her skin still with gooseflesh even though she feels burned to the touch.

Ava crouches beside her and rubs her shoulder. 'You going to tell me your name now?'

'Millie,' she says, her voice cracking.

'Okay, Millie. I'm Ava, and here, this is Max with a lovely cup of tea for you.'

She takes the cup, only half full. Sensible, Ava thinks. Saves the spillages. Millie stares into the cup, the steam collecting around her face, and she blinks a film away from her eyes. Ava walks over to the desk where Max stands.

He raises his shoulders. 'What the?'

'Social services said they'll be a couple of hours. I could hardly just leave her.'

'Well, I've got actual work to do. Three guinea pigs need grooming, and there's that massive dog I still haven't started. They want him smiling with his teeth on show, but his teeth are gross, so I need to scrub and whiten them.'

'And what's that?' Ava asks, pointing to a thick wad of paper on the front desk.

'Those are the place names for the funeral banquet for that cat that came in three days ago. You know, the ginger tom that smells like piss. They want a banquet for fifty. I think it's a business meeting. Very formal. Look at the place names. Mr Khan, Mrs Glover. No first names. People are weird.'

Ava picks up the paper and flicks through it. Including organising the wake as part of the service was meant to be an easy add-on, but these demands are way more than anticipated. A sit-down three course meal, projector screen so they can display photos of, what's the cat's name, Tiger, gift bags for all the guests to include—Wow! Designer fragrances and engraved silver pendants, and a singer performing numbers from *Cats* the musical.

Ava checks the customer's paperwork to confirm that their Life Score code has been included, so she can source everything, and yes, Max has been thorough. It's all there. 'Well,' she says with a slow exhale. 'As long as they're paying, who are we to judge? Carry on with the grooms. I'll start organising the wake up here so I can watch Millie.'

Max doesn't need telling twice, and he turns on his heel and runs toward the cold room.

Ava logs on to the accounts page and sees that turnover isn't too bad. If clients were putting on funeral banquets for pets, there was definitely scope to up prices and improve margins. Poor Max has logged his hours, and he's doing way too many.

A ten per cent price increase could pay for another member of staff. She goes about drafting up a new price list and adjusting the website, adding some more pictures of peaceful fur babies lying on soft beds or snuggled up to their wealthy-looking owners, jewellery in the shots. It's amazing what you can pull off stock photography sites these days, Ava thinks when her attention is snapped back to the reception again by the screaming coming from outside. Ava starts, stands, then realises Millie is gone.

Ava looks in all the usual dumb places people do—under the desk, behind the coffin display. Then, that screaming again. She rushes to the door. Out on the street, the old woman has a child by the hair and is holding the scissors to his neck. Ava's scissors. She hadn't even noticed her snatch them. The child's mother is screaming as Millie backs away from her but keeps the child pulled in tight to her waist, the scissors denting the little boy's skin.

Despite the general public's disapproval of children, no one can stand to see one hurt. The child is frozen except for his trembling. He looks about six years old. Ava only has a side view, but that's enough to see his wide eyes wet with tears, squinting from the pain of his hair being yanked up. Millie's night dress blows in the breeze, her now bare feet stepping through the debris that litters the side of the road. The traffic has come to a standstill as Ava makes her way outside.

'Millie!' she says, loudly, but with the softest tone she can manage. 'Millie, stop this. Put the scissors down.'

'Shut up!' She winces at the noise but doesn't put her hands to her ears this time. She cowers low, doubling over. 'Stop being so loud. Where are the proper police? The ones with guns?'

'You don't want them here, Millie. Just let the kid go.'

'I need the ones with guns! Where are they?'

Ava sees it, the man sneaking up behind. A street worker, by the looks of it, what appears like the end of a pneumatic drill in his hands.

'Millie, look at me. You need to put him down. Now.'

The man is creeping closer, long strides, landing on his tiptoe, then heel.

'You don't understand,' Millie says. 'None of you understand. You all need to shut up. I can't stop the noise. It's all just too loud. Too bright and too loud. I just want it to stop.' She lifts the scissors. The man with the pneumatic drill strikes her across the head, and her skull caves in as if it were made of bread.

Chapter 22

'The success of this latest campaign by XL Medico is revolutionary.'

The presenter's voice is plastered with a smile but is otherwise expressionless. Her screechy excited voice conveys the enthusiasm her face fails to, a testament to anti-ageing treatments before Pres-X-2 was released.

Ava turns the volume up as she idles away her morning, watching the news on her work computer, and she soon regrets it. Is she the only one in the entire Society who can't see the point in making herself look twenty years younger? She can't take her eyes off the screen though. It's a distraction, a welcome one. It keeps the image of bread head away, and stops the screams ringing in her ears.

'Crime reporting is up seven thousand per cent, making our Society much safer,' the presenter continues, her fashioned smile not reaching her eyes. Her crisply ironed baby-blue suit is as starched as her face. Even in a gale force wind, nothing on the woman would move. 'Purchases have increased even more than that—women's fashions and homewares especially. The majority of our female citizens over forty have maxed out all their available credit and are working hard to source more. That is boosting our economy at a faster rate than ever seen since records began. An extra fifty billion pounds have been taken in VAT in the last week alone. The wonders of Pres-X-2 have no bounds.'

The camera leaves the studio to show the lines in every shop, the 'out of stock' signs that label every online purchase, the empty shelves of the most expensive produce in the supermarkets. Alongside is a chart with a red line shooting up, in case anyone needed to see what extra tax money looked like in the form of a child's drawing.

Back in the studio, the camera zooms out to show another person sat with the presenter. A man, above the age at which Pres-X-2 becomes available, wearing a suit that shows he clearly has a Life Score high enough to afford it. Next to him, a young woman, maybe twenty years old. Ava recognises her from somewhere, a TV advert or something, though she can't place her with certainty—some Z-lister with more ambition than skill, most likely. Right at that moment, Ava wants to know everything about this woman. Where she's from, where she shops, what her last job was, who she's fucking. Why is that? Two minutes of watching crappy daytime TV and she's hooked. She moves to turn it off but resists, eyeballing the beauty of the guest instead. She looks so smug, like she's just been awarded an extra 100 Life Score points for simply sitting there. If she's famous, she probably has.

The presenter now directs her question to the man, shifting round in her seat, her face still unmoving. 'And the first citizens to take the new drug, Pres-X-2. How are they getting on?'

'The regression years are nothing like they are for the original Pres-X. The change is much more subtle. The bright pink skin is just a minor tinge that fades quickly, and the cultural adjustment is minimal. Celebrities first in line such as Monika Skye and Alana Miley, are delighted.' The man's smile looks more like a sneer. The blackness of his suit seems like a poor choice under studio lighting. It makes his eyes look even darker. He probably had little choice, she realises as the camera catches the glint of the Eyes Forward pin on his lapel.

'And here in the studio we have Isla Sharp.' The presenter faces the woman now as the camera moves around to zoom into Isla's face, uncomfortably close, as if to prove she's wrinkle-free, and her pores are totally clear. 'Isla, how are you?'

'Great, Sandra, Malcom. Simply great. Never better, actually. No longer having to bother with cosmetic injections and treatments. I have so much more time without my usual anti-ageing regimen being necessary.' She gestures animatedly as she speaks, like a kid on too much sugar batting away a fly. Ava notes the implant in the back of her hand glowing gold.

'What do you make of all these celebrities who're denying they've had Pres-X-2?'

'Well, Sandra, I say that's just silly. Shout it from the rooftops. There's no shame in it. Be proud! Let the rest of the Society know the wonder that is Pres-X-2.'

'And of course. . .' Malcom leans in close to Isla, securing his spot on camera. 'For the likes of women like Isla, appearing at their aesthetic peak *and* being at safe age opens up a world of opportunities career-wise. They're also much more likely to find a partner, if still single.'

'He is totally right,' Isla says. 'Before Pres-X-2, I was limited to starring in TV commercials. But since Pres-X-2, I've been offered roles in sitcoms and soap operas. There are so many parts that have opened up to me now. So many more acting roles to choose from, since most acting roles on TV are for young women. Older women just aren't written about. They don't make for such good telly. I'm soon to start filming a college comedy. Can you believe it? A college student role, at my age. It's marvellous.'

Ava's eyes start to smart from lack of blinking, and she leans in to turn the damned show off, worried she'll completely wear down her molars, until the presenter's tone changes, dips, ever so slightly. The change draws her in again and she leans back, still staring. At least she's had a blink.

'Wonderful Isla. Congratulations,' the presenter says before directing her attention once more to Malcom. 'Now, Malcom, I ask only as our viewers at home may be wondering. Why is the male take up so much lower?'

'Obviously, we can't speak for every male out there, but we assume it's because for a husband and wife to both take the treatment, it would be hard to fund. So, they prioritise the woman, naturally. Since they are the ones to benefit the most.'

'Meaning?'

'Meaning women's careers are more hindered by their aesthetic age and fertility. There are many scientific studies to back
this up, studies from a hundred years ago and up until today.
Women are most productive and employable when well-presented and without babies on the brain.'

'If men take Pres-X-2, is sterilisation compulsory?'

'No, of course not.'

'Why? Women must be safe age to have the treatment. Why
shouldn't men be safe?'

'Because men are not the ones causing extra burdens on the
Society by breeding. That is the women.'

'But—'

'Look, I know what you're getting at.'

Ava gasps when he says this. The tone change cuts right
through her. 'The feminist movement is trying to make waves
again, but it is good for women to have the peace of mind to
know that they are sterile. It would be extremely naïve of a
woman to trust a man who says he is sterile. Far better she takes
responsibility for herself and her own actions.'

It's the first time Ava heard of some feminist movement,
making waves 'again.' When did it make waves before? The
ruddy-faced Malcom looked quite appalled at the thought. If
the presenter's face could move, Ava thinks she would have
shown similar emotions to Malcom's response. She must have
invested too much in looking young when Botox was the only
option. Was her questioning just bitterness? The Botox would

wear off soon, and surely, she'd have a high enough score to have Pres-X-2. If she wants it. Though perhaps she doesn't. Perhaps Ava isn't the only one in the Society who thinks it's all a load of nonsense. Or, after a second of contemplation, perhaps she just wants to make sure the men take it too.

The news goes to some minor stories of looting and general vandalism, trivial stories letting all citizens know there is plenty of Society Police work to do, if they want it. The Eyes Forward slogan, *All Eyes Are Our Eyes* scrolling across the bottom of the screen constantly, the walled-in eye spinning on some invisible axis. Ava shivers. She never really considered how creepy that was before.

Between the Eyes Forward notices are XL Medico commercials, blending seamlessly into the Society Policing adverts. XL Medico is clearly upping its branding and its adverts are everywhere. Then, after more stories of minor crime, the news covers a more pressing matter, after the celebrity interviews and more XL Medico adverts.

The health minister, with the spectacles he wears just for show and his overly made-up pink skin, says, 'The recent acts of violence by those given Pres-X—original, not the new formula—is a clear sign that the lower Life Scorers simply need some adaptation time. The reality of a whole new lifetime by people who have, erm,' he actually pauses, 'not experienced all the wonders life has to offer is a lot to take in. But this will not alter their plans to give everyone in the nation who has a clean criminal record the chance at a longer life. B-Well, the new revolutionary medication by XL Medico will be available for everyone.' He clearly wishes to reiterate this point. The dosage correlates to Life Score. You want to feel happy? Then strive to Score! Max out those credit cards, buy the things you want, upgrade your property, and don't get in trouble with the police, and you too can live a long and happy life!

A statement was necessary, Ava surmises. Millie wasn't the first, nor the last. Eight incidences of elder violence in Berkshire alone in the last week since Millie's abrupt demise—all sub 750s who'd recently received Pres-X. Despite the feeling of tragedy, Ava can't help being a little annoyed all those killed were sub 700, so they won't even come to Ava's funeral home.

Still, the pet business is starting to take off.

Max comes into work, seeming a lot more upbeat than recently. Not a tough change though. If he was any lower, he'd sink into the floor.

'Morning, boss.' He has a bounce to his step, a sparkle in his eye.

'Who are you, and what have you done with Max? Your girlfriend must finally be cheering you up.'

'Ha! Of course she is.' His cheeks blush, only slightly, which makes Ava smile. 'I'm just feeling good. Got my B-Well. Doctor wrote me a prescription a couple of days ago. Took a while to kick in, but now I am feeling great! Thirty milligrams a day for my 300 Score.'

'Wow. Hey, that's great. I'm really happy for you.'

'And Nan gets her Pres-X tomorrow. She's actually agreed. Can you believe it! I was going to ask if I can have a few hours off. She said she'd go on her own, but I'm worried she'll bail.'

'Of course you can. That's great news. She worried? These stories are coming in a lot since poor Millie.'

'She'll be fine. I mean, they're rolling out the B-Well too. She'll get sixty-five milligrams for her Score. She's going to be great. I know it.'

Max's optimism is drowned out by the news report carrying on in the background, the person being interviewed whole-heartedly disagreeing with Max's point of view.

'Lower Life Scorers simply cannot cope with a longer life. They're not mentally designed to think so long term. If they were, they'd have a high Score.'

Ava curses at the interviewee and reaches over to turn the stupid thing off, finally, kicking herself for not doing so hours ago. As much as Ava's pleased Pres-X is being rolled out, it seems the general consensus is one of concern. The demographic shift, more talk of it being against evolution, and the cost of B-Well on the health service.

As Max goes to the cold room to try to figure out how to embalm a goldfish, Ava puts her elbows on the desk and rests her chin in her hands, her mind turning over and over with the news of lower Life Scores and violence. That wouldn't happen to Zia, of course not. Not to Erin, either. They are both such gentle and kind women.

Still, it would be best if she did her due diligence and makes sure it's safe and that there's nothing that's been overlooked. So she can make sure Zia's recovery will be as painless as possible.

What had the guy in the lab said? The Joan Porter effect? She Googles the name, but it turns up nothing. Nothing of note, anyway. A few Joan Porters exist, but nothing that rings any alarm bells. She taps her fingers on the desk, shifts her weight, then Googles again. Nothing. It's gnawing at her insides though. Who has no online presence? That alone is cause for alarm. The only conclusion is all record of her has been wiped. That would be a big job only capable by the biggest of companies. And XL Medico is as big as they get.

XL Medico is the place to find out more, she's sure of it.

Chapter 23

6 years before the Great Unrest

'Open the bloody door, will you, Lu?' Ken shouted through the door.

It was ten p.m. and Lucia was in bed reading. Hardly in the ready position to run to the front door, as he clearly expected. She took her time, slippers on, grasping at the banister with every step.

He forgot his keys, he can damn well wait.

Lucia tightened her dressing gown before she found her keys and opened the door, letting the cool January air invade her home.

'Shit, Ken. What the hell happened?'

'Some git. Some bloody git.'

Lucia found her reading glasses and inspected his face, the piece of clear glass still stuck in it. A sodden handkerchief was doing little to stop the bleeding. Across his forehead were more smaller cuts and blood was dribbling into his eye.

'Get the antiseptic,' he said.

'This needs a bit more than antiseptic, Ken. You should go to hospital.'

'Can't.'

'Don't be so stubborn.'

'Can't go. If I do, I could lose my job.'

'Oh, Jesus.' She rested on the armrest of the sofa. She was too tired for this nonsense. 'What sort of crap have you been up to?'

'I can't blow my cover, Lu. Where's that damned antiseptic? A bottle of whisky too. Wash your hands.'

She did as she was told as he sat at the table. In the first aid kit she found Steri-Strips, doubtful that'd be enough, but she grabbed them anyway. She handed him the whisky, and he took a swig. From the smell on him, she doubted it was his first of the night.

'Okay, now, just pull it out and we'll go from there,' he said.

'Just pull it out. You're actually serious?'

'Pull it out, rinse and dress. That'll have to do.'

'You going to tell me what happened?' She folded her arms and waited. He created all this drama, telling her what happened was the least he could do.

'Some bloody baby lover overheard us talking, me and some of the Eyes Forward. We'd infiltrated this group. A load of idiots meeting in the pub in the evenings, trying to say they're going to cause trouble and stop Pres-X, like they could bloody do that. Twats. I mean, it's government approved for Christ's sake. They didn't know we're government, obviously. We just joined in and listened to their crap. They didn't like our ideas. I only said about banning babies to curb population instead. Sensible, really. They were probably some paedos worried about where they were going to get their fresh meat.'

She poured antiseptic over the glass and skin around it as Ken gritted his teeth and gurgled a groan. Good. She hoped that hurt.

'And so this person bottled you? Sounds about right.'

'He shouted a lot first. I told him he was a prick, and it went from there.'

'A bar fight. At your age. Jesus, Ken. You're in your eighties.'

'Well, some people don't like being told their kid is a waste of resources.'

She pulled out the glass in one swift movement, and immediately wished she'd twisted it a little on the way out, caused the man some more pain. His pathetic scream that followed was not anywhere near guttural enough for Lucia's liking.

'You said what?'

'It's true. Bursting at the seams, this bloody planet is. And here is some guy, in a bar, at night, with his kid screaming the place down. Bloody thug. And he has the audacity to say Pres-X shouldn't exist because his kid is more important. Like I said, twat.'

She held tissues and swabs up to his chin to try to stem the blood. Some of it dribbled on the table. More cleaning up for her to do. 'You're a belligerent old fool, Ken. How could you say such a thing?'

'Hey! It's not long until I'm going to be Preserved. You think the Society can support more damned babies when the people already alive are going to live longer? It's just sensible planning. That's what we were talking about. Give priority to the living, not the unborn. Little screaming brats.'

She took his hand and held it up to his chin. He could at least try to help. 'Priority to those *artificially* living, you mean. You're actually considering mummifying yourself like you're Tutan-bloody-Khamun. You're not seriously going through with it?'

'I am. The Eyes Forward are supporting their most loyal mature employees to have the first treatments.'

'Mature people don't get into bar fights.'

He copied her sentence in a high-pitched squeaky tone.

'You're going to be a guinea pig,' she said.

'Don't be daft. Thousands have had it already. Millions probably. Don't you get it? This is the new norm, Lu. Like antibiotics and flushing toilets and whatever else in human history that's been invented to save lives.'

'It's not God's plan.'

'Whatever. You should be excited to have some young man for a husband again.'

'With the attitude of some old bigot.' She stuck the Steri-Strips over. The cut would probably scar. That would ruin his soon-to-be young face.

'The world is changing, Lu. XL Medico has changed it. This drug is going to do wonderful things. Immortality, that's what they're offering. Like gods. Like bloody gods—Ow!'

She squirted the antiseptic into one of his smaller wounds, some dripping into his eye. She handed him another wad of dressing and tutted as she walked off. 'Bloody gods can patch up their own wounds.'

Chapter 24

10 years after the Great Unrest

That night at work, Ava sets up the lab equipment, then logs onto the work computer, her access to XL Medico's intranet finally granted. Her colleague is nowhere to be seen yet, so thankfully, she has a few moments alone to search for answers. She finds her way around the software, browses the files containing order sheets, holiday time, health and safety, all the sort of stuff she should have been presented with on day one, if she wasn't such a danger to be around. It was her orange time then, she reminds herself. Understandable.

After a little more browsing, she finds the staff forum. It's unnervingly outspoken and uncensored. Maybe XL Medico allow this space for its staff to let off some steam. Still, she must be careful to watch what she types. She can't afford to lose this job. Even browsing, she has the prickling feeling of eyes on her. Snooper's paranoia.

Scrolling through the many, many topics moaning about staff shortages, labs being left a mess and deadlines too difficult, she finds a mention of the Joan Porter effect. She pauses and hovers the curser over this thread for a while. She reads and re-reads. The Joan Porter effect is dropped in casually, as if everyone knows what it is and there's no reply to question it. Other lab staff have written about the news stories, touting concerns about the latest spell of psychosis among some patients. There's the odd staff member chiming in, reminding everyone of the marvels of B-Well, but still, it's a sombre read.

Ava devours the forum, then continues searching and search-ing, under files and old articles, but Joan Porter's name never comes up again in anything more official. All her search results turn up is more posts on forums mentioning the Joan Porter effect, with no information as to what the origins of such a name for the malady may be. By the time her colleague arrives, she has a neck ache, dry eyes, and little patience left. Frustrated, she stands, stretches, and begins swapping out some equipment.

'Sorry I'm late. Stuff came up,' Edgar, Ava's new and already lax lab assistant says with panting breaths, his receding hairline glinting with sweat.

'No worries,' she says with a shrug, then continues to piece together the equipment.

He puts on his lab coat and walks around, like he's looking for work to do but unsure what. Clearly not someone who can work without instruction, Ava points him in the direction of the glass-washer. He's obedient, if not motivated.

After a long enough break from being on the computer so as not to arouse suspicions, she leans on one hip and asks in her most aloof tone, 'Hey, who's Joan Porter?'

He stands still a moment, resting his scrawny frame against the counter, as if he needs a break already. 'You've never heard of Joan Porter?'

'Only as a verb.' She puts a conical flask in the sink along with some other glassware. She'll leave all the washing up to Edgar.

'Kind of urban legend around here,' he says, idly fiddling with the glassware.

'Enlighten me.'

'Well, she invented Pres-X.'

Ava's jaw drops, and with it the test tube she was holding. It rolls across the countertop, and she lurches to catch it before it rolls off the edge. 'Really?'

'Yeah, but she was working under XL Medico, and they never credited her. It was around the time Life Scores came in, and hers was low.' He moves toward the sink and looks mournfully at the amount of cleaning there's already to do.

'I guess they didn't want some low Scorer being credited with such a huge thing.'

'Exactly. And she was pretty old by then anyway, like maybe ninety. It was her life's work. You've really not heard of her?'

Ava shakes her head and upturns her mouth. 'Nope.' Still so casual.

'They scrubbed her name off everything, so I guess I shouldn't be so surprised. I swear there's some AI filter that

continually searches her name online in case anyone types anything about her. Can't help word of mouth though. Anyway, I
think she was just too old for Pres-X by the time it was ready.
You know, too senile, and it doesn't work.'

'I know.'

'The story goes, she took it and went bat-shit crazy. I think
she basically turned into an alcoholic in her old age and died
in some psychotic episode. That was about thirty years ago, so
before my time here. You'll have to ask one of the older staff if
you want specifics.'

'So. . .' Ava shifts her weight to her other hip, slouching more,
looking as chilled out as she can. 'The Joan Porter effect is just
what happens if you go nuts after taking Pres-X?'

'That's it.'

'A bit like what's been in the news lately?'

Edgar gives a long exhale, pausing from loading up the washing tray, his eyes glazing over for a moment. 'It seems the lower
Scorers are susceptible, for sure. I wouldn't go 'round saying
such things though. That's one way to get banned from ever
getting your dose. The hysteria on some of the news channels is
really not helping. And it doesn't matter anyway. With B-Well
available now, it's fine. The newly Preserved just need some rest.
Some time to adapt.'

Ava shakes away the image of Millie's brains across the tarmac, her shoulders cracking as she forces herself to look relaxed,
stiff as a board in her arched state. She's used to blood and
guts, but there was something so much worse about seeing the

before and after, without even so much as a gleaming mortuary table to sanitise the view. With the new flasks in place and the liquid syphoned off, Ava's fingers twitch over the keyboard once again as she considers another search. She then remembers her mediocre Life Score and thinks better of it. Losing her job is not an option. Not with Zia needing Pres-X, not with Zia getting closer to the threshold of when they decide treatment will not help. The only person she can think to ask is Mrs Constance. She must have been around then, when Joan Porter was, but she hasn't seen her in a while, and it would be inappropriate to just call her up for no reason. Mrs Constance might think her intentions are somewhat different, and that idea makes Ava itch and fidget.

For the rest of her shift, the sparse information she has swims around her head. Joan Porter invented Pres-X, though never benefited from it. How senile was she, is what Ava needs to know. What is the link really between low Scorers and their sanity post treatment? She refuses to believe the nonsense that low Scorers don't have the mental bandwidth to compute living longer. That idea makes her grasp a beaker so tightly, she nearly cracks the glass. No. The Joan Porter effect is something more than that. Something in the formula doesn't make sense. Ava has a master's in chemistry. She can spot a dodgy formula a mile off. And this formula is unbalanced. It just doesn't add up.

Joan Porter is dead, and dead people leave a trace. XL Medico may have scrubbed her existence off the internet, but this is the

Society, and what Society can exist without paperwork? There's a trail somewhere, she's sure of it.

***

As luck would have it, Mrs Constance comes to see Ava the very next day. In the funeral home, carrying a box containing her dead cat.

'It's just so awful,' Mrs Constance says, wiping her eyes with her XL Medico handkerchief. 'I think he never recovered after Ted died. He just gave up on life.'

'I'm so sorry,' Ava says, pulling a chair out for Mrs Constance. 'Why don't you come and have a seat?'

'Poor Stanley. Poor, poor Stanley.'

The box is open, and Stanley is lying on a tartan blanket. His half-chewed ear on show, bald patches of fur, scrawny legs curled up underneath.

'He certainly was a handsome boy,' Ava says. 'I'm sure you gave him a wonderful life.'

'He obviously needs a service to match my Ted's,' Mrs Constance says between sobs. 'The full works. And a lovely groom. His fur became a bit matted of late.'

Max will have his work cut out for him with this one, thinks Ava as she takes the box from Mrs Constance, sure she spots a flea jumping around in there. 'Why don't I take Stanley across the hall where he'll rest for now? Here, read these leaflets on what we offer in the meantime. Let me just make you a cup of tea.'

Ava hands Mrs Constance the leaflets, then takes the box to Max, who's giving a final brush to a Labrador whose service is tomorrow—shine enhancing hairspray over his fur and a clear polish on his claws.

'Got another one for you,' Ava says as she places the box on the side. 'You remember Mrs Constance?'

'No?'

'Sure you do. Her husband was the last human client we had.'

'Oh, the bus accident, head smashed in. Sure. I remember. And now her cat. That's a shame.' He peers into the box. 'At least the cat kept all his brains in his head.' Max's attempt at humour can't hide malaise. Ava sees it in the film over his eyes he keeps blinking away. His brief spell of happier moods seems to have ended already, and his pale face sinks with a frown.

'What's up with you?' she asks.

'Me? Nothing. Except they reduced my dose of B-Well. Can you believe it? I need to up my Score so I can get more.'

'No! Oh, Max, that's awful.'

He resumes polishing the Labrador's claws, the intensity of his concentration the same tactic Ava has seen him use before to divert his mind. 'Frida has been really supportive,' he says in a monotone voice, not an intonation of stress at all. 'But it's just hard. I was feeling so good, and now it's like my insides have been ripped out.' He puts the polish down and brushes the dog's tail instead.

'It's good you have Frida at least.'

'I missed a credit card payment. Just one. Well, I've missed one before, but that was months ago. I opened a new bank account and just forgot. Simple as that. And since the credit card was in mine and Nan's name, they've taken fifty points off both of our Life Scores.' He slams his grooming brush on the counter, his actions showing the rage his voice hides. 'I'm just so annoyed.'

'How's Erin doing?' Ava asks, concentrating on the positives.

'She's been really quiet. Her treatment went well, so they said. At least she got that in before they knocked the fifty points off. She's slept a lot since and she has that pink face like she's meant to. She hasn't really spoken much. I'm sure she'll be fine, just a bit in shock. She has her B-Well, but again, a lower dose since my screw up. I'm just pleased she actually went through with it.'

'Well, if you need to take some time—'

'No. Really. It's good to be at work. At home I'll only mope around, and Nan will give me hassle. She wants it quiet, she said. Like, super quiet. Even my footsteps were annoying her. I wouldn't mind leaving a little early tomorrow though. Frida's coming over. She needs to talk to me, apparently.'

'No problem,' Ava says, hoping to God that Frida doesn't have any bad news for Max. A new girlfriend saying 'We need to talk' is rarely a good sign.

Ava arms herself with a cup of tea, then makes her way back to Mrs Constance, who sits wiping her eyes and looking through photos on her phone. 'This was Stanley in his prime. If he could look like that for the service, that would be wonderful. He was such a scamp. Loved chasing balls of string. Perhaps he could have a ball of string in his casket?'

Ava smiles at the photos and wonders if Max has a magic wand. Some fur extensions and plumping collagen injections are going to be needed. 'Gorgeous boy. Why don't you email those to me, and I'll see what we can do.'

'I suppose it would be quite inappropriate for me to ask you out again, now that I'm a client again.'

It was quite inappropriate the first time! Ava's back stiffens but she doesn't have time to answer before the front doors crash open, or rather, someone crashes into them. With a wail, a woman falls into the building, screaming, limbs flailing, hair a mess, clothes hanging off her in shreds.

'Oh, my God.' Ava rushes over. 'Are you okay?'

The woman jumps up and growls at her, only her mouth visible under her curtain of tangled hair, baring teeth and hissing like a cat.

Mrs Constance jumps off her seat, then backs into the wall. 'What in God's name—'

'Fucking God!' the woman screams. 'God! What kind of God lets people do this to themselves?' She runs at the reception desk, then smashes her head against it.

Ava hurries to her and takes her by the arms, holding her back. 'Stop it! Let's get you some help. You need to stop it!'

The woman kicks Ava in the shins, then pushes over a display of leaflets and flowers, the vase smashing across the floor. Falling to her knees, she screams, 'Why? Oh why! What have I done?' Her knees cut into the shards of vase, blood dribbling onto the floor, her bright pink skin smudging with claret.

Ava crouches next to her, softly hushing her, rubbing her shoulder. She pushes her hair off her face, smearing blood from her head wound at the same time. Then, with her bright pink complexion, Ava snatches her hand back as she recognises her. 'Erin? Oh, Erin! What's wrong?'

Erin thumps the ground so hard, Ava hears her knuckles crack—more cuts from the broken glass. Erin wails and pushes Ava away as she tries to comfort her.

Mrs Constance doesn't move, just stands, staring with the widest eyes.

'Max!' Ava shouts at the top of her voice. 'Max, a little help out here!'

'Quiet!' Erin says, bloodied hands going to her ears. 'Oh, Maxy! Maxy!' Erin screams, copying Ava, before standing again and once more proceeding to smash her head against the table. As Ava goes to her again, she snaps around and raises a fist. 'Don't think I won't hurt you, young lady. I'll hit you! I will! Bitch! I can see you! Clear as day, I see you. Right through you!'

'Nan?' Max appears in the room, body shaking when he sees her.

'Maxy!' Erin staggers to him, squinting, reaching for him, blood smeared across her palms and dress. 'It's just awful, Maxy. Make it stop. The noise. The glare. Please, make it stop.'

'Nan, your meds. Have you had your meds?' He holds her wrists, wide eyes aghast at the state of her.

She shakes her head, slowly at first, then faster and faster. 'No. No, no, no. I didn't take them. Not many. I saved them for you, Maxy.'

'Nan, you need your B-Well.'

Her knees slacken, and she crumples in front of him. 'I just want it to end, Maxy. I'm done. Please, make it stop.'

Ava grabs her coat, then drapes it around Erin's trembling shoulders and helps her back to her feet again. 'Why don't you take her home, Max? Call the doctor?'

Erin buries her head into Max's chest. He's so much taller than her, she looks birdlike next to him. They stand there a moment, Erin's body convulsing with her cries.

'You need some rest, Erin,' Ava says, barely above a whisper. 'Just some rest and your meds, and you'll be right as rain again.'

'Come on, Nan.' Max puts his arm around her, then leads her away, mouthing sorry to Ava as they walk past the carnage.

Mrs Constance has been sitting silently throughout, pressing her back into the chair, leaning as far away as she can by the looks of it.

'Apologies, Mrs Constance,' Ava says as she fetches a broom. 'Give me a minute to clear this up, and I'll be back with you.'

'Joan Porter effect. It's happening everywhere.'

Ava almost drops the broom when she hears that. 'You know about Joan Porter?'

'I assumed you did, since you work at XL Medico.'

'Before my time.'

'Well, it'll get out eventually. These things have a habit of doing so.' Mrs Constance sips her tea for an agonising moment as Ava waits with bated breath. 'Let's just say that Pres-X doesn't agree with everybody. Still, with the B-Well, it should be fine. That poor woman needs to take her meds.'

'It does seem to be the lower Life Scorers who are susceptible.'

'I wouldn't believe that. Just random. Not even genetic. I seem to remember Joan Porter's daughter adapted fine to her Pres-X.'

Ava's brain is working overtime as she takes in this news. Her well-practised sympathetic and interested face is plastered on so well she must look like that frozen-faced newsreader. 'Well, anyway. Shall I leave you with the leaflets, and you can get back to me?'

'No need. I'll take the deluxe package. Only the best for my Stanley. And as soon as possible. It would be wonderful if you and I weren't just enjoying each other's company in a professional capacity again.'

Chapter 25

***

Ava receives a selfie from Dan to show her his treatment result. He looks much the same at this stage, a rosy hue to his complexion, that's all. His grin is wider than she's ever seen it though, all delight and mischief. She zooms in close to pay attention to what he suggests: his hairline. Some new hairs are already sprouting, narrowing his forehead by a millimetre or two. Too excited to wait the few days for full regression, he insists she meet him at Jeremy's that evening.

'Well?' he says as he opens the door, holding his hands on either side of his face like he's a picture.

'Gorgeous as always.' She laughs, then gives him a peck on the cheek.

'I mean it! Can you see the improvement already?'

'You look happier. Does that count?'

He tuts so theatrically, he almost trips over as he takes her coat. 'Just jealous, you are. Come inside and check out my face under the bright light.'

His excitement is contagious, and she follows him down the never-ending hallway. 'Where's Jeremy?' she asks.

'In his room. He's not doing so great. Everything is too noisy for him. The lights are too bright.'

That explains the dimmer switches, Ava notes as she struggles to walk in near darkness. She swallows as she remembers Erin's outburst and Millie sprawled on the street. At this rate, she'll be in need of a B-Well prescription for herself. 'He's okay, though?' she asks, trying to hide the worry and hope from her voice. 'Sane?'

'What? Yes, of course. Don't believe all the nonsense you see on the news. It's like the old Time's Up terrorists are in on it again.'

She opts not to tell him she's seen the mental state of a newly Preserved first hand. Twice.

The food smells delicious. The sort of delicacies she can only imagine having the Life Score to buy.

'You know, I looked in the mirror an hour ago, and I swear I have fewer lines than I did even this morning. Look, don't my cheeks seem like they have more collagen?' He pokes a finger around his face. 'And my hairline is coming back down so fast. Look at the stubble that's poking through.' He leans in too close for Ava to focus so she tilts back and squints. Yes, he's right, soft little baby hairs are edging lower down.

'Yep,' she says. 'Your youthful hairline is returning. How old were you when you started losing it the first time? Twenty-two? This should give you an entire year of fabulous forehead photos.' As much as she delights in teasing him, he isn't exaggerating. Less than forty-eight hours since the treatment, and the years have already begun to melt away. 'So, you get the job?'

'Yes!' He pours them both a glass of red, and they clink glasses to that. Ava sips. It's the most divine wine she's ever tasted.

'You look knackered though.' Dan screws up his eyes to peer at her. The lines disappear when he widens his eyes again. They don't stay like dug trenches as Ava's do. 'Overworked?'

'Of course. Pets dying left, right, and centre.'

'Jeremy says if your services were around when his Misty died, he would have loved to have given her a funeral. That's Misty.' He points to an oil painting of a dog with long white fur tied up in ribbons. 'Says he loved that dog more than anything.'

A loud crash comes from upstairs, making them both jump. When Ava's heart has leapt back out of her throat, she checks her glass and exhales as she's not spilt a drop. She has a sip as another crash ricochets from upstairs, and this time she's not so lucky, and red wine splatters across her top. At least it's black. Dan's left the table and is running for the stairs before Ava's even put her glass back on the table.

'Jeremy?' Dan calls and keeps running. 'Jeremy, darling?'

Ava catches up from behind, and there's another crash, cursing, the cries so shrill, it's like Ava's in some recurring nightmare.

'No!' she says to herself, just a whisper, rubbing her temples. 'Not again.'

Jeremy's on the landing, face wild like some feral dog, hands digging into his ears. 'Make it stop! Please, make it stop.'

'Your B-Well. Jeremy, where is it? Have you taken it?' Dan runs to the bedroom, then brings out a blue blister pack of pills. He looks at Ava, shaking his head. 'He's up to date. He's had them all. A high dose too. Eighty-five milligrams.'

'Why did I do this?' Jeremy cries. 'Why? Tell me?'

It's all too familiar to Ava. She swallows back some tears as Dan takes him by the hand, brows knitted, a sheen of moisture in his eyes. 'You're okay. It's me, Dan.' He sniffs. 'I'm going to look after you. Ava, there's a doctor's number on the pinboard in the office just there. Can you call it?'

Ava rushes to do just that as Dan sits with Jeremy on the floor, his arms around him, Jeremy burying into him. Dan mutters to him softly as Ava makes for the door to call the doctor in another room. She dims the bedroom lights lower, only one more notch until they're in complete darkness. No wonder Jeremy fell into the cabinet. She can't see shit, and her eyes are decades younger.

She goes into another room, a spare bedroom by the looks of it. All grandiose furniture with a layer of dust. At least she can turn the light up in here so she can read the doctor's number. The bulb buzzes as she turns up the dimmer switch, then flickers like she's in some horror movie, while the floorboards creak underfoot.

On the walls hang pictures of people, a younger Jeremy, with who she assumes are siblings. *Were* his siblings, she corrects herself, alongside parents and aunts and uncles. The backgrounds and landscapes are unfamiliar, from the nicer bits of Berkshire where she's never visited, most likely.

She dials the doctor's number and is on hold for a few minutes, a tinny version of Greensleeves playing down the line. She uses that time to pace the room and gaze at the photos, into the eyes of people long gone. Dan said Jeremy has no family to pass his Score on to, which means he has lost so many. All of these faces, the smiling and the serious, jaunty poses and cheeky grins, a wedding in the midst, no, two weddings, their personalities captured with the lens, immortalised only in memory. Jeremy must have cried a billion tears for these people. Ava knows that feeling.

The fear in his eyes she saw just then, it wasn't any reaction to the drug or adapting. It was fear of the lonely years to come. Another lifetime ahead, with his entire lifetime behind, his new relationship with Dan not enough. His ghosts are all around, whispering. That's why the Preserved want quiet. They're listening for the whispers of their past, while the future bombards them with noise.

The doctor arrives within half an hour, breezing right past Ava and making his way up the stairs like he has night vision goggles. He sits next to Jeremy, utters some 'there theres' and gives Jeremy a sedative injection. It's seconds before Jeremy is flopped over Dan's shoulder, his sobs abated, his jerking movements stilled. Dan and the doctor lift him to his feet, then drag him back to the bedroom where his snoring begins immediately. Dan stays with him, stroking his head and his hand for a while, speaking some gentle words that Ava can't make out from the hallway. As the doctor re-packs his bag, Ava turns up the light, then rights the cabinet—a broken panel, a door off its hinges. It's probably an antique, she thinks. Still, nothing a screwdriver won't fix. She re-organises the photo frames, some of Misty, some more of family and friends, tokens of recollection, images of a time before. She brushes the dust off with her jumper, then shows the doctor out.

'I've seen people like this before,' Ava says. 'Saying the same thing.'

The doctor stiffens and glances at her hand, the implant just starting to turn orange. 'This gentleman is a high Score. He would not suffer the psychosis of the lower Scorers.'

'But he did. It was just the same.'

He twitches his nose, then upturns his mouth. 'You've been drinking during your orange time.'

Her face heats, sure she looks pinker than Jeremy. 'It only just started turning orange a moment ago.' She inwardly kicks herself for not noticing the date and takes a step away from the doctor.

'Probably hormones. Fertile women say all sorts of things when their hormones are acting up.' He reaches into his bag and takes out a blister pack and leaves it on the side. It's silver, rather than the blue packet Dan looked at earlier, and says B-Well+. 'A few extra milligrams of B-Well. He'll be right as rain in no time. There's an adaption period, that's all. He needs some rest to recover. Good evening.'

Ava nods as he turns and makes his way to his car, a sleek black one—personal car, so rare these days. The Eyes Forward logo gleams on the side.

Chapter 26

After a busy morning in the funeral home, trying to find a singer willing to perform the musical score from *Cats* the musical, Ava very much regrets adding bespoke pet wakes to the business model. But she receives happy news via a text message to say her Life Score is now at 590, thanks to maxing out her credit and her extra wages form XL Medico. So, so close to 600. The Pres-X rollout is still only at 650, but that score is within touching distance.

There are blue-black bags under her eyes, and her grey roots are already beginning to show again. Combine that with the fact she's on her last pair of underwear and has had no time to do laundry, shows how hard she's been working. In a Tupperware containing not just today's lunch but also remnants of yesterday's—as her washing up was done in such a rush the evening before—Ava picks through her poorly made packed lunch, promising she'll treat herself to something a hell of a lot tastier than burned pie crust and a near-death apple once she hits 600. Even a cup of tea isn't enough to make the pie crust wash down easily. The wilted vegetable filling tastes more like compost than food. At 600, she'll be able to shop in that deli that gets the vegetable stock in almost a week earlier than the 500 plus shop.

Her eyes glaze over at the thought as she picks a desiccated ex-pea from her molar, imagining the delight on Zia's face, a younger Zia, regressing, eating the freshest and finest food, laughing over a cup of single origin loose-leaf tea. If Zia is happy and adjusts well. If she doesn't suffer the adaption anxiety of so many. The Society's elders are making the headlines daily now with their mild acts of anarchy, disrupting traffic being the most common. No more violence, but still, the mental turmoil seems a common consequence.

Short term, the experts are saying. All fixable. They're keeping an eye on it. The newsreader chuckled when they said this, the old Eyes Forward pun still not wearing thin for some. Suddenly creeping up the score ladder and getting closer to making the list for Zia's Pres-X seems scary. Too soon, perhaps, yet still not soon enough. What if there's a problem and the Joan Porter effect is more harmful than they are saying? It's not like Zia can delay though. Last night, Zia forgot the oven was on *again,* left the bath running *again*, and thought Ava was still in a relationship with Mandisa. *Again.*

Ava can still smell the smoke billowing up from the oven through the apartment, hear the fire alarm ringing. The burned pie crust, an unpalatable reminder.

When Joan Porter died, she must have had a funeral. That's what Ava concluded a while ago, but has been too busy to consider further. But now she has a lull in her day, a blessed few moments where she doesn't have to consider the appropriate level of mourning for a goldfish, and she can do some more research. There will be records of Joan's death. Paper records, the kind that the Eyes Forward can't simply delete. And luckily, Ava's in the funeral business.

It's easy enough to get a rough date. According to Edgar in the lab, her Life Score was low, too low for XL Medico to mention her. And she died about the time Pres-X was first approved. After a quick internet search, she finds seven funeral homes catering to lower Life Scores in Reading that were in business at about that time, five of them still in business now. She assumes Reading as she worked in Reading, and people don't travel out of county for something like work or for anything anymore. Not for years. If it's not Reading or is one of the closed funeral homes, she has no chance of finding out more.

She grabs the work phone, then dials. The funeral home business is a close-knit enough community that Ava's on first-name terms with the owners of the other homes. The staff, not so much. Turnover is high. Many don't last but some move from home to home, and she's employed some of their staff in the past. They've all helped each other out at some point over the years. Florist introductions, helping with staff shortages, references, even sharing embalming fluid when stocks were low, moving around corpses when clients switch homes. She'll be at the centre of funeral home gossip for asking, but she'll have to live with that.

It's the third home Ava calls that gives her a lead. The owner, Kim, poached Max's predecessor, one Ava had trained, offering a higher salary than Ava could manage at the time. Max is better though. There are no hard feelings now, not from that anyway. The hard feelings might be from when Ava broke up with her after a brief relationship years ago. Kim said she loved her job as half the business was burying men. Not that she's a man hater, she claimed, just that she'd never met a man she liked. One night out with Kim and Dan, and it was clear the relationship had no legs. Shortly after the breakup, Ava met Mandisa, and Kim hired that staff member. It was nothing personal, Kim had said, all sweetly through her painted-on smile. She needs to work on her solemn face, Ava thought.

'Yes, I have the records here,' Kim says. Ava can picture her toothy face as she speaks. She makes little squeaky noises with every S. 'Her daughter is indeed next of kin.'

'I have a client who wishes to speak to the family. An old family friend. Perhaps I can leave you my number to pass on?'

There's a pause. The kind of pause that makes Ava feel like she has some loose hairs down the back of her shirt. With the amount of fur that Max was transplanting onto Stanley earlier, she probably does. Ava keeps her fingers crossed and hopes Kim won't ask any more of her. She bites her lip and waits it out until Kim clears her throat. 'There's a shortage of embalming fluid at the moment, you know? Are you still making your own?'

The itch subsides at the bribe, and she relaxes with fresh relief. Nothing too awful. Nothing she can't make time for. 'Thanks, Kim. I'll drop a few litres in for you.'

'Fair deal. Thanks. I'll email you.'

***

When Ava arrives home, she catches Zia on the stairs. Zia, who's walking up past Suzanna's now empty apartment. Zia out and about on her own.

'Zia!' Ava says when she sees her, bolting up the few steps between them to catch up. 'What are you doing?'

Zia lifts her arms to show her full bags. 'I just went to get some shopping.'

Ava looks her up and down. Shoes on, coat on, hair plaited, and she made it home. 'By yourself?' Ava says, still questioning, concern overriding the obvious facts. 'You shouldn't do that by yourself.'

'Why not?' Zia purses her lips at Ava's comment and continues to climb the stairs. 'I am quite capable, you know. Especially since this medication.'

'What medication?'

'The injections for my brain I've been having,' she says, as if this is common knowledge. 'The doctor came and gave me them ages ago. He's been coming around once a week. I completely forgot to tell you. But now I remember, clear as day.'

Ava drops a step behind Zia, needing a moment to take this in. 'Well, what is the medication? What's it called?'

Zia pushes the door open with her whole bodyweight as Ava dashes to assist, unnecessarily, as Zia manages by herself. 'My memory still isn't that good, dear. They give medicines such funny names. Memorr… Menzip… No, I can't remember.' She laughs and dumps the shopping bags on the counter, waving away Ava's attempt to help. 'Ironic, really, that I can't remember the name of the drug to help my memory. Anyway, I've been feeling a lot better this last week or so. You'd know all about it if you were ever around. I think I have a leaflet somewhere. You hungry? Dinner is on.'

The apartment is tidy. No tea spills or crumbs anywhere. The temperature is acceptable, and Zia is right, the slow cooker is on with dinner almost ready. Ava steps back and watches her put the groceries away, mostly in the right cupboards, then peer into the lid of the slow cooker with acknowledgement rather than surprise. Ava hasn't come home to such organisation in years. Zia's complexion is normal, not the bright pink hue of Pres-X. Yet here she stands, demonstrating the mental faculties that have been absent in her for some time.

Zia rifles through a drawer that contains mostly useless junk that they never know what to do with, then hands Ava a leaflet about her new medication. It's called 'Memorexin', a medication specifically aimed at improving cognitive function in those over seventy. Ava reads it and beams, her joy ousting her guilt for being so absent at home, and her chest inflates with the lightness of hope. Maybe something really is helping. Maybe something can buy Zia some time before she qualifies for Pres-X. Then she reads the smaller print. 'Specifically designed for those with a Life Score sub 600.

'Zia, this is pauper's medication. Did the doctor tell you any more?'

'It's working, dear. What more can I say? I feel wonderful. You're always so busy, I didn't want to bother you with it. Oh, I remembered we were talking about the Time's Up meetings.'

Ava's breath catches. She figured out that they were Time's Up meetings, but hearing Zia mention it so flippantly sounds brash, treasonous somehow. She said it without a hint of caution or shame.

'There're some more documents in a folder that I came across. It's on the table. Help yourself. I have some more somewhere, I'm sure of it. I had an orange folder with some bits in it. Can't find it now. Anyway, that's what I have at the moment. Those Time's Up were a noisy bunch in those days. Impassioned. Rather vocal about the cause. I'm sure they're still knocking around somewhere, having meetings, if you wanted to get in touch. They were all quite friendly. What did you want them for?'

'Just to say hi,' Ava says absentmindedly, reaching for the folder.

It's a substantial wad, and Ava catches some loose pages that try to escape. Sitting at the table, she flicks through the paperwork. Unsigned peace treaties. Her parents died before the Great Unrest ended, did that hinder progress? Were they that influential? There's what look like contracts, also unsigned, the Eyes Forward logo a header at the top of each page. She skims the paragraphs. They talk about roles in the Society, Score progression, and exclusivity deals. Most of the legal jargon goes way over Ava's head, not that her comprehension matters since the proposals they suggested were never ratified. There are a few red underlines and question marks, areas crossed out by her mother's hand. She recognises the way she wrote some letters, her M dipping below the line, a little curl to its limbs.

Ava bites the inside of her cheeks, blinks away some nostalgia, then carries on flicking through. NDAs. Those are signed, by her parents and representatives of the Eyes Forward, and by names she doesn't recognise. Underneath the latter names are their titles in the Enough movement. Ava does a double take when she sees that, her eyes retracing that word, the stern, angular font so familiar, the diagonal exclamation mark that follows. She traces the signatures with her fingertips, as if somehow touching those lines would help her understand, to feel some message from her parents.

That message doesn't come through, all Ava knows is that Enough founders and chairs had signed the same NDAs as her parents and Time's Up. They swore not to reveal anything they discussed in their meetings, though exactly what that was seems to have been kept purposely vague, 'to be announced', it says. Basically, they signed never to mention a word about any meeting ever, the specifics of which infuriatingly not written down. 'Any interaction with any member of any faction or Eyes Forward representative shall never be discussed.' The paper it's written on is as secretive as the meetings.

Ava still thinks of her parents and Time's Up as two separate entities. Lumping them together is like pouring salt on a wound. Her heart cannot accept what her brain knows. Her heart still says that her eyes are lying.

She shuffles the papers and comes back to the same one, that NDA, and considers all the secrets it was made to cover up. She angles the page to shine it in a different light. Its shadows are still there, murky secrets spilled in black and white. Representatives from the Enough group had co-signed the document on the same day as her parents. They must have been standing right next to each other, in touching distance, breathing the same air. What did they talk about? Did they smile? Compare notes on how many lives had ended as a result of their campaigns? Her breath shudders as her mind's eye wicks away that image. Not her parents. There's no chance they would have condoned such actions.

Enough is enough! That slogan sprayed onto buildings and bus stops is an image she recalls well—some have only recently been painted over. The slogan from the group that her parents hated so vociferously. The time they spent in whatever room signing this document would have caused their hairs to bristle and jaws to clench. That is what she can imagine. Her parents did what they had to, to stop the killing. Peace-seekers is what they were. Anything to end the violence.

'Zia,' Ava calls, then goes over to her. 'These documents, the NDA, what was that about?'

'What's an NDA?'

'It's a non-disclosure agreement. It means you signed to say you'd keep a secret.'

'I don't know why I signed that. I keep all my secrets quite well.'

'Yes, Zia, but what was this one about?' She holds up the form and Zia puts on her reading glasses.

'What am I looking at here?'

'This is the NDA.'

'What's an NDA?'

Ava lets her arm fall to her side. She should have assumed as much. 'Nothing, Zia, don't worry about it.'

'Your father might know. When's he home? You can ask him then.'

Ava doesn't correct her and walks back to the table. Whatever secrets they promised to keep on that day likely died with her parents. Despite the moderate temperature of the room, Ava shivers. Perhaps she's used to it being too hot in the apartment, or perhaps dredging up ghosts comes with an unearthly ambience. Her hands prickle with cold as she places the papers on the table, then rubs the gooseflesh from her forearms.

She fans out the papers, spreading them across the entire table surface, running her hands over the sheets that her parents had once touched, had once lied about. Not lied, she reminds herself. Just not discussed. Kept secret. She knows they were against the roll out of Pres-X, certain it would never become so popular that they opened a funeral home specifically for the high Life Scores. Seems dumb now, to doubt Pres-X's popularity.

Not God's plan, her dad used to say. Nature will prevail. *Yeah, right.* She stifles a laugh at the thought, remembering her dad's thick accent and animated gestures as he said this. Since when has nature had a chance against the onslaught of humankind? Leaves rot, branches snap. Nature is brittle, whereas humans can light fires.

All such documents should have been burned years ago. Without signatures, how could Ava know if such contracts ever came into existence? But the ideas were there, ideas spawned by Time's Up. Her parents may have spoken out against the atrocities of Enough, but Time's Up bombed old folks' care homes during the years of the Great Unrest. They were responsible for millions of the Society's elders' deaths a decade ago. And her parents were part of it. If these contracts are to be believed, the Eyes Forward were also on their side. The Eyes Forward sought peace and delivered, this Ava knows. No one wants to go back to those years. The murders of young women that were never even investigated, the mandatory sacrifice of an elder for a child to be born, the bombings and stoning of whichever age group you didn't approve. Real police were even recruited. Mounted and armed. Protests turning to riots, turning to arson, turning to. . .

No. No one wants to go back to that. The Eyes Forward working with the factions of the Great Unrest resulted in peace, the peace that still remains. Compromises were necessary.

Her implant catches her eye, the sharp prod she can feel under her skin not letting her forget for long. The compromises women have been forced to make to accommodate the views of the Enough are clear. There was little argument back then. Safety trumped any concerns over discrimination and equality and other such terms that were trendy before the Great Unrest. The Enough movement made their demands, and they were listened to, their collective voices louder than that of women. The Enough movement who murdered pregnant women, who beat their swollen stomachs to the point of termination, who banned women from going outside, are responsible for the rules around fertile women now. Stunted careers, baby licences, the whole safe age mantra. The Enough movement hardly had to compromise. They were pandered to.

But the Time's Up? Ava's wondered before... What did they gain out of the peace treaties? No one questioned it at the time, not really. Too inebriated by the idea of the violence ending that no one stopped to ask what the Time's Up had demanded. What silent compromises does the Society live by now?

Ava stares at the NDA, willing the answers to jump out at her, but she can think of nothing. It seems the Time's Up just conceded. As simple as that. She sits back a moment, watches Zia put the kettle on, then pushes back her loose strands of hair. Perhaps soon she can ask her such questions. Perhaps soon some more of whatever is locked away in her mind will resurface. Ava gets up, then pours herself and Zia cups of tea. Zia asks again about Mandisa before inquiring about Ava's dad, then puts the milk in a cupboard rather than the fridge. Ava's heart sinks a little. Sure, Zia seems improved, but she's not completely better.

Sitting back at the table, Ava holds her tea in both hands, letting the heat take away her chills, yet continues to scan the paperwork. She scrunches her brows to strain her thoughts, wishing like never before that her parents were still here to talk to. She has a sip of tea, scalds her tongue, then curses her own stupidity. What does any of this matter? It's in the past. Her parents meant no harm, she's certain of that. Knowing all the ins and outs of such meetings would serve no one and achieve nothing except satisfy her curious mind. Her father would chastise her for being nosy, for dwelling on things that aren't important. She can hear his voice, loud, stern, telling her to stop wasting her time with fantasies and do something useful. To behave.

She always behaves.

She gets up and helps Zia serve dinner just as one last piece of paper catches her eye—her parent's Score inheritance certificate. The certificate said her parents' Score was higher, much higher than she believed. They were 700 pluses.

'Zia,' Ava calls through to the kitchen where Zia's plating up dinner. Still so organised, but Ava has too much else going on in her mind to notice. 'Zia. Why did I never see this letter?'

Zia takes the letter and looks over it, rolls her eyes, then carries on serving up. 'Because I never showed you.'

'It says here we, us, or at least one of us, should have inherited their Score.' Ava points to the line that states that, clear as day.

'I can see that. You want some olives? I have a jar somewhere.'

'Sure. But listen, their Score was 760. Your Score is 490 and mine is 590. Where did the rest of their points go?'

'I rejected them. And now I can't find them. Have you seen them?'

Ava's eyes bulge. 'What!'

'The olives.'

'Sod the olives, Zia. Why did you reject my parent's Score?'

'Why do we need such a Score? It's stupid. They thought so too. They only got that Score because that man, whatshisname, Porter gave it to them. But he was killed, or died, or something.'

Ava takes a second to process that. She knows that name. 'Porter? As in Joan Porter?'

'No, it was a man. Joan is a woman's name, no? Anyway, we're happy with our Scores, so no need to take theirs. High Scores lead to trouble, trust me. We're fine without some silly Score. Oh, look. I found them. Green ones though. I wanted black ones. You mind green ones?'

'You never asked me! I should have been told about this.'

'Well, I'm asking you now. Are green ones okay, dear?'

'Yeah, green are fine. You never asked me about the Score.'

Zia shoves a full and heavy plate into her hands. 'I'm sorry, dear. How is it? Your Score?'

Ava puts her plate back on the counter, the weight of it too much for her trembling hands. She looks at Zia. How much is she understanding? It's like she's here one second but gone the next. 'Fine. But if we had a high Score, you would've qualified for Pres-X ages ago.'

'See what I mean! High Scores mean trouble. High Scores mean low ethics. I don't want that drug, and I don't want to feel obliged to have it just because of a stupid number. You want some salad with this?'

'Sure, and Zia, I've been working my butt off to increase my Score so I can finance Pres-X for you.'

'You never asked me.'

'I did.'

'Well, I never agreed. Dressing? Oily or lemony?'

'Lemony. And you have to have Pres-X. You'll die otherwise.'

'We're all going to die, Ava.'

'But sooner. I can't lose you. You're all I've got.'

'What about having a baby? You'd be a good mum.'

'Not this again. Zia, please, you have to think clearly.'

Zia takes her plate to the table and Ava follows, clearing a space with one hand in the scattered paperwork.

'Just leave it,' Zia says. 'I'll put the mats on top.' She does that, putting placemats over the letters and documents, covering up Ava's parents' signatures with food. Zia puts a forkful in her mouth, dressing dripping down. A little splatter gets across some pages like they mean nothing. She's always been a messy eater.

'I know I never had children,' Zia says with her mouth full, more splatters. 'But things were different back then. This was a country, not the Society. We travelled. But that sort of thing ended years ago. You're not burdened with such other desires now. Family, that's all that matters now. Not adventures or work or silly things. Family.'

Ava takes a napkin and blots the splatter, a futile attempt to keep the paperwork clean. 'I am trying to save my family,' Ava says. 'That's you. You're my family. That's much more important than making new family.'

Zia puts her fork down a moment. Ava can feel her eyes boring into the top of her head as she keeps hers on the paperwork, wiping away any blemish. 'Listen, Ava. To quote your parents, when my time's up, it's up.'

Ava doesn't push it anymore, the lump in her throat is already stubborn enough.

Chapter 27

6 years before the Great Unrest

Keisha and Ian were having their breakfast in the café the next morning. Lucia served up extra-large portions for Keisha since she was eating for two, and Ian always pinched a bit. She'd first noticed at one of the meetings with the cake. Lucia assumed he'd stop that when she got pregnant, but he still did it. Lucia was exhausted from Ken waking her up late with his stupid bar fight injuries, so she sat with them, cup of tea in hand. The café was quiet, and the other customers had all been served so she could afford a few moments off her feet.

'There are other groups,' she said, leaning in, not much louder than a whisper. 'More trouble-causing groups by the sounds of it.'

'How'd you hear?' Ian asked, talking with his mouth full.

'My shithead of a husband told me. He'd been spying on one of them.'

'Maybe we should, you know, reach out?'

'No,' Lucia said. 'No, I don't like the sound of it. This other group, Ken said, were going to cause trouble.'

'You have to cause trouble to get results. Look at all of history. A protest, that's what we need.'

Keisha finished chewing before she spoke. 'Joining forces would make us louder. More people might listen.'

'To be honest, I think I'd be happier in a group that was willing to actually do something rather than just sit around and gossip,' Ian said, much more loudly. 'We're not achieving anything.'

Lucia looked around. The other diners didn't seem to have noticed anything. 'Well, I don't know where they meet or anything.'

'Ask Ken?' Ian said, sticking his fork into some of Keisha's hash browns.

'How do I do that? Without making it sound like *I* am running meetings?'

'Bring him to book club,' Keisha said. 'Let us tease it out of him.'

Lucia pondered this for a while. It could work. Ken did used to like reading, and it would help maintain her cover. If he had any doubt she was actually going to book club, his presence there would deal with that. She sipped her tea even though it was still a bit hotter than she liked.

'Okay,' she said. 'I'll ask him.'

And so it was decided. They messaged the other club members so they could play along. They even chose a book. The

Sirens of Titan, by Kurt Vonnegut. Lucia suggested this one as she'd read it and already had the paperback on her shelf, and she knew Ken had read it before. He quite liked it, he'd said at the time. And it suited the club's fictitious theme. She felt quite proud for thinking of a book that ticked all those boxes.

The next day was Lucia's day off. Thank God. Her feet were killing her. She got up early to get a nice breakfast ready, then laid the paperback out on the table.

'Morning,' Ken said and slumped down into the chair, immediately slurping his coffee.

'Morning,' she said, and passed him some toast. 'We're doing that book on Thursday. You've read it, haven't you?'

'Years ago. I think I liked it.'

'You should come along. You might enjoy it.' She tried to keep her tone casual and breezy, and she was doing really rather well. 'You certainly can't do any more Eyes Forward work with your chin so sore. They should give you some time off.'

He sat back in his chair and pondered this a moment. 'You're probably right.'

'We always have nice cakes too.'

'Fine,' he said, and took a bite of his toast. 'Thursday.'

***

Thursday rolled around too fast, and Lucia's voice quivered with nerves whenever a customer tried to speak to her. It's stupid to be nervous, she kept telling herself. He was her husband. And it wasn't like he'd never been to the café before. It was just book club, like how it used to be. Nothing to be worried about.

By closing time, she'd cleaned the café, baked fresh rock cakes, and was awaiting Ken's arrival. Everyone else was expecting him too, and they had all remembered to bring their books with them. Some had even read it.

When Ken arrived, his face was red from the outdoor chill, which made his sore chin look even worse. He huffed as he came in and handed Lucia his coat.

'So, cake?'

'Have a seat,' she said, hanging up his coat. 'The others are just out back.'

The oven pinged, a little later than planned. The cakes would still be too warm to eat. She cursed herself for that. Everything was meant to be perfect.

The staff room emptied out into the café floor, and all attendees took a chair, then moved them into a circle. Lucia sat next to Ken and gave a brief apology that the rock cakes would be another few minutes to cool down before introducing her husband. 'Everyone, this is my husband, Ken.'

They all smiled and said hello.

'Gosh, Ken. What happened to your face?' Luigi asked.

'Some idiot at the pub glassed me. No respect, people these days.'

'That's awful,' Ian said. 'I didn't know the Red Lion had such a rough crowd.'

'It wasn't the Red Lion, that's why. It was the White Horse.'

Lucia wanted to air-punch at that. She looked across the seating area and clocked the others smiling to themselves. It was as simple as that. Although she couldn't shake the feeling of dread that this other group was up to no good, the others must be right. It's about time they started doing something, taking action. The Pres-X thing was getting entirely out of hand across the Society.

The time for idle chitchat was over.

Chapter 28

10 years after the Great Unrest

The next day, Ava still hasn't heard anything from Kim. Every time she hears a noise outside, she looks up, expecting to see her walking towards the door, wanting payment in more than just embalming fluid. Ava discontinuing their relationship was met with enough snide back then, she can't imagine Kim isn't going to want some form of payback. She'll have to drop that around at some point. Maybe that's when Kim will reveal her real intentions. She forces that thought out of her head, as well as the stomach knotting unease she gets whenever she has a 'what was I thinking' moment. Ava looks at herself in the mirror a second, then laughs at her paranoia. She's no catch. Kim will just be enjoying having some hold over her, that's all. At least she didn't ask about a male client.

The stories of Society's elders' psychosis still make up the bulk of the minor stories, underneath all the wonder reports of Pres-X-2 and B-Well. She does her best to avoid the news and distracts her mind from her impatience.

On-edge and frustrated, she cleans the funeral home, polishes the display coffins, sends service chairs to be reupholstered, then orders another lot of flowers that aren't needed. All jobs that don't need doing, not now anyway. But they keep her mind busy, her fidgeting fingers away from calling up Kim again and chasing. It would be impolite to chase after such a short time. Be patient, she tells herself as she fluffs coffin pillows, cleans non-existent smudges off windows and straightens the already straight leaflet displays. She finds some air freshener, a floral scented one, and sprays generously to cover up the already pleasant smell of flowers.

She mutters to herself as she vacuums for the second time, convinced she can see dog hairs reappearing even though no dogs have been in for over a day. 'It's quite likely Joan Porter's daughter is hard to find. People change email addresses and phone numbers all the time.'

If Max notices her odd behaviour, he doesn't say anything, which makes Ava wonder if she's usually more unhinged than she thinks. Perhaps this antsy behaviour is normal for her, but she's normally too relaxed to realise. That thought makes her rearrange the coffin display and polish underneath the desks.

It's the following day, as Ava's dusting all the surfaces she only dusted the day before, that she receives an email.

Hi, this is Joan Porter's daughter. I understand you wish to speak to me about my mother?

Ava's hands freeze over the keyboard as her stomach lurches at the words. Joan Porter's daughter. Her mouth dries like she's speaking face-to-face instead of via email. Her mind is blank, and she curses herself for not planning her next move. So desperate she's been for answers, she hasn't really considered the questions.

The footer of the email gives an accountancy firm in town, Friar Street, of all places. An accountancy firm sandwiched between betting shops seems like a bad joke. After instructing Max to man the front desk and phones, she makes her way there.

It's a short walk, and ambling in the slow lane gives her a few moments to think what she needs to ask. What is the Joan Porter effect? Does that explain the adverse reactions? Why does she think her mum reacted so badly? Is Pres-X safe? The short walk isn't really long enough for Ava's adrenalin to abate, and she soon arrives at a small office building advertising business and personal accounting, located, as she suspected, behind some betting shops, complete with their unsavoury clientele. Ava enters and is greeted by a child playing, tapping away at a laptop.

'Hello,' the child says, standing, all smiles, dark curls falling over her face.

'Oh, hi. I'm looking for the accountants.'

'My mum says I'm not to talk to anyone.'

'Sensible advice.'

'But you seem nice.'

'Is your mum around?'

'Iris!' the voice comes from the office behind. 'I told you not to talk to anyone.' From the office a woman appears, about Ava's age, maybe a couple of years younger, though who's to know these days. 'I am sorry. Iris is having a tough time at school at the moment, so we're attempting home learning for a while.'

'Sounds tricky.'

'Impossible, really. But it should only be for a week, maybe two.'

Ava sees the tattoo marking on the little girl's arm. Stretched and distorted now as she's grown, but the symbol of the Eyes Forward is clear enough. She's a child from the time of the Great Unrest. They had a life sacrificed to have her. Could that have been Joan?

'How can I help you?' the woman asks, tiredness in her voice, flicking her red plait over her shoulder, a style reminiscent of years ago, when such a look was so popular, it was almost mandatory.

Ava fidgets and thinks on her feet. 'I'm after some accountancy advice for my business.'

'Why don't you come through this way.'

They go to her office, and the nameplate on the door reads Mae Taylor. Porter must be her maiden name.

'Yes, so, erm, well. . .' Ava stumbles over her words, kicking herself for being so unprepared for this part. 'You had a donor for your daughter, I see. Would that have been your mother or father?'

'No,' she says flatly. 'So, accountancy?' Mae's eyes narrow, her pale cheeks slightly flushed.

Ava fidgets some more, wrings out her hands on her lap.

'Let me guess. . .' Mae leans back in her chair with folded arms and huffs. 'It's you who got in contact about my mother. You're not after accountancy advice at all.'

Ava bites her lip. 'I'm sorry for the dishonesty. I truly am.'

'What do you want? My mother and I were not close.'

Ava swallows, and finds her words, wishing she was as blunt as Mae. 'I am concerned about the rollout of Pres-X. I'm close with my aunt, and she'll qualify soon. I understand your mother reacted badly to Pres-X, whereas you did not.'

Mae purses her lips, her freckled cheeks now ablaze. 'My personal use of Pres-X is not widely known. How did you learn about this?'

'I work at XL Medico.'

'Then you have access to all the information you need.' Mae turns her attention to her computer, as if Ava isn't there at all.

Ava waits a while, thinking perhaps Mae will acknowledge her again. When she doesn't, Ava speaks so quietly she sounds like a mouse. 'My job at XL Medico is menial, but people talk, you know.'

Mae dips her chin, her shoulders slouch. 'What do you want from me?'

'What happened with your mum? Should I be worried about my aunt? She's all I have. I don't want to lose her, but people at XL Medico talk about the Joan Porter effect.'

Mae snorts a small laugh at this, then shakes her head. 'Mum would hate that.'

'I'm sorry. Not my choice of words. There's nothing about her anywhere. I just want to know if my aunt will be safe.'

Mae's lips twitch. She snaps a band on her wrist. 'I was estranged from my mother for most of my life. My first life. I only got back in touch with her when she was in her nineties. I wanted to make my peace with her. She begged me to take Pres-X, to give me another chance at life since my first had been so miserable. I was seventy-one at the time. She promised us a life together, to start over.'

'But she died.'

'Pres-X was her life's work. We were among the first human trials. It was just a few days later when she went from trying to build on our negligible relationship, saying she wanted to make up for lost time, to being abusive and drinking heavily. She died a few weeks later from alcohol poisoning. I tried to stop her, but she was aggressive. You have to remember, I was fairly frail myself then. I had a pink face, but regression takes years. She was violent towards me and herself. She never showed me any love or care throughout my childhood, but those last weeks were her worst.' Mae says all of this without a hint of emotion. There's no sadness in her face. It's like she's reading a grocery list. Ava can't help but admire that, her ability to move on. To not be ruled by hurt.

Ava takes a few breaths, digesting it all. 'I'm so sorry. My aunt hasn't a high enough Score. I assume you've seen the news about the lower Life Scorers? The sub 750s?'

'I have. I don't know what you want me to say. I'm no chemist. It could be just as they're saying, adaption issues. But the new B-Well sounds like it's effective.'

'You were a low Life Scorer yourself.'

Mae's lips purse slightly. 'Yes.'

'No psychosis after taking it?'

Mae shrugs, her gaze still on her lap. 'I have never been neuro normal. The adaption is tough though. I had years of worsening hearing, lower contrast vision before the treatment. That all creeps up on you slowly, you barely notice it. Then all of a sudden, those senses come back. But the brain takes longer. The joints too. It was like someone turned the lights on and the volume up. I shut myself away, locked myself in a room alone for the entirety of the rest of my regression.' Mae looks up a moment and Ava catches a split second of eye contact. 'I'm sorry,' Mae says. 'I'm not sure what help you think I can be. I just took the drug my mother gave me. I have no knowledge of anything else.'

Ava nods. Mae has a warmth to her she's trying to hide, Ava is sure. The news stories haven't escaped her concern. 'The way the Society is going, everyone—all women, at least—will be on Pres-X-2 before long anyway.' She says this will all the spite she intends.

Mae doesn't answer for a while, only stares past Ava and snaps the band on her wrist. 'I really don't want anything to do with that drug. I have a daughter. I hoped for a better world for her.

The Society does nothing but turn back the clock. The ideals they're enforcing on women. . . I don't want that for her.'

Ava looks out the doorway towards Iris, still tapping away at the keyboard. 'She's a cute kid, for sure.'

'Sorry to rattle on,' Mae says. 'I have so few people to talk to. Not many parents around, especially mothers, since, well, you know.'

'I know the feeling,' Ava says as Mae's words probe the tenderness of ancient scars. The Great Unrest wiped out so many women her age. Beaten to death just for being fertile age. Ava was lucky to escape unscathed. So many of her old school and university friends did not. 'It's refreshing actually. Everyone I speak to seems to be excited about looking young. It's like that's all that matters.'

'My mother would have thought the same. Please, I value my anonymity. My mother being discredited was a blessing.'

'What about your father?'

Mae visibly stiffens at the mention of her father, then shakes the words off her shoulders. 'I haven't seen my father in decades. He's probably dead for all I know.'

'He could be alive—if he'd taken Pres-X.'

'If you discover as such, I don't want to know. He's nothing to me. He had nothing to do with Pres-X. He was totally against it. In fact, he and my mother fell out about it.'

'Was he from Enough?' Ava doesn't mean to sound like she's interrogating Mae, the questions just roll off her tongue.

Little Iris comes running in, her looks such a stark contrast to her mother's. Dark hair next to Mae's red, and a happy face next to Mae's drawn one.

'Mum, I've finished all my maths. And I did some coding, see?' She passes up the laptop to Mae.

Mae looks at Ava, eyebrows raised, her eyes darting from Ava to the door. All warmth has gone.

'Thank you for your time,' Ava says.

***

Back at work, Ava can't settle. She cleans, rearranges leaflets, and tries to update the website, but the urge to pace and wrack her brain is greater than any other motivation. Joan Porter's daughter made an impression, and she can't think about anything else. In another life, perhaps they could have been friends. Ava doesn't have many of those. So many old school friends were bludgeoned to death during the Great Unrest. They were the target age back then. God only knows how Mae survived. Mae never answered if her father was Enough, but from the look in Mae's eyes, the fact she didn't answer said a lot.

A Preserved couple come into the home asking about funeral services for their poodle, who's on his last legs. Being prepared, they say. Their complexion is patchy pink. They must have had Pres-X a few years ago. Some lines in their faces still remain, the odd tuft of grey. The regression years used to be a time of hiding away. Now the complexion is paraded around proudly, dog walking and making plans. Ava attempts to engage, to sell her services and be interested in their concerns, yet she's more vacant than she should be, not listening as intently. The poodle's name is Horace, or Holly, maybe Hugo . . . she forgets as soon as they leave, forgetting also the level of service they requested. At least she took down their details.

Acknowledging that her brain might as well be made of lumpy custard, she leaves work early, sticking a sign to the window and telling Max to lock up when he leaves. The streets are warm, warmer than the home, and she misses the air con as soon as she leaves. The dense lanes of people leave the air stale and sticky. Rain is due, a storm by the feel of it. She mounts her bike as a bus trundles past, its exhaust fumes making the humidity worse. The mugginess does nothing to freshen her mind on her cycle home, and the uphill route leaves her clammy and irritated. She wishes things made sense, that everything fit together, that her insides would uncoil from their tight spring. The titbits of information she has are clogging up her thoughts. Perhaps an aspirin will help.

As Ava arrives home, her phone pings with an email from an encrypted email address. Titled, *This Mae Be of Use.*

Mae.

She opens it and attached are photos, like the ones that Zia sent her but more. People hold banners saying, Enough is enough! They stand shoulder-to-shoulder with the Eyes Forward, their logo visible on their lapels. All men, of course. No women and their dangerous uteruses present.

That man is there again. The same man with the scar down his chin. He wears a brimmed hat tilted, blocking half of his face. The same man from the Time's Up photos.

She can't trust her own memory. Lots of people have scars, so she loads up the hard drive when she gets home. Zia's watching TV but only half watching. The other half of her is doing a crossword, well, glancing at it anyway, holding it upside down. After a brief greeting, Ava looks through each photo, comparing. That scar is identical. It must be him. Eyes Forward, younger looking now than he was then, meeting with both the Time's Up and Enough groups.

It's common knowledge that the Enough tried to buy out XL Medico and hold Pres-X to ransom to bribe those in power to follow their ideologies. There were videos posted online of wealthy Pres-X takers standing on platforms shouting, 'Enough is enough!' The news at the time of the Great Unrest made it sound like Time's Up and Enough were rivals. But the papers Ava saw made it seem that the Enough had a relationship with Time's Up. Certainly, there was some cohesion that bought about peace. Chin Scar's presence across all three certainly supports this idea. A Pres-X taker, a Time's Up member, a high up employee of Eyes Forward, and here, photographed with Enough. That seems valid evidence that the three are working towards the same cause, or were. That cause once was to depopulate, not on the whole, not originally. The depopulation was aimed at the low Life Scores, those who couldn't finance Pres-X. But now they're rolling it out more. That's a real slap in the face to Time's Up. That part just doesn't make sense.

It's not the only part she can't wrap her head around. Her parents were peace loving and wanted the best for their daughter, and the Society's future. Zia says they fought for her right to have children, not that she ever wanted any, but that's not the point. It's what they stood for, she was sure of it. They stood for that so much, they were trampled to death in riots trying to protect their town. They weren't the sort to bomb old folks' homes and condone the sacrifice of the Society's elders years ago. They rallied for the working classes, since they had come from nothing themselves. Yet they had accepted a bump up in their Life Scores. Their part in a faction of the Great Unrest bought them elite privilege. Perhaps their lack of scruples bothers Ava more than she thought.

Ava stares at photos a while longer, boring her eyes into those 2D representations, trying to gauge the plastered on facial expressions and poised body language. What were they thinking? What made the Time's Up agree to peace? Standing next to Chin Scar in the Time's Up photos is a woman that Ava hadn't recognised before. Why would she recognise her? She's changed so much since then. Fifteen years younger, mostly black hair instead of entirely grey, lines from smiling rather than worry.

In the centre of the Time's Up meetings is her Zia.

Chapter 29

That night, Ava paces her apartment, restless and worried. She can't shake it and her muscles knot, her back as rigid as an ironing board. She stretches, to no avail. She's too wound up, too tense. The documents she read play over and over in her mind, tightening her forehead and neck. The NDA especially. The rest, the contract and treaties are still a mystery, and she fights the urge to go back to the folder and read again. She does some push-ups, sit-ups, then some more push-ups, but no amount of down-dog and reps can sweat the tension away.

The photo of Zia, her parents, and the Eyes Forward man with the scar on his chin sitting with the Time's Up comes to mind again. The man who has so obviously taken Pres-X. It just doesn't sit right. She can't picture the scene, how it must have played out, like she's wearing the wrong reading glasses. Headlines of the killings from a decade ago flash before her mind as she paces and paces, then shakes her head, wishing her brain was a sieve and would just let all those images fall through the holes and away, ditching the noise and leaving her with just lumps of facts and information. Right now, it's all a congealed mess.

She resists no more and gets the documents out again, dropping a few on the floor, watching them flitter down and land by her feet. She bends to pick them up, and under the cabinet, there's a flash of orange. What had Zia said? An orange folder somewhere? She reaches underneath and grabs it. A thin folder, not much in it. Just one document, a sheet from the contract that she had seen before, but this sheet was hidden somewhere else. Kept separate, not for prying eyes. She reads it and almost drops it again as the letters form words which form an unbelievable pain in her chest. The document adds another layer of confusion, but in that mental chaos are these words, the words that make her miss her parents more than she ever has. It's a promise from Eyes Forward, stating that their Score would be increased, as Ava already knew. But this document is more than just a promise of increased wealth. It's a signed statement by the Eyes Forward that, once they hit eighty years old, they would receive complimentary Pres-X.

Ava's knees buckle, and she slumps to the floor. She swallows back a wave of nausea and suddenly she's hot, too hot. The heat rises from her toes and envelops her completely. Sweat pours from her forehead and stings her eyes, as if they weren't welling up enough already. She pushes the tears away with her thumb and reads the document again. Her parents never wanted to die. They never wanted their time to be up.

Standing again, slowly and fanning her T-shirt, Ava resumes pacing, then finds a cold beer in the fridge, a budget brand, not the best, but it'll do.

Her parents didn't want to die so soon. No one does. But her parents had the chance to live long lives. They should still be here. That thought makes the beer taste sour and not cold enough. Her throat burns and her hands sweat so much, she puts the bottle back on the counter. She bends over and takes some deep breaths.

Her parents were never meant to die.

Was that her parents' bargain? Silence the Time's Up and they'll get Pres-X? It's one obvious explanation why the Time's Up made no demands. They were bought. Not that Ava cares they were planning on taking Pres-X. Screw their lack of scruples. That doesn't matter a jot. All that theory does is fill in some blanks. If they really were so important in Time's Up, perhaps that was what brought about peace. Everyone would take Pres-X if they could. Everyone except Zia. Zia, who's smiling in the front row centre of the Time's Up photos. Was she the ringleader? Is that why she thinks she doesn't want it?

There's too much trauma in her head, too many mental images of people suffering and hurting themselves and each other. And still too many stories on the back pages of the news about adaption issues with Pres-X. But she's met Mae. She was fine. So many are fine. Just a minority suffer. Peace and rest are all that's needed. She's sure of this now. Her Zia will see sense eventually. Like her parents did.

Yet still her stomach knots. As many questions as she answers, she has more to ask.

She decides to go Society Policing to distract herself. Her implant has just turned green again. There is next to no chatter on the dark web. It'll be potluck if she finds anything. She cycles down the hill towards the centre of town. The dark streets are deserted except for a pair of screeching cats having a ruckus in the road. No doubt one of them will be a client for Ava soon. She hopes it's the one with its back arched, swiping at the smaller one. She's a sucker for an underdog.

The town centre has a few central pedestrianised streets, and the road adjacent is a prime target for drive-by gang violence, a speedy getaway almost guaranteed. Old CCTV cameras hang lifeless and smashed from their mounts, relics from times before policing was largely handed over to the people. Society Police posters with the Eyes Forward logo have replaced them. And Society Police are everywhere again. Her usual spaces overlooking the eateries are rammed. She opts to find some lower-level crime, a bit of vandalism perhaps, and cycles down towards the bus-free zone.

The orange glow of artificial lights gives the effect of dawn, blinding Ava as she tries to look down Broad Street. She squints through it, edges a little farther down the street on her bike before choosing a spot on the corner of Cross Street.

The approaching footsteps aren't light and swift like she's used to hearing. They're like dragging feet and wheezing breaths. There are some cries and groans as the shadows approach, emerging from the light. At the intersection of the two streets in front of her is the monument. A seven-metre statue of the Eyes Forward logo, the static eye looking straight ahead, but instead of the walls either side, the XL Medico's open hands cup the eye.

The footsteps get closer, the people still silhouetted against the dusky streetlights. Ava tucks herself into the shadows, then gets out her phone and loads up the Society Police app and waits.

The voices are audible now. The usual gangs approach silently, sneaking up on their target like an ambush predator. These lot must be amateur, Ava assumes, until she sees in the dusky streetlights they all have pink faces.

A glint of metal in each of their hands, the shiny blades catching the light. They walk and shuffle towards the monument. When they arrive, they fall to their knees and wail. Millie's wail was a kitten's purr compared to this noise. Ava can feel this wail in her bones, shaking her core.

They circle the monument now—about twenty by the looks of it—all kneeling, facing the Eyes Forward eye.

'Make it stop!'

'We just want it to end.'

'No more drugs.'

Ava keeps videoing despite the lack of crime. What are they doing? Is this worship, all facing the monument? But no, their cries say otherwise.

'We're done! All of us, we are done!'

That glint of metal again in the streetlights, higher now. Knives are raised to the air, the shards of light hover there for a moment before they're plunged downwards and into their own necks.

Ava gasps and almost drops her phone in shaking hands. She runs towards them, weaving through sprays of blood and bodies falling to the ground. She steps over one woman, then crouches down to her, takes off her jacket, and pushes it into the wound. A futile move. The blood soaks straight through. In her final moment, the woman pushes her hand away.

The last word comes out as a gurgle. 'Leave me be. I want to be at peace.' With bloodied hands, Ava calls for an ambulance on her phone, smeared claret blocking her view of the screen. She runs to the man next to her, his eyes already glazed in death. She's used to seeing dead bodies, the sight of blood does nothing to turn her stomach normally. But this. *This* is something entirely different. The next woman along still has breath in her, the blood not pulsating like the others. Perhaps she missed her artery. Her face is in pain rather than peace.

Ava grabs her hand and squeezes it. 'I'm here. You're going to be okay. Help is coming.'

The operator is on the phone. Ava puts it on speaker and shouts the address.

The woman attempts to release her hand from Ava's grasp, moans, then pulls away. 'Let me go, please. If you must help, then help me go.'

A weak hand holds up the knife, pushes the handle towards Ava. 'Help me go, Ava.'

Ava's eyes widen. She brushes hair and blood from the woman's face. 'Erin? Oh, God, no. Erin, please, Max needs you.' She presses her jacket into Erin's wound, the blood just a trickle, but Erin is quick, too quick, too determined, and stabs the knife into her leg at the top, hitting the artery. Deep red spills out, blanketing Erin's torso and colour drains from her cheeks in seconds, her mouth frozen in a smile as her final breath leaves her.

Chapter 30

The ambulance staff appear unfazed by the sight. They move unhurriedly, heavy breaths, speaking little. Armed with body bags, they roll each corpse into one, leaving the blood on the street for the impending rain to wash away. No real police turn up to tape the area and investigate, no news crew. Ava's video uploads to the Society Police app. The rain arrives, just a drizzle, sending pools of blood trickling through the cracks.

Twenty-one elders had dragged their souls across town for this. In front of the Eyes Forward-XL Medico monument. All twenty-one body bags are loaded into ambulances, no lights flashing nor sirens blaring. Silently they drive back through the night, leaving the streets as deserted as they were just half an hour before.

Ava sits on the monument a while, praying for the erasure of time. She watches the blood dilute, marbling with the rain and street grime. Erin's blood. She can still feel her hand in hers, still hear her voice. Her bright pink skin burned into her retina.

She gets up, cycles home, slowly, her stomach cramping with the pain of what she just saw. Max, poor Max. Can she tell him she was there, that she failed to save Erin? The authorities will inform him. Perhaps it's best to let them do their job. What would she say anyway? Her words can only make things worse.

She arrives home to Zia, kisses her forehead as she sleeps, then puts an extra blanket on her. She watches her chest rise and fall a moment, ashen eyelids closed, a contentment in her slumber.

Ava sits on the sofa, staring at the wall. Everywhere she looks she sees the pink faces of despair, her mind repeating one word over and over: why? She turns the TV on, no volume, just flicking through the channels, trying to find the breaking news stories. Somewhere there must be headline news of a mass suicide of Society elders. There's nothing. Not yet anyway.

There's a knock on the door, and she looks at the time. One thirty a.m. This can't be good. She opens the door. It's two men in suits plus one woman with a matching buzz cut, that familiar logo embossed on all their jackets, their mouths tight in the menacing arrogance that people in power seem to always display. They glance at her implant's green colour before speaking.

'Ava Maricelli. You must come with us.'

She doesn't question, doesn't resist. What would be the point? She follows, locking the door behind her.

Expecting to be taken in for questioning, to sign an NDA perhaps, get a lecture about not inciting panic, to do her bit for the Society, she assumes they'll arrive at an Eyes Forward building. The suits don't explain anything, don't talk among themselves. From the icy ambience, she can tell any questioning would be unwelcome.

The drive is short, only twenty minutes. It's the first time she's ever been in a private car, not that she has any notion of enjoying it. The blackened windows hide the outside view and the outside's view of her. How typical of the Eyes Forward lackies, in their matching suits and matching, expressionless faces and indistinguishable, monotone voices to want to camouflage themselves further behind tinted glass. There's immortality in such a disguise. One drops off and another can seamlessly take its place like some never-ending being. A conveyor belt of homogenous flesh.

What's the collective noun for a group of Eyes Forward representatives? There should be one. A herd of cows. A flock of sheep. A murder of crows. . . Ava chokes on her own spittle at that thought, then clenches her fists and grinds her teeth.

She looks at her lap, her hands, at the dark window. She should be more nervous. Her heart should be racing. Yet she feels heavy, a weight bearing down on her, leaving no room even for dread. That ambivalence is overridden by concern when she steps out of the car and instead of being at Eyes Forward, they're at the XL Medico labs. The home of potent drugs and all manner of scalpels and noxious gases. Perhaps they just want her to tell them her recipe, the midnight calling a way to intimidate her into conforming.

They step forward and through the doors. Still silent, Ava looking up at them for a clue, a tell, anything.

Nothing.

No employee card to scan. The receptionist buzzes them straight through. No questions. No fuss. They walk through the corridors, past her usual lab as she ponders, somewhat hopefully, that she's merely in trouble for leaving some equipment out, spilling something, but no, she's sure none of that is the case.

The corridor carries on, past B-Well labs and farther than she's wandered before. They round some corners before they get in an elevator. Silently, they step inside and descend.

Has her snooping been noticed? Has Mae been speaking to people? *No.* She blinks away the thought. Why would they care? She's done nothing wrong, not really. There's nothing this can be about except for what she just witnessed. They're taking her somewhere to silence her.

The basement smells damp. Exposed lintels and breeze blocks instead of the usual white-washed and chrome surfaces. The rough concrete floor feels cold even through her shoes. The huge warehouse-style space is mostly empty except for shelving units, a swivel chair with a missing wheel, and a three-legged desk. It seems this is the place they send things they want to forget about or can't be bothered to fix.

Ava swallows, tenses her muscles, then squares her shoulders. She glances at the men out of the corner of her eye. She's ready to fight her way out of this if she has to. She could take them, individually at least. Maybe not the woman. She has the girth of someone who trains more than Ava. But Ava thinks she'd have a chance, maybe, if they don't have guns. Three of them together though. . . she'll need a bit of luck.

After exiting through a locked door, they enter a more clinical room. It smells faintly of bleach, the lights dazzling and glaring off the white walls and furniture. There's a single plastic chair in one corner and a chrome table in the opposite one.

'Sit,' one of the men says.

Ava obeys but doesn't slouch. She's poised to stand and run if she needs to, though looking around she knows there'd be little point. Her mind spirals as fear fills her gut. Is this it? Is this how she dies? In some backdoor room of XL Medico, never to be seen again? What about Zia? She'd be so confused. Faced with internment, Zia is all she can think about. The irony of it almost makes her chuckle. She's been so caught up with trying to make sure Zia's safe and will live longer. If she snuffs it first, it was all for nothing.

They shut the door behind them. A countertop runs the length of the room with cupboards underneath. The man opens a cupboard, then takes out a hypodermic needle.

'Jacket off. Roll up your sleeve.'

The needle is empty. No lethal injection then. A shot of air to an artery? Again, Ava obeys, trying to relax her bicep so she doesn't look like she's about to punch him. The man takes the needle from its packaging.

'What is this for?' She snatches her arm back, an instinctive reaction, but he grabs her wrist, and with the other man, they pin her arm in place.

'To test your follicle-stimulating hormone levels.'

'All this for a menopause test?' She tries to hide the relief in her voice.

'All this to see if you are eligible to be a candidate.'

'For what?'

He doesn't answer. Ava grits her teeth through the sharp prick of the needle and watches the syringe fill with blood, sure he doesn't need that much.

'Your phone, please,' he says when he's finished.

'Why?'

He says nothing, but his colleague steps up. He's broader and standing closer, he more than doubles the amount of human Ava is looking at. He holds out his hand, and Ava gives it to him. He holds the phone up to her face to unlock it, scrolls through, then deletes her record of the video.

'Sign this.'

A document Ava knows well. She saw a similar one just recently. The standard Eyes Forward NDA, pretty much un-changed since the one Zia signed. She doesn't question it, just takes the pen and signs.

The Eyes Forward smirks. 'Good girl.'

Girl! She lifts her top lip like a snarling dog.

'Francine will show you out.'

Ava had forgotten all about Francine. The woman hoists her up by her armpit and shoves her towards the door. Her knees are weak, and she takes a moment to right herself as she stumbles through the door. *A stupid blood test! Is that it?* Despite the hideousness of the evening, she's light. After seeing so much death, she's warm with life. Giddy. A blood test. All of that for a damned blood test.

They walk in silence through the warehouse, up the elevator, then down the corridors, Ava lighter on her feet now, her sweat drying. Theatre, that's all it was. A scare to keep her quiet. She could laugh at their showmanship.

Francine grunts with every step. She seems more tired than burly now. Ava sneaks a peek at her ruddy face. Yeah, she could definitely take her.

They make it to reception, and Ava steps through the turn-stiles. 'It's been lovely getting to know you, Francine. Let's grab a coffee sometime.'

Francine's narrow eyes could freeze the sun. She eyeballs Ava as the doors shut, and Ava backs away into the night.

Ava turns her back on XL Medico and faces the dimly lit road ahead. *Dammit,* she curses as she realises she'll be walking home.

Chapter 31

5 years before the Great Unrest

The meetings were taking their toll on Lucia. More and more people were turning up, but not all the right sorts of people. Angry people. People who wanted to do harm. Not just to moan about Pres-X and possibly start a petition to stop it. People who wanted to take dangerous courses of action. Some had gone to the other groups at the White Horse, and it was as Lucia feared. . . they wanted to hurt the Preserved, to take away their life even. It didn't seem right. To stop the drug was all she wanted, to stop it working, maybe. Some even wanted to harm elders who hadn't taken Pres-X. Lucia counted the years left before she would be at that age. Only ten. A decade until people hated her for no reason. That meant she had a decade to stop this madness.

She missed the early meetings when it was just the seven of them. Ian and Keisha didn't even come anymore, too busy with their baby. And the last meeting Mo attended, she was so distracted looking after her baby that Lucia couldn't count on her for support. Lucia was feeling quite alone at the meetings these days and wondered if she should suggest they find another venue, one where she didn't have to host, so she could not attend if she wanted.

But no. That would be silly. At least attending the meetings, she could listen and have some say. If she wasn't there, she'd have no input at all. And they all did love her rock cakes very much, so she still felt worthwhile.

Tonight's meeting had ended early, much to her relief, after Thomas and Steve got in a row. Always so rowdy, those two. Luigi tried to step in, but to no avail. Perhaps if Daphne would say something once in a while, everyone would listen. Lucia had known Daphne for years and never heard her say much except offer tea. Luigi was old-fashioned like that. 'There's enough to say without women putting their oar in,' is what he'd always say.

Lucia had quite forgotten what the argument was about now, such was her memory of late, but it left her quite rattled for her walk home. Everyone had left so abruptly, there were even some cakes left, so she wrapped them up and took them home for Ken. Perhaps he'd be home and awake when she arrived back. They rarely seemed to cross paths these days, both so busy with their projects. Ken never told her anything about his Society work, and she never told him the truth behind her meetings. He didn't really enjoy the fake book club he attended. Said it was 'too high-brow and boring', which would have upset her if it weren't entirely true. They didn't want to make it fun for him. She certainly didn't want him attending another.

She was sure he was up to no good. No good ever came from working with the government. But she wanted to know. If she could get some inside gossip, that could be the focus for their next meeting, instead of all the bickering.

So, a box of rock cakes tucked under her arm, she made it home and in the front door to find Ken sitting in the living room with the lights off. No TV on either.

'What are you doing home so early?' he asked.

'It's eight p.m.'

'That's early for you.'

She went to flick the light switch.

'Leave it!' Ken barked from his chair.

She snapped her hand back in surprise. 'What? Why? I can't see a bloody thing.' She flicked on the switch and almost dropped the box of cakes. 'Ken? No. No, no! You haven't!'

'I have, and I'm delighted. I'll have no judgement from the likes of you.'

'You've actually gone through with it.'

'I told you they were rolling it out for staff. I've been such a good employee, I deserve this.'

'Deserve this! This? You've poisoned your body with that. . .that. . .drug. That zombie tortoise drug. And now look at you. You look ridiculous!'

Ken turned away from her, shielding his eyes from the light. 'The pink skin will pass eventually. Then I'll be a new man. Young again. I feel rejuvenated. My hearing is already better.'

'Well then, maybe you'll start listening to yourself. You're crazy. Damned to hell, you are!' She got a rock cake out of the box and threw it at him. 'Get out! I don't want you in my house! Get out.'

He laughed. He actually laughed! 'I'm not moving out, Lu.'

'Get out!' she screamed at him again, wishing the cakes were actual rocks.

He held his hands in front of his face, swatting the soft projectiles away. 'I'm going upstairs, Lu, to work on the computer. I'll sleep in the spare room until you see sense.'

He walked up the stairs as slow as ever, thought Lucia. Energised with rage, she went to the master bedroom and took out the suitcase, the suitcase they haven't used in ages as they never went anywhere anymore. She filled it with his clothes, his spare glasses, his tablet, and that stuff he put on his hair that didn't even make it look better, then dragged it down the stairs. *Thump, thump, thump,* it went all the way down. She left it on the front porch. He'd get the hint. If he wanted to be a young man, he could go live in a hostel.

Chapter 32

10 years after the Great Unrest

Max never arrives at work the next day. Understandable, thinks Ava, the image of Erin's final moments still flashing before her. She's scrubbed her skin raw, changed her clothes, yet she can still smell the blood. The copper aroma has left a stain on her senses. She can still feel Erin's hand in hers turning cold. Nothing of the mass suicide is reported on the news, only a few very public events of newly Preserved psychosis among the minor news stories. The incidents they can't cover up so easily with multiple witnesses in broad daylight. The sort of public display that a gentle kidnapping and needle can't keep quiet. Ava rubs her arm where her blood was taken. It left a bruise as a reminder. Useful, she thought when she woke up and had a fleeting moment where she assumed it was all a bad dream. Luckily, the man hadn't been the most delicate-handed.

Stanley is still in need of a groom, as well as the other pets they have in the cold room. Ava checks her bookings list and realises that it's only Stanley and the Labrador at the moment.

The guinea pigs have had their services, the extravagant cat wake was a few days ago, and besides the singer being half an octave flat, it all went well. Checking the accounts, it's clear that pet funerals will not keep the business afloat, even with their hiked-up prices and steady business. There's only so much she can justify charging for embalming a hamster. Lowering the Life Score may be against her father's vision, but she can no longer appease a corpse. A new licence for a little lower, say, 600 pluses could make a big difference. It would also allow Max to use them for Erin's funeral. Sure, Ava swore she'd never lower. Her father had visions of providing grandiose funerals for the Society's wealthiest. But times change, and right now, with the mass suicide not being reported, Ava suspects that the number of deaths of Society elders publicly known is just the tip of the iceberg.

The licence is mercifully easy to apply for, only a twelve-page document that takes a couple of hours, leaving her the rest of the day alone to think. To think of Zia and remember her from her younger days when she used to go jogging and make the best pastries, when she used to laugh along with the TV and take a young Ava on trips out to the theatre, when she used to be able to stand without pain. And now it seems like the cure to her suffering is resulting in a whole new type of suffering in others, for Ava hasn't a doubt in her mind. Mae might have coped after treatment, but that was decades ago. Ava's convinced there's something very wrong with Pres-X.

She glances up at the picture of her parents, then angles herself away, slightly, as if trying to avert her father's gaze. Her mum would understand—she was always more amenable. Less stubborn anyway. The right sort of woman, the Eyes Forward would say. If there is something wrong with Pres-X, her father would approve. He'd shout words of joy and I told you so's. She can still hear his voice, disparaging, opinionated, always black and white. Her mother's voice is lost to Ava now. It was always so quiet. Ava remembers her as a half-smile and a nod. The ghosts of the Great Unrest are all around. Old school friends and university friends, and women who never survived. Such violence is like a hologram that descends decades and leaves an afterimage.

Perhaps her father should have thought more about the future instead of wallowing in his own morality. An angry thought, but one she uses to justify her actions. She's never going to please everyone, certainly not the past and the present. Yet she can't shake the guilt of letting down her parents. Now she feels like the future is always demanding to know what she's doing and why, like it's the only time period that ever matters. The past whispers, the future shouts. The present just gets lost in the noise.

Ava searches more news articles, reads chemistry papers, and peer-reviewed studies to find answers, clues, anything about why some Preserved are suffering to the point they end their lives. She finds nothing but the benefits of Pres-X and its combination with B-Well. Had all these people simply adapted poorly and not taken their B-Well as Erin hadn't? But Pres-X has been around for years, and B-Well mere moments. Something in the formula must have changed. The lack of information, and the opaqueness with which the media are reporting on the psychosis incidents though makes it clear to Ava.

This is a cover-up.

The news is awash with stories of more celebrities and Pres-X-2, some denying but more and more touting the benefits. Millions added onto their wages for the next film, album, TV show. Take Pres-X-2 and it reignites your career, apparently. The sports section in the news is in heated discussion about athletes taking it. It has no performance enhancing qualities, it says. It only gives them back what time took away. A short career lasts longer. Legends can shine again. And those who have taken it enjoy more camera time, better sponsorship deals. The top grossing athletes aren't the best at their sport anymore, it's the ones who look the youngest.

Ava huffs and turns the broadcast off. At this rate, they'll be wanting people to look like toddlers.

With work quiet, she messages Dan. In between jobs, he's sure to have some free time to meet for coffee. She shuts the home, hangs a 'Be back in an hour' sign on the door, then joins the pedestrian traffic making its way towards the High Street. It's as dense as ever, the outside air stuffy with breath and body heat, gruffs and tuts from the crowds as they elbow-graze and shoulder-swipe each other as they go past. The lanes are organised, at least, and Ava keeps up with the fast lane.

When the lane filters through to Broad Street, she takes the turnoff and the traffic eases slightly. Ava can see through gaps in the people, straight ahead instead of just the rooftops. She approaches the Eyes Forward statue, or XL Medico, whichever it's supposed to be, and notices a woman in Hi-Viz clothing working in the standing area. Soapy bucket next to her, scrubbing brush in one hand and bin bag in the other. Ava does a double take before crossing the white line to say hello.

'Suzanna?'

She straightens her hands, pushing on the small of her back and almost drops her sponge. 'Oh, Ava sweetie. Hi.'

'How are you?' It's supposed to be a polite thing to ask, but Ava regrets it instantly. The fact that she's scrubbing the streets answers her question.

'Well, I avoided a custodial sentence, so that's good news. I'm trying to concentrate on the positives.' Her skin forms natural crow's feet around her eyes, highlighting her smile. She looks quite content and less stressed. 'How's my old apartment? Anyone moved in yet?'

'I haven't seen anyone, but I've been busy.'

'I suspect you have, clever thing like you. They've stuck me in some god-awful building with neighbours fresh out of prison. All sorts of reprobates. I've lost all my points, all of them. Can you believe it?' She makes a little sigh and gazes up, like she can see her points flitter away. 'I'm on powdered rations. Can't even buy real food. I have a few points now that I'm working, but I've had to start all over again.'

'Oh, Suzanna. I'm so sorry.'

'It's fine, really. I can build them up again, I know it.' Her smile tightens as she says this, her lines digging deeper from the effort. 'You don't suppose, I mean, I hate to ask. . .but if a widower, or widow, I'm not fussy, if one comes into your work. . .put a good word in for me? I always swore I'd get there on my own, but now, well, needs must. And I think I'd make a good wife.'

Ava's shoulders drop, but she's not really surprised. She should start a dating service for Score-diggers and lonely elders. Actually, that's not a bad business idea. 'I'm sure you will. I'll keep you in mind Suzanna.'

Ava steps back into the traffic and is whisked away with the flow in seconds, almost tripping on her own feet as she looks over her shoulder at Suzanna resuming her scrubbing. Cleaning Erin's blood stains away, most likely. Any last trace of evidence gone.

The fast lane is now so fast, she almost misses her café, the Lunch Lounge. It's not her usual place for a coffee but one that has a more extensive lunch menu, at Dan's request. She pushes her way out of the lane and into the marked loitering area of the pavement to see Dan sitting by the window, rosy-faced and waving at her through the glass. Ava steps up to the doorway, phone in hand, ready to show her Score ID. She offers the ID to the barista, who ignores it and instead, reaches for a large device, lights running up either side, then holds it in front of her face like a giant camera.

'Look straight ahead,' the barista says.

Ava obeys, too confused to protest. The lights leave little rings as an afterimage.

'Sorry, miss.' The barista folds his arms across his chest and puffs himself up, looking more like a security guard. 'You can't come in.'

Ava takes a step back, her brows knitted. 'This is a 500 plus café. I'm 500 plus.'

'Not Score dependent now, miss. Well, not entirely,' the barista says without a hint of an apology. 'Computer says you appear over forty. We only allow people who look under forty to dine in here.'

'You *what?*'

'Come back when you've had Pres-X-2.'

The barista turns his back on a red-faced Ava, and Dan comes to join her.

'Hey,' Dan says, putting his hand on Ava's shoulder. 'She's with me. I'm accompanying her.'

'Well, accompany her somewhere else then. She looks too old to drink here. Even with someone younger. We have other customers to please. Eyesores are bad for business.'

Eyesores! Ava clenches her fists at her sides, her biceps too. She'll give him a sore eye, wipe that smirk off his perfectly smooth skin. Fucking kid. In her anger, Ava can't find her voice. Her mouth hangs open, eyes wide, swallowing gulps of air down her dry throat. 'Dan. . . I. . . what. . .'

'Come on.' Dan takes her by the arm. 'We'll go somewhere else.'

Slow lane this time. With her anger simmering, Ava's legs are weak, her body not responding. She needs a sugar hit, some caffeine. Baristas shouldn't be able to give such news without also giving a coffee. It's just not fair. After a few minutes of wobbly steps, they enter a grotty café near Zinzan Street, a place Ava's never sat in. Its sub 300 décor is made up of more chewing gum than paint, and the seats look like they'll buckle with even Ava's slight weight.

'What do you want?' Dan asks. 'I'm buying.'

Ava just stares blankly at him.

'Never mind. I'll see what they have.'

He returns a few minutes later with tepid, weak tea, sugar sachets and two shots of Sambuca. Her surprise at the odd combination is short-lived and quickly the beverages Dan has selected seem like the most sensible choices ever. Ava downs the Sambuca straight away, grateful the staff didn't inspect her implant and tell her she can't have alcohol. The aniseed makes one eye close and the other water. Then, she necks the tea.

Her vocal cords re-oiled, she finds her voice. 'I just can't believe it, Dan. How many times have we been to that café? And now because I look my age, I'm not welcome? I just can't believe it.'

'I don't know what to say. The world's gone crazy with this new drug.' He looks a little crazy himself, wearing a green tweed suit and a brighter green shirt. No doubt he thought the green would neutralise the pink.

'How's Jeremy?' Ava asks.

'Speaking of crazy?'

'That's not what I meant.'

Dan looks at his hands and fiddles with a napkin a while before answering. 'He's much better, actually. The doctor gave him some new B-Well, so his moods are basically fine. It's just, he sleeps loads and when he's awake, he's like a zombie. This isn't what I signed up for. I thought having some old guy and being with him while he regressed would be fun, but I'm just like his caregiver at the moment.'

'Sounds tough.'

'And it's not like I can dump the guy.'

'Dan!'

'What? Under usual circumstances, if I was with some really boring guy, I would. But he financed my Pres-X-2. If he bails on that, I'll end up in debtor's prison or have all my points taken away.'

'Sounds like you rushed into the commitment.'

Dan downs his Sambuca, wipes his mouth, and his words come out with a gurgle. 'Yeah, yeah, all right. I don't need preaching to, especially not by the grim reaper.' His usual jibe at her clothing doesn't carry the same comedic weight it usually does.

'I'm not preaching. Just, well, sounds like you're stuck. I'm sure Jeremy will be fun eventually. You'll just have to wait.'

Dan nods and lifts his chin up a little, turning his head to the side. 'And I look great, right? I've got this new job starting next week too, so I'll be super busy at the university until Jeremy recovers.'

If Jeremy recovers, is what Ava thinks. She rests her weight on her elbows, ignoring the spills soaking through her shirt, then leans closer, lowering her voice. 'Listen, Dan. I need to tell you something.' She peers around. No one is paying them any attention. No one looks like Eyes Forward lurking in the corner. With their slicked back hair and pristine suits, they wouldn't be caught dead in a place like this. 'It's not safe for me to tell you, but you need to know. Please keep this between us.'

Dan puts his ear closer to her mouth, and she recounts the night before. Erin, Millie, Joan Porter. All she knows. He's so close, she can't read his expression, but he stays still, listens to every word, and doesn't so much as make a joke.

'It's a cover-up, Dan. I know it. Something is wrong. Really wrong. I'm working at XL Medico tonight. I'll try to find out some more information.'

***

Edgar is already in the lab when Ava arrives at XL Medico, doing nothing in particular, just sitting at a desk. Her instant irritation at seeing him swaying back on two legs of the chair, idling away, is unwarranted as it soon occurs to her that he doesn't know how to make formaldehyde-rose. It then occurs to her that if he were to know, she'd lose her advantage. Ava can't imagine her patent means anything to a company in bed with the Eyes Forward.

'Evening, Edgar.'

'Evening,' he says, and she swears he flinches at the sight of her orange implant. 'Fifty litres today.'

'No problem. You get what we need from the fridge, and I'll set up the glassware.'

The fridge is low on stock. She knows this from their last shift, and there's little chance anyone else would have stocked up. He'll have to go to the stockroom fridge to resupply.

'That's not going to be enough methanol,' he says, exactly as she predicted. 'I'll go get more.'

With the glassware almost entirely assembled in record time, she sets up some extra stages but doesn't connect them to the main system. A bogus lot, just to throw Edgar off. The guy is clueless enough not to notice the decoy. She grabs some saline from the fridge, adds a small amount of calcium carbonate and phenolphthalein, then sets it to simmer. Distilling some nonsense should confuse him for a while. If he asks, she'll make something up.

With Edgar taking his time, Ava seizes the opportunity to search through the computer again, but not looking for Joan Porter info this time. She wants anything, any studies on Pres-X, and the difference with Pres-X-2. She finds the recipe for both. Not how to make them, the exact recipe is still protected, but the ingredients. As she suspected, there's no formaldehyde-rose in regular Pres-X. The amount of regular formaldehyde needed is more than she thought though, and the recipe does require vanadium. There appears to be no alternative.

She shuts down the computer and assembles the last of the glassware, pausing to scratch her head and think. There is no vanadium. That ran out a few years ago when the oil ran out. So how are they making the original Pres-X? Have they subbed her solution for the original? That hasn't been tested with the original formula.

Edgar arrives back, a full tray of bottles jingling.

'Edgar, are there any labs here making original formalde-hyde?'

'Don't think so.'

'So how are they making Pres-X?'

'They're not, as far as I understand. Just using up stockpiles at the moment.'

'But vanadium ran out two years ago, so does that mean stockpiles of Pres-X are two years old?'

Edgar starts measuring out the methanol. 'Not our job to ask questions, Ava.'

Ava nods, notes his reaction to the distraction equipment she set up, then gets to work. There's no need to speculate further. The answer why people are reacting badly is as clear as day.

The formaldehyde in Pres-X is too old. The drug is past its use by date.

It's nine-thirty p.m. by the time they finish. Fifty litres are bottled up, and the smell of sickly-sweet is stuck in Ava's sinuses. Her dyed hair is now a sweaty mess stuck against her scalp and her face blotchy from tiredness and heat. She exits the lab and walks down the corridor, making no attempt to rectify her appearance. So many of the glass windows are reflective, mirrors beaming her state back to her. Were they always like that? Just the lighting, perhaps. Then, coming the other way, she sees Mandisa, looking like she just stepped out of the beauticians rather than a humid lab. Matte skin and shiny hair. Why is it that switching those around makes your appearance so much less attractive?

'Ava. Hi, you're working late.' Her voice is so smooth it's like she gargles honey.

Ava clears her throat, yet her voice still comes out like she's swallowed gravel. 'As are you.'

'I was just checking over a few things, that's all.'

Ava looks around to see that Edgar has gone. She didn't even notice him walk on, too lost in her awkwardness.

'Your product launch for B-Well has gone, erm, well.' Ava winces at her stupid sentence and wishes there was some way to make herself smell better.

'Thanks,' Mandisa says.

They stand in awkward silence for an uncomfortable amount of time. Over her own post-lab aroma, Ava notes Mandisa's vanilla perfume, her crisply ironed and well-fitted shirt, her shiny shoes.

'Pres-X-2 must be on the cards for you, then,' Ava says.

'Next week, actually. You should consider it. It'll do you the world of good, career-wise.'

Ava winces, although her words don't contain a tone of malice. Her dyed hair, though, is clearly not enough in Mandisa's eyes.

'Thanks,' she says. 'I don't think it's for me.'

Mandisa gives the subtlest of nods, then walks away, her light footsteps tapping softly on the tiled floor.

Ava waits a second before plodding away. Her dad always told her she sounds like a herd of elephants when she walks. After a few paces, she turns back to watch Mandisa just as Mandisa glances back over her shoulder. Ava blushes and snaps her head back, facing forward. How rude is Mandisa! Suggesting Ava should take Pres-X-2! Was she always so rude? Probably. Ava was too infatuated with her before to realise. Now she's not. Now she sees her for the haughty, judgey cow she is.

Ava checks her reflection in the polished windows as she walks back towards the exit. Her roots are showing. She'll touch those up later. A bit more makeup, perhaps. Not to impress Mandisa, of course not. Just to be presentable. Professional.

Stupid Mandisa and her perfect complexion. Rude. Bitchy. Ava hopes she never has to bump into her again.

Chapter 33

The confirmation comes through that the funeral home can now serve lower Life Scores and Ava gets to work early the next day to adjust the website and advertising. The sun is only just up, the pedestrian lanes only partially full, and the scurry of bikes is so much calmer than at her usual commute time. Even the Score-diggers haven't gathered outside the home yet. A lower Life Score licence may put them off completely, Ava hopes with a grin. Not much point in bagging a sub-700 elder these days. As she walks unimpeded through the front doors, she thinks that alone is worth dropping the Score requirement. The sliver of light coming from the cold room tells her Max is already in.

'Hi, Max?' she calls down the hallway.

He steps out of the cold room, red eyed and pale faced, chin down, an unwashed look about him. 'I was just spending some time with Nan. . .'

'I heard. Max, I'm so, so sorry.' She steps forward, intending to offer a hug, but he tilts his body away, guarded, not wanting to give in to it. That's the thing with pain. More of it doesn't make the old pain go away. Pain shared isn't pain halved. It congeals. Sticky. Like some curdled mess of pain. That's how Max's face looks now.

He fidgets a bit, finding his words. 'I know she's not a 700 plus, but I didn't want her to be anywhere else.'

Despite his standoffish body language, Ava hugs him anyway, not a usual gesture for either of them, but what else can she do? He doesn't reciprocate, his stone-cold limbs frozen to his sides. 'Erin was the kindest and most wonderful woman.'

He backs up, keeping his head angled away from Ava. There's no shame in tears, but he obviously wants to hide them. 'She was taking her B-Well. She was going to be fine. I don't know how this happened. What an awful accident.'

Accident? 'What did happen?'

'A bus crash. A load of newly Preserved going on retreat, to take some time out to adjust, you know? Glass shards from the window got her right in the neck and her leg.'

Ava's chest tightens. She struggles to speak through gritted teeth. 'What are the chances?'

'I know she's not a 700, but is there a way to let her stay with us?'

'I'm lowering the Life Score of the business. Needs must. Nan is welcome to have her service with us, if that's what you want.'

Max half-smiles a little, looking slightly less sad. 'At least she didn't get depressed, not really. Not like some of them. You heard about those up in Sheffield? It was on the national news.'

'What were you doing watching the national news?' Ava says with a frown.

'I was watching it last night. Before. . . anyway. . . I don't know why. I just saw it. Seventeen Preserved have killed themselves so far this year in Sheffield. They reckon it's an adaption thing—they can't get used to it. Or that Sheffield is just so busy, it was noisy for them when their hearing came back. But some of them had perfectly fine hearing, their family said. Or it's that the wisdom of age isn't suited to the lifestyle of youth. Something like that, they said. And there's pretty much no decent mental health services anywhere, no matter your Life Score.' His last words catch in his throat despite his attempt to smile them away. He doesn't need to put on a brave face, Ava thinks as she looks at him. A young man trying to be older. Weakened by grief but trying to be stronger.

'You don't have to be here, Max. Take some time off.'

'No. I'd rather be busy. I can't go home. I don't want to be there.'

She can understand that. The echoes of an empty house are heart-breaking.

'Have you told Frida? Maybe you can spend some time with her?'

Max stiffens, then Ava remembers they were meant to be having a talk. 'She. . .well. . .she's got a lot on her mind at the moment. It doesn't matter. I can't really bother her right now.'

A double blow for Max. Ava bites her lip as his posture sinks lower. The scant amount of therapy he'd managed to have may have smoothed out the sharpness of his sadness, but it still weighs him down like a rock. And now that rock is even bigger. 'Well, if you need a break, if you change your mind, just go, okay?'

He nods, then returns to the cold room, shutting the door behind him. She'll drop a coffee in later, maybe a sandwich. Although the thought of seeing Erin in there makes her hollow in a way she can't explain, like the dishonesty has ripped out her insides. Integrity takes up more internal space than she knew, some spacious ex-lodger, leaving her insides as vacant as an empty house.

Ava has no time to mope, nor does Max, for that matter. Within half an hour of opening, once their advertising has been updated, Ava's taking calls for more services. She collects four clients that morning with requests for more still coming in. Max works like a trooper, still insisting he doesn't need time off and Ava's grateful. She would struggle without him. Max works without complaint. That's until the cold room is full.

'That cat and dog are taking up an entire unit each,' he says. 'When did the owners say they want the service?'

'The Labrador's is all arranged for the day after tomorrow. The cat, Mrs Constance didn't say yet. I'll chase her up. Maybe he can go in with someone?'

'You want to double up?'

'Well, it's not really double. It's just a cat. He can go in with the dog.'

Nine people and a cat and dog. It's the busiest they've been in a long time. All the people are elders with 650-700 Scores, all with bright pink faces and freak accident wounds. The families come in muttering, 'Such a shame,' and, 'They had their whole second life ahead of them.'

To cope with the extra demand, Ava and Max work tirelessly, pulling in favours with caterers and florists to get funeral times turned around quickly. Erin's is the first, at Max's request. He'd chosen a pale blue summer dress she'd loved, music that was played at his parent's wedding, an urn to match her daughter's. The service is moving and well attended. Max flitters between staff and family, not wanting to relinquish his responsibilities, seeming professional, using work as a shield. Ava stands at the back of the room to mourn, to remember, trying not to allow the questions to play over and over again, attempting to relax her clenched fists every time she hears the words 'freak accident.' She fears she'll have nothing left of her molars by the time the day is out.

It's not the first newly Preserved client they've had, although it's been a while and rare. Before the service, Ava checks the details from a few years ago, a Layla Dean who was murdered by her husband weeks after her treatment. The burn rate was as any other Preserved, the same as Mr Constance. Yet when Erin is moved to the crematorium, the burn rate is long. Far longer even than Mr Constance and the usual Preserved. As the cremations continue throughout the week, it's the same. The new Pres-X takers take almost double the time to turn to ash. By the end of the week, Max notices and acknowledges with an eyebrow raise to Ava. The extra furnace time will eat into their margin, for sure, but Ava isn't thinking about margins now. She has other things on her mind. □

Chapter 34

An email arrives from the Eyes Forward at the end of the week, welcoming itself into Ava's business inbox with the three-tone jingle that makes her groan on reflex. What do they want? Some new law or rule is the usual cause for that jingle. Those three tones sound cheerier than they make her feel, less ominous than they should. Ava clicks to open it and another groan escapes. A link to a shop where she can buy the required supplies. How thoughtful of them. She must buy several metres' worth of reflective backing for her shop's front windows. By decree of the Eyes Forward, business premises' windows must now have seventy-five per cent dedicated to mirrors instead of windows. That means that the stretch of glass the funeral home has facing the street must now be three-quarters reflective. *To allow our Pres-X-2 citizens to constantly enjoy the benefits of their treatment,* it states. Or to highlight the lack of Pres-X-2 for the ones who don't want it, Ava thinks. The fines for not complying aren't worth the argument. A disgruntled letter to her local MP is all the power she has, and then orders the required materials.

Max's emotions have been up and down since Erin died, but the last couple of days he seems a little more upbeat, enjoying moments of less gloom at least. This morning though, he comes into work seeming totally crushed. He doesn't say hello to Ava on his way through, not even a wave, then races straight to the cold room.

It's the day of Stanley the cat's funeral. Mrs Constance had delayed due to her tight schedule, but the mourners are now arriving thick and fast to pay their respects. The ceremony room looks lovely, flowers everywhere, Stanley curled up on a squashy bed, noises of birds and trees faintly playing over the speaker. Well-wishers leave small bouquets of flowers, tins of fish, more blankets to wrap him in. Some bring their own pets, too, living ones, to say goodbye. The snarling and hissing tell Ava they were probably not the best of friends, but it's touching nonetheless. She listens to the service while facing the wall. The Eyes Forward members in attendance never tell her to do so, not verbally. It's like they have some repelling shield. She doesn't want to face their way, doesn't want to wait for the disgusted glare or the belittling instruction. Conditioned, she realises she is. Obedient now, saving them the bother of instruction. Out of the corner of her eye, occasionally, she's sure there's a flash of gold breaking up the orange glow of her implant.

Throughout the morning, Ava still hasn't seen Max. As the service ends and most leave, she makes her way to the cold room to find him. The body of a 650 is lying on the table, Max mid-embalming, a young woman sobbing in the corner.

'Erm, Max?'

'Ava, this is Frida.'

Ava jolts upright, then looks over at the woman. A pretty thing, as Erin had said. Even with her tear-stained cheeks, she looks attractive with her high cheekbones and well-styled hair. Such a mismatch for Max. 'Hi, Frida. It's nice to meet you, but you really shouldn't be in here.'

'We just needed to talk,' Max says, not looking up from his work.

'I just had to come and speak to him. It's quite time critical,' Frida says between sobs, lacking the lovely manners Erin had been so complimentary about.

Max and Frida lock eye contact with each other, and Ava is left feeling as out of place as the corpse.

'You going to tell me what's going on?' Ava asks, sounding more like she's addressing a child than a couple of adults.

Max raises his eyebrows at Frida, who stands rigid with pursed lips.

'She might know how to help, Frida.'

Frida glares at him, as if the room wasn't cold enough already.

Max huffs, shakes his head, then looks at Ava. 'I don't know what to do. Frida won't listen.'

'We know exactly what to do. I've come up with a really good option, and we need to hurry up,' Frida says through her teeth.

'That's a crappy option, Frida.'

'Okay,' Ava says, holding her hands up. 'I don't know if I can help, but I definitely can't if you don't tell me what's going on.' She's surprised at how authoritative she sounds, like some nagging parent.

Frida's posture sags very slightly, and she nods at Max.

Max puts his tools down, then leans against the wall. 'Frida's pregnant. Unlicensed, obviously.'

'Oh,' Ava says, shuffling on her feet, the room suddenly feeling a lot hotter. She sees it then, Frida's implant glowing blue. She had assumed their problem was some legal probate, Score-kind of problem. Not this. This is way out of her knowledge and comfort zone. 'Well, I think you can just walk into the clinics—'

'I'm not getting rid of it,' Frida says.

Ava chokes on thin air at that. 'Oh. Wait, what? Seriously?'

'You see our problem,' Max says.

'But. . .' Ava mumbles a moment, needing time to process what she's hearing. 'But you can't just have a baby. You know you can't.'

'We can, if we go to France or Scotland,' Frida says.

Max throws his hands up. 'How though, Frida? You might as well say, let's get a billion dollars or learn to fly. It's just not that simple, is it, Ava?'

Ava looks from Max's face to Frida's, both staring at her, like her ignorant opinion is somehow going to solve this. 'Erm, well, no. Honestly. That's all quite far away and your implant is blue.

You're going to hide that all the way? And I'm fairly sure they shut their borders to pregnancy refugees years ago.'

'I've read stories online,' Frida says, nodding in her certainty. 'People make it.'

'And those that don't lose everything. *Everything*,' Max says, slicing his hands through the air like he's cutting himself loose. 'Score reduced to zero. Nothing. No. It's too big a risk.'

'But there are people you pay that help. I've read about it.' Frida's voice cracks, and her eyes fill up again.

'There are also people who want the Society Police points and snitch. Ava, tell her.'

Ava takes a step back. This is the shittiest time for Erin to be dead. Why couldn't she still be here advising on this? What would she say? 'This is definitely not my area of expertise,' Ava says, making the understatement of the century. 'My gut feeling is that it sounds reckless.'

A small cough makes them all jump and turn around. Mrs Constance is standing in the doorway.

'I'm not interrupting, am I?'

Ava steps toward her, holding out her hand to shake. 'No, Mrs Constance—'

'Flick.'

'Flick. Yes. No, you're not interrupting.' They shake hands. Mrs Constance's grip is firm, and Ava's feels somewhat slack. 'Let's go out this way.'

Ava walks down the corridor, leaving Max and Frida to their debate, Mrs Constance following behind.

'I just wanted to thank you for the service,' Mrs Constance says, holding her silk-gloved hands to her chest. 'It was a wonderful tribute to Stanley, and a lot of very important people came along. Some ministers from the Eyes Forward and board members from XL Medico. All quite appropriate.'

'No less than he deserved.' It hadn't gone unnoticed to Ava, the Eyes Forward logo on the suits, the XL Medico merchandise. Even some of the pets that attended had XL Medico collars. Even from her position facing the wall for most of the service, she could feel the wealth and pomposity of it all. Ava glances at the fur collected across the floor. No matter how wealthy and important the pet owners are, they still leave a mess.

'I shall be in next week to collect his ashes.' Mrs Constance pulls her black coat over her shoulders. It looks like it has been made out of poodle.

'I'll let you know when they're ready.'

Mrs Constance takes Ava's hand again. Ava's quite sure her sweat will leave a stain on the silk. 'I'll be in our favourite bar some nights this week. They're so friendly there. Just thought I'd let you know.'

'That's nice to hear,' Ava says with her most practised smile. 'See you soon.'

Mrs Constance glides across the floor and out of the front door, all the while Ava suppresses the desire to violently shiver. She turns around and Max and Frida are standing in the corridor, watching with wide-eyes and open mouths.

'Don't look at me like that,' Ava says.

'Hey, boss,' Max says. 'Your personal life is your business.'

Chapter 35

During the Great Unrest

Lucia brought her scarf up to cover her face on her walk to work. The smoke from the fire was still drifting through the air. It smelled of ash, of molten plastic, and dead people.

So many dead people.

Every building had graffiti on now, more and more over the last year. The spray paints had been dividing up the city. Her group made up a large portion of that. Not her actual group, the original group, but what it had become. Time's Up. It was too catchy, that was the trouble. The other groups, the more violent ones, had adopted the name as soon as they'd heard it. They'd bombed buildings under its banner.

So many dead people.

The care home down the road, Thistledown Manor, was gone, plus all of its elderly residents. Fifty of them had burned or choked to death. Oakwood Hall, gone. Daffodil House, gone. Sheltered housing blocks were torched, and there was street violence too. Time's Up was chanted outside town halls and government buildings. No one wanted her rock cakes anymore. All they wanted was death.

Ever since the government made the life donation policy. That was probably Ken's idea. It sounded like something he'd come up with.

It all escalated from there, and there was no amount of calm talking and reasoning Lucia could do to stop it. People wanted blood—from which end of the age spectrum depended on where their viewpoints aligned.

Poor Ian and Keisha hadn't left their house in months, terrified for their little boy's safety. Lucia had only seen photos of him, not even managed a cuddle in person. Keisha's tummy didn't flatten out much after she had him. She'd be beaten on the street if people thought she was pregnant.

Mo. No one had heard from Mo. Last time Lucia saw her, she'd popped into the café with her gorgeous baby girl. Lucia can't remember the baby's name, but she'd looked just like Mo. Curly hair and bright eyes. Mo had visited ever so upset to say that poor Donny had died. It was terribly sad, but Mo didn't stay long. It was a 300 plus café. Lucia wondered if that was why.

She opened the café with a huff, heaving open the door and wondering if there was any point in opening today. She had few ingredients to work with, thanks to the group campaigning for more moderate consumption. What did they call themselves? Pre Green, Pro Grow, she can't remember. Too many factions. Too much unrest. Names and slogans weren't worth the brain space. It was such language that was causing all the bother in the first place. She was getting too old for all of this.

Ken would say to take Pres-X, if he was still really her husband. Husbands don't betray their wives like that. Husbands don't just run away. He'd gone to live in some protected camp for pink-faced idiots nearly a year ago when the Great Unrest began, and all the Preserved started hiding away with security and whatnot. 'I'll be back when this all calms down,' he'd said as he'd left. As if she cared.

She had enough flour, at least. Not really enough sugar, but there was no harm in putting in less. She'd put up a sign saying *reduced calorie cakes*. There's no orange juice either. Her stockpiles of coffee would last another week. She doubted she'd have enough left over to bake some fresh goodies for the meeting tonight. Because, despite everything, they were still having their meetings. And tonight's was set to be a biggie.

The Eyes Forward were coming. They wanted to talk.

Chapter 36

10 years after the Great Unrest

Everywhere Ava looks, the craziness around Pres-X-2 is rife. Empty shops, excitement on the news and well, all TV really, Zia mentioning it at home. It's like a jamboree of nonsense that Ava can't wade her way through. Job adverts posted on social media are saying Pres-X-2 takers only.

In what is now a rare moment of calm in the funeral home, Ava gets her calculator out. The burn rate—the length of time to turn a body to ash—it just doesn't add up. She scours old documents from previous Preserved cremations, and the numbers are as different then as they are today. She briefly considers asking other funeral homes when she remembers hers is the only one that caters for a high enough Life Score to cremate the Preserved. Not that she was relishing the thought of pulling more favours with Kim anyway.

She does her sums again and calculates the energy needed. Based on her calculations, the corpses of recent cremations must have been made almost entirely of polytetrafluoroethylene. She laughs at herself, her private joke. She loves it when chemistry and cremation come together. She loves it even more when it makes sense. Has the formula gotten stronger? Are they somehow overdosing on expired Pres-X? Is that what's making them go mad?

It can't be. A stupid thought. Why would they give them more of the drug they covet so much, more of the drug that is going to be dwindling in supply, since there's no one making formaldehyde, since there's no more vanadium?

No more formaldehyde.

No more vanadium.

She ruminates on that for longer than she should, her brain working too slowly. The formaldehyde is old. Too old. Formaldehyde breaks down into formic acid and carbon dioxide. Formic acid. . .irritates the eyes, the nose, the ears, causes confusion. Carbon dioxide. In the corner of the room is a fire extinguisher. A carbon dioxide fire extinguisher.

Ava stands, then bolts to the extinguisher, holding the bright red cylinder in her hand, the answer smacking her in the face.

The gas used to put out fires.

As quickly as they were burning the bodies, the bodies were emitting dry ice, cooling the flames.

She walks back to her seat again, slowly, and sinks into the chair. Could it be as simple as that? It's not simple, she reminds herself. It's really quite complicated. There's a ton of other stuff that goes into Pres-X, other compounds that she has little knowledge of, and it would take her a decade to explore all the options alone. XL Medico is more than just one scientist though. They have teams of scientists and researchers. It seems ridiculous to think that Ava's out-of-practice scientist brain could figure this out, even though she's probably the only one who knows about the burn rates.

The only one who knows.

That thought sends a shiver across her shoulders, and suddenly she feels less clever and more vulnerable. Would XL Medico know about burn rates? Would the Eyes Forward?

Do they know I know?

She loads up the data for each of the cremations, then edits the details, adjusting the costs. Making it so her balance sheets do not add up is a pain, but a ruckus with an auditor is a hell of a lot more appealing than a ruckus with the Eyes Forward. She'll think of a way to make the numbers add up later. She has enough other puzzles to deal with.

It still makes little sense why Eyes Forward is rolling out Pres-X to the general population. XL Medico banking the money is the only explanation, and they in turn bank rolling the Eyes Forward. Again, is it that simple, using up old, expired stock and banking a pretty penny for it?

How on earth can they be claiming that B-Well would help against this potent mix?

She should stop thinking about it. She knows she should. Stop meddling. Curiosity kills the cat. But her mind is in overdrive. She calls down to Max.

'What?' He comes out of the cold room, looking exactly like he's been in there embalming corpses all day.

'How's Frida?'

'Angry. Why?'

'No reason. Hey, I was wondering, did Erin leave some B-Well? Could I have a look at it?'

He pulls his head back. If he had any meat on his bones, he'd have a double chin. 'You can get a prescription pretty easily, you know.'

'I know.'

'Okay. . .' He elongates this word, making himself sound as confused as he looks. 'Well, hang on.'

He comes back out with a rucksack and rummages until he finds a fistful of blue blister packs. 'How many do you want?'

'Just a couple. Is that. . .are you sure that's B-Well?'

'Yep. See, says it on the packet. Now I've got Nan's Score, I get a lot more. Needed, really.'

He pops a couple of blue pills into her hand. The blister pack that the doctor left Jeremy was silver. Not blue like Erin's. Jeremy's blister pack had B-Well+ written on it.

'All okay, boss?'

'Yeah,' Ava says, pocketing the pills. 'Sure. Yeah, everything's great.'

***

She needs to get to the lab and see exactly what's in this B-Well. She also needs to get a sample from Dan. With the cold room almost constantly full of 650 Preserved, business is as busy as it's ever been, leaving Ava little time to do anything else. Then, just as she's sweating through her shirt, trying to arrange the bespoke wakes that she's kicking herself for not taking off their service range when they dropped the Life Score, the door opens and in walks Kim. Ava hasn't seen her face-to-face in years. That *what was I thinking* mindset really knocking on her now.

'Kim, what a lovely surprise.'

'Did you think I wouldn't claim my end of our deal?'

Ava's mind is blank for a few seconds, then she smacks her forehead. 'Oh, I'm so sorry. We've been swamped here, and I totally forgot about the embalming fluid.'

'I can see. Business is booming, by the looks of it. Lucky you.' Kim's tone is tinged with admiration. Just a tinge, the rest has the cool pitch of resentment. 'I'll bet you get all sorts in here. Widows and widowers of the Society's highest Scorers. Haven't got a lonely old 750 plus knocking around here by chance?' She laughs in a way that doesn't convince Ava she's joking.

'Ask the Score-diggers outside. They don't seem to have much luck though.'

'Less of them than there used to be, I guess since you lowered your Score requirement. Shrewd move, by the way. Although Paul, over at Funerals for You, is a little put out.'

'Paul can handle a little competition, I'm sure.'

Ava keeps her eyes on her screen, idling away with the curser while mentally doing some crude sums. She knows why Kim's here, and she's well aware her own supplies of formaldehyde-rose are dwindling, and she has a full cold room to embalm. 'I am sorry, Kim. Can I drop you some embalming fluid 'round next week? I'm getting a little swamped here.'

'Forget the formaldehyde-rose. Our sub 500 funeral home doesn't really require such quality stuff.'

'Okay. Well, if you're sure.'

'There's something else you could do for me though.'

Ava winces through her smile. 'Right?'

'Dinner? Or even maybe drinks, say, tomorrow? I did break data protection rules for you by contacting that client.'

Ava tries to stop her chest from visibly deflating. So much for not being desirable. It's only that she seems to be desirable to all the wrong people. But then, as quick as she's sickened by the thought, a plan forms in her head. Kill two birds with one stone, so the saying goes. She stifles her wince and attempts to make her smile look more genuine as she locks eyes with Kim. 'Sure. Love to. I know just the place.'

Kim makes her way out of the door, swaying her hips more than she usually does and is still standing just outside when the cars pull up. All three of them. The reflective glass still allows her to see through, even if the outside can't see in. Kim stands among the Score-diggers, gormlessly staring at the Eyes Forward suits making their way in. *Great.* She'll definitely be the gossip of all the funeral homes now.

They come in, walking in unison, all six of them, led again by the man with a scar down his chin. Ava waits until the front doors close behind them before she sits again, then faces the wall before she's asked. The chairs don't move, no heavy scratching noises across the floor and no sigh of the cushion as they sit. Yet she feels their looming presence behind.

'We are here to congratulate you on being the highest performing Society Police app user this month.' Chin Scar is talking. She'd recognise that voice anywhere now.

'Oh. Thanks.'

'And, as such, you are to be rewarded. You have been selected to receive complimentary Pres-X-2—a gift from the Eyes Forward. This is a marvellous opportunity for someone of your stature, as I am sure you will appreciate. Your blood test shows you are now suitable.'

'I'm all right, thanks. I don't want it.'

'You will start your treatment after your next cycle. This is an honour. And an excellent development for women especially. Research has shown that visibly ageing women feel less fulfilled, strive to Score less, and are less productive in the workplace. They are less attractive and suffer more as a result. Eyes Forward have pledged to ensure the entire Society live long and happy lives. Even women.'

Even women. 'As I said, I am quite happy *not* taking preservation medication at the moment.'

'You will be collected when your implant is gold. Your blood tests show that is imminent. The conditions of this opportunity will be emailed to you. Good day and congratulations.'

'Do I get a choice here?' she calls as she hears the sound of their suits making their way to the door.

'The Eyes Forward makes the best decisions for you, as they do for all their female citizens.'

A pit forms in Ava's stomach, and the room starts to spin. Her chest inflates, yet she struggles to find her breath. She has no choice. That is what they said. Traffic noise fills the space as the doors open. Ava stays sitting, still facing the wall, words now escaping her. She continues to face it until the doors close, silencing the world outside.

Chapter 37

Ava knows she should go Society Policing. A free evening off from XL Medico and the brief look at the dark web she saw earlier tells her it could be a lucrative night. But she gets side tracked from checking for planned lootings and vandalisms. Instead, she reads posts from other people unhappy with the attitude toward women and Pres-X-2. That forcing women to look younger is a way to restrict women's rights, not empower them. Ava feels a flush of pride, a sense of belonging, that she's not the only one who thinks the whole Pres-X-2 thing is madness. There are women saying that word again that she heard that TV presenter say, *feminism*...what had he said? That movement making waves again? It seems he was right. There's so much chatter, mostly from some group called Sisters and Spies, but Ava is too tired to read it all.

She makes her way home, still pondering Society Policing, but the thought of the dash in and out, a brief snack and hello to Zia, then back out again, makes her legs ache before she's even done one pedal stroke. She yawns all the way home, rubs her quads when she stops at the lights, and considers not bothering Society Policing that night. She's orange anyway—sort of orange with some gold finally creeping in. Curfew sounds like a blessing right now.

With all her doubts about Pres-X, she can't stop hoping that it will be okay for Zia. XL Medico will sort it out. They'll adjust the formula to have her formaldehyde-rose used instead to get around the lack of vanadium somehow. Tweak the B-Well, maybe. All these justifications are what keeps hope alive—the belief XL Medico will sort it out soon. They'll realise the formula is off and readjust. Plenty of people haven't adjusted badly. She just can't lose Zia.

But what if Zia does react badly?

No. She shakes that thought away as soon as she has it. Ava will figure out how to fix it even if XL Medico doesn't. Quite how she'll manage such a task is beyond her comprehension in her tired state. But she'll figure it out. She knows she will. As soon as she's caught up on some sleep, she'll be back to investigating. Just a decent night's sleep is all she needs, then she'll figure it out.

She just can't lose Zia.

Sod curfew. There must be points to be earned somewhere. She cycles through the bad end of town, piles of boxes outside the buildings being snatched away as quickly as they are taken indoors, and the cries of the new residents as they move into their new homes. Dormitories, some of those. Bedsits if you're lucky, the streets if even less so. Ava doesn't stare, or tries not to, sure she recognises a family from across the street of her building. The boxes of clothes and kitchen equipment certainly imply a downgrade. Another family most likely gone the same way as Suzanna.

At her apartment block, she chains her bike up at the empty bike rack before crawling her way up the stairs. The hallway is quiet and cold. There's an emptiness to the place, a hollowness. Eviction signs are attached to doors, ripped from others, the yellow square of paper flapping on a pin is enough evidence though. Ava's been too busy to notice the emptying out of the middle-Scoring area. The highest Scores will be all right for sure, 750 plus is worn like armour. Get to 800 and you're almost untouchable. That Score is like Kevlar. The vulnerability of the middle-Scorers is clear now. As everyone buys more and more, to strive to Score, their business props up the super Scorers to their own detriment. Ava's apartment building has had its insides scooped out. There's a chill where a beating heart used to be.

At least Ava's apartment is still well-lived in and paid for. Ava can make rent easily at the moment, which is one less thing to worry about. As she walks in and through to the kitchen, it's clear that Zia has outdone herself. With Ava's busy work schedule, she's had little time to help with the cooking and cleaning, yet she arrives home to Tupperwares lined up, labelled with the days of the week.

'I thought I'd make sure you're eating all right,' Zia says, snapping the last of the lids on. 'So, there's lunch for every day this week. All home cooked, no processed junk. I went to that food shop that still sells to sub 600s. It's quite good, really. No-nonsense stuff, but got lots of vegetables and some basic cheese. It's a bit rubbery but cooks up okay. It's so busy walking there, even the slow lanes seem fast, but that's probably my knees more than their pace. Anyway, I never know what time you'll be around for dinner, so thought I'd make some dinners too. You can just heat them up as you like.'

'Zia. . .' Ava stares at all the boxes, blinks away some tears. 'I can't believe you've done all of this.'

'And all the laundry is done too. I'm pooped, being honest with you. But at least I know you're going to be eating properly and wearing clean clothes.' Zia loads up the dishwasher, bending slowly.

'It's my job to look after you, Zia. Not the other way round,' Ava says as she goes to help.

Zia swats her away. 'Pah! Why? I've not much else to do. And this new medicine is working wonders. I don't lose track of things like I did before. I can actually remember what needs doing.'

'It's amazing, Zia, really.'

Zia sits, allowing Ava to finish off and turn the dishwasher on. Not all the pots fit, so Ava fills the sink. She pours the washing up liquid from a full bottle. New. Zia must have replaced it when Ava had forgotten.

'All this work you're doing must be upping your Score quite a bit,' Zia says, munching on some dried fruit. 'You'll be booking in for that youth drug soon, I assume? I've seen the adverts on the telly. Looks like a wonderful thing.'

'No, Zia. My Score is to finance your treatment, not mine.'

'Don't you dare. I don't want it. I've told you this.'

Ava turns to face Zia, a face full of hurt. It's false, Ava's sure of it. Of course, she's heard Zia say such things before, but she can't mean it. Zia just doesn't want Ava gifting her points. Zia doesn't know what she's saying. She doesn't understand. Ava just needs to make her. She doesn't even remember her brother is dead half the time, so she doesn't know she'll be leaving Ava all alone. Once she's had the treatment and is young again, she'll realise then. 'But—'

'No. I'm fine. I'm happy being an old fart. Leave me be. It's you we need to think about. Your future is what matters. You're not an old fart, but you seem like you want to look like one. You are never going to find love if you don't start taking care of yourself. You should at least use some face cream.'

Face cream. Like that's really what's important. Ava shakes the soap off her hands, then drains the sink, pushing her hair out of her face with her still damp hands. 'I think I have a bit more to offer than being pretty.'

'But that's the first impression they get. It's important.' Zia stands again, then takes the cutlery out of the drawer, only to put it back in again, going on to do the same with the mugs.

Ava walks into the living room, then plonks onto the sofa. The seat groans, the padding is going. It'll probably need replacing soon. Still, it looks okay. Passable, not too stained or weather-beaten. She turns the TV on, and the first advert to come up is XL Medico's latest campaign for Pres-X-2. It features young women smiling and laughing like they really are teenagers. They probably are. The only difference is they're all up skyscrapers, looking down on the view below.

'Want to look your best? Of course, you do! With Pres-X-2'

Ava snarls at the TV, feeling more irritated than inspired as Zia nods along from the doorway. 'Aesthetics are just a temporary fix to a long-term problem,' Ava says to the TV or to Zia, she's not really sure. More to herself. 'The issue is that women are seen as a problem. Staying pretty solves nothing.'

She shifts her weight on the lumpy sofa. Her knees are a little stiff. She put her back out a month ago, but nothing that worries her, nothing she's ever given a second thought. She reaches for her reading glasses more often these days, which is the only part of her ageing so far that's remotely annoying, and even that is minor.

Rather than stay at home and listen to another lecture about being single, she opts to take her tired legs and go Society Policing. Or at least pretend like she is. Maybe the glint of gold in her implant will stop her from getting in trouble if she's caught out past curfew. She rides her bike out into the dark towards the better end of town, dodging the crime hotspots and usual vandal sites. She Society Polices with little enthusiasm, but in her mind, it justifies her time away from home more than simply needing fresh air.

A little further up the hill and over the roundabout, she comes to the end of town that is far more exclusive than hers—houses rather than apartments, each with their own front garden, some even with their own cars parked outside, all with lights on in their windows. There are no evictions at this end of town. Once you've made it this high up the ladder, the trap door closes behind you. Your fall is always broken. But it's impossible to make it this high when single. One wage, one Score is rarely enough to soar so high. Not that Ava cares. The grandiose things don't bother her, absolutely not. She needs none of it. All she needs is her Zia, and for Zia to stop nagging her.

She watches a couple walk their child inside from the bus stop to their front door, the kiss they share on the doorstep, the tender way they hold hands. The evening is warm, yet Ava shivers a little and folds her arms over her body, pulling her collar up to protect her neck. But instead of pedalling away to keep warm, she continues watching. Despite her dismissiveness to Zia about wanting a partner, she still imagines herself growing old with someone. Staying young with someone doesn't have the same ring to it somehow.

Chapter 38

The good night's sleep Ava needed turned out to be about five hours of tossing and turning, filled with frustrated dreams and getting up to pee. A poor rest, and she didn't actually do any Society Policing. A wasted night. She kicks herself for being lazy and unenthused. That is not the attitude of a 700, she's sure of that. If she'd done a stake-out, cycled some more, perhaps she would have slept better, exhausted herself into a contented night's sleep instead of feeding her growing discontent. Cycling around, staking out wealthy homes, was in no way useful and not even inspiring. She leaves for work with a gnawing sensation of inadequacy and tiredness, pushing on her bike pedals as if her knees were made of jelly. At least it's mostly downhill.

Her commute takes her past the mismatched gentrification that's taking the town by storm. Some low Scorers fail to buy groceries at their usual shop. Its new 400 plus sign hangs above the door. The powdered rations delivery truck is doing the rounds already, early for that service. More boxes of personal items are piled up outside budget housing and temporary accommodation before she gets through this part of town and into the streets where everyone has a pinkish hue to their skin, or the dewy glow of the hue recently subsided.

Ava tries not to stare, to watch the bikes and buses ahead rather than the busy throng of pedestrian traffic, but the change is so remarkable, it keeps drawing her attention. When she's not gawping at other people, she's catching way too many glimpses of herself, the mirrored windows now everywhere. The pedestrian lanes have been shoved a metre or so over, away from the storefronts to create a new viewing area. An area to loiter and gaze upon your reflection. Some stores have gone all out and painted ornate picture-frame designs on their mirrored windows, enjoying a queue of people lining up to see themselves. The wind is light today, her cheeks reddening with the cool chill of the morning, her crow's feet deepening from her wincing against the low sun. All of this she knows too well. She's reminded of it constantly as she cycles along. As if she isn't feeling inadequate enough already.

The crowd of Score-diggers is absent as she walks through the doors of the funeral home. Good thing, too. She's about as in the mood for that as she is for a kick in the crotch. That small blessing lightens her mood a little, but not as much as her phone pinging. Despite her lack of Society Policing points, her phone pings at 9 a.m. to say she has crossed the threshold into the coveted 600 club. Her extra wages at XL Medico, and the funeral home doing so much better, have given her the extra ten points she needed to cross that threshold.

She air-punches and takes some joy in the small win. She celebrates by going back to Beanies, showing Kris her Life Score and grinning as he serves her coffee, just the way she likes it. He hasn't forgotten. They'll bring face scanners in there too, no doubt, like almost everywhere. But for this day, she can hold her tired-looking, loose-skinned face high. She returns to work, walking in the slow lane, her coffee cup logo on show just in case anyone wants to know she's now a 600.

When she sits at her desk, she places the cup in front of her. The extortionate price means she probably won't justify a second cup from there today, but she could refill it, perhaps. She swivels the cup around, pondering which is the best angle to keep the Beanies logo on display.

She's savouring the last sip when the front doors open, and she looks up and almost chokes on the now tepid coffee.

'Mandisa!' Ava says after a phlegmy cough. 'What are you doing here?'

With the sun casting its glow through the door frame, Mandisa is a golden-framed silhouette, sleek and glamorous, walking as if gliding. Ava's cheeks flush as she continues to cough up the last bit of coffee but manages to not spill any. For once, she's actually looking reasonably well-presented. Her well-ironed clothes and freshly washed hair have recovered from her cycle into work, nothing like the sweaty mess she usually appears at the lab. She has some clients coming in today for visits, but Mandisa isn't who she's expecting to see.

'Hi, Ava,' Mandisa says, her voice smooth as if it's made of honey.

Ava bends to wipe her mouth on her sleeve out of sight under the desk. 'I'm so sorry. I wasn't aware you'd lost someone. Who are you here to visit?'

'Oh, I'm not visiting anyone. I mean, I've not lost anyone. I've come to see you, actually.'

'Right. Well, here I am.' Ava bites her lip at her stupid comment. Why does Mandisa always have to smell so good? And look so good. Even with her new pinkish tone, she looks perfect. 'I can see you've had your treatment.' Another stupid comment.

'Yes. Really does work wonders, doesn't it?'

Not that she had so much as a wrinkle before, but any effect of gravity has disappeared. Her eyebrows are higher and her jawline lifted. There's a plumpness to her skin that makes her cheeks look like they're bursting with vivacity instead of shrinking away from life. Ava swallows and fidgets on the spot, then nods. 'You look great.'

Mandisa smiles and doesn't return the compliment. 'I hear you had a meeting with some Eyes Forward the other day.'

'Weird news travels fast.'

'Anyway, you're welcome.'

Ava pulls her chin in. She shouldn't do that; it makes her jawline look worse. She stretches her neck out again when the surprise at Mandisa's comment has worn off. 'Excuse me?'

'I put in a word for you, to get you the treatment.'

She almost pulls her chin in again at those words but subdues the reflex. 'What? But I don't want it.'

Mandisa chuckles, a little girl kind of laugh. 'Oh, don't be daft. Of course you want it. Everyone wants it.'

'You know they're forcing me to have it.'

'I pulled a lot of strings for you. You could at least sound grateful.'

'But you never asked me. It's just a cosmetic thing. It's really not for me.'

'It's so much more than that,' Mandisa says, looking up at the ceiling. 'And it opens up so many doors, literally. New bars and cafés, respect—'

'Mandi, seriously.' Ava's tone is curt. She swallows and softens her voice. 'None of those things are important to me. Do you not know me at all?'

'But imagine what it could mean for us.' Mandisa steps forward and looks at Ava now as she takes Ava's hands in hers and stares into her soul. Ava's anger dissolves into something else, something softer, needier.

'You're almost 600 now,' Mandisa says, so close, her breath blows across Ava's face. So fresh. So welcoming. 'There's so much more to this that you can't possibly comprehend. Your hormone levels are perfect for treatment now. Imagine, we could be together again.'

Those words hang in the air, sweeter than Mandisa's perfume, softer than her hands, more welcoming than her touch.

The room spins for a second as Mandisa's words envelop her. Ava wobbles for a moment, then blinks hard, twice, and rights herself. 'I am a 600, actually. And we could be together despite those things, Mandisa. Those things only matter to you.'

Mandisa drops Ava's hands and backs away. Still smiling, more smug now than welcoming. 'You'll see soon, Ava. It's not about what matters to me. You're all that matters to me. But this is bigger than that. It's about what's good for the whole Society.' She turns away. She's at the door, about to leave.

Ava swallows and stiffens as she realises she's letting her leave. Her words *You're all that matters to me* are dancing in the air like wisps of dust catching rays.

Mandisa flicks her hair and looks over her shoulder to say her parting words to Ava. 'When you open your eyes, come find me. I'll be waiting. I've waited this long.'

When the doors close behind her, Ava finds a chair, her knees going slack, and her breath gone. Mandisa. Holding her hands. Saying they could be together.

No. No. Ava thumps her temples. Why is she feeling so tempted? She and Mandisa were over ages ago. She's not going back down that road, not under these conditions. Ava is how she is. Mandisa wants her to be someone else. No, *something* else. Desirable. She doesn't think Ava is desirable as she is. Mandisa.
. .

Her thoughts stop there for a moment, that name lingering like some drug.

Mandisa. Her scent still hovers around. Ava takes a deep breath in, then licks her lips.

Mandisa.

Chapter 39

During the Great Unrest

There were no cakes for the meeting, not that Lucia cared. All sorts of nasty so-and-sos were meant to be coming. They didn't deserve cakes, especially not during times like these. How many poor innocents had been killed now because of this government and their rules, because of the extremist views held by some? She couldn't shake a sense of responsibility. She was the brainchild behind the Time's Up. They may have acted under her title, but the group was not the one she founded. Not by far.

Yet still, the Eyes Forward thought she was influential. And they wanted to talk.

Not just the Eyes Forward but the Enough as well, those nasty people killing young women. It had sent chills all over her when she'd heard they were coming. They didn't even give her the choice. The Eyes Forward just told her all these horrible people would descend on her café, and she could either like it or lump it. They'd said it in a more formal way than that, but she'd gotten the idea.

She still hadn't heard from Mo. She didn't live in the same house anymore since she'd had another baby, and her Life Score dropped so she couldn't afford it. She hadn't replied to any emails or texts and Lucia feared the worst. Lucia could help with the children if she knew where Mo was, but no one had heard from her.

Lucia had kept knowledge of this meeting quiet, as the Eyes Forward instructed. Only the most influential were to attend. Lucia wouldn't even count herself as one of the most influential, but she supposed it was her café, so that gave her some say. Therese, Thomas, Selina, and Steve would come, along with Luigi and Daphne. That was all. Mostly the more mild-tempered of the group. To be fair, the more ill-tempered rarely came to the café anymore. All their time was spent frequenting the White Horse from what she'd heard. Nasty business.

Four men arrived first, big men with ruddy faces and broad shoulders. Lucia thought they must have bought their T-shirts when they were a few sizes smaller. And they all wore the faces of men who thought so highly of themselves, yet they couldn't even buy the right size clothes. She felt glad there was no cake. Lucia tutted and shook her head when she saw them, forgetting her manners entirely.

'This the meeting with Eyes Forward?' One said in a higher voice than she imagined for such a brute.

'It is. Please take a seat.' Lucia checked her watch, wishing that some of her own party would arrive quickly. They all sat in silence, Lucia not daring to meet their gazes. She tapped her foot and bit the inside of her cheek, trying to think about what she'd have for dinner and what chores she needed to do around her house.

Luigi and Daphne turned up just as the ambience was getting frostier than the icing in the fridge. They greeted Lucia with a kiss on the cheek each.

'What's this meeting about, Lucia?' Luigi asked, Daphne peering in.

'I was contacted. Someone called… Oh, I'm bad with names. It begins with a K. Anyway, the Eyes Forward want to speak to us, and—'

Ian arrived then. Lucia hadn't even expected him. 'Ian. What a surprise.'

'The other White Horse lot will be here soon. Some guy, Kylan Morris, told us to be here.'

'That's his name.' Lucia slapped her forehead. 'Why did he invite you?'

'Beats me,' Ian said.

Lucia wanted to ask about Keisha and the baby, but when she looked up, in the doorway, pink-faced and his chin scarred, was Ken. Lucia gasped and backed away as Ken took a step closer.

'I never wanted to see you again,' she said in a hissing whisper.

'I'm trying to help you, Lu. Listen to what we have to say. You think I didn't know what you were planning? We're all here to help you put a stop to this madness, to make you see sense—to give *us* a chance again.'

'Us?' The word came up her throat like bile. 'You are not my husband. You can never be the man I married.'

Lucia took a step away from him, then turned her back.

'You've got a nerve. A damned pinkie coming to a Time's Up meeting,' Ian said to Ken.

'This isn't a Time's Up meeting,' one of the big men said. 'We're Enough.'

Lucia's knees gave way, and she took a seat. To be faced with one. . .to be in the same room as one of those. . .those. . .killers. It was too much. 'You. . .you baby murderers, in my café. Get out, the lot of you.' She wished she sounded more authoritative or could at least stand to confront them, but her body wouldn't allow it. It was like being near such evil sucked the blood from her.

Another couple of men arrived, wearing the same suit as Ken, the Eyes Forward logo stitched to the front. 'No one is going anywhere,' said one. 'We are all here for the common good. You're also here by orders of the Eyes Forward, so settle down.'

'We are here for the common good,' said Luigi, pointing at Lucia and Daphne. 'Those brutes are here for themselves.'

The Eyes Forward didn't respond as more people arrived, people Lucia didn't recognise, introducing themselves as Time's Up. But they weren't her Time's Up. They were the ones that caused trouble. They didn't even deny it. They boasted about it when they came in.

'Got another block.'

'Me too. Wiped out nearly a hundred yesterday.'

'Well done all.'

There were handshakes and backslaps and grins. Lucia cowered, shivered, and fought back tears.

Killers were in her café. Everywhere.

Finally, Therese, Selina, Thomas, and Steve arrived and joined her in her corner. Fancy being outnumbered by brutes in her own café. There were so few women in the room. In fact, there were no women besides her little group. She was surrounded by glowering men with power on the brain. At least she got a seat. No way should these thugs get one.

The Eyes Forward cleared his throat. 'Good evening, everyone. My name is Kylan Morris, this is Lloyd Porter and Ken Wickes. We are here because the unrest is escalating. Your factions are wreaking havoc across the Society. Of course, there is no doubt that your methods have been effective. The population is plummeting faster than we anticipated thanks to your actions. For that, you are all to be commended.'

Commended? For mass murder? Lucia wanted to shout out. Her mouth made moves to speak, but there was no sound. Just the presence of the Eyes Forward silenced her like some submissive. She hated herself for that, for her cowardice.

'However,' Kylan continued, 'the time has come for us to consider how to bring about peace. The Government must maintain control. Firstly, this meeting is highly confidential, an NDA is being passed around which you all need to sign a copy of. Now then, before you start arguing, remember that all factions have caused violence and deaths. All of you in this room have blood on your hands.'

Lucia looked at hers. They were clean, she knew it. Sparkling clean.

'The unrest does need to stop,' he continued. 'The damage to infrastructure is getting too much. It's going to be too costly to repair the Society at this rate.'

Damage to infrastructure? Lucia thought the government might have other priorities. Hoped, anyway.

'That's those damned Time's Up vandals,' one of the big men said, pointing to Lucia's side. 'The Enough never damage buildings.'

'You blew up a maternity ward in a hospital,' Luigi said.

'Well, there'll be no need to rebuild that if we get our way.'

'You murder women.'

'And?'

'Stop!' The Eyes Forward said, holding up his hands on either side like a fight was about to break out. 'We have come with terms, to bring about peace. All of you here, as ringleaders of the factions, will end your terrorism and will persuade your peers to do so. In return, we have come up with these compromises.' He passed around some papers.

'Sorry if I'm a bit grouchy,' one of the other big men said. 'I couldn't get my coffee this morning because those Pro Grow twats won't let deliveries in. They won't be happy until food is spread so thinly we're all eating nothing but cabbage soup and flavoured air.'

A small man in the corner, who Lucia hadn't even noticed come in, stepped forward. 'Yet here you are, living and breathing, no worse for wear.'

The big man laughed. 'Oh, piss off. I'll bet the Pro Grows stock-piled coffee before they blockaded shipments. Like it's so easy just to live on less.'

'Quiet, the lot of you!' Kylan Morris said. 'Please, take the paper and read our terms. I think you will all be happy.'

Lucia got her reading glasses from her pocket and read. She blinked, wiped the wetness from her eyes, and read again.

Enforced sterilisation of all girls.

Pres-X will continue to be available to high Scorers, but its roll out across the low Scorers will never happen.

Food will be more tightly rationed, with powdered, nutritionally balanced sachets available as a sustainable food source.

As a reward for your help towards peace, all people in this room will have their Score upped to 750, with the option of having complimentary Pres-X when they reach appropriate age.

Her chest tightened. Her stomach twisted. 'No!' Lucia said, shaking her head, more tears in her eyes. 'You'll maim girls? Take their choices away? No, this can't happen!'

'I agree,' Luigi said. 'My daughter should have the option to have children if she wishes.'

'Children? Plural?' one of the Enough men spat. 'What planet are you on? Fucking foreigner.'

'And to bribe us with Pres-X?' Lucia said, her voice breathy as her lungs struggled from shock. 'Like we can be so easily bribed!'

'Well, that part, it's worth considering,' said one of the brutes, and out of the corner of her eye, Lucia saw her own friends, Selina, Steve, Therese, Luigi and Daphne all nodding along. At least Thomas didn't.

'Judases, the lot of you.' She folded her arms and turned away from them. In front of her was the pink face of her husband, smiling, those stupid pleading eyes still trying to sway her. 'Ken Wickes, you're dead to me. Dead!'

'There will, of course, be more actions taken—to empathise with the Time's Up. These actions are of a more sensitive nature. Many of you would not benefit from knowing what they are. If you would rather not know, you may step out now. For those that wish to be informed, here is an extra page.'

Kylan laid out some paper on the table, printed side down. Lucia's hands stayed steadfast to her sides. She was sure she didn't want to know. But then, maybe knowing would be best, at least then she can try to stop it. She lifted the sheet, read the words, though it was hard as she was shaking so much. What they were promising was despicable, awful, simply cruel.

Or was it?

A headache formed in her forehead and spread to her temples. She always had a headache these days. Her scalp, even her jaw cramped. She was being torn in half, the ends and means at odds with each other. Her mind was splitting from her morality.

The meeting ended shortly afterwards. They all had copies of their NDAs, should they dare discuss the awful things they heard, and the offer letter from Eyes Forward. Lucia wanted to burn the lot of it. She walked home in a huff. Betrayed, dejected.

When she got home, she fell asleep almost instantly, exhausted from her anger. She forgot all about making dinner.

Chapter 40

10 years after the Great Unrest

Want to look your best? Of course, you do! With Pres-X-2
One of the core values of XL Medico

***

Ava's implant switches back to green just in time for her Friday night plans. She wants to stay out anyway, some place where the Eyes Forward are unlikely to find her. Any day now they'll come for her. The thought makes her back itch and her neck crack.

The bar is heaving on Friday night, full of faces still pink or people who look like teenagers. Ava makes for the toilet as soon as she arrives to rub some cream into her face, then a little shimmer blush. It's more than she'd usually wear, but the gentle sheen is supposed to blur out lines, so it says. Not that she cares. She used to be able to blend in, her dark clothes helping her melt into the background. Blurring out her lines isn't to make them disappear on her face, blending makeup isn't to make her facial features indistinguishable. Every hint of age now is like cat's eyes in the road. The brightly coloured marks of some poisonous toad.

Dan is already there, sitting at a centre table in full view of everyone, no corner to hide in, no shadows for company. Ava curses to herself but walks over and joins him, taking a gulp from one of the two drinks in front of him, assuming one is for her. She then leans over and gives him a hug. His pink face has calmed already, and his hairline is down another inch from when she last saw him. It's like gravity is pushing up instead of pulling down on his cheeks and eyes.

'Well, it certainly has made a difference!' says Ava as he looks at her for comment.

'I know, right? So, how long before you've a high enough Score to get it?'

Ava rolls her eyes and takes another gulp of the pint. 'I don't want it, but they're forcing it on me anyway.'

He manages to lift his eyebrows without wrinkling his forehead at all, and she retells the entire story.

He holds his hands to his cheeks, his mouth hanging open as she finishes telling him. 'Wait, hang on. You're getting free Pres-X-2, and you're upset about it?' If Dan's eyes bulge anymore, they'd plop from his wrinkle-free sockets.

'I'm not being given a choice. I should have the right to choose, shouldn't I?'

'So make the right choice. Ava, this is amazing. You don't have to bind yourself to some right old bore to get the drug.'

Ava winces at his description of Jeremy. 'Jeremy any more lively?'

'Barely. The B-Well is still working, so he isn't wailing like some deranged cat. You wanted a sample? Here, I brought you one.' He hands Ava a blister pack, and it's as she remembers—B-Well+ in a silver packet. 'Why on earth do you want that anyway? Anyone can get it on prescription if you really need it.'

'I just want to test it, see what's in it. Glad Jeremy's doing better.'

'He is better. But. . .well. . .I was just expecting him to be a bit more exciting, or excited, looking forward to being young again, playful, you know? Instead, he just wants the lights off—'

'Oh, yeah. . .'

'Not for that. We haven't even done *that*. Libido isn't the first thing to come back, it seems. Not that I'd want to right now. He still looks ancient.'

'Good things come to those who wait,' Ava says. 'Anyway, there was another reason I wanted to come here tonight. I'm meeting someone—'

'Oh, God. Hide!' Dan says. 'That awful woman you dated ages ago just came in. What's her name, Kam or Lin or—'

'Kim! Hi, over here.' Ava stands and waves, glaring back down at Dan, who mouths *What the fuck?* back at her.

'Ava, lovely to see you.' Kim plants a kiss on Ava's cheek, then looks at Dan with eyes that could freeze the sun. 'I thought it would just be us two.'

'Dan just happened to be here. Isn't that right, Dan?'

'Lovely to see you again, Kim. It's been too long,' he says through a painted-on smile.

Kim purses her lips and replies with a 'Hmmm.' She steps around to stand with her back to Dan. 'Oh, why don't I go and get us some drinks, then you can tell me all about those Eyes Forward trucks coming to your home the other day.'

'Sure. Thanks, Kim.'

After she's walked away a few paces, Dan pokes Ava's arm. 'What the hell? You're dating her again?'

'No. Listen, I just owed her a favour, and this is it. But it's okay. I have a plan.'

'Unless your plan involves chucking your drink over her, I hate it.'

Kim is still at the bar when Mrs Constance walks in, wearing snug beige trousers adorned with a gold belt and a low-cut red top falling an inch or so above the trouser waistline, her golden hair cascading in fresh curls over her shoulders. Again, Ava stands and waves.

'Who the bloody hell is this now? Although I instantly approve more of this one than the last.'

Ava shushes him and pulls up another chair for Mrs Constance. 'Flick,' she says, remembering her first name just in time. 'How wonderful to see you here.'

'You too, Ava. And who's your friend?'

'This is my good friend, Dan. Dan, this is Flick.'

'Pleasure,' Dan says, shaking her hand, his grin as wide as it can be.

Kim arrives back from the bar with a tray of drinks, which she nearly drops at the sight of Mrs Constance. 'Oh, hi. . .' She wobbles as she places the drinks down on the table. 'Ava, why don't you introduce me to your friend?'

Ava does the introductions and looks at Dan, who bounces his eyebrows at her.

If Mrs Constance wanted any sort of interaction with Ava, it proves impossible due to Kim's smothering affections. She spends the evening showering Mrs Constance with compliments, laughing at everything she says, playing with her hair and being the exact kind of idiot Ava imagines all Score-diggers to be when dating, Dan included. After a few hours in the bar, Ava makes a discreet exit, meeting Dan outside as she assumed he'd follow, leaving Kim and Mrs Constance to their conversational flirting, laughing their whole way home.

***

Saturday at XL Medico, and it's time to get on with her investigation. She has B-Well pill samples she's kept in some cling-film from Max, and the blister pack of B-Well+ from Dan. She necks some aspirin to take away the lingering headache from the drinks the night before and arrives an hour early to get some private lab time before Edgar arrives. Her early start proves unnecessary as the testing takes her just a few minutes. The pH of the tablets is vastly different, so different she double-checks the results, but her hands shake, and she drops the litmus paper. The pills that were prescribed to Erin have a neutral pH. Jeremy's, they're alkaline. And the only reason she can think for this is to rid the body of formic acid. In fact, it's the perfect pH to do this.

In the stock fridge, she rummages and finds some formic acid and tests it in the lab with the B-Well—child's play. She knows she's right. But she just wants to see it, to really visualise it for herself. She dips the litmus paper in the end, then reads the neutral result. It confirms her fears. XL Medico knows the Pres-X is off and is handing it out anyway, literally poisoning them, making them go so crazy, they take their own life instead of living the vastly longer one promised. The high Scorers have the antidote to the acid mixed in with their happy pills. They're safe.

She needs to tell someone, anyone who will listen. Perhaps it's just an error in the B-Well manufacturing. She needs to get word to them, to their product development team. She needs to speak to Mandisa.

Mandisa.

Ava slaps her forehead, then screws her eyes shut as she's forced to believe what she wishes wasn't true.

Mandisa with a B-Well product development badge.

Mandisa is brilliant. A far better chemist than Ava. Meticulous to a fault. Perfect in all that she does.

Mandisa knows. XL Medico knows.

Has this been part of the Eyes Forward plan all along? Their secret NDA-protected way to appease the Time's Up? To stay quiet for a decade, wait until enthusiasm for Pres-X is really high, then allow the drug to go bad. Fossil fuels and vanadium running out was forecasted for ages. This has been planned for a decade, since her parents were alive, since they signed that NDA. There is only one conclusion that Ava can come up with, only one that appeases the Time's Up without riling the powerful, high Scoring citizens.

The cull of Society's elders during the Great Unrest never ended. It just became more covert, more menacing. The Eyes Forward never stopped the killing. They just covered their tracks.

***

As Edgar cleans and organises the lab, Ava makes sixty litres of formaldehyde-rose before she cycles home, frustrated, yet pedalling slowly, still needing time to process, to come up with any other solution than the glaringly obvious one. But there is no other. However many times she cuts up and rearranges the facts, she comes up with the same answer.

XL Medico knows. Mandisa knows. This was planned.

She cycles up the hill, legs tired yet barely noticing the gradient, so lost in her thoughts. When she arrives outside her apartment block, the flashing blue lights don't distract her mind, and the white and yellow vehicle in the street goes unnoticed. She walks up the stairs, the commands being shouted from the top floor apartments not registering. It's only when she finds her apartment door open and filled with people in green outfits and medical bags scattered across the linoleum that her attention is snapped to the here and now.

'Zia?' she cries out, but Zia doesn't answer. A woman goes to Ava, a stranger, holding her back from walking any closer. 'Zia!' Ava calls out again. The still body lying on the floor gives no response.

The voices from the medical staff sound distant, as if underwater, saying words Ava shouldn't be hearing, machines making noises that shouldn't be coming from her apartment. Beeps and zaps. There's some blood on the side of the table, a broken cup on the table, and some spilled drink pooling on the floor.

'Zia! Please, tell me she's okay.'

The woman says some words, then nudges Ava to sit. She does. She has little strength to argue. She trembles in the chair as they work on Zia, then move her onto the stretcher and carry her down the stairs.

***

The plastic chairs in the hospital are cold and uncomfortable. No matter, Ava wasn't planning on sleeping anyway. She sits for a while, paces for longer, leans against the wall, then sits again. Perhaps she does doze off for a bit. Time passes so erratically, she's unsure. One moment she's been there for minutes, the next, hours. Then another moment and it's been mere minutes again.

Doctors and nurses move from one room to another. Still no news.

'Ava Maricelli?'

Ava jumps at the sound of her name. The doctor smiles, not in the solemn way people do when dealing with grief. Ava knows that look all too well. This doctor looks like she's caring for the living rather than consoling for a corpse. 'You can see her now.'

'She's okay? She has a history of giant cell arteritis and vascular dementia.'

'I am aware. She's had a mini stroke and has a head wound from banging it when she fell. She's incredibly lucky she managed to call the ambulance before she lost consciousness. I am optimistic she will recover from this latest episode.'

Ava sits again when she hears that, and tears tremble their way out. She struggles to draw breath as relief shudders through her. *She's going to be okay. She's going to be okay.* She takes a moment before going to see Zia, composing herself, wiping the tears from her cheeks, blowing her nose, still pinching herself.

Zia's not dead. She hasn't lost her. Not yet. She's still okay. For now.

Chapter 41

On her way to work on Monday, while Zia is still in hospital, Ava wonders if there's any worse guilt than being away from a sick loved one. She had cleaned the blood and spilled tea off the lino when she arrived back home, picked up the broken glass, then cried into a bottle of beer. If she'd been home on the Saturday like most people, she could have made sure Zia was okay. She may have noticed the earlier warning signs of the mini stroke.

It's pure luck Zia isn't worse off. Some more medication, the doctors said. Zia's head is partly shaved from stitches, and her face is all purple and swollen with bruising, making it look worse than it is, they reassured her. The gash missed her eye. She didn't lose too much blood. A miracle, the doctor said. A few days to recuperate in hospital and she'll be fine.

Fine.

What an awful word. Zia hasn't been fine in ages.

Ava stayed with Zia until the early hours of Sunday, then was back again that afternoon until Zia told her to go home. Zia insisted Ava continue as normal, not to worry about her, that she needs to up her Score so she can get Pres-X-2. Ava didn't dare tell her it's being forced upon her for free. In fact, that thought barely entered her mind. All she could think about since seeing Zia is how she can get her the private treatment with the neutralising B-Well. She came far too close to losing her. There's no way she's going to risk actually losing her now. At least for the time being, Zia's being looked after in hospital, so Ava can dedicate her time to working, upping her Score, knowing Zia is currently safe.

The whole horribleness of the weekend plays over and over again in Ava's head as she cycles to work. What she could have done. . . what she *should* have done. That they said Zia will be fine. That Ava thinks Zia needs to be damn well better than fine. That doctor, with her pink skin fading into normality, looked like a child when she told Ava the news. It felt more like a playground gossip than a doctor-patient discussion. Some professions should be exempt from Pres-X-2, Ava thinks. How can she listen to a doctor who looks like she's a teenager?

When Ava arrives at work, it's not yet opening time, but there is a queue outside. Not the sort of crowd the Score-diggers create, but an orderly line of people, all facing the front door. Assuming they're only there to check their image in the new reflective glass, Ava ignores them and lets herself in, locking the door behind her.

She switches on the computers, has a quick vacuum and dust, welcomes Max, who makes straight for the cold room, puts the kettle on, then at 9 a.m., opens the doors. The queue shuffles forward, entering the funeral home one at a time.

'Can I help you?' Ava asks the man who's just come in. It's no one she recognises from her current client visitor list. He wears the cheerful face of someone not in mourning, with brightly coloured clothes to match.

'I'd like to buy a funeral please, on credit. I hear you do payment plans?'

'We do payment plans, yes. Who is the deceased?'

'Well, no one yet. But I'd like to get ahead of the game. I'm planning ahead, you know. I'll take a package on credit, please.'

'For who?' Ava appraises him, thinking perhaps he's sick, though he looks nowhere near ready for the cold room. 'We tend to do prepayment plans for the over sixties, unless there are special circumstances?'

'It's for me. I'm forty-nine, and my special circumstance is I'm being organised.'

Before Ava has time to respond, the next person in the queue comes in and shouts over the top of the first customer. 'Striving to Score, you see. There was an article in the Sunday Score Supplement, advising on some untapped credit sources most people aren't taking advantage of. I'm a 600, so I do qualify for a funeral here.'

Another person enters, and another, all shouting now, holding up their Score app to show their 600 plus Score, none of them anywhere near the usual age to start paying for a funeral. Before Ava has time to process, the entire queue that was lined up outside bundles in to take up the whole reception area, and still more people flock to the doors. All middle-aged, 600-750s, planning years ahead for their funeral.

'Max!' Ava shouts to the cold room. 'Can you come out here and give me a hand?'

She hears Max curse as he arrives at reception, but doesn't even have a minute to turn and greet him. The first man is getting impatient, the rest of the queue, currently less so, but the agitation is heating up.

Ava loads up licensing documents, unable to find anything that prohibits taking payments this early. Inflation is what's hard to figure out. A ten grand funeral today will likely cost double that or more by the time these people are old enough. She does some numbers, crudely, and explains that only the full deluxe package is possible for such advance payment plans. That's thirty grand in today's money, but by the time their funerals are needed, who knows? She strains her forehead, thinking of interest as well as inflation, impossible to know burn rates, for God knows what the burn rate is going to be for a Pres-X-2 taker. She pulls figures out of thin air, drafts up a contract in front of a waiting room rammed with people impatient to throw money at her, then decides fifty grand is about right.

No one quibbles. In fact, maxing out that much more credit makes them yelp with joy rather than pain.

Max shoots Ava a look, which she shrugs off. What is she meant to say?

By the time the morning is finished, they have set up forty-five payment plans for people who probably aren't going to die for decades.

'Well,' Max says, locking the front door and putting a 'closed for lunch' sign in the window. 'That was the weirdest morning at work ever.'

'Yeah.' Ava exhales slowly, leaning back in her chair. 'I mean. . . I don't even know what to make of that. With this and the lower Life Scorers in the cold room, business is the busiest ever.'

'Yeah. . . About that. . .'

Ava looks at Max, notes his hunched shoulders and fidgeting hands. 'Max. . .what's wrong? If you're going to bail on me, I need to know.'

'Sorry, yeah. Been meaning to bring that up. Just been busy.'

'And—'

'So, Scotland seems like the easiest route.'

Ava sits upright in her chair and leans over the desk. 'You're actually going to go?'

'I guess so. It's what Frida wants. I can't really abandon her.'

Ava nods and smiles. Erin would be so proud. 'Good for you, Max. Not every man would be as decent.'

'Well, it's what Nan would want, I'm sure. Frida's going in a week. I'll join her a while after. Couples draw more attention, apparently. She can sneak through easier on her own.'

'All that way,' Ava says, not even being able to imagine going so far. Like most, she's never left her county. Berkshire is big enough. Scotland is just incomprehensibly far. 'How's she getting there?'

'Trains, bike hire, more trains. Mixing it up is the best way to stay undetected. It'll take ages.'

'Shit.' Ava rests her chin in her hands. 'That's really tough.'

'If you find a new employee, I can hang around for a bit to help with the training.' The intonation at the end of his voice makes a question out of this statement. Ava can't ask anything of him. He's been through enough.

'Thanks,' she says. 'Appreciate it. But you just concentrate on you. And thanks for this morning. That was crazy. I'm going to have to get an accountant to manage all of this. It's a lot more complicated now.' Luckily, she knows one and has been meaning to visit her for a while.

Ava grabs her coat and goes to switch her computer off, her finger hovering over the standby button as the news show comes on. Reports of the economy doing so well, VAT payments sky high, and the entire nation embracing the 'trend to spend' is still making headlines. What grabs her attention isn't the usual scoop, but when they cut to the entertainment news. Monika Skye is there, alongside some other celebrities Ava can't name off the top of her head, shouting about their new show. A live audience claps, the glee on the presenters palpable.

'Some lucky Society Citizens have been awarded Pres-X-2, and we're going to be showing their treatment, regression and journey for you all to see.'

'That's right, Monika. Three lucky winners will be commencing their treatment in two days' time. And we'll show you everything, live on air. Now why, you may ask, have these three people been so lucky?'

'Good question, Berenice. Each lucky winner has displayed marvellous credentials, making them worthy of such a prize. Let's take a quick look at their profiles.'

'Shit! Shit, shit, shit!

'First up, we have Jenny.' A full frame photo dominates the screen of a blonde woman with a kind face, looking tired yet smiling. 'She's a fifty-one-year-old carer with a low Life Score, but who has nursed many Pres-X takers in their pre-treatment years.'

'Second up, we have Meenal, who used to have a Life Score of 700, but lost it all just before Pres-X-2 was released. Bad luck Meenal but we've got you now!' Meenal's picture pops up, a well-presented woman with the fakest smile Ava has ever seen. Two down. Maybe it won't be her. Maybe her treatment will be private.

'And thirdly, we have Ava. Who is a dedicated Society Police and has the highest record of prosecutions in Berkshire. Keeping our streets safe! Well done, Ava.'

Shit!

Chapter 42

Ava leaves Max in charge and walks to Mae Porter/Taylor's business address, resisting the urge to buy another coffee from Beanies. She doesn't want to be seen anywhere anyway. And coffee isn't what she wants. More Sambucca would be more suitable to take the edge off what she's just seen. She pulls her scarf up to cover half of her face and the hood on her coat down to cover the other half, leaving only a narrow slit to look through. Her face is so red, everyone will think she's had her treatment already. She could kill Mandisa for setting her up for this. No one likes Society Police. She's going to get stoned in the street by low Scoring thugs.

An odd scuffle is breaking out in the lanes ahead, which she manages to avoid by lane weaving, a frowned upon method of walking but not something that should get her docked any points. Although, perhaps being docked a few points would be a good thing right now. Maybe that'll get her out of doing the

TV show. She starts to wonder if Max wants company on his way to Scotland.

A cursory glance in the shop windows reveals several 'out of stock' signs and a few more with 'stock arriving soon! Reserve your slot' banners decorating their entranceways. Business is clearly booming for most, not just hers. The news reports of the economy flying high seem to be true, as does the desperation in people's faces as they shout at shop assistants, trying to hand over credit cards, begging to pay now to reserve stock coming in later. 'It doesn't even matter when it comes in, just let me pay for it now!'

On top of the buildings are more posters for credit card and loan companies being erected as quickly as it takes to read them, all in garish colours like they're handing out sweeties rather than debt. Despite the fast walking pace and body heat from the other pedestrians, Ava shivers. She's always strived to Score but has also always erred on the cautious side with debt. She has plenty, but manageable. She can still hear Suzanna's cries, still see the sight of her scrubbing the asphalt. And she'll still have to repay what she owes. Debt is inherited as well as Life Scores.

Ava walks past one restaurant for 700 pluses. It never used to cater so high. The food was good, Asian fusion, and now it's gone top end. The sweet and spicy smell fills the street. If she gets to 700, she promises to eat there again—if she can be seen out in public at all when everyone knows her as Society Police. The sign in the window says you can pay for a meal on credit now and use it when your score hits 700. You can even sort it out online. She licks her lips and puts a reminder in her phone to do just that. She could even use one of her new credit cards.

Someone's shopping bag pokes her forearm, while another catches her foot from behind. Looking around, it seems Ava's the only one not completely giving in to the 'trend to spend.' She ruminates over the crazy morning at work and wonders realistically how many funeral plans they could take on credit, dreading how busy business will be in fifty years, or maybe a hundred and fifty, depending on the evolution of Pres-X-2. Planning a business model so far ahead is more daunting than she originally thought. In fact, she hadn't originally thought much about it at all. If some mass die-off happens again like the Great Unrest years ago, how would the business cope?

As she's keeping pace, she gets out her phone, then loads up the Sunday Score Supplement article, accidentally stepping on someone's foot, her mouth too dry to apologise. The article is expired, and she can't read it without subscribing with enough details to make her uncomfortable, yet headlines elsewhere quote the article, and every social media platform is awash with new and exciting ways to expand credit you didn't even know you had and up your Score. Regular flower deliveries, cinema membership, ordering a new bicycle years before that model is manufactured, booking holidays years in advance, home insurance paid years in advance, fiftieth birthday party, sixtieth birthday party, in fact, she could book celebrations for every single birthday she's likely to have for the rest of her life. How long that life will be is the question. Zia's birthday is coming up.

That's one she could do. She bookmarks the page and mentally plans to arrange something later, then puts her phone away. She's not going to get into the credit maxing trap. Just those essentials are enough.

Past the betting shops, which are also now taking bets on credit, Ava makes it through the crowds outside and into the accountant's office. Mae's daughter is absent this time and Ava's greeted by a woman with the tidiest plait Ava has ever seen.

'Can I help you?' she asks, in a tone that does not imply she wishes to help.

'I'm here to see Mae.'

'She's busy right now.'

'I'll just have a seat and wait.'

Ava sits before the woman has time to protest. If she's learned anything from the tactics of the Eyes Forward, it's not to give people choices. She picks up some leaflets and flicks through them. The business accounting advice seems sound, sensible even, a far cry from most companies' overzealous promises and empty statements. When she's read them all, she starts on the posters. *Business accounting you can trust! Save with your self assessment. Strive to Score? Strive to succeed!* Ava winces at that last one. Meddling with an Eyes Forward slogan seems crass.

'Mae will see you now.'

After sitting in awkward silence for so long, the receptionist's voice makes Ava jump which she fails to disguise as she stands, then walks towards the office door.

Mae's shoulders sink a little when she sees her. 'So, not a client then.'

Ava remembers why she liked her so much the first time they met—such honesty is a rarity these days. 'I would like to be. I've lowered the Life Score requirement of my funeral home from 700 to 600. Business is very busy. I have some spreadsheets and accounts here.'

Mae narrows her eyes slightly and takes the paperwork, scanning through it with pursed lips. 'Prepayment plans for people this young?'

'They want the credit, apparently. What can I say? It's good for business. That and lowering the Score requirement.'

'Sensible move, given the current situation.'

'The situation being that sub 750 Preserved seem to be extremely accident prone?'

'I wouldn't know. I try to ignore the news.'

'Also a sensible move.'

Mae continues to scan through, inputting some figures onto her computer while Ava sits patiently, noticing with a degree of awe the tidiness of Mae's desk, the precise placements of every piece of stationary, not a speck of dust on the bookshelf.

'I can have a better look through this in a couple of days and get a management pack over to you,' Mae says.

'That would be great, thanks.'

'Although just from initial impressions, this could boost your business's worth considerably. And your Score, of course.

I'd say carry on like this, and you could be hitting 700 in a year or so.'

Ava sits a little straighter and squares her shoulders. 'I'd like to hit 700 now, or as soon as possible. How many prepayment plan sign-ups do you think I'll need? I also need to employ at least one other staff member.'

'Keen to get Pres-X-2?'

Mae's bluntness makes Ava's posture bow for a second before she rights herself. 'It's not for me,' she says, enunciating careful-ly. 'It's for my aunt to get Pres-X.'

'Well, that's just down to 650 now, so you could hit that—'

'No,' Ava's interruption sounds sterner than she intends, and she takes a breath. 'She has to have the high Score treatment. What we spoke about before. . .' Ava leans in close and dips her voice. 'I figured it out. There is a difference—'

'I don't think it's okay for me to be hearing this,' Mae says, leaning away, shaking her head.

'I won't say anymore. But I need to get to 700, 750 to be sure, in case I don't qualify for employee discount. Can you tell me what I need to do?'

Mae looks at Ava for a while, a rare moment of lingering eye contact from her. 'Of course. That much is my job. But you should also know that businesses where the staff have taken Pres-X-2 are already becoming more successful than those who haven't. There was a study published just today. You should check what your competition is up to.'

'Yeah, thanks. I'm getting free Pres-X-2.'

Mae's mouth upturns. Ava can't tell if she's impressed or mocking. 'Congratulations,' she says. Definitely mocking.

'Piss off.'

Mae snorts a laugh and Ava follows, surprised at her own brashness.

'Why you?' Mae asks.

'Best performing Society Police, apparently. Plus, my ex put a word in.'

Mae's mocking face morphs into shock. 'You're a Society snitch?'

'Don't judge. Life is hard. I don't even want it.'

'Well, you'll be the envy of the Society,' Mae says, so much ridicule in her voice.

Ava smirks. 'It's not like I even have a choice. Any suggestions on how I can get out of it?'

'Maybe be like one of the poor people you spy on and commit a crime. What is it, two strikes and no Pres-X?'

'That applies to Pres-X-2 as well?'

'I was joking. As a professional, I am obviously not condoning you commit a crime. And they'd probably strip you of your Score as well.'

Ava slumps, pressing her back into the chair. 'Hey, thanks for the photos, by the way.'

'I don't know what you're talking about,' Mae says with a wink.

'I've read stuff online, you know, on the dark web. Other women are unhappy. Secretly. They're not pleased with the way things are heading. There are rumours the Eyes Forward are planning to curtail women's rights more. There are still people out there wanting to fight this, some called Sisters and Spies.'

A sharp intake of breath from Mae as Ava's words snap her attention. She stays very still for a moment before shaking off whatever she was thinking. 'Well, getting involved with that is probably a good way to have your Pres-X-2 treatment taken away.'

'Sounds like a plan then.' Ava laughs.

'I'll get back to you about the accounts. I'll send you an email when your paperwork is ready.'

Ava thanks her, then leaves, an uneasy feeling bristling up her back. There was something there, something Mae wanted to say but didn't. She walks back down Friar Street, past businesses with mirrors on the outside, empty shelves on the inside, ruckuses breaking out on the street as phones are held up, antagonising each other, striving to Score in the most malicious of ways. At least the extra money will be enough to cover some new locks on the doors and CCTV cameras inside the home. With this level of hype and stress on the streets, she's going to need it.

Chapter 43

During the Great Unrest

Lucia never signed her peace treaty. It'd been a couple of months since that meeting, and she still wasn't tempted to sign it. Nonsense treaty, she called it. Backwards treaty. Discriminatory treaty. She had all sorts of words for it, none of which were peace. And why should she sign it? She hadn't caused any trouble. None. Not one bit. She told them to stop the trouble ages ago. And she didn't need some stupid high Score to make her be a good person. Those scoundrels in the meeting were after a bribe. Is that what all the talk had been about? Using it to get wealthy and Pres-X? Oh, she wanted to spit on their doorsteps.

She could rely on Luigi and Daphne. They wouldn't be so easily swayed. They had a daughter to think of. She was still young enough to have a family. They'd fight for her right to have children, to keep her body autonomy. She met them at their funeral home at close of business one Friday, planning on dinner after. When she arrived, some protests in the street were heating up.

Luigi was kneeling on the floor when she arrived, a large sheet under him, paintbrush in hand. 'Oh, Lucia,' he said as he startled. 'I forgot you were coming today.'

'Luigi!' she said, staring at the sheet. 'What are you doing?'

'It's a peaceful protest, there won't be an issue.'

'But. . .but. . .you don't mean it. Surely you don't mean it.'
He couldn't mean it.

Sterilise women, save the Society!

'It's for the best, Lu. Don't you see? There won't be peace
when we're at each other's throats. This is a compromise.'

'Compromise?' She snarled that word through her teeth.
Bloody compromise. 'You want women sterilised? No. I can't
believe that. . .' Then she realised. 'You've sold out, haven't you?
For that drug! For that bloody drug!'

'They've promised they won't roll it out to everyone. The
world won't be taken over by Preserved. Just some select citizens
get to live a longer life—'

'But you were so against it.'

'I was against universal rollout, for sure. But a few people
having it—where's the harm?'

He was speaking so calmly and rationally it was like he
should be saying something else entirely. He couldn't mean
those words, he just couldn't. 'What would Ava say? I barely
recognise you.'

'I'll even lower the Life Score of this place, so business will be
fine.'

'Business! That's all you care about. What about nature?
What about God?'

Even through the thick windows across the front of the business, the chanting from outside was loud and clear. Not the

words, as they were all so mixed up. The hate, though, the anger. The banging on windows and stamping feet.

'There have been far less killings these past couple of weeks. Don't you see, Lu. This is for the best—for the whole Society.'

'You were brainwashed by that man, whatshisname, I've forgotten. And the other one. And my Ken. They're evil, Luigi. My brother wouldn't think such things.' She held her hands to her ears and shut her eyes, squeezing them so tightly they hurt. Her pulse banged through her temples. 'Not my brother,' she said, over and over. 'Not my brother.'

When she opened her eyes, the door was swinging shut, the funeral home empty. Her head still hurt, a mixture of pain and numbness, a cloudy patch in her vision that she couldn't blink away. What was she to do? Where had Luigi gone? He was there just now. The keys were on the front desk, so she went and locked the door. But she couldn't take the keys, that wouldn't be right. Luigi would need them when he got back from wherever he went. Where was he going? She struggled to remember. She screwed up her forehead, trying to remember. Walking down the hallway, she checked the office, then out back, calling his name and Daphne's. There was no answer.

So she sat and waited.

Hordes of people marched past the home, so many, faces were squished against the glass, banging on the windows. Troublemakers, the lot of them. She turned her back. No way was she going to let them in. It got dark quickly, and when she turned, all she could see was the imprint of cheeks and hands against the window, accompanied by plenty of screaming. Oh, these riots always had plenty of screaming.

Luigi and Daphne must have gone home. She'd wait until the march stopped, then join them. If only she could remember where they were going.

Lucia dozed off for a while, waking with a little drool on her chin and even more confusion in her head. Her cheek felt numb on one side, her temple throbbed on the other. Where was she? She looked around. The coffins and the leaflet displays reminded her. The funeral home. Why was she here? She was probably meant to see Luigi. That daft brother of hers. He always was quite inconsiderate.

She decided to leave, not really sure why she'd stayed. What day was it? Was she working today? Maybe she'd pop in and see Mo and her little dog. Her baby must be due soon.

Chapter 44

10 years after the Great Unrest

Afternoon at the funeral home is slightly less busy than morning, and Ava manages all the prepay sign-ups without Max's help. He has a full cold room to prep, and if he's going to be gone soon, she needs him to be on schedule now. She hasn't had a moment to advertise for any new staff and makes a mental note to do that as soon as she can, though Max seems quite irreplaceable at the moment. She's gutted, if she's being honest with herself. She wishes there was another way.

Ava spots Frida come in towards the end of the afternoon, and Frida gives her a little wave as she walks through. Ava waves back but has no time to stop her with another client sitting with her. It's not professional for Frida to be back there.

Just as Ava's closing the doors, exhausted, and having taken more money than she ever imagined in one day's trading, an Eyes Forward truck rolls up outside. Not the usual sleek SUV style truck, but a barred-window truck with a bolted door at the back and only the cab doors opening, still jet black with the Eyes

Forward logo on the side. The men exiting aren't in the usual suits, but black trousers and shirts with a stab vest over the top. Ava starts to sweat. Is joking about committing a crime now a crime?

They make no pleasantries as they enter, all three of them, hands hovering over batons.

'Can I help you, gentlemen?'

They don't reply straight away but walk around the reception area, looking behind coffins and displays. 'Anyone else on the premises?'

'My employee in the cold room, and his girlfriend—'

'That's them! This way!' The three men pick up their pace and run down the corridor, opening the office door first, then the cold room, Ava chasing after them. 'What's this about?'

Max and Frida startle as the men burst into the cold room, and Max puts his arm over Frida as the officers approach, Ava standing useless in the doorway.

'Frida Simmons?'

'Yes?' she replies, her voice just a squeak.

'You are under arrest for attempting to flee the country illegally while pregnant. You will come with us to a termination facility immediately.'

Ava exhales as though she's been winded, and while Max's arm stiffens around Frida, his legs weaken and his eyes are as red and wide as they can be.

'No!' Frida screams, wrapping her arms around Max. 'Max, stop them! No! I can't!'

There is little she can do to resist. Max is no match for the three of them and their batons. One man has his baton raised above his head, his eyeballing stare more intimidating than Max's. Two of the men grab Frida's wrists. They'd yank her arms out of their sockets before they'd let go. Her feet drag along the floor, her body contorting as her skinny arms are held in place.

'Max! No!'

Max cries from behind, 'Frida! Please, let her go!' His voice is small, pathetic really, his scrawny frame no more than a mild annoyance for even one of them, let alone three. Ava steps to one side, letting them pass as Frida continues to bawl and kick. As quickly as they entered the home, they're gone, a trembling Max left standing at the doors watching the truck drive away.

'Max. I'm so sorry—'

'You bitch! It was you, wasn't it? You're some big-shot Society snitch! No one else knew! She'd kept her implant hidden. It was only you we told.'

'No! Max, I would never—'

'How could you!'

He runs out of the door in the direction of the truck, leaving Ava alone, shaking.

***

Ava waits at the funeral home for an hour after closing, in case Max comes back for his jacket, phone, or anything else he left behind before running off. She makes a cup of sweet tea while she waits and when that doesn't settle her, she does some push-ups until she's sweated through her shirt. Raising her heart rate doesn't calm her, but it funnels her anger, clears her head of all the *maybe it's for the best* nonsense and laser focuses her attention on what she just saw. It's not the first time she's seen a woman carted off by people who see her uterus as a threat, but it's the first time in a decade.

The closed-door dealings of the peace treaties are so reminiscent of the Enough rallies years ago when seen from such a close angle—when it affects someone she knows. It's been easy to assume the Society got it right, and the Eyes Forward settled the Great Unrest when the consequences of such were hidden from view. Most consequences.

Her implant still feels foreign under her skin. Is this peace or appeasement? The years since the Great Unrest don't feel like the idiosyncratic era of calm and prosperity the Eyes Forward would have everyone believe. It's just history repeating itself, as it always does. Sometimes it takes weeks or years or centuries, but it always does, like some cyclical time-warp of anti-women crap.

Her arms hang limply by her side, and she wishes she counted how many push-ups she's done. Must be a new record for her. Max still hasn't returned, and after Ava has paced the whole place a hundred times, she sends him an email and locks up to leave. There's still an hour of visiting time left, and Ava races to the hospital, arriving empty-handed and out of breath, legs burning from the effort. She dreads the docked Life Score points she may receive from dodging red lights and cycling too fast.

Zia is sitting up and chatting to her ward neighbour when Ava arrives.

'Ava, dear. How lovely you're here.'

'Zia.' She gives her a kiss on the forehead, avoiding the bruising. 'How are you?'

'Oh, never better. You know they bring me cups of tea whenever I want.' Her face is still swollen and purple, her speech a little slurred but really, she's looking a hell of a lot better than Ava imagined.

'What have the doctors said? Is your head wound okay? They said you had a mini-stroke.'

'Load of nonsense. I'm absolutely fine. You look a little flushed, though, and pale. How do you manage that combination? Is it makeup? Are you low on iron?'

'I'm fine, Zia. I'm going to speak with the doctor.'

Twenty minutes of precious visiting time is wasted roaming the corridors trying to find a doctor, but when she does, the childlike looking doctor is kind and attentive. 'It was a very minor stroke, we think. We're keeping her in just tonight for observation. She can likely go home tomorrow.'

'She's taking this medication, an injection, Memorexin. She's due her dose in a day, I think. Is that what caused the stroke?'

The poisoned Pres-X is on her mind, and she can't discount that thought. What if they're trying to bump off all the elders?

'That is not a risk with this medication,' the doctor says, resolutely, but Ava can't quell her doubts.

'And the stroke, it won't affect her eligibility for Pres-X?'

'Not this time. She will have to forgo a treatment or two of the Memorexin. We don't want to shock her brain right now. Her memory might slip a little more without maintaining the doses.'

'But Pres-X. Not too much of a slip to interfere with Pres-X?'

'It will, as always, depend on how much damage there already is. If it were more serious, then it could. It would be best to consider Pres-X treatment as soon as possible.'

Ava bites her lip, annoyed—even the doctor knows so little. 'Thanks, doctor.'

She walks back to Zia's room, then stands in the doorway for a while. Zia's laughing with the patient in the bed next to her. If it weren't for the bruises, she'd seem completely well. Ava's chest inflates, and her heart warms, just a little.

With her score increasing, work going well, and Zia recovering, Ava feels the most hopeful she has in a long time.

Chapter 45

Ten points deducted for her haphazard cycling skills, the morning message tells Ava. That sweet time in the 600 club was all too brief. She arrives at work already tired, anticipating another busy day like the one before and unsure if Max is going to be around to help. Her email pleaded her innocence, but she can't blame him for thinking the worst of her. The whole damned Society will hate her when she ends up on TV in some XL Medico publicity crap.

When she arrives, the lights are off except for a torchlight. In the early winter dimness of the morning, this seems odd. A power cut? Perhaps Max is in already, and he's looking for his phone. She lets herself in, then walks through to the cold room. The open office door catches her attention on the way. All the paperwork is on the floor, the filing cabinet overturned, and a framed photo that was on the desk is smashed to bits.

Her heart races as she backs against a wall. A break in? Surely not. Who breaks into a funeral home? She loads up the Society

Police app on her phone, then grabs a wooden chair leg that has been broken off. One of her father's chairs. The solid wood is so heavy, she struggles to hold it with one hand. She takes a few breaths, reminds herself that she is well trained for this sort of thing, and the trembling in her hands eases. She stops and listens for a moment. A faint rustle comes from the cold room. On tiptoes, she skulks towards the door, waiting outside a few seconds before kicking it in and shouting, 'FREEZE!'

Max sits on the floor in a crumpled puddle of his own tears.

'Max! What the—' She drops the wooden chair leg and crouches beside him.

'They gave her an abortion. They knocked her out, killed the baby, then dumped her on the doorstep of her flat like a bag of rubbish. Took half her Life Score points and half of mine. Nan's. What she'd left me.'

'Oh, Max. I'm so, so sorry.'

'She won't speak to me. Thinks it was me. I told her it was you, and she blames me for that too.'

'I didn't, Max. I swear I would never.'

He shuffles farther away. 'It's over. All because we told you. I never should have trusted you.'

'Oh, Max. I never told anyone. I'm so, so sorry.'

His body convulses with sobs. She can't be mad at him for trashing the place. The poor thing. She rubs his arm and attempts to console him, missing Erin more than ever.

From the reception, someone calls out, 'Hello?'

Dammit. Why didn't she lock the door? She checks her watch. 8:55. With a sigh, she props Max up against the cupboard. 'Wait right here. I'll be back in a moment.'

She walks hurriedly to reception and almost stops dead in her tracks when she sees Mrs Constance standing there, all smiles.

'Ava, you're looking a little peaky. You getting enough rest?'

'Mrs Co—Sorry—Flick. How can I help?' Ava says, walking towards the entrance to guard the door. The queue outside is already forming, and she wants no more early customers. She turns her back on the door, grateful they can't see in through the reflective glass. As Mrs Constance faces Ava, her perfume wafts around. Almonds, lilies, hibiscus.

'I just came by to say hello and to say what a lovely time I had the other night. We should certainly do it again some time.'

'You and Kim seemed to get on well.'

'Oh, she's fine, yes. But it was sitting with you I enjoyed the most. I've just reached a Score of 900. Can you believe it? And there's this very exclusive restaurant in Henley I thought we should go to. Just you and me this time.'

Ava can't help but raise her eyebrows at that. '900. That's quite an achievement.'

'Yes. Sixty points I was awarded for informing the Eyes Forward of just one illegal pregnancy. They do take these things awfully seriously, you know.'

Ava's stomach knots, and she fails to draw breath. 'I'm sorry. You? You snitched on a pregnancy?'

'Yes. Nasty business, these unregulated pregnancies. The Enough made very sensible demands, I think. And, from the sounds of it, that employee of yours didn't want the baby anyway.'

'Max's baby!' Less of a rasp now, more of a retch. 'That was you?' Ava's head hurts. She squeezes her eyes shut and rubs her eyebrows.

'And sixty points as a reward.' The smugness in her voice makes Ava recoil. 'Now, how are you set for—' Her sentence doesn't finish. Instead, a dull thud and squeaking yelp comes from Mrs Constance.

Ava stops rubbing her brows and opens her eyes. Mrs Constance isn't in her view at all. Max is, trembling, red-faced, with the wooden chair leg in his hand. Ava follows the blood dripping from the chair leg down onto the floor where Mrs Constance's head looks remarkably like Mr Constance's did when he arrived.

Ava's once again exceedingly grateful for the reflective strips over the glass windows. The crowd gathering outside is none the wiser.

Max is unmoving besides his shaking arm, struggling with the weight of the chair leg that's still in exactly the same place it was when it collided with Mrs Constance's head.

Shit.

Ava thinks for a moment. *What to do. What to do. What to do?*

She steps toward the front door, opens it, then shouts to the crowd gathering, 'Opening late today. Sorry, power issue. Come back at ten o'clock.' Somehow, she manages to say that without a single quiver.

As she closes, then locks the door, Max still stands there, knuckles blanched over the wooden leg, staring at Mrs Constance lying on the floor, transfixed by her vacant stare. Ava bends, moves those caramel curls out of the way, then checks for a pulse. Stupid to check really. Her brains litter the floor.

'Max?'

He still doesn't move. Doesn't respond.

'Max!'

He jumps, like he hadn't even known Ava was there before. 'Yes, boss?'

'Fire up the furnace. Go, go. It's just like a normal cremation, okay? Luckily, we don't have any other cremations today.'

'Now?'

'Yes, Max,' she says, softly coaxing. 'Go on.'

Ava follows him part of the way, then collects a trolly from the cold room. When Max is back, without a word said between them, they lift Mrs Constance onto the trolley, wheel her to the crematorium, then tip her into the furnace. They turn up the flames, and Ava's chest sizzles with guilt as she watches the fire engulf the body. Guilt for the killing, guilt for what befriending Mrs Constance has led to but, mostly, guilt for visualising Mrs Constance's points turning to ash.

900 Life Score points crumbling to cinders, wasted. The fact that she mourns that loss makes her as bad as any of them. Yet she can't shake the feeling, can't rid her heart of its frugality of benevolence.

Compassion is an emotion for the wealthy. Anger is more economical. And Ava is angry at damn well everything. The flames spit and crackle in a wrathful dance of deception and squander. The effluvium of Mrs Constance's life drifts up the chimney, filtered and purified, to fumigate the atmosphere with their crimes.

Ava steps away, swallowing back the thick soup of emotions that threaten to inch their way up her throat and spill onto the floor. Her breath shudders as she wills her heart to slow, and she rubs her cheeks, her temples, forcing the blood to reflow, for the fug of vexation to lift. Max is standing just behind, silently trembling. In the corner of her vision, she sees him wiping his eye, blowing his nose.

Still without a word, they collect cleaning supplies and mop up the mess on the floor.

At 9.50 a.m. they put the cleaning supplies away, then stand in the corridor for a moment. Max's trembling is barely perceptible now. Ava gets them some sugary drinks from the fridge they usually reserve for clients after particularly teary moments.

'Max?'

'Yes, boss?'

Her lips move a moment, tight, unable to unclench before she finds her words. 'This never happened. Okay? If Frida asks, you still have no clue how the Eyes Forward found out. Assume they intercepted your internet searches. You hear me?'

'Yes, boss.' His eyes are on the floor where the blood once was, the stain in some invisible part of the spectrum the two of them will always be able to see.

'You okay to help me with pre-plan sign-ups for a couple of hours?'

'I think so.'

'It's just business as usual.'

After a couple of breaths and checking her reflection, Ava opens the doors, then lets the queue in.

What's the worst that can happen? She wonders as she loads up the prepayment plan paperwork for client after client. She's now a criminal. Maybe they really won't make her go on that god-awful TV show after all.

***

Ava's face is now adorning the front page of several social media channels, the envy of the Society, it says, to be receiving free Pres-X-2. It's her ID mugshot where she looks more like a criminal than Society Police.

If the slipper fits.

She doesn't read the comments, can't bear to see what the citizens will be saying about her. Calling her a grass, a snitch, some Score-digging traitor, elitist. She can only imagine. As soon as her face pops up, she scrolls past it, turns the TV off, whatever is needed to take her face off the screen.

In moments, she's looking at her computer anyway. She has a long line of prepay clients to deal with. The news and social pop-ups, as she loads up their forms and ID checks, doesn't give quite enough time for idling at her computer. She exits what she can, minimises everything else, then arranges another twenty-two prepayment plans.

Every new client that comes in, she expects to look down their nose at her, to treat her with scathing suspicion and make some joke or quip about her Society Policing. But the ones that do mention it, thank her. They actually thank her, shake her hand and say she's doing a marvellous job of keeping the streets safe, of helping to do away with the scourge of low Scorers who cause so many problems. Ava's solemn face thanks them in return, and she gives a small nod, hoping her cheeks aren't as red as they feel.

At lunch, they shut the doors, hang the 'be back in an hour' sign in the window, then put the kettle on. Max has been working in the cold room for the last hour, and Ava goes in to check on him. He's busy, working quickly, frantic even. Six corpses embalmed, all with their hair and makeup done and cheeks filled. The cold room is a mess though, clutter everywhere and Max is losing things as quickly as he's finding them.

'The cremation is complete,' he says with a jittery voice. 'So much quicker than Nan and the other Preserved. Super quick, really, compared to today's times, so not too bad for the finances. I'll pay, of course. If you want. Dock my wages. But it's done, anyway, all gone. Like it never happened. Haha. What never happened? Nothing! Ha! Just like we said. My baby is dead and so is she. Who? No one! And the burn rate was like the old days. Same time as Mr Co—' He stops short at saying his name. 'Same time as the old, high Scoring Preserved.'

Of course it's the same burn rate. Mrs Constance had Pres-X before it was past its expiry date.

Max is still talking, rambling on, barely stopping for breath. She steps up and grabs his shoulders, grasping with all her strength and digging her nails in.

'Max. Shut. Up.'

His eyes meet hers, and through her taut fingers she feels his tension ease off a little. His chest rises more slowly, the loud exhale that follows long and controlled. 'Sorry, Ava. I'm sorry. Shit, I'm sorry. I'm so fucking sorry.'

Her hold on his shoulders isn't enough to stop his shakes, and his body convulses. She draws him in for a hug, the same way Zia did when she learned her parents had died, when Mandisa broke up with her, when she grazed her knee as a child. The way that is done by parents and aunts and family to console and offer empathy when their hearts share in sadness, when they want to make you feel supported and that they're there with you, when the thin film of happiness pops like a bubble and all the sorrow spills out. For that's all she feels at that moment when Max's jittery ramble collapses to despair.

'It's okay, Max,' she says, soothing as his tears wet her shirt. 'It's okay. It's all going to be all right.'

Chapter 46

Ava's implant turns gold just as she locks the front door, then starts to clear up, and it stays gold, not just a flicker. Finally, her fertility is negligible enough for her to be acceptable. She considers briefly going out for a drink to celebrate until she remembers that Zia got home from hospital a couple of hours ago, and a celebratory drink after covering up a murder is perhaps bad karma.

A cold chill shakes through her at that last thought, but she shuts it away. Never think about it again. Compartmentalise life's traumas. It's done. She sent Max home once he calmed down, once he stopped apologising and his tears dried. She told him to take his B-Well and get some sleep—to take a double dose, triple if needed. She'll figure out how to get him more later.

She almost laughs when she recalls her conversation with Mae. Commit a crime. They'll never give you Pres-X-2 then. Ha! Convenient. Although a crime of this magnitude, they'll probably never let her see the light of day.

Before she logs out of her computer, a news headline flashes across her screen. 'New initiative by the Eyes Forward!' She clicks and Monika Skye, complete with an entourage of smiling women behind her, fills the screen.

'Women are truly valued in the Society. Preserved or not, fertile or not. And to show that value, all public sector female employees who are not yet of age to take Pres-X-2 are to have their wages altered. The women lucky enough to work in these fields are to have half their wages given as beauty credits. That's right! Beauty credits. They will have a catalogue of products and treatments to choose from and will be first in line with orders. This will save all public sector employees from suffering the stock shortages and empty shelves we have seen of late. Women will know that the Eyes Forward have their best interests at heart.

'This bonus will obviously stop once the woman becomes of Pres-X-2 age. But this prescription will help women look and feel their best throughout those difficult years and keep the Society looking its absolute best!

'The beauty credits will be non-returnable or transferable. Ladies, they are just for you! So, make the most out of them!'

Ava rubs her ears, blinks a few times, just to confirm, yep, she definitely heard that right. Damned beauty credits. For a moment she considers loading up the dark web and searching for reactions from the Sisters and Spies, thinking of Mae and her little girl. But then, what's the point? If that's what's happening, she knows there's little she can do about it, and she wouldn't want to. As Mae said, getting involved with such a thing would be bad news. If they stripped her Life Score, Zia would never qualify for Pres-X. It's a strong bargaining chip the Eyes Forward have. A ransom. What more effective way to make people behave than to punish them with mortality if they don't?

She groans and turns her computer off, thankful she's not a public sector employee. How long before they insist on this rollout everywhere? The streets are lined with mirrors, and the Eyes Forward enforcing vanity on all citizens makes Ava swallow back bile. As always though, she's hollowed out, powerless, alone in her views against the Eyes Forward. The odd few that seem to agree are hidden behind dodgy internet and code names. For the rest of the Society, more and more women are turning into ornaments.

She cycles home without the heavy dread and guilt she should have. She actually feels lighter. The news won't affect her as she's finally of safe age. She has one less problem. Is that her fertility or Mrs Constance or Max knowing she didn't snitch on Frida? Maybe all three. Maybe it's that Zia's home. She races up the hill, though keeping to the rules of the road. When she called the hospital, they said a friend picked up Zia. God knows who, but it was what Zia wanted. Another sign that her memory is coming back, remembering old friends.

Parked in the bike rack at her apartment block is a white and purple bike Ava recognises but cannot place. Must be a friend of Zia's from years ago. She runs upstairs through a now almost completely empty block, then bursts through her apartment door.

'Zia! How are—' She cuts off when she sees who's sitting with Zia. 'Mandi?' Mandisa is there smiling, in a well-fitted trouser suit, her XL Medico 'product development for B-Well' badge pinned to her lapel.

'Ava,' Zia says. 'Look who came to see me in hospital and took me home. I got on a bus! My old friend, Mandisa. She hasn't changed a bit.'

Ava pauses a while, then looks from one face to the next, her own pinching. 'She's not really your old friend though, Zia.'

'Oh, but she is. I remember it clearly now. Your parents adored her too. How happy they would be if they'd known you two got together.'

Ava screws up her eyes, as if squinting would turn Mandisa into someone else. Nope. It's still her. All smiley and beautiful and confusing the hell out of Ava. 'What? My parents never knew Mandi.' She shouldn't bother arguing. She knows she shouldn't. Zia's memory is filling in the blanks with nonsense, that's all.

'Of course they did,' Zia says. 'From the meetings.'

Meetings?

'Ava!' Mandisa says, giving Ava no time to think. 'Oh, my. Look at your implant.' She stands, then walks to Ava. 'That's it then. They'll be collecting you for your Pres-X-2 soon.'

'Oh, that's a shame,' Zia says. 'I always hoped you'd have a baby. Too late now. Still, good news about your treatment.'

'I've been waiting for you, Ava,' Mandisa says. She looks younger than she did when they first met. Her cheeks are lifted, her eyelids tighter. She takes the final step towards Ava. She's still smiling, her lips slightly parted, so close now, Ava can smell her soapy freshness. It's hard to think about anything else except Mandisa's scent. 'I wanted to protect you, you know—from all the Time's Up stuff. You'd be on their radar, what with your parents. . . Anyway, none of that matters now. I had to leave, you understand? To progress with them, to get promoted, so I could complete my work. But now, now you work for XL Medico. They trust you, which is great for our cause. I'm so excited for what this all means for us, Ava.'

Her breath is on Ava's face, so close. Ava's eyes are transfixed, her heart hammers in her chest.

'You understand now, don't you? Once you have the treatment, you can climb the ladder at XL Medico too. There's so much good we can do together.'

Ava can't say a word, can't even move, she's zoned in on those soft, slightly parted lips, her stomach fluttering, her lips dry.

'It's you and me, Ava. It was always going to be you and me,' Mandisa says, then kisses her firmly on the mouth.

Ava holds the door frame as her knees slacken. Mandisa leans in closer, her body pressing against Ava's while Ava suppresses a groan and reciprocates the kiss, greedily, her body turning to jelly. Mandisa pulls away, leaving Ava wanting, and suddenly acutely aware that her elderly aunt is in the room. She holds onto the door frame tighter, righting herself.

'I'll see you soon?' Mandisa says.

Ava means to say, 'Yeah, sure. Soon,' but what actually comes out of her mouth is something like 'Yehumoh. Sho.' She turns around the door frame as Mandisa shimmies past, calling good-bye to Zia as she leaves.

'How wonderful,' Zia says. 'I haven't had time to make dinner. Shall we get takeaway?'

'Huh?' Ava says, still looking in the direction of Mandisa. 'Yeah, sure. Wait, hang on. Can we talk? Meetings? As in, Time's Up meetings? Mandisa was at those?'

'Oh, yes. She was really helpful. Such a lovely girl. I told her about that peace deal years ago, even though I said I wouldn't.' She holds her finger to her lips in a childish way.

Ava runs to the cabinet, then takes out the paperwork Zia had given her before. The contracts. She flicks through, much she doesn't understand, but still she reads, skimming, so many mentions of brotralapram welloxatinine. Then she reads another part. Brotralapram welloxatane. She says that, again and again. Such a small difference almost looks like a typo. She kicks herself for not noticing it before. It's there in black and white, all her suspicions confirmed. An alkaline form and a neutral form of B-Well. The contract is dated seven years ago, as an extension of the peace treaty. The Time's Up consented to this. Mandisa worked for XL Medico then. She consented to this.

She reaches for Zia's cup of tea and finishes it, wishing the caffeine was stronger, then reads again. They always knew the vanadium would run out. Of course they did. Everyone knew.

The B-Well had been planned all along. The alkaline form for the high Scorers. The low Scorers were never meant to cope.

'Zia! The Pres-X. It was always meant to expire. The Time's Up knew it would go bad. The Eyes Forward knew.'

'Of course. Such ghastly stuff. Not natural at all to live so long. People expire. Medicines expire. It's God's way.'

'And the treatment, the B-Well, they're only giving the good B-Well to the high Scorers.'

'I don't know what that is. B-whatever. That's all gibberish to me. But that Pres-X is a menace. Pizza or curry?'

'Pizza. So, you, Mandisa, the Eyes Forward, the Pres-X roll-out—'

'Oh, dear. They're shut today. Curry then?'

'Sure. So listen, Zia, the Eyes Forward and the Pres-X rollout, they're harming people with the old Pres-X. You, they, planned this?'

'Oh, look at you.' She takes Ava's face in her hands. 'You look quite stressed, dear. Looks like you're getting a hot flush. Shame. I always hoped you'd have a baby.'

***

When Ava goes to bed that night, she should be thinking about the contract and the peace treaty or about Mandisa's ploy with the Eyes Forward to poison the low Scoring elders. She should be tossing and turning in disgust and anger, reeling from what Mandisa's done. But instead, she dwells on their kiss, on what Mandisa said, *It's you and me, Ava.* It hasn't been her and Mandisa for so long, yet when Mandisa said it, every fibre of her body wanted it. She still wants it, though as much as she desires another kiss, she can feel Mandisa's hands around her neck, affectionate at first, then a noose waiting to tighten. Millie and Erin's pink faces of despair flash before her, their cries and wails of misery.

Ava thumps herself on the head, trying to rid her brain of the hurt and the sadness. But, if she's being honest, it's not the pain she's trying to banish from her mind. It's desire. Mandisa broke up with her ages ago. There is no Ava and Mandisa. Mandisa doesn't want Ava as she is. She wants her younger, richer. Mandisa wants a different Ava, a high Score Ava. Mandisa wants Ava prettier, like she's not good enough now. Mandisa wanted to protect her. Ava wants Mandisa. . . No. She didn't mean to think it that way round. She shakes her head and starts her thought process again. Ava wants Mandisa. . . *Dammit!* When she rethinks it, it comes out the same. Ava wants Mandisa, she does, but Mandisa from before, before she changed into the safe age high Scoring ambitious woman, before she knew Mandisa was poisoning Society's elders. Ava wants the old Mandisa, how she was when they first met. Innocent and brilliant. Not this Mandisa.

She gets out of bed, turns the bedside light on, then looks in the mirror at her droopy breasts and lined face. A far cry from the Ava that Mandisa first met. It crushes her when she thinks that perhaps Mandisa wants the Ava from before she changed too.

Chapter 47

3 years after the Great Unrest

Lucia stopped working in the café a while ago. It was shut down and turned into a betting shop. It wasn't her fault. Not really. She left the oven on a few times. The fire brigade was cross, and then there was the whole expiry date incident. Everyone forgets what year it is sometimes, but the health inspector disagreed. She was due to retire anyway. Now, she thought, she might actually have time to read all those books.

She rose slowly today, a bit earlier than usual. The sun had not yet come up. She walked downstairs to find some suitcases and boxes in the hallway. Careless. A trip hazard. She moved around them and found a note on the counter:

Zia, just to remind you, we move into that apartment today. Removal company will come and collect the boxes later. There's coffee in the cupboard, and I've left you out some lunch. Ava. xx

Ava. She hadn't seen Ava in such a long time. Or was it yesterday? Such a lovely young woman. Luigi must be so proud of her.

Her chest ached a little when she thought of Luigi, though she couldn't place why.

After her coffee and the breakfast cereal that had been left out, she decided to walk to the library. A new book would take that chest ache away. Something with a happy ending and a nice couple, a young couple with their whole lives ahead of them. On the way, she stopped at a bakery and bought some bread for Ken, before she remembered she hadn't seen Ken in a long time. He'd turned into a bad man, somehow. Maybe he cheated. It was something awful, she was sure of that.

Then she remembered he'd died. She remembered her last words to him: You're dead to me. She didn't feel that sad about it. She'd grieved already, she thought so anyway.

There was a woman, very pretty thing, standing by the bakery. She smiled when Lucia approached and called her name in the most delicate voice.

'Lucia?'

'Yes.'

'It's me. Mandisa. Remember me from those meetings?'

'No.' Lucia couldn't remember any meetings.

'I was always the quiet one. We met the other day too. Said we'd catch up today.'

'Ah, well...since you're here anyway.' She seemed like a lovely girl, and Lucia could do with a good chat.

As soon as they sat, Lucia remembered everything. Almost everything. There was something about being somewhere familiar, indoors rather than under a dazzling sun that helped her brain to work again, something about the smell of tea, the rock cakes the bakery served up that sparked her memories.

'You should meet my niece, Ava. You'd like her. Let me show you a picture.'

'Sure,' Mandisa said. 'Again, every time, sure. And I really hope to meet her one day.'

'How have you been, dear? The new job going well?'

Mandisa nodded and swallowed her bite of cake. 'Nature has come through for us. You saw the news this morning?'

Lucia shook her head.

'The vanadium. It's totally gone now. The Pres-X is finally going to expire. It's what we've been waiting for.'

Lucia held her chest, a swell of hope filling her. 'It's going to run out? No, they'll find a way.'

'The Pres-X is going to expire, and we have a treatment for that, but they won't give it to everyone.' She took Lucia's hand then and leaned in close. 'You understand what I'm saying, Lu? It's the best I can do. Better than nothing, though. A compromise.'

A compromise. Someone else had promised her one of those once, and she was sure that wasn't a good thing. Still, this young lady said it so nicely. What could go wrong?

'Let's not confuse things,' Mandisa said. 'I have a meeting with the Eyes Forward and XL Medico later. I've worked with them for long enough now. They know I was part of your Time's Up—the peaceful Time's Up.'

'We never wanted any trouble,' Lucia said, looking into the distance, like she could see the past now.

'There are many Time's Up working for Eyes Forward. You remember Ian and Steve? They're quite influential now. We've figured it all out. How to stop Pres-X. People won't want it when they see the harm it does. I have it all written into this contract,' Mandisa said, handing Lucia some paperwork. 'It's all ready for them to sign. Here, take a copy in case you need to remember later. In case anything happens to me. Hide it away. Keep it safe. We're in this for the long game now. It'll be a few years before the plan will start to work. We'll have to wait.'

Lucia took the paper and slipped it straight into her bag. 'It sounds like you have it all under control, dear. I'm very proud of you. Have you seen my niece, Ava? You'd like her.'

Chapter 48

10 years after the Great Unrest

Sisters and Spies are all over the dark web, as well as whispers of discontent at the Eyes Forward, some messages in code and some plain as day. Like the latest Eyes Forward announcement, it was one more pebble falling into a pond, the ripples piling on top of other ripples. Small women's voices getting louder, bolder. Ava, piece of toast in hand, reads post after post of disgust and annoyance, talk of elections needed, and for equality to be installed.

Ava has barely finished her toast when there's a knock at the door. She slams her laptop shut and wipes butter from her mouth. Zia doesn't seem to hear it, too busy fiddling with the TV, trying to get it to turn on. Ava has unplugged it, not wanting to hear the news today, not wanting to hear any more minor stories of psychosis among the Society's elders, not wanting to hear the reality TV show hype and see her picture plastered across the screen. It'll take Zia an age to figure out what's wrong with the TV. Perhaps she never will.

EMMA ELLIS

Another knock at the door. She can't run. They'll know exactly where she is. She chews some more of her toast, swallows, then goes to the door. It's Chin Scar, another Eyes Forward representative, and the delightful Francine.

'Congratulations. Today is your big day,' Francine says, without a hint of excitement.

'You mean you and me are going to get that coffee?'

Francine doesn't understand humour, obviously, none of the Eyes Forward do.

Ava grabs her coat and two of them move to leave. Not Chin Scar. He stays put, staring into the apartment. Staring at Zia.

'We need to go, Ken,' Francine says.

'In a moment.'

Ava startles as she detects a hint of emotion in him. His usual robotic mannerisms morph into something entirely different.

He steps into the apartment and Ava moves in front of him. 'Erm, I didn't invite you in.'

He steps around her, as if she were a bit of furniture. 'Lucia?'

Zia looks up, turns her back on the telly, and stares at Chin Scar, her lips pinched shut.

'Lucia. It's been so long.' There's a neediness in his voice then, a quiver of longing.

Ava looks at his scar, knows he knew Zia from years ago. They were in the same photos. But this youthful-appearing man in front of her looks like no one she ever knew. But the name, Ken, she knows that name from years ago. *It can't be.*

'Lucia, don't you recognise me? It's me, your Ken.'

Zia takes a step back, waving the remote control in front of her. 'My Ken died years ago. Get out, you, before I knock you out!'

Ava steps in front of Chin Scar, a wide stance this time, her arms out on either side. 'She said leave.'

Chin Scar angles his head down, slowly, and takes in Ava's face for the first time, not just a cursory glance at her implant. 'You said all your family were dead.'

'I said my father was dead.'

He narrows his eyes at this, then his face softens as he looks past Ava, then back to Zia who is now backed against a wall. 'It's not too late, Lucia. I can get you treatment. Safe treatment. Lucia, look at me!'

'Hey! Leave her alone,' Ava says, not backing down. She'll knock him out if she has to. 'Get out of my apartment now.'

Francine grabs his arm. 'Come on, Ken. We have to go.'

Chin Scar straightens, a couple of blinks and he's back to his old self, young self, usual self. 'Yes. Quite right. Hurry up then. Let's get this done.'

Ava shuts the apartment door, craning her neck around for as long as she can to make sure Zia is okay. She's resumed pointing the remote control at the unplugged telly.

In the car, Chin Scar sits in the front, Francine next to Ava in the back. From this angle, she can't see his face, can't stare and try and place some recollection. She hardly knew her uncle, can't remember seeing him in her adult life. He never had any-thing to do with her family. It was Zia who was always there.

Zia, who took her on play dates and trips and showered her with love throughout her childhood. Zia, who moaned about her husband later in life. Zia, who was at Time's Up meetings while her husband went and had Pres-X. Ava remembers Zia's words, 'I mourned the man he was.' Ava's heart sinks a little. If she was so against Pres-X that it cost her her marriage, no way is Ava going to be able to convince her to have the treatment now.

The studios are an hour's drive and the four of them sit in stuffy silence. The sat nav giving directions is all there is to break up the awkward atmosphere. How is it this hot in early winter, Ava wonders as she fidgets and rubs her itchy back against the seats. The air con is rubbish, might as well not be on. All the questions she has for Chin Scar, she knows there's no point in asking. She's learned her lesson. Curious women don't get good answers. They become burdened with knowledge and morally torn. When Pandora opened that box, she wasn't enlightened; she cursed the world. So, Ava sits, silently. Like they said when they took her blood.

Good girl.

In the low morning sun, Ava can make out some view out the windows, the buses, pedestrian lanes, everyone going to work, getting on with their day, a normal day. They're not about to be paraded as a Society snitch live on air and be given pharmaccu-ticals against their will. Ava doesn't want Pres-X-2. She doesn't think so anyway. She could tell them now, about Mrs Constance, that she killed her. But she wouldn't want to get Max in trouble. Maybe they could DNA her ashes for proof. *Prison or Pres-X-2, Prison or Pres-X-2?* Ava repeats this to herself over and over. Mrs Constance snitched on Max. That trail would be there. The Eyes Forward would rather send down a low Scorer like Max than an almost 600 like Ava. She can't protect him if she doesn't keep her mouth shut. Prison would be crap anyway.

Despite her shower this morning, she can still taste Mandisa on her lips, still feel her body pressed into hers. She knows the price for that again is Pres-X-2.

The studios are bright, glaringly so. Ava's welcomed by some much friendlier people than the Eyes Forward representatives she travelled with. They still escort her though, like she's some flight risk. This is the Society. All eyes are our eyes. Where on earth do they think she could run off to? She gazes at the fire exit, then another, all too far. She'd be dragged back and chained to a seat if she tried to leg it. And then, as she's looking towards another exit sign, there's Mandisa.

'Ava,' the producer says. 'Here is a representative from XL Medico. Mandisa Johnson.'

Mandisa holds her finger to her lips when Ava starts to say she knows her already, then holds out her hand. 'Ava, so pleased to meet you. On behalf of XL Medico, thank you for your service to the Society.'

Ava takes her hand, shakes it with little enthusiasm. 'Right.'

'And congratulations on entering safe age. Quite a milestone for a woman.'

The producer walks away, instructing someone to show Ava to her dressing room, and Mandisa leans in a little closer. 'It's an angle. Quite a genius one, don't you think?'

'What?'

'Take Pres-X-2, find love. Best keep our feelings secret until after your treatment. Once you've regressed, we'll go public.'

'You're making a marketing thing out of this?'

'I know. Clever right?' Mandisa sneaks a peck on Ava's cheek, then walks away with a wink as the runner leads Ava to her changing room.

'So, this is our Society hero!' the woman in her changing room says. There's a rack of clothes, a beauty stand full of cosmetics next to some blinding spotlights, and two people to help get her ready.

'Easy on the makeup, Val,' the runner says. 'Don't go making her look any younger before she has the treatment. Just take the shine away.'

Val laughs and ushers him away. The other woman looks Ava up and down and picks out some outfits. Snug, fitted clothes in shiny materials. *Colourful* shiny materials. Accessories that look like a choking hazard and shoes she could never run away in. The sight of it all gives Ava a headache.

'Jules, go for that yellow and pink dress, the fitted one. It looks like she has a figure under this tent,' Val says to her colleague while untucking Ava's shirt. 'We want something low-cut to see her décolletage. Pres-X-2 works wonders on the décolletage. Isn't that right, Jules?'

Jules nods and holds the dress up to Ava, squinting her eyes, tilting her head to check the sizing.

'Is there any point in me protesting?' Ava says.

'Oh! They never said you were so funny!' Val says, sitting Ava at the beauty stand. Val stands behind and scrunches Ava's hair. 'Now, what to do with this? Nice to see some greys here. We'll highlight those for the cameras. That'll make the before and after shots really stand out. Show me your teeth?'

Ava pulls her lips back.

'Hmmm, not so bad. Don't show them off too much if you can avoid it. We really want them to see the worst of you now.'

Ava's phone pings, and she takes it from her pocket. It's Dan. *OMG is today your big day? Good luck!! You deserve this!*

She doesn't reply. Instead, she texts Max, asks him to open up or not—just deal with work. Based on their current takings, a closed day won't be the worst thing. There's no funeral booked in for today at least. She recites the names of the clients they have in the cold room, along with the dates booked for their services. Anything to take her mind off what Val is doing, rubbing her face, brushing on powder, lining her eyes. Anything to stop her thoughts that keep coming to the front of her mind, screaming she doesn't want this.

But the Eyes Forward have decided for her. And since when has females' body autonomy been a match for what men in power want? History repeats, she reminds herself.

Ava squints under the studio lighting, sitting on a recliner that forces her head to lie back and her eyes to look down to face the front—probably the most unflattering angle possible. Monika Skye and Berenice Whatsherface are all smiling, jiggling around on the spot like they need to pee. Ava is alone. This is her special day, she is told. The other winners will have their own show dedicated to them. Ava tucks the pink dress between her legs to save the cameras that view. The mic attached to her neckline is on, she was told before she sat. She doesn't dare to even breathe.

'One of the true heroes of the Society, don't you think so, Monika?'

'Absolutely. My favourite deli was vandalised a few weeks ago, and it was only due to the bravery of our Society Police that the perpetrators were punished.'

'And what a noble way to strive to Score! Good for the Society and good for your Score. Remember that everyone.' Berenice blows a kiss down the camera lens.

'This is why today's lucky winner is so deserving. Ava, you must be so excited?'

Ava looks from the camera to Berenice, then to the camera again, unblinking. They are standing right next to her, but Ava is so alone. 'Erm, yeah, thanks.'

'Wonderful. And just look at her. Can we get the camera here? Zoom in nice and close.' Berenice uses a long, manicured finger—the nail of which looks like it could slice through her jugular—to point out Ava's crow's feet, her wrinkled forehead, and her grey roots. 'No need for that hair dye after today!' She uses her thumb and forefinger to pull at Ava's eye bags and jawline. Just as Ava's eyes start to well up, the camera pans away, leaving Ava out of shot to talk about Society Policing, the wonders of Pres-X-2, and how spending is still trending.

Ava scans the studio audience. The bright lights and her reclined position make it impossible to search every face, but she tries. She needs to find someone who can look at her, not just her age and her marketing potential, but someone who sees through all of that and notices her. For someone to make her feel like she isn't so alone.

'For years humankind did not understand that avoiding UV was best, and that vitamins were needed to survive,' Monika says, in a way that implies she thinks she knows about everything. 'And now, we have learned so much more. Times have moved on. Creams and injections and face masks are stone age weaponry in the war against ageing. Our knowledge has evolved faster than our flesh.'

'You are so right, Monika.' Berenice nods along. 'What a time to be alive. A time when we don't have to fear time itself.'

Ava's toast threatens to rise up her throat at that comment.

A nurse comes over to rig up the IVs. One in each arm. One taps into her vein to remove her blood, the other into her artery to pump the Pres-X-2 in. Ava laughs silently. It's just like embalming. It's like she's a corpse.

'You'll feel a little light-headed. Feel free to relax and nod off.'

Ava turns her head to her side and there, in the wings of the studio, her eyes still searching for kin, she sees Mandisa. She's smiling at her, giving her a double thumbs up. Ava doesn't look at the IV bags then, nor at the nurse or presenters or Chin Scar standing next to Mandisa. She gazes into Mandisa's eyes as the room swims around her.

All else blurs away, and as she slips into sleep, all she can see is Mandisa.

Chapter 49

In the darkness of Ava's room, her phone flashes. It's on mute, the sound too annoying. The glare and noise aren't bad, she's just tired. So tired. She's been ignoring her phone for days, scared to look at the news in case there's a search for Mrs Constance. So far, nothing. No one has missed her, which gives Ava relief but also sadness. She was as lonely as she seemed. Also, she's afraid of seeing updates on herself. The TV show, clips of her treatment wearing that horrible dress, attempting to smile under the glare, smile away the lies, smile so widely that there's nothing else left of her except a smile. The rest could just disappear. What else is needed but a grinning mouth for show? That's all anyone seems to care about.

When ignoring the flashing becomes more annoying than looking at her phone, she reaches for it and reads the email.

Your Score has been updated. I have arranged your accounts. Come by my office to go through the figures. Mae

Would an email not suffice with all that information? But Ava's bored to tears and a trip into town is at least something to do. Three days she's been resting in her room, milking her recovery for all its worth, not wanting to talk to Mandisa or Zia. Mandisa has dropped off food, but mostly she sits in the living room chatting with Zia.

Ava watches a moment, hoping she'll always remember Zia this happy, remember her voice, her smile, the way she throws her hands around in gestures and laughs through her nose and forgets and remembers. How she looks at Ava with more care than anyone ever has. She's mourning Zia before she's gone, counting the hours as if there are so few. For it's the unknown now that adds weight to the days. Internment bulks up every day to bursting, yet leaves a hollowness that can never be filled. It's indescribable, the waiting for loss, a shadow casting across the days with a sun moving at an indeterminate speed, haphazardly snaking in the periphery, licking its way closer. Ava feels that chilling touch, whereas Zia notes it as a life fulfilled. It's a difference they will never reconcile, yet Ava struggles to accept it. In her new, youthful state, Zia feels further away from her than before.

Ava scrapes her hair back, her dark roots already overtaking the grey, but she puts a hat on anyway, pulls on some jeans and a jumper, then sneaks out of the apartment.

At Mae's office, the little girl is there, two laptops in front of her this time, coding across the screens. She stands up as soon as Ava enters.

'You again,' Iris says, her smile broad enough to show the gaps in her teeth. 'Hello.'

'Hi. Is your mum here?'

'Yes. Do you want to see what I've done on my laptop?'

'I don't think I'd understand it.'

The little girl does a one-shoulder shrug, then gets back to her work.

Mae appears in her office doorway and gestures to Ava. 'Come in.'

Ava walks in, then sits, keeping her head lower than Mae usually does, hoping the brim of her hat obscures her face. 'Bright kid you've got there.'

'She has some innate ability. Gets it from her great grandmother, on my husband's side.'

Ava remembers the tattoo on the girl's arm and wonders if that's where her life donation came from.

'So, I have all your figures here,' Mae says.

Ava takes the wad of paperwork. 'You could have just emailed these to me.'

'I know. . .it's just. . .' Mae bites her thumbnail a moment, then leans in over the desk. 'I was thinking about what you said last time. And then that announcement about women's wages. . . I can't believe they've done that. And the whole bloody Society seems delighted.'

'Not the whole Society.'

'That's what I wanted to talk to you about.' Mae's eyes dart from side to side, her lips twitching before she finds her words.

'The group, Sisters and Spies. I've had dealings with them before. Years ago. My husband's grandmother was part of them.'

Was. Ava notes the tattoo on little Iris's arm again. 'That's
where she gets her skills from?'

'She has a gift.' Mae says, then drums her fingers on the
desk. 'You asked who my father was. Lloyd Porter. That was my
father's name.'

Ava looks blank.

'Google his name.'

Ava does that, and her whole body stiffens. She checks her
spelling, then Googles again. Lloyd Porter. 'The guy who invented the Life Score algorithm.'

'Yep. the guy who marginalised anyone without inherited
wealth.' Mae leans back like the reveal has lifted a boulder from
her shoulders. 'I know the formula. Or I did. It's evolved a bit.
But I reckon I can figure it out.'

Ava raises her eyebrows, impressed at Mae's knowledge but
clueless as to the point. 'What use would that be?'

Mae's eyes go to the doorway, to the little girl engrossed in her
laptop. 'I want a better world for my daughter. We can't keep
going this way because of men like him.'

A lump forms in Ava's throat. A better world. Like that's
really possible. The Eyes Forward have too much power. 'I don't
see that there's much we can do about it. Knowing the formula
doesn't stop it being used.'

'Not now, maybe. But one day. If we plan. If we pool what
we know. If the SAS will help.'

A collective. As Mandisa said, XL Medico trust Ava now. She's branded as an upstanding member of the Society. She's no genius, but she must be of some use. 'A mathematician, a chemist, and a group of hackers. That's a formidable force. But still, the Eyes Forward are a fortress.'

Mae nods, but her face is resolute and stern. 'One day, we'll figure it out. Even if it takes years. We'll figure out how to break the system.'

Chapter 50

It's the first time Mandisa holds Ava's hand in public. This time around, anyway. And the last time they were together, it was rare. Certainly, towards the end of their relationship, it was pretty much unheard of. Mandisa didn't want to be seen with Ava then, not wanting to be tied to an unsafe woman. A low Scoring, unsafe woman.

That wasn't it, Mandisa has insisted again. I was protecting you and protecting my work from your Time's Up family ties.

Ava wants to believe her, to allow her longing to chase away her doubts. But she has many desires. Desire for Mandisa and all that comes with a relationship. And desire for justice. That latter desire claws at her skin, tenses her muscles, and makes her eyes water. Only rarely can she relax into other desires when the need for integrity is so profound. When Ava looks at Mandisa, she sees the headlines of everyone driven to madness from taking the expired Pres-X. 'If they didn't take it in the first place. . .' says Mandisa. Every cause has casualties, she says.

The ends and the means clinging on to each other with the thinnest whisker of justification. It was the Eyes Forward's idea for a solution, Mandisa says. If it were up to her, Pres-X would have just been stopped. Pres-X-2 would have replaced it entirely. Looking young is fine, becoming younger is not. The subtlest of differences sound like she's misspeaking. Such duplicitous words give Ava a headache and make her crimes blur into the background.

Now their implants glow gold, and they tilt their hands to display them proudly. With the cameras ahead of them, Mandisa grasps tightly. Ava holds on but less firm, not wanting to overpower her. Happy for the hold to loosen.

The camera doesn't disappear when they get to the funeral home, nor do they cease to follow when they go for brunch at Lunch Lounge. The face scanner isn't even brought out. No need now. There's no ambiguity. Ava and Mandisa look like they're only just legal to drink the wine they've ordered.

Ava wonders if she's ever seen Mandisa smile so much and wonders if it's purely herself who's responsible for that smile. The smile fades later when they're alone, and the cameras are gone, but not entirely. It's just less painted on, more relaxed maybe. Ava looks at her when they're pottering around one of their apartments, discussing work, social plans, trying to figure it out. . . what is it Mandisa wants from her, and what she wants from Mandisa.

One hundred more points they've been awarded each since the TV show special, which aired two months on, interviewing the lucky winners and how their lives have changed since having treatment. Ava and Mandisa's blossoming romance made headline news. They've been booked on daytime and evening TV shows, radio programmes, and invited to cut ribbons and attend functions.

Society Police trainers have asked Ava for tips and to endorse their spyware and apps. Everyone knows her for what she is. Was. She has no need to go hustle for a place in the alleyways at night anymore. She agrees to have her face adorn the latest night vision phone attachments and dark web decoder app. Why not? Mandisa says. Might as well cash in. The fuss will die down, Ava's sure. The busy timetable is good for her. It keeps her mind busy, stops her dwelling.

The post treatment fatigue only lasted a day. Her pinkish skin pales back to normality after a week, and her grey roots disappeared under the black regrowth. It all happened so quickly. It made her think that the ten-year regression of original Pres-X had its benefits. It left time to adjust. For Ava, she feels thrown back into the deep end of youthful insecurities and a life she grew out of years ago.

She's yet to look in a mirror—besides the one they presented her with live on air or the ones that line the street—really look. Part of her terms and conditions was that she would avoid looking until the show two weeks later, when she could gaze upon herself fully regressed in front of a live studio audience. For authenticity, they said. It worked. Her tears were real.

Four employees from other funeral homes approached Ava for work, and she hired them instantly. The workload is crazy high. Prepayment plans still make up the lion's share of their working day. At least the bodies that come in are limited. They can only hold ten at a time, and ten is what they always have. Always recently Preserved elder citizens. An accident-prone bunch. That's what the news says, anyway. Max reluctantly took on his colleague, Yasmine, a few days after Ava's treatment. Although, now he seems more pleased to be shut in a small room with her. The combination of Yasmine's company and a higher dose of B-Well has brightened his days. Ava smiles when she sees the sparks between them. That cold room is not so cold these days. Frida's never returned his calls.

With her gold implant on show, Ava visits the lab in the daytime now. She's no threat anymore. Her uterus is as expired as the old Pres-X. She's up to a hundred litres of formaldehyde-rose a week now with some help from Edgar. He's not bad to work with, not really. He does what he's told. Now the funeral home pretty well runs itself without her, she has more lab time, more than is needed to make formaldehyde-rose, and her chemist's brain is full of ideas. With her safe age status and youthful appearance, those in charge have actually listened to her suggestions, and she has some freedom to develop products and run tests. The satisfaction of finally working with the living instead of the dead makes her arrive for work early every day, and her face is a lot less solemn than it used to be.

Today, Mandisa comes in the lab, looking as polished and professional as ever.

'You taking lunch, Ava?'

Ava smiles. 'Sure.'

She leaves Edgar in charge of the equipment, hangs her lab coat on the back of the door, then makes her way to the canteen with Mandisa. Some Eyes Forward are walking down the corridor. She searches for Ken, but he's not there. She doesn't know why she always looks for him. To try and suss him out, perhaps, to look for some familiarity. Some family vibes rather than the stone-cold looks from the rest of the clones. The odd time she has seen him, she's received nothing of the sort. It's silly to keep trying.

They walk past the B-Well labs, where they make two types of B-Well: one to save lives and one that does nothing to help the elders who take it.

'I've been thinking,' Mandisa says.

'Yes?'

'Look.' Mandisa gets out her phone and shows Ava pictures of houses—not apartments. Houses with gardens and driveways and space.

Ava screws up her eyes, missing her reading glasses. Pres-X-2 doesn't get rid of the need for those. 'What am I looking at, Mandi?'

'We could live here. If you want. I've always loved the look of this neighbourhood. It's quite exclusive. Only the top Scorers

live there. The delis and cafés there are to die for. We make the
Score requirement, the two of us together.'

'What about Zia?'

'She'd come too, obviously. She could have her own bedroom
and bathroom. You could leave that pokey apartment behind
and live in a lovely home. With me.'

Ava searches for her words. 'It's just—'

'What?'

'It seems so soon. We've only been together a couple of
months.'

'*Back* together. We've really been together for ages. It was
always a temporary split. I just couldn't include you with my
plans, *our* plans. I had to climb that ladder, or I never would have
been able to do my Time's Up duties.' She takes Ava's hands, her
eyes locking with Ava's. 'We've been through so much already,
but you still don't seem to understand. I never stopped loving
you. Our time apart was nothing, just a temporary necessity.'

Ava thinks about their time apart. That seems so long ago
now. The time when Mandisa needed Ava out of the way so she
could help with the development of a drug that would help a
few and not help many more. All the while, in the knowledge
that the Pres-X would drive people crazy.

'It was necessary, Ava. You know that? We didn't hurt anyone.
We just didn't stop it. It was always the plan. We had to wait
a while, that's all. Some plans take ages to unfold. Restoring
balance is worth waiting for.'

Ava looks into Mandisa's dark eyes. They glisten with sincerity. Mandisa's right. Restoring balance is worth waiting for. Ava bites her lip and nods. A year apart is nothing in the grand scheme of things. A blip in the long-term plan.

'Right. Yes. Of course,' Ava says.

'Shall I call then—about the house?'

Ava looks at Mandisa's lips as she speaks and licks her own. 'Yeah. Sounds amazing.'

***

Zia's latest Memorexin injections are still working, for the most part. She has good days and bad days. She put her back out yesterday and hasn't gotten off the sofa all day. A carer comes to visit her. A young woman possessing enough patience to cope with Zia's repetitions and judgements, and a good enough sense of humour to make Zia laugh. It's conversation for Zia at least.

'Ava!' she calls out as soon as Ava gets in through the front door.

'Yes, Zia?'

'Come meet this woman. I don't know who she is, but she wants to talk to me.'

'That's Claudia, Zia. She's here to look after you.'

'She overcooked the spaghetti. You tell her. I don't want to be rude.'

Claudia bites her lip to stop her laughing as Ava mouths, *Don't worry*. The place is spotless, and Zia is fed, clean and entertained. That's all that matters.

'You know what she tells me?' Zia says.

'What's that?'

'She says that she wants a baby. You should get to know her. Look, she's green.'

'Mandisa and I don't want a baby, Zia.'

'You dad wants a grandchild. He'll tell you when he gets home.'

The injections aren't working all that well today then.

Ava walks over to Zia and kisses her forehead. 'I'll make you a cup of tea.'

She goes to her bedroom and stands in front of the full-length mirror, looking at the carpet, her toes scrunching the pile. Claudia has vacuumed in here too. Ava wonders how she ever coped without her. After a while, and a few breaths, she lifts her chin up, then her eyes, and gazes upon herself. She inspects her face and her figure, then she takes her top off. No need really. Her top was fitted enough. No more of her baggy shirts and boyish trousers. Mandisa took her shopping a few weeks ago and picked out some things. Flattering, she'd called them. Modern. It makes Mandisa happy for Ava to wear such things, so she does, dutifully. Ava still draws the line at colours though. The blackness of her clothes is the one part of her she's maintained.

'It matches your soul,' Dan said a few nights ago. Ava didn't laugh like she usually does.

She leans in close and looks at her skin, radiant, as youthful as it was over twenty years ago, despite feeling dehydrated today. She didn't sleep well last night, though it looks as though she did. No dark circles, no puffiness. Her boobs stay where they are when she takes off her bra. Her stomach has lost the little fat it had. She still looks like her. Sort of. Better? Not really, she doesn't think so. Just more desirable, according to everyone else. And isn't that what's most important? Everyone else?

But she doesn't feel like herself. Her skin is too tight, like it's not hers. She doesn't know what's right, her thoughts too smeared with hypocrisy. When she actually was the age she looks now, she was certain she was always right. Now she's older, apparently wiser, and she's riddled with self-doubt and questions everything.

***

Ava visits Mae again, on Mae's request, under the guise of accountancy advice and after several email requests. She's starting to feel more like a friend than just an accountant. So many women lost during the Great Unrest left a vacuum for female camaraderie, and Ava takes delight in having such a bond again. Perhaps that was part of the Eyes Forward plan years ago, to disassemble women's groups, to stop the gossiping. There's power in rumours. Like planting a seed. An acorn turns into an oak tree if left unchecked. Ava pictures Zia years ago in her café, hunched over a pot of tea and piece of cake, filling the space with whispers of discontent. Such whispers spawned riots, fuelled the Great Unrest and years later are still having an impact.

The smallest utterances can grow into the loudest chants.

Ava's been reading too much on the dark web, she thinks. It's hard to determine what's gossip and what's fact. Sisters and Spies blur those lines as much as the government.

Mae is jittery when Ava arrives, an excitable nervous tension shaking its way out of her.

'There's so much chat,' she says. 'Feminism. Have you heard of that? It might be before your time. But it's coming back. Women. Rights for women. The SAS, they're bringing it back.'

Ava nods. What Mae wants her to say is unclear. The SAS are making up words, that's all she understands. The young child still sits on the floor, playing with her computer.

On a business card, Mae has written a code. ASAS84739. Ava picks it up and inspects it. 'What's this?'

'Your username,' Mae says, as if Ava was expecting such a thing. 'Download the Shadownet browser, Nebula. You heard of that?'

'Sure, I think. The untraceable search engine?'

'It's a lot more than that. Anyway, download that. It's safe. Trust me.'

Mae's trembling hands don't give rise to much trust. She takes a sip from her coffee, the bags under her eyes telling Ava she's been up all night, and the caffeine is what's keeping her going. Ava leans back in her chair, away from the skittish mess that Mae appears to be.

'You understand?' Mae says. 'It's self-explanatory from there. Once you log on, you'll see all the chat about it. Check it from time to time. To keep up to date. It's not going to be overnight but sometime. This way, you'll know when it's happening.'

Ava frowns. 'When what's happening?'

'The revolution.'

Ava's grip on the card tightens. Another word she never expected to hear, but she knows what that one means. She can't believe it'll ever come true, but a little niggle inside tells her to hope, to cling on to it, that there is a way to right the wrongs. 'Restoring balance is worth waiting for.'

***

It's hard to think about any sort of revolution when life is treating Ava so well. She hates that she was forced to take Pres-X-2, hates that the Society limit your options depending on your Life Score. But having a high Score is nice. Too nice.

She wants to enjoy that for a while, to relish in it, to stretch her legs in her new stride.

It happened bit by bit. So slowly, Ava can't pinpoint when it started. Her sense of comfort and security. When she no longer felt like she needs to squirm out of her own skin, like a snake needing to shed. But the day she acknowledges it completely, is the day they move into their new house.

Mandisa and Zia are in the kitchen chatting in a way that old friends do. There's so much unpacking to do, and Zia gets on with it, finding the perfect place for the cutlery, finally her repetitive habit discovering its use. She unpacks the cushions and lays them out, in one order, then another, debating the best places for them around the house. Mandisa watches, keeps talking to her, about old friends they had, the meetings they used to go to. Zia looks content and worries less. Once the kitchen things are unpacked, they make rock cakes. Despite all Mandisa has done, she makes Zia happy, and for that, Ava is grateful.

Mandisa looks at Ava with eyes of adoration and speaks to her of the good things Time's Up have done, how important her parents were, tells Ava she's so pleased she can include her now, finally, how she'd missed her so much. And Ava nods, mesmerised, feeling useful somehow. Worthwhile. That's more important than feeling powerful, she tells herself. To be useful, to contribute something, to build rather than break.

At bedtime, Ava and Mandisa go to their room, shut the door, then do what so many couples do. When Ava wakes in the morning she sits up, yawns out her sleep, stretches, then feels that her skin fits. She looks at Mandisa just beginning to stir, and her heart swells like it never has before. Only one of her desires is present. Zia is up already, the TV blaring out some early morning gossip show. Ava leans back on the headrest and thinks about her day ahead in the job she loves, stroking Mandisa's hair as she looks up at her and whispers 'Morning,' then pulls her back under the covers. Ava feels like she's exactly where she's meant to be. Not because of her reflection, Ava has made her peace with that. She realised that if she doesn't care how she looks, why should she care about looking younger? And it's not because of the much larger house she has awoken in. She knows now that Zia won't be around for decades more, and that's okay. That's her choice. But the one fear that Ava has always had is gone.

She doesn't fear being alone anymore. She's found friends.

The dark web is still alive with chatter and on the Shadownet, she's found a community. Women who've been so long lost from her inner circle but on the Shadownet, they can communicate freely. She stretches her fingers and types away, scrolling through posts, reading about other women who share her disgust, then writing her own tale down. There are women there who understand, who can relate. That Shadownet username has linked her to many people. Even in other counties, there are women that won't let her forget. Across the entire Society, she's conversed and bitched and gossiped and planned.

It's not just her. She's not alone.

Women are shouting louder than they have in years. Sisters and Spies write that word—feminism—over and over and over until Ava can almost believe it's a real word that's been lurking in their language all along, that a revolution is coming. Until then, she's a spy with some of the greatest access to XL Medico.

Did she do the right thing? She still wonders from time to time.

You had no choice, remember? The Eyes Forward forced you. They took away your choice.

And they are doing much worse things.

She needs to remember it. She needs to remember Mandisa's part in it. When Ava reciprocates Mandisa's smile with her mouth and her eyes, when her arms reach for her with desire, when she sinks into the sofa with a feeling of belonging, those smiling eyes are open like never before. They see more, and her vision is razor-sharp. As much as she may indulge in the perks of their relationship, her gut still twists when she thinks of the elders. Erin and Millie's faces still haunt her dreams.

She cannot get too comfortable. A brief hiatus to unwind is all she can afford.

This is a blip in the long-term plan.

The revolution that Mae spoke of is coming. Some plans take ages to unfold, she reminds herself.

Restoring balance is worth waiting for.

Ava's lack of choice may take her guilt away, but it feeds her desire for justice. The casualties of the cause have left scorch marks across her soul. She will not forget. She is a Sister. She is a Spy. Though according to Mandisa, to XL Medico, to Eyes Forward, she did what she was told. She's a shining example for the Society. She's a model citizen, for now.

Good girl.

A note from Emma

Please scan QR code to review this book.

Preserve is the second book in the Eyes Forward Series. If you enjoyed it, please consider leaving a review on Amazon and Goodreads. Reviews are so vital for indie authors such as myself and knowing you enjoyed my work makes it all worthwhile. The third and final book, Rebel, is available now. It's set eighteen years after Preserve and has some new characters for you to meet. You'll also get to spend some time with the ones you already know and love—or hate! The story gets a whole lot more sinister. Check out my website and Facebook page for updates.

Subscribers to my website receive a free spin-off thriller nov-elette, featuring Mrs Constance as the main character. It was so much fun to write and I hope you enjoy it.

If you are in the mood for some more twisted dystopian, my first series, The Raft Series, is available now.

The science in Preserve is obviously all fiction, although the study of senescent cells and how they contribute to ageing is a growing area of research. Perhaps one day some aspects of ageing will be curable. Let's just hope that access to such treat-ments isn't only for the 'high Scorers.' If Pres-X was available, or Pres-X-2, would you take it?

Acknowledgements

Preserve would not be in print without the help of my wonderful betas and critique partners. Thank you to Maggie, Mitra, Danica, Emily, Natalia, Barry, Elizabeth, Vickie, Laura, Caitlin. . . and I am sure I have forgotten someone! Their time and honest feedback made this book what it is today. Thank you also to my editor Shannon K. O'Brien, for being so incredibly thorough, and Natasja Smith for her proofreading skills.

Thanks especially to my partner, John, for giving me the space and time I need to write, for his support, patience, and encouragement.

And thank you for reading it.

Made in the USA
Monee, IL
11 August 2024

63598852R10239